ULTIMATUM

OSGUARDS: THE GENESIS LEGACY

THE OSGUARDS UNIVERSE

OSGUARDS: GUARDIANS OF THE UNIVERSE
Book 1: Homecoming
Book 2: Revelations
Book 3: Armageddon
Book 4: Revenge

OSGUARDS SHORT STORIES:
Awakening
Induction of the First Osguard
Consequences
Cancer

OSGUARDS: THE GENESIS LEGACY
Book 1: Ultimatum

ULTIMATUM

BOOK ONE
OF
OSGUARDS: THE GENESIS LEGACY

MALCOLM DYLAN PETTEWAY

Rage Books LLC
www.ragebooks.net

Osguards: Ultimatum

ISBN: 0-9843645-4-4
EAN-13: 978-0-9843645-4-1

Printed in the United States

Rage Books LLC
www.ragebooks.net

A good leader can engage in a debate frankly and thoroughly, knowing that at the end he and the other side must be closer, and thus emerge stronger. You don't have that idea when you are arrogant, superficial, and uninformed.
– Nelson Mandela

PROLOGUE

Tasman Sea
Between Australia and New Zealand
Planet Earth, Millmum Galaxy, Rojam Os Cluster

The full moon seemed to hover like a giant white balloon over the Tasman Sea between Australia and New Zealand. Its light caressed the water's surface like a silk sheet covering a waterbed. A cool breeze raced west over the water, chasing what was left of the lingering heat from the day's sun wretched blaze. While the picturesque beauty of the water played out above the surface, deep within the water the seabed rumbled, destabilizing the landmass underneath the Tasman Sea known as the Norfolk Ridge.

Suddenly the rumble turned into a crack as the ridge shifted, sending ooze and dirt into the Norfolk Deep, a trough that ran more than 4000 meters below the surface of the sea. The underwater earthquake pushed and shook the ridge, dismantling it with the fury of a small nuclear weapon. The energy it created ripped to the surface like lava from a volcano.

A fifty foot wall of water bubbled from the quake, releasing one of nature's most feared enemies to man…a tidal wave. The energy continued to burst through the water producing tidal wave after tidal wave. After a few moments, it was clear that the energy released from the underwater earthquake created a train of tidal waves that pushed out in two directions…east and west.

The disturbance in the night had given birth to a Tsunami…a Tsunami on a direct collision course with Australia to the east and New Zealand to the west.

***

**Universal Security, Science and Trade Association of Planets'
(USSTAP's) Lilly Station**
Atlantis Continental Self-Atlantic Ocean
Planet Earth, Millmum Galaxy, Rojam Os Cluster

Lilly Station, the home of the Earth Forces of USSTAP, sat one thousand two hundred and fifty fathoms, on the Atlantic floor near the Ramanche Trench of the continental shelf, once known as Atlantis. The old Kulusk station was the spherical hub, housing the command section and gate portal rooms. Several wings extended from the hub like spokes of a wheel, housing different corps.

Extending at the end of the wings were concourses where the sea cruisers and the newly minted sea protectors docked when in port, and where the startram catcher was also housed. The current commander of Earth Forces USSTAP, also known as the world general, General Akbar Zandi, a British national of Iranian descent, had just finished his shift and was weaving through the maze of corridors to his quarters to begin one of his five daily prayers as called for by his Muslim faith.

He was a Sunni Muslim, a direct descendant from the Balochi Sunni minority population in Iran. He was six feet and two inches tall and slender, with dark olive skin and straight black hair salted with several beautiful lines of gray. He wore a stencil mustache that highlighted the fire that sparkled from his dark brown eyes when he let out a hearty laugh. His face, weathered with years of service to USSTAP, somehow maintained its youthful glee and wonder, which was ever so evident when he smiled; which seemed to be a constant in his demeanor.

Akbar had never visited or seen Iran. He was a second generation British-Iranian, born and raised in London. His parents had raised him with access to and appreciation of all things western, but with a firm adherence to his Muslim religion. Akbar walked a fine line between the two throughout his childhood, until he went to university. Like most young adults away from their parents overbearing watch, Akbar recklessly experimented with his freedom and strayed away from his religious upbringing; until that fateful day...the day the world learned they weren't alone...the day that Michael David Genesis, the Chief Executive Osguard of USSTAP, the First Osguard of Rojam Os, revealed to the people of Earth USSTAP's existence.

That was the day Akbar realized there was something bigger than him and it frightened him. This thought brought him back to his religion, and he'd prayed to Allah for guidance for hours that night. The next morning he woke up with an epiphany. Allah had answered his prayers. No matter what it took or how long it took, he knew in his heart that Allah had directed him to join USSTAP.

Since Akbar had joined USSTAP, he'd lived every second of his life to the fullest, which is why a smile was a constant to his demeanor. When he turned the last corner heading towards his quarters, the voice of the watch officer rang in his surgically implanted Artificial Intelligence (ARIT) Communication Device (CD), "General Akbar, this is the Watch Officer."

Akbar tilted his head to the right and tapped the transceiver hidden behind his lower earlobe, activating his CD transmit function, "This is Akbar."

"Sire, the ARIT watch indicates an underground earthquake is happening right now in the Tasman Sea. It looks like it triggered a tsunami heading to both the east coast of Australia and the west coast of New Zealand."

"Alert One! Ready all available ships to gate portal into the area. I'm on my way." Akbar tilted his head to the right and tapped the hidden transceiver behind his earlobe again to deactivate the CD, turned around and sprinted back down the corridor.

Two minutes later he emerged in front of the control center. The smoked double-glass doors had a sign, "Control Center (1A001) in Chaktun." Akbar stepped up to the doors and placed his hand in a device on the right side. The doors opened, sliding apart into the door frame. Akbar stepped in and signaled to the door guard not to announce him.

He took a deep breath and scanned the room. The room was circular in shape. Three chairs sat in the middle of the room facing each other. The chairs had a control ARIT attached to each of them. There were two stair steps up to get to the chairs. The Watch Officer, Centurion Richard Gray saw Akbar and automatically moved from the middle seat to his designated seat to the left. Centurion Gray was a South African, with piercing blue eyes, buzz cut blond hair and a body that looked like it survived on a diet of a daily weight lifting routine.

Akbar nodded to Gray and continued to scan the control center. On the outer walls he saw all twelve control stations with ARIT ports manned with his topnotch controllers. Gray must have recalled the day watch to handle the disturbance. Akbar made a mental note to somehow assuage the hurt feelings the night watch must be feeling for being replaced during this new crisis. As the door closed, he witnessed the professional fury of activity his day watch was performing. He took his seat in the middle of the activity, and swiped his hand over his control panel on his right armrest. A holographic depiction of the area displayed on the main board popped up in front of him.

"Play back the incident," Akbar commanded.

"Tiah!" the chief controller, Colonel Abraham Epstein, seated in front of him responded. Colonel Epstein was a third generation Israeli American from New York City.

Epstein had a penchant for practical jokes and was well known for his spirited sense of humor. But at the moment neither characteristic was present in his deportment. Currently, he was all business and very professional. Epstein tapped his glass control console and waived his hand over it, biometrically pushing his display to Akbar's 3-D holographic presentation.

"Should we notify the Aussie and Kiwi Governments?" requested a voice from behind Akbar.

Akbar turned around just in time to see his Centurion of Operations, Jessica Jansen, make her way to her seat to his right. Jessica was an American from Wisconsin with twenty-four years of service to USSTAP under her belt. She was a brunette with short curly hair. The sparkle in her eye was the opposite of the stern professional demeanor she wore like a badge.

Akbar gave her a nod of acknowledgment and then turned to Centurion Gray. "How long until the Tsunami hits land?"

"ARIT Approximates that in two hours it will hit the Northern Island of New Zealand between Kaitara and New Plymouth; and three more hours after that it will hit Australia between Brisbane and Sydney."

Akbar raised his head in thought, then took a deep breath and exhaled. "The 2029 Earth Pact amendment requires Earth governments to officially request assistance from USSTAP before we can render aid during a natural disaster," Jessica added.

Akbar could feel her eyes staring at him. He imagined them to be pagenay beams boring through his head. He also knew with the political atmosphere between USSTAP and the United Nations, the bureaucracy, such a request would have to go through, would take too much precious time to process. The delay would, unnecessarily, endanger lives and property.

"There's no time," Akbar finally responded. "Besides, they know it is coming. I'm sure their meteorological equipment, satellites and ocean sensors have sprang into warning mode by now. No, don't contact them. Besides, I plan to handle this in international water." Akbar took a breath and put his fist to his lower lip, "But we should send a notification report to Millmum Capital Station. See if they can get a starship here to lend a hand."

"Tiah," Gray responded as he worked on his ARIT console to send the notification report.

Jessica nodded and broke her self-employed protocol of never smiling. Akbar took that as a sign of agreement and a moment of solidarity. He quickly laid out his plan to shift the tsunami south on his ARIT tablet and let it calculate the particulars.

He reviewed the plan and with a swipe of his hand over his tablet, pushed the plan to the chief controller. "Distribute these to the subs," he commanded.

Akbar moved his hand over the ARIT controller and suddenly another 3-D holographic projection appeared. This one was of the tsunami above the surface. He bit his lower lip in anticipation and pushed the execute button on his tablet.

Lilly station was equipped with a submarine fleet of forty sea cruisers and ten sea protectors. The sea cruiser was coated with a special black substance called *slitanium* that absorbed light and sound. Red power rods covered the seams. When in stealth mode ten, they ran with their lights out and porthole windows blackened.

The sub was one mile in length and half a mile in width, with eight decks. The engines were cylindrical and ran three quarters length of the sub on the port and starboard side. Each engine melded into the main body of the sub at three through five. The main sub was elliptical on all sides with three hexagon cabins connected by an elongated pentagon. A directional aileron sat ten feet on top. The bow was arrowhead shaped, which sat on top of a reverse pear shaped bridge. Its weaponry consisted of four pagenay blasters—two in the front and two in the back—and two coronet cannons.

The sea protector was a larger version of its sea cruiser cousin. It had fifteen decks, and was one and half miles long, and three-quarters of a mile in width. One other difference was that it carried two five-ship squadrons of waterblades: single-seat fighter submarines. These subs silently patrolled the Earth's waterways, seas and ocean. Upon Akbar's execution, these submarines separated by miles of oceans, activated their ship gate portal systems, projecting a white light and opening a gateway through innerspace. The white light shining like heaven's glow illuminated the murky waters. Each submarine lumbered forward into the light, swallowed by innerspace until they completely disappeared, only to emerge out of the angelic light in a per-designated position in the Tasman Sea.

Akbar watched as Jessica called off the entry of every submarine into its spot. "Sea Protector Atlantis in place; Sea Cruiser Gauntlet in place; *Sea Cruiser Poseidon* in place; *Sea Protector Nautilus* in place..."

Jessica named each sub and marked their placement on the ARIT tablet which automatically projected at the Chief Controller's position and on Akbar's 3-D rendition. After fifteen minutes all USSTAP submarines were in place; making a perfect horseshoe formation around the tsunami with the opening pointing towards the south.

***

Tasman Sea
Between Australia and New Zealand
Planet Earth, Millmum Galaxy, Rojam Os Cluster

Situated one hundred miles outside Sidney in the Tasman Sea was the Australian commercial cruise liner, *Australian Delight.* On board she carried eight-hundred souls, unaware of the impending doom that lay in front of her.

One passenger, Kerri Knight, a reporter for the worldwide World Media News (WMN) walked the starboard deck soaking in the radiance and beauty of the full moon. She took this cruise to celebrate her final divorce decree between her and her now ex-husband, former companion newsman from WMN, Jerold Washington.

Washington had moved over to the more controversial news outlet Freedom News Network (FNN) two years ago. The move had added strain to an already tense marriage, due to their competitiveness and individual career goals. The addition of the third ingredient…politics, doomed their marriage for good, leaving no exit ramp but divorce.

As she gazed out onto the horizon she discerned the up-swell of the troubled seas. Immediately, her reporter instinct went into high gear. She searched her purse for her common. The common was three evolutionary steps above the smart phone of the early twenty-first century. With a common, an individual could do all the things that a smart phone could, plus high resolution 3-D holographic projection, X-ray, biological imaging similar to the magnetic resonance imaging (MRI) that hospitals practiced years before, as well as containing a small computer, printer, fax and copier.

She found her common, a gold-silk like cloth with Velcro strapping, slipped it around her wrist, and activated it. It produced a holographic keyboard that floated above her wrist. She pointed her arm to the horizon and selected a few keys to enlarge and project the image. A three inch by two inch holographic screen displayed above the keyboard, displaying a five hundred power zoomed image of the oncoming tidal waves.

"Call headquarters," she commanded. Her common connected her to her news headquarters in Miami Florida with an electronic squeal.

"WMN producer's desk," the voice said over the common's invisible speaker.

"Manny, this is Kerri. I'm connecting you to my common. Let me know if you see what I see."

A moment of silence covered them both as the common captured, projected, and then sent the images to Manny in Miami.

"What is that?" Manny asked over the connection.

"My common is telling me I'm about fifteen miles from a tidal wave. Squelch that, several tidal waves…fifty foot tidal waves."

"Kerri, get *out* of there!"

"Manny, where am I to go? I'm on a ship in the middle of the ocean. Not many places I can go."

"Get to safety then! Warn the others!"

"No, if I'm going to die out here, I might as well report it."

"Kerri!" Manny yelled. "Get your ass to safety now!"

"Sorry, Manny, you better tape this or, better yet, go live with it; because I'm getting ready to report this."

As if to punctuate it, the ship's emergency call system began to wail, warning all passengers to go to their designated shelter points.

"Kerri, get to safety now!"

"Manny, don't let me die for nothing! I'm sending you this! You better get it on tape!

Another moment of silence between them seemed to overtake the wailing of the emergency horn and the captain's voice over the loudspeaker ordering all passengers to go to their designated shelter area.

"Okay Kerri, I'm taping. But I'm not going out live. I will need to edit this, in the case we get to see your crazy ass drown," Manny said with despair.

"Okay!" Kerri yelled. "We are doing this on one…two…three." Kerri moved to the railing and placed her fist towards her face to ensure the common captured her and the background in the same frame.

Her long brunette hair fluttered with the wind, accentuating her live reporting was a death defying event. Her green eyes sparkled in the common's light as she plastered her best reporter smile onto her face. "This is Kerri Knight for WMN. I'm in the middle of the Tasman Sea off the east coast of Australia on the *Australian Cruise Liner Australian Delight*, where I believe we are about to encounter the scourge of a sudden tsunami."

***

USSTAP Lilly Station
Atlantis Continental Self-Atlantic Ocean
Planet Earth, Millmum Galaxy, Rojam Os Cluster

"All cruisers and protectors are in place as you ordered," Colonel Epstein announced.

"Great," Akbar huffed. "Have all controllers signal their subs: Chromerion Fields activate."

On the big board, and on Akbar's 3-D holographic depiction, reflected the fifty USSTAP submarines in the Tasman see activating their Chromerion Fields. The fields surrounded the ship, providing them an energy shield against enemy fire and natural phenomenon that could harm the submarines or life aboard the subs. Both displays depicted in the control center presented chromerion fields as lines of energy, when in reality the fields were invisible to the naked eye.

The submarines, which lay ten fathoms under the surface of the water, distorted their fields towards the surface of the water. The fields stretched upward, still engulfing the subs, but extended the area of protection. With each fathom of stretch, the fields weakened by a factor of .034 percent.

Akbar used the ARIT to determine the optimum range the subs should be and still provide enough energy to the fields to protect the submarines, and hopefully stop the force of the tsunami waves. He could only provide an educated guess on the force of the waves, based on their speed and height. From there he had the ARIT calculate the rest.

The fields broke through the surface of the water and spirited towards the sky. They stretched in height and width, interlocking with each other like invisible hands clasped in a handshake. The fields pushed towards the sky, fifty…sixty…seventy…then finally ninety feet high, building a seawall of energy.

"Barrier in place," Epstein announced. "First wave…five feet…should hit the barrier in five…four…three…two…one…*now.*"

The depiction displayed the wave hitting the horseshoe barrier on all sides. As the wave smacked the barrier, it transferred power to the barrier. Blotches of energy dispersal shot through the barrier in white sparks. After releasing its energy onto the barrier, the wave retreated in the opposite direction with less energy and much smaller. A quarter of mile in its reverse direction the next wave swallowed it. As the waves continued to smack against the barrier, they became much stronger, bigger and violent. Each time the barrier absorbed the punch and sent the wave whimpering back. Meanwhile, underneath the water surface, USSTAP sea cruisers and protectors strained to maintain position and to maintain connectivity with each other's generated field.

"I'm getting reports from all controllers, submarines' field generators are weakening! The strain is enormous!" Epstein blurted out.

"All subs maintain position," Akbar commanded. "In the next two minutes, I want all subs to divert remaining power to the fields…including life support."

"What?" Jessica huffed

Akbar turned to Jessica knowing he need not explain his orders, but still feeling obligated, "The next two minutes contain the nexus of the tidal waves; the next three tidal waves are the most powerful and most violent. Now that we sent the smaller waves back into them, they should have lost some of their intensity. We only need to maintain optimum power for the next two minutes as the ripple effect tears those waves back down to size. Then the subs should be able to re-engage life support and maintain control of the smaller waves until the harmonics completely wipes them out."

"Tiah," Jessica responded.

The USSTAP submarines did as requested. Inside the subs, the sound of the engines straining, the generator sputtering and the hull stretching echoed throughout the submarines as the tidal waves pounded the fields above them. The tidal waves beat on the fields in an unsettling rhythmic pattern, like the devil beating at the door to a human soul.

Each hit, bit at the nerves of USSTAP sailors and their controllers back on Lilly Station. Then the pounding began to abate. The pattern became less intense.

"All submarines are cleared for regular energy pattern; energize life support at will," Akbar pushed. "Maintain position and field coordinates until further notice."

"Tiah," Gray responded as he stood. He marched around the room checking all controllers' boards and individualized the order as it pertained to each submarine.

"Good job, sire," Jessica said. "Now what?"

"Now we hope no one saw that," Akbar pushed as he looked around the room. "Even though we completed this mission in international waters, someone may still call this a violation of the 2029 Pact."

"We just saved thousands of lives, you think someone will complain?" Jessica questioned.

"Look, for the last thirty years, I've seen the spirit of cooperation the governments of Earth are willing to give USSTAP wane and wane. Political barracudas, especially from the Earth First Freedom Party, will jump at the chance to make some anti-USSTAP movement from this."

"I hope not," Jessica stated after a few seconds of silence, "I pray that the governments of Earth have common sense people who understand, we just saved lives today."

18

"You and me both, Centurion…you and me both."

***

Tasman Sea
Between Australia and New Zealand
Planet Earth, Millmum Galaxy, Rojam Os Cluster

"Did you *see* that?" Kerri screamed. "Did you get that?"

"Yup, we got it all," Manny responded. "What was that? What happened?"

"USSTAP, baby! I bet you it was USSTAP…and I got it all on film."

CHAPTER ONE: HAPPY BIRTHDAY

Outside Vedar City
USSTAP Compound
Planet Chaktun, Millmum Galaxy, Rojam Os Cluster

The white light of innerspace washed over his body, bathing his chromerion protective bubble with benion particles. This was his favorite part. The moment where the entrance portal shut and the exit portal had yet to open. It was his moment of solitude and inner reflection that always calmed his inner being. There was something cleansing about the white light…something godly. It was almost a spiritual moment.

Every time he used the gate portal, Michael David Genesis II, also known as Deuce, became emotionally drunk with delight. He simply loved traveling through gateportals.

As usual, before he could fully enjoy the moment the exit port opened. The light shone over the six foot-two inch, twenty-year-old like a spotlight. He stood in the light with his hands naturally cupped to the side of his pants. Even though he was part Tuit, he looked like a younger version of his grandfather: mahogany complexion, tall, broad-shouldered with a sparkle in his catlike eyes and a gleam in his smile.

In front of him sat USSTAP Rojam Os Science Academy, formally known as the Chaktun Science Academy. Deuce stepped through the portal and took in the beauty of the Academy. The Science Academy sat on the southernmost edge of the planet's main continent. A lush rainforest and the smooth aqua blue waters of the Merrimack Ocean surrounded it.

The octagonal building was five acres of polished stone, smooth metal and lustrous glass that reached into the heavens, twenty-five stories high. White polished stone pillars that spanned the full height of the building engulfed all eight sides, dominating the exterior like gods holding open the gates to paradise. The building housed the best minds Rojam Os had to offer. Multiple laboratories sprinkled each floor and each section testing technological, medical and scientific theories.

On the east side, about two marks away, sat the rest of Vedar City. Here was where his grandfather, Michael Genesis, his grandmother, Michelle, and what was left of the original sixty Osguards had come to live out their golden years. Today was his grandfather's birthday and he and his family were visiting to celebrate it.

Before he could catch his breath, eight more portal openings, sprang to life, illuminating the area with the angelic white light of innerspace. One by one, his family stepped out of the lights. First he saw his father, Osguard Edward Samuel Genesis, and his mother, Osguard Kalina Freeman Genesis. Ed was presently the Osguard of the Angel Galaxy in Rojam Os, and Kalina was presently the Osguard of the Plax Galaxy in Tuit. Next he saw his aunt, Osguard Sharyla Genesis, and her daughter, Cheyenna Genesis. Cheyenna was a product of ARIT DNA baby bank management.

During the Tuit reconstruction years, Cheyenna's natural mother, a Tuit from the planet Lashall, had Cheyenna removed as a fetus with the aid of gateportal technology and placed in an ARIT baby bank chamber. There, the ARIT provided the proper environment to allow the fetus to mature. When Cheyenna's natural mother decided she did not want a baby and put her up for adoption, the baby bank programmed the ARIT to suspend her maturation. Rumor had it that Cheyenna's maturation was suspended for years.

Nonetheless, Sharyla, who never married but loved children, adopted Cheyenna from the Tuit baby bank. Once adopted, the ARIT introduced Sharyla's DNA into the fetus, allowing Cheyenna to claim Sharyla's bloodline. Cheyenna, a mixture of three parents, was a beautiful tall but slender girl, who had Sharyla's sunflower skin coloring and auburn hair. But her eyes were distinctly Tuit, with the yellow tint and catlike pupils.

To the right of Sharyla and Cheyenna stepped out his other aunt, Osguard Kashara Genesis, and her daughter, Tynala. Like Cheyenna, Tynala was a product of a baby bank adoption. Kashara had never married either. Tynala, also the by-product of three parents, had a hint of vampire teeth from her Gigantur natural parents. But, like her cousin, she adopted her mother's dark golden complexion and auburn hair.

To the right of them, Deuce's maternal grandparents stepped out from the light. Retired Osguard Adam Freeman and his wife retired Osguard Jenna Freeman. They were the original Osguards in the Tuit Galactic Cluster. In fact Adam was the First Osguard of the Tuit Galactic Cluster, and the first Tuit to befriend Michael in the opening days of the Tuit War. Adam and Michael remained friends ever since, as evidenced by the union of their children, Ed and Kalina.

"You're late," came a voice from behind them.

Deuce swung around and saw his grandmother, Michelle Genesis peering at them with a scowl on her face. After all these years, she still maintained her beauty. Her face remained young without a wrinkle in sight. She had added a few pounds to her frame, but she still had the sexy shape of a model. Her hair was shorter and wavier with several streaks of gray to highlight her seniority in life, but all in all her appearance screamed she was still a force to be reckoned with as a person and leader.

"You were supposed to be here ten minutes ago," she continued to lecture.

Immediately Cheyenna and Tynala ran towards her with open arms. They grabbed her, and smothered her with love and affection while screaming, "Mama!" at the top of their lungs.

Deuce knew this ploy would melt what anger resonated in his grandmother's heart. She could never resist her granddaughters. He counted to three, knowing Michelle would wrap her arms around them and start to cry. As soon as he counted to three, Michelle fulfilled his expectations.

He dropped his bag and walked over to them, feeling a slight watering in his eyes. It had been three years since he saw his grandmother and all of a sudden the feeling of how much he missed her bubbled up to the surface. Michelle looked up and caught Deuce's eyes and waved at him to come closer, which he did.

As soon as he was close enough, Michelle reached out and grabbed him and nestled him between his cousins.

"I'm so glad to see you guys. Boy did I miss you," she whispered.

"Hey mama," Deuce spurted out trying to hold back his sobbing. "How are you doing?"

"I'm great, now that you are here," she responded, trying to put back some bravado in her voice. "Your grandfather will be pleased to see you. He doesn't know I summoned you guys here for his birthday party." Then she looked up at her children, who appeared to be patiently waiting with smiles for their turn to hug their mother.

Deuce sensing this, tugged at his cousins and they stepped aside. The scene played out once more, this time with the elder Genesis children. Deuce watched as his grandmother squeezed his father, mother, and aunts, with such ferocity of love; it brought more tears to his eyes. He did not understand why he was so emotional.

All his life he'd trained himself not to show emotion, no matter how mad, sad or afraid he became. But at this moment in time, hugging his grandmother seemed to delete all that training. Now he felt embarrassed he did not have this type of emotion, when he reunited with his other grandparents on the station yesterday.

In a moment in which he wanted to rectify this embarrassment, he moved over to Adam and Jenna and gave them both a bear hug. "Thank you," he whispered.

Adam looked puzzled, but pleased as he patted Deuce's back, "For what, son?"

"For being my grandparents," he responded. He kissed his grandmother and grandfather on their cheeks. "I also want to thank you for being surrogate grandparents to Cheyenna and Tynala. I know that you didn't have to do it, but you did it anyway."

Adam moved Deuce's head so he could look him in the eyes. "Thank you son, I hoped you understand why."

"Yes, I do," Deuce pushed. "You wanted them to know they were loved by the Tuit side of the universe. You wanted to ensure they knew about their Tuit roots, like you did me. You wanted them to feel complete."

"That's right Deuce," Jenna smiled. "I knew you understood."

Deuce nodded with a smile.

"Adam…Jenna!" Michelle screamed as she walked over with open arms to greet them. "I am so glad you came! Michael is going to be so happy."

She threw her arms around them and gave them a big loving hug, as she did with her grandchildren and children. After a few seconds she released her grip. "We need to go, the party will start in two hours and you may want to freshen up a little. I will take you to my house first; you can drop your bags off there, rest a minute, freshen up and then we will meet Patricia, Debrlina, Joe, Mitiah, and Maji, and all their kids, in the executive dining room of the Science Academy, and give Michael the surprise birthday of his life."

"Right now Shawn has him in the lab going over the unity project, so he doesn't suspect a thing. Matter of fact, because we have been living on universal time, I'm not sure he knows it is his birthday today in Earth years, which makes this especially delicious."

The group collected their bags and hopped into the ground-tram. Deuce and Tynala sat up front with Michelle. Cheyenne, her mother, and her aunt sat in the second row; and in the fourth row sat Deuce's parents, Adam, and Jenna. The ground-tram was a bullet train car type vehicle that hovered one foot above the road.

It interacted with the road to ensure steady speed and direction through an ARIT control panel. Michelle punched in the destination in the holographic 3-D control panel, with the stipulation of fastest route and let the ARIT select the path home. When the green light illuminated, Michelle looked around to ensure all were buckled in their seats. Once satisfied, she tapped the light and the ground-tram lurched into motion.

Soon the road cleared the forest and pushed onto a clearing where several grand framed houses stood. The houses reflected earth's brick and mortar architecture, with elevated roofs. The yards contained manicured lawns with borders of shade trees. The houses themselves were two and three-story mansions with at least three to four thousand cubic square feet of living space, and garages. Some houses had horse stables, gazebos and pagodas.

"How was Vedar City created?" Tynala blurted out as she took in the scenery.

Deuce knew, Tynala and Cheyenna like him were raised and educated on star bases and starships all their lives. They only visited other planets under ambassadorial rules; and seeing such grandiose and beautiful living arrangements, surrounded by an ocean and the rain forest, was something to be admired.

Michelle simply smiled and began to tell the story, "The Chaktun government deeded the land on which Vedar City was built, as a settlement for the Rillion Osguard incident in which the Maxum of Chaktun conspired to kill your grandfather and usurp USSTAP under Chaktun rule."

"This was done under the arrangement that the land would not be used to conduct USSTAP business or governance, maintaining USSTAP claim of no territorial domain and therefore, no state governmental recognition. After the Earth United Nations and the United Universal Science, Security and Trade Association of Planets Pact of 2029, disallowed USSTAP owning land in any country on Earth accept for ambassadorial quarters and workspace. USSTAP evacuated Osguard Gardens in Danville Virginia and Osguard Village in Victoria Texas, thus leaving no retirement community for the

Earthborn Osguards to retreat to upon the end of their service to USSTAP. Therefore USSTAP, with the concurrence of the Chaktun government, built Vedar City for the Earthborn Osguards as a retirement community."

Deuce knew the transition for his grandparents was difficult, but his grandfather had no say in it. The UN-USSTAP Pact of 2029 was agreed upon after his grandfather's retirement, and by another First Osguard of Rojam Os; who was of Chaktun descent and ratified by the Chief Executive Osguard of USSTAP, who was from the Provello Galactic Cluster. He remembered that much from his history lessons.

The ground-tram glided into the center of the community, where a large green field, similar to those found in New England towns, captured his attention. It was a rectangular patch of manicured lush green grass bordered by a red brick walkway. Along the walkway sat redwood benches facing the center of the green, where statues of the three great founders of USSTAP, Laurona, Nausona Osguard, and Ortho Chting, adorned the center.

Laurona and Nausona were the twin daughters of Vedar Osguard, who escaped to Earth from the war-torn Chaktun, lived as slaves in the antebellum American south, and returned to start USSTAP. Ortho Chting was their successor whose personal search discovered Michael and his relatives, who turned out to be Laurona and Nausona's descendants. He trained the original sixty Osguards to take their place at their ancestors' helm and guide USSTAP into the future.

The statues of these magnificent leaders stood upon a cloud of stars with their backs to one another, gazing into the heavens. Between them, were waist high pillars upon which globes of the planet Chaktun and Earth revolved. This monument towered over eight flags, waving with pride that represented the eight galactic clusters that made up USSTAP.

On the east side of the green sat shops and stores with English writing, depicting a taste of America that existed in years gone by: a cafeteria named the *Sugar Bowl,* a barber shop named *Perfect Cuts,* a beauty salon named *Looking Good,* a food market named *Vedar City Market,* a hardware store named *Hammer and Nail...* as well as other stores that served as a quaint reminder of life in the United States.

On the west side sat a large church that dwarfed the green. Deuce knew from his last visit, this church had several sanctuaries to accommodate the different religious affiliations of the retirement community. He remembered his grandmother telling him that they were Baptist; but the church also accommodated Methodist, Presbyterian, Catholic, Muslim, and some others he did not remember.

As for Deuce, he was raised to respect all the religions he had encountered, but did not devote his life to any specific one. He worshiped with his father as a Baptist, his mother as a Firelar, and as a Chaktun Disciple of Jus. But the prevalent religion throughout the stars was Kindredness: a belief that the universe was controlled by spirits in communion with one another, bidding and thinking as one entity, but working as many.

Kindredness seemed to explain the differences in all the federated religions that flooded the universe and integrated them into one coherent, believable, and sustainable force in the universe. Deuce, as well as his cousins, was beginning to shy away from the family teachings on religion and adapt to Kindredness. With this thought flying through his mind he turned quickly away from the church, hoping that his grandmother would not insist on him participating in a service during their visit.

The ground-tram took a right onto North Main Street and pushed forward several blocks, before it entered another region of houses. Then it took a left onto New Haven Ave and slid two more houses down. When it stopped, they were in front of his grandfather's house.

It was a large, five thousand square foot shale gray stone house, with two floors, a finished basement, six rooms, five baths, front wooden-covered porch, back yard deck and patio and other amenities one could not achieve on a space station or a starship.

"Retirement is sure good to you, Mama," Deuce blurted in awe.

"Adam and Jenna have similar accommodations on Tuit," Michelle said. "Lifelong commitment to the universe is good to all who serve. USSTAP takes care of its people, whether they serve a short term or serve long enough to retire," she added for emphasis.

***

USSTAP Science Academy
USSTAP Compound
Planet Chaktun, Millmum Galaxy, Rojam Os Cluster

The smile on his face was illuminating. He had just discovered what until now was considered the undiscoverable. Michael David Genesis, the former Osguard of Millmum Galaxy, the former First Osguard of Rojam Os, and the former Chief Executive Osguard of the United USSTAP, double-checked his figures once again before pushing the analysis into the ARIT.

Even with his eighty years of age, Michael still carried the confidence and command presence of a leader. His auburn hair was now gone, replaced by the silver shiny cover of gray. Bags and wrinkles now bordered his eyes, and slackness invaded his once stern jaw line and chin. However, he maintained the exuberance of youth and the appearance of strength through his tone, fit body frame, which could be attributed to his daily workout routine.

"What is it?" his brother Shawn asked.

Shawn, who had turned eighty-two two months earlier, also appeared to maintain the mantle of Osguard leadership. He too was grayer with wrinkles and a slower step, but like his brother maintained the sharp intellect of a thirty year old.

"In the famous words of Archimedes, eureka!" Michael exclaimed.

"You mean you found the point?"

"Yes, my brother. I found the point. And I'm calling it the Unity Point," Michael said.

"Really!" Shawn gasped as he stepped closer to his brother.

"Really. Not only have I found the point of equilibrium between outerspace, innerspace, and ultraspace, but, I have found the equilibrium between those three and the etion energy well phenomenon.

"Thus, I say dear brother; I found the spot in which the universe first sparked to life. I found the source of benion, trachion, restion, and etion radiation—or at least where the source is."

"Where?" Shawn asked as he picked up the ARIT tablet and reviewed the results.

"Believe it or not, it is where the zero point coordinates of all four dimensions meet."

"What? How'd you figure that out?" Shawn pushed in disbelief.

"It was a side project of Billy Red's that I picked up when I went through his lab several years ago. I was getting bored living the retired life, so I thought I would snoop around in this old dust bucket of a lab and see what the greatest mind of our time was working on besides killing me."

"I came across his records and found his notes detailing his search for the galactic Garden of Eden…as he called it. In reality, he was looking for the source of the universe, or at least where the source may have begun. I've been tinkering with his notes off and on for the last three years. But lately, I've been motivated to find out if there was something to this galactic Garden of Eden idea Billy had."

"So you have a set of coordinates, what does that prove?" Shawn asked, handing the ARIT tablet back to Michael.

"Nothing, I guess," Michael responded. Then he turned to face Shawn and flashed his most hypnotic smile, "But it could be one last adventure. What do you say we grab an old scout ship and check it out…you, Patricia and me?"

"You're crazy," Shawn huffed, staring his brother down. "We're too old to go gallivanting around space in an old scout ship by ourselves."

Shawn didn't know it, but those words only fueled Michael more. He did not like to be considered too old to do anything. It hurt him to his soul to accept retirement twenty years ago, and it hurt him more to know USSTAP was able to continue without his input. All his adult life all he had ever known was USSTAP…ever since Ortho plucked him off the New Haven Green on that fateful Fourth of July. That was the night he almost threw his life away on a vengeful quest against Billy Red. Ortho stopped him and the voice in his head stopped him.

"Look Shawn," Michael pushed further, "God has connected Billy Red and me together since the beginning of all this. Billy became Mezhak Zyder and I became the First Osguard for a reason. I believe this is the last chapter God has written in the story of Billy Red and Michael Genesis. I need to follow it through. I want to do that with you and Patricia. But if I can't, you know I will do it alone."

Shawn shook his head in defeat, "Give me some time to think about it."

Michael smiled, for he knew he had the upper hand in this debate if Shawn had to think about it. But he had to play it off and give the illusion that he was unsure. He gave a deep sigh and slowly nodded, "I'll give you until tomorrow afternoon. After that, I can't promise you what I will do."

"Great…until tomorrow afternoon then," Shawn responded with relief. "Now let's go get something to eat. I think the executive dining hall is still open."

"Okay, I could eat now," Michael said. "Just let me record this and close up the lab. It should only take about ten minutes. I'll meet you down there."

"No, I'll wait," Shawn responded. "Here, let me help."

"Fine," Michael relented.

It took approximately ten minutes before Michael looked around and decided they were ready to leave. "Shawn, let's go," he commanded.

Shawn looked up from his ARIT terminal and nodded, "Let me just save and close this last file."

Michael nodded and closed the drawer he was inspecting. He then walked over to Shawn and gazed over his shoulder at the holographic scout ship displayed from Shawn's ARIT terminal. "Yeah, that's the one," he said, smiling with anticipation. "Good selection."

"I know," Shawn responded. "It fits all the parameters. She is a mighty fine ship. Her top speed is MOP 45. She has gateportal engines and eight pagenay cannons for protection."

"Good!" Michael said, almost salivating at the thought. "Let's put in a requisition order tomorrow, after I put together my exploration proposal."

"Do you think the Guardians will approve this?" Shawn asked as he stood. The holographic picture of the ship disappeared as the ARIT flipped off.

"They already have," Michael giggled. "They approved it when they approved me reviewing Billy's work here. In the fine print, it gives me full authority to select a project for further investigation and probable implementation. I select this project for further investigation. I can't help it if that investigation takes me back into space."

"Okay…okay," Shawn sighed. "I forgot how devious you can be when you want something." Michael shrugged.

"I'm starved," Shawn continued, "Let's talk about this tomorrow. For now I want to get to the dining facility and get what's left over from the meatloaf special."

"Augh!"

Michael turned and headed towards the door. Shawn followed in silence. The door swished open and the two left the lab that once belonged to Mezhak Zyder, also known as William "Billy" Red—the smartest man the universe had ever produced, and the deadliest foe Michael ever came up against.

As they walked to the dining facility, Michael's mind flashed back to the multiple encounters he had with Billy Red. He flashed back to the knife fight he had with Billy that almost killed him, but ended up being the morsel of evidence that connected him to USSTAP and ultimately led him to the position of First Osguard.

He remembered that fateful Fourth of July where Ortho revealed to him his destiny, and stopped him from exacting old fashion street justice on Billy. Ortho had Billy arrested by USSTAP, tried, convicted and sent to a prison planet; where he escaped with the aid of the Moslecks.

He flashed back to the space battle he had with the Mosleck starship when he was on his orientation ride as an Osguard-in-Training. He found out later that Billy was on board and that Billy almost lost his life then. Billy could have died, if it wasn't for his longing for revenge against Michael and the other Osguards. Michael's memories jumped to the fight he and Billy had in a New Haven Connecticut park. The fight traversed the streets and ended in an abandoned house that ultimately blew up from a gas leak.

Michael thought Billy had died in that as well. He did not know that Billy escaped only to become Mezhak Zyder, the well renowned Chaktun professor and inventor. With the aid of his Kulusk and Chaktun enemies, Billy's Omega 244 DNA was activated just enough to stimulate his brain and forge a life on Chaktun as the universe's greatest mind.

Nonetheless, the ache for revenge was strong for Billy. From all their encounters, Billy had only came out on top on one…the first encounter. After that, Michael repeatedly beat Billy, leaving him more battered and bruised than ever. So Billy, with the help of the Chaktun Maxum, devised a plan to kill Michael in the Unity Stream during the first ever virtual meeting of all the Osguards, and galactic ambassadors.

But as luck would have it, a zeshion storm interrupted his plan, sending both Michael's and Billy's consciousness to an alternate universe. That last battle ended with Billy losing his life at the hands of Michael's daughter, Kashara.

Ever since then, Michael had maintained a feeling of guilt. He wondered if he had reacted differently, done something differently other than accepting Billy's challenges to fight, would he have turned his life around enough to see the fruits of his labor. Michael didn't want to see Billy's scientific work get lost with the man, so he continued to honor the man in any way he could; including adopting Billy's lab and life work.

It wasn't a secret that Billy Red and Mezhak Zyder were one and the same. But, it was a secret that Mezhak Zyder attempted to kill Michael. It also was a secret that Vedar City was the price the Chaktun government paid to maintain their part in the plot a secret as well.

This barrage of memories, engulfed in guilt, was a daily mental dance Michael went through every time he entered or left the lab. It played on his conscience and whittled away at his nerves.

The door to the executive dining facility swished open and Michael stepped in, still lost in thought, fighting the memories, playing to the guilt when the lights popped on.

"Surprise!" yelled the crowd from inside the room.

Michael snapped back into reality as his heart skipped a beat. He looked over the crowd with his mouth agape. He saw the banner with the words, *"Happy 80th Birthday."*

His mind went into full throttle. He did a quick conversion from Universal Date to Earth Date in his mind. Then he laughed…a full belly hardy laugh. It was the sixth of August back on Earth. It had been so long since he used the Earth calendar system that he forgot it was his birthday. All this time, he had been using the Universal calendar system, which would have made his birthday still six-months away.

As Shawn slid from behind him, Michael scanned the room and saw his immediate family in one place for the first time in ages. He saw all his grandchildren, his children, siblings and in-laws and their children and grandchildren. Tears sprung from his eyes and a slight screech bellowed from his mouth.

Michelle walked up to him and grabbed him by the hand. She gently kissed him on the lips and whispered, "Happy Birthday, honey."

CHAPTER TWO: STILL HERE

FNN Headquarters
New York, New York, USA
Planet Earth, Millmum Galaxy, Rojam Os Galactic Cluster

Jerold Washington's face scrounged up with anger as he watched his former wife report on the tsunami from the Tasman Sea. His naturally smooth mahogany wrinkled face produced an ugly frown. The tension seared his forehead with lines of hate as he listened to his ex-wife's voice ring from the monitor's speakers. To him, it was like listening to nails scrape across a chalkboard. Finally her closing remarks pushed him into a full frenzy.

"What you've seen is not natural. The tidal waves from the tsunami appeared to hit an invisible barrier and dissipate into the sea. This reporter does not have any direct evidence why this happened, but I would venture to say USSTAP may have saved thousands of lives tonight; including this reporter's. If I'm correct, I would like to be the first to thank them for their service. Reporting from the Tasman Sea, this is Kerri Knight for WMN news."

Jerold pounded his desk with both fists. Anger seethed from his lips as he hissed. The news had been free of USSTAP stories for over ten years. That's when the world seemed to accept the UN-USSTAP Pact of 2029, which relegated USSTAP to a faceless entity, with no voice and no power on Earth.

Certainly, there still were several human interest stories on how USSTAP provided medical treatment to the terminally ill folks throughout the world. But that had been happening since U-Day – the day Michael David Genesis took over the airwaves and announced their presence. There have been so many of those human interest stories that people have become immune. There was no real danger to his plan of letting those stories go unchallenged. Anyway the viewers may have deemed him a monster if he did.

It didn't matter to him, because it was always some new or up and coming reporter, who needed to sink his or her teeth into the business, doing those stories. No reporter with any real credentials would be caught dead pushing those human interest stories. Then he flashed back to the days of his early reporting years. The thought of those days began to ease his anger.

He gushed on the inside, as he reminisced how he'd cleverly twisted the facts to suit his private agenda of turning the viewers against USSTAP. His first reports targeted Michael Genesis and the Osguards. His reports had the viewers believing the Osguards thought themselves royalty, and expected the people of Earth to worship them as so.

The fact that Michael Genesis introduced himself to the people of Earth as, *"Your Osguard,"* on U-day only fueled his storyline.

He'd created the fear in some, that U-day was just the first step of USSTAP's plan for world domination. In the beginning, and as a direct result of Jerold's constant plea for caution and restrain to his audience, USSTAP's negotiations with Earth's governments became problematic and the Firstie cause took root in America.

Next, he moved onto USSTAP's organizational structure. Jerold called them socialists in some reports, fascist in others; and on those rare occasions when he had his viewers in a panic, he threw out the word, "communists."

He knew he wasn't consistent, but it didn't matter. The fear was there, he just added fuel to the fire. His reports disturbed the socialist governments of the world, who saw their grip on their people fading; and created fear in the capitalist driven economies, which saw a real threat to their survival. Consequently, the banking industry and financial markets took heed and began hoarding their capital, leading to a worldwide market depression; which, Jerold aptly blamed USSTAP for causing.

This is when he caught the eye of the Earth First separatist movement. This movement's objective was to terminate USSTAP's involvement in Earth's affairs. For what reason, Jerold did not know or care. All he knew was that they were so enthralled with his reporting skills and tenacity, that they sponsored his documentary on religion in USSTAP. The documentary was theatrical release that became the number one documentary, worldwide, for eight weeks.

Afterward, the DVD and common releases sold millions. This was truly his crowning achievement. He won several accolades and awards for his in-depth reporting. But that wasn't the prize. The prize was this documentary pushed many religious leaders of every faith and denomination to turn against USSTAP. The documentary made the religious faithful fear USSTAP as an evil instrument, out to destroy their beliefs and way of life.

The very existence of life on other planets, other galaxies and other clusters questioned the fundamental beliefs of many religions. Accordingly, the fact that billions upon billions upon billions of people practiced a multitude of religions that didn't resemble any religion on Earth—was sacrilege to their faiths.

Soon there were other reporters that jumped on the bandwagon. Racking USSTAP over the coals became a ratings bonanza – so much that Dr. Claude Chenault, a French psychiatrist turned business executive, created FNN. He dedicated FNN to the complete destruction of USSTAP's image on Earth. FNN was the catalyst that propelled Dr. Chenault into politics and eventually to his selection as the U.N. Secretary General.

Within one year of Michael Genesis' retirement from his second term as USSTAP Chief Executive Osguard, and seeing no real opposition in USSTAP leadership, Dr. Chenault used his influence, political savvy, and the power of the media from FNN, to force USSTAP's new Chaktun-born Millmum Galaxy Osguard to the bargaining table to draft and sign the U.N.-USSTAP Pact of 2029. This effectively banned USSTAP from meddling in Earth's affairs without invitation by the United Nations.

At first when USSTAP failed to respond to world disasters – and lives were lost, where lives would have been saved – people revolted against Dr. Chenault. But he stood his ground and weathered the protest, marches, and threats, from governments like the United States, Russia, Great Britain, and China. He simply stated that the U.N. did not have the power to enforce the Pact of 2029. If USSTAP really wanted to save people during natural disasters, they could and there was nothing the U.N. could do about it. Therefore, it was USSTAP's decision not to interfere, not his.

After a while, and with much coaxing from his reporting, people either bought into the statement or gave up fighting the statement. Nonetheless, without input from USSTAP, the protestors did not have a leg to stand on. Now, all of a sudden, his ex-wife and rival news reporter blasted the airwaves with news that USSTAP intervened in a natural disaster, and saved lives.

He thought, '*Surely this is against the Pact of 2029.*'

Then it struck him. He needed to go on the air and openly charge USSTAP of violating their agreement with the U.N, and ask, "Why now? Why not before? What's different now? Why didn't they help in the New York flood of 2030; or the San Francisco Earthquake of 2032, or the Moscow blizzard of 2035?"

He pulled out his common tablet and began typing down his thoughts. He had to deflect any notion that this was USSTAP. He knew USSTAP would not own up to it. So he had to give credit to someone else for stopping the Tsunami. His fingers glided over the holographic keypad with mad skills. As fast as his mind could capture the thought, the thought was displayed on the holographic see-through display.

His eyes jumped from the keypad to the display and back down to the keypad. His mouth moved as he silently mouthed the words he was typing. He was in the zone. He was pushing every synapse to the fullest as he conjured up lie after lie, woven within fact. He knew the best way to move the viewer to his way of thinking was to sprinkle truth within the lie.

He smiled and whispered, "I gotcha, witch! I got your damned USSTAP and raise you with a solid Australian, New Zealand secret emergency response system."

He stopped and reviewed what he wrote. Each word he read filled him with an evil glee. His smirk transferred into a wide-face grin. The grin turned into a hearty laugh. His laugh echoed within his office for twenty seconds. When he finished laughing, happiness returned to his inner-being as he caught his breath. Then with one stroke, he hit send and his story went to the producer, with a note, *Put me on live in ten minutes.*

Now it was time to practice. He needed to make sure his voice and demeanor was convincing. He wanted to exude the confidence that would command the attention of his viewers.

He read his masterpiece out loud: *"Good afternoon. This is Jerold Washington with late breaking news. It is (insert time) Saturday, 6 August 2044. Approximately four hours ago an earthquake, measuring 6.1 on the Richter scale occurred in the Tasman Sea about one hundred and fifty miles east of Brisbane Australia. It triggered a massive tsunami with tidal waves of over fifty feet heading east towards New Zealand and west towards Australia."*

"Coverage from another news outlet captured the devastation as these waves barreled towards the commercial Cruise Liner 'Australian Delight.' That footage captures the unbelievable stoppage of that tsunami by what looks like an invisible barrier. We at FNN are grateful that the tsunami was stopped in its tracks, prior to pursuing a

path of destruction; and our hearts and prayers go out to the passengers and crew of the 'Australian Delight.'"

It must have been a horrific experience to come so close to death and have it staved off by an unknown force. To some, it must seem like a miracle. To others, including the reporter from WMN, it appeared to be the work of the men and women of USSTAP. I wish I could confirm either today, but I cannot. What you saw was an untested prototype capability, built by the joint effort of Australia and New Zealand's Emergency Management.

"Oh, they will deny it, because it was a secret venture and because the capability was untested prior to them authorizing its use in this deadly situation. But it is true."

"Two governments of Earth produced this wonderful capability, and activated just in time to stop the ghastly damage that was in the wake of a surprised tsunami. With precision timing and expert execution, the great men and women of the joint emergency management stopped one of the most horrendous forces of nature; and because of political winds they cannot take credit for their actions."

"Well, let me be the first to thank them and give them credit where credit is due. Thank you...thank you...thank you."

"And for those who believe USSTAP had a hand in this, let me assure you that you are dead wrong. It has been almost 15 years since the UN-USSTAP Pact of 2029 was signed; and in all that time has USSTAP ever lifted a finger to save lives or property during a natural disaster? No...they haven't. They have steadfastly adhered to the Pact, because they knew then, as they know now, we can take care of our own."

"Remember, the United Nations, under Dr. Chenault, was transformed into the world class peacekeeping force it was always meant to be. They have answered the call during these disasters in the past, and they will continue to answer the call in the future.

Furthermore, with the intellect, the ingenuity and integrity of our own people of Earth, as displayed by the Australian-New Zealand Joint Emergency Management in this crisis, we don't need aliens from another planet, or their surrogate brainless earthborn, twits to help us. We help ourselves."

"So I guess what we witnessed today was a miracle – a man-made miracle, ushered by the grace and love of God. Therefore, don't believe the hype pushed by the other news network. USSTAP had

nothing to do with today's events. Believe in me...believe in you...believe in us...believe in Earth First."

"Stay tuned to FNN for further news on tonight's event. My colleagues will be with you all day and will report the facts as we get them. Stay tuned to FNN to get the real truth. I'm Jerold Washington for FNN."

"Wow, I think that's it," Jerold said. "I think that will do."

***

Earth First Headquarters
Paris France
Planet Earth, Millmum Galaxy, Rojam Os Galactic Cluster

Dr. Claude Chenault eyed his guest with caution. Dr. Chenault was a powerful man—a self-made man; driven by hatred and revenge. But even his cold heart had to take pause in the presence of his guest.

Dr. Chenault was a doctor of psychiatry, who'd practiced for a short eight years before the allure of public life called him. He'd founded the Earth First movement in 2015, just a couple of short years after Michael Genesis announced the presence of USSTAP to the world.

Using his Earth First as a global political party, he was elected to the French Senate, then as Prime Minister, and finally to the Presidency of the Republic. He resigned as president to accept the position of U.N. Secretary General, where he served as the youngest Secretary General for two terms.

Under his tutelage, the U.N. charter changed. Dr. Chenault used his power of persuasion, coupled with his fear-mongering tactics he perfected with Earth First, to manipulate, cajole, and blackmail member nations, into transforming the U.N. into an organization with teeth. The charter modifications included permission for the U.N. to buy surplus military equipment from member nations, and the ability to conscript a militia under the same rules as the famous French Foreign Legion. This terminated the U.N.'s dependency on the military of member nations. U.N. Peacekeepers' was name formally changed into the U.N. Foreign Legion.

During his tenure, Dr. Chenault approved the U.N. buying and outfitting five aircraft carriers, a tank battalion, a wing of Mirage fighter jets, a squadron of tankers, cargo planes and other surplus material that the member nations wanted to offload for payment. Additionally, the men and women of the renovated U.N. Foreign Legion, who answered only to the Secretary General, were based throughout France, for no other nation wanted an armed militia within their borders that they had no control or command. It is at this time the U.N. Foreign Legion unofficially became known as the Chenault Legionnaires.

With this military might and newfound firepower, the U.N. bolstered Dr. Chenault's will with ease, even when challenged by the member nations or the U.N. Security Council. Even today, he still had his tentacles within the legionnaire force; in which his will would be executed without a moment's hesitation.

Dr. Chenault returned to running Earth First and his media mogul empire after his second term as U.N. Secretary General. As a media conglomerate, he boasted of owning eighteen newspapers in ten countries: including France, the United States, Great Britain, Canada, Australia, South Africa, Germany, China, Japan, and Italy. He also owned satellite radio stations, as well as the worldwide FNN that reached out to these countries and more that he used to spew out his anti-USSTAP sentiment across the world.

Even with this power, he still felt uneasy sitting across from his guest, known to him only by one name—Phillip.

Dr. Chenault's office was elaborate, to the point of ostentatious. The white marble floor and mahogany wood carvings were something straight out of a Shakespeare scene. The cavernous room carried a chill that no modern HVAC could correct. Even the silent act of breathing echoed from the walls. Paintings, adorning the wall, captured an era in France's history that beckoned for nobility and royalty to rule the world. But even this was demure, compared to the evilness that surrounded Phillip.

Dr. Chenault sat behind his grand desk, his bald head beaming with sweat and his lips quivering with anticipation, as he tried to play the posturing game with Phillip. He noticed Phillip kept his hands on his knee and his legs crossed. Dr. Chenault steadied himself as he played in his mind the many occasions when he was the most intimidating person in the room. He needed to summon that strength once again to deal with what he knew would be a most unpleasant meeting.

Finally, after two minutes of playing the posturing game, Phillip spoke: "We have to move up our time table."

"What do you mean, move up our time table?" Dr. Chenault pushed before he knew it.

Phillip uncrossed his legs and leaned forward. "My boss doesn't like that USSTAP is still integrated here on Earth. It's been twenty-eight years since we picked you for this mission and you have yet to deliver. My boss has been more than patient."

His girth seemed to cast a shadow on the entire room. His eyes were round but small; some would describe them as beady. His eyebrows were thick, and his hair was cut short but stringy; almost oily. The craters on his face looked like small boulders had pummeled him as a child.

His voice was deep...baritone deep; so deep that the cavernous room just didn't echo when he spoke, it seemed to shake. "My boss has done so much for you. He has ensured your rise to power in your political maze. He quietly made sure you were selected as General Secretary of the United Nations. Basically, all that you have is because of my boss's generosity."

"I know that," Dr. Chenault piped-in, "and I am grateful. However, I've done all he has asked."

"All you have accomplished is to activate a non-interference clause with USSTAP!" Phillip bellowed. Then he paused to capture his composure.

"USSTAP's influence on Earth is almost non-existent," Dr. Chenault interrupted. "Before this incident with the Tsunami off the coast of Australia, USSTAP was a forgotten memory."

With a sigh Phillip continued, "Believe it or not, this non-interference clause is a basic agreement USSTAP has with all member planets. You have achieved nothing but the status quo. USSTAP is still here. They move with stealth in your oceans, in your cities and in your skies. The agreement my boss had with you was to drive USSTAP from Earth, not drive them underground."

Dr. Chenault bristled as he watched the anger ooze within Phillip's words. "I've done all that your boss has asked. What else can I do?"

Phillip leaned back in his chair, displaying a catlike grin, "In two weeks, USSTAP and the few people of Earth who still honor the occasion will celebrate the thirty-second anniversary of that day, commonly known as U-Day," Phillip announced. He again crossed his legs. "My boss wants you to make sure this is the last celebration of U-Day."

"What? How?" Dr. Chenault pushed.

"I don't know, but it has to be something big, something destructive...something that finally drives USSTAP away."

"And untraceable to you or your boss?"

"That goes without saying," said Phillip.

"What's the time table?" Dr. Chenault asked, already hatching a plan in mind.

"Six Earth months," Phillip responded with a cold chill to his voice. "If USSTAP is still on Earth in six months, you won't be here in seven."

Dr. Chenault squinted and took a deep breath; and as he released it he responded, "Threats don't motivate me, Phillip. So keep your threats to yourself. I understand what you want, and I will deliver. But if you ever threaten me again, or by chance you carry out on some blind system of revenge on me, rest assured your boss won't like it."

Phillip uncrossed his legs and stood up. His huge frame looked like a giant about to devour a goat.

Dr. Chenault picked up a common chip from his desk and threw it at Phillip. Phillip caught it with his big clunky hands. "What's this?"

Dr. Chenault stood, knowing he was about to play the last chip he had in his hand, so he had to make it look and sound real. "That is one of four hundred copies of data—data tying your boss and the Tri-Galactic Resource Distributing Company to the actions of Earth First; me and all we've done with the United Nations."

"It has every correspondence we have had since that fateful day you chose me to be your surrogate on Earth. It ties you and your boss to every action and deed done by Earth First, the U.N., and me for you against USSTAP."

Phillips eyes narrowed and the smug smirk on his face disappeared, "Four hundred copies?"

"Yeah, four hundred copies," Dr. Chenault reiterated. "You can keep that one. Because if anything happens to me, four hundred of my foot soldiers, spread throughout the globe, will post these on the world wide common for all to see; even the idiots in USSTAP will get to see it. And knowing the penchant for revenge that is part of the Osguard code, I hate to imagine what will happen to Tri-Galactic Resource Management, you or your boss."

Phillip sneered. "Are you sure you want to play this game?"

"You created the situation and made up the rules. All I'm doing is working with what you gave me. If you call that a game; then yes, I'm happy to play it."

Phillip sighed and turned away. He looked over his shoulder and warned Dr. Chenault, "As you say on Earth, welcome to the big leagues. I hope you have what it takes to play."

He reached in his suit pocket, pulled out a portable gate portal and activated it. The white light from innerspace flooded the room and blinded Dr. Chenault so much he had to raise his hands to cover his eyes.

Between his fingers and through squinted eyes, Dr. Chenault witnessed the white light swallow the giant beast. Then with the majesty and awe of a heavenly miracle the invisible door closed, shutting the white light from view.

"I'll never get used to that," Dr. Chenault whispered, as he sat back down in his chair.

He grabbed his common access device (CAD) and turned it on to FNN. The CAD displayed a 3-D holographic image of Jerold Washington about a foot in front of his face. It was like he was talking right to him. This was the psychological effect of watching news on the CAD. It appeared you were having a one way conversation with the anchor.

Dr. Chenault peered into Jerold's eyes, and saw the distinguished appeal of loyalty and truth—the very ingredient necessary for a good anchor to develop a rapport with his viewers. Dr. Chenault listened with intensity. He wanted to know how Jerold would handle the mess his ex-wife created by bringing USSTAP back into the global conversation.

"So I guess what we witnessed today was a miracle—a manmade miracle, ushered by the grace and love of God. Therefore, don't believe the hype pushed by the other news network. USSTAP had nothing to do with today's events. Believe in me…believe in you…believe in us…believe in Earth First.

Stay tuned to FNN for further news on tonight's event. My colleagues will be with you all day and will report the facts as we get them. Stay tuned to FNN to get the real truth. I'm Jerold Washington for FNN."

Nicely done! Dr. Chenault thought, as he deactivated his CAD. He was able to introduce God and Earth First…back-to-back.

He silently praised himself for bringing Jerold into the fold, with a salute and a one-person toast of his thirty year old scotch.

***

USSTAP Lilly Station
Atlantis Continental Self-Atlantic Ocean
Planet Earth, Millmum Galaxy, Rojam Os Cluster

Gate Portal Room Four illuminated with the white light of innerspace. The controller managed the board as if it was a piano and he was playing Beethoven's Symphony Seven. On the stage a huge man emerged from the light, almost blocking out the light. When the gate portal door closed, the large behemoth of a man, known as Phillip stepped down.

"Good evening, Commander. How was your visit with your father?" greeted the controller.

Phillip nodded, "It was...challenging, Lieutenant."

"Sorry to hear that, Commander."

"No big deal. I'm sure things will be better next time."

"I'm sure it will, Commander. These things always work themselves out."

"Yeah, I guess they do...I guess they do," Phillip responded.

Phillip walked out the gate portal room and weaved his way through the maze of corridors to his quarters. Outside the door, it read *Commander Phillip Rand.* He stepped in and went to his desk. He pulled out an encrypted communicator from inside the right hand bottom drawer. He activated it, "This is Philip. We have a problem."

CHAPTER THREE: CARDS ON THE TABLE

House of Michael and Michelle Genesis
Vader City
Planet Chaktun, Millmum Galaxy, Rojam Os Galactic Cluster

The smell of bacon broke through his sleep, like a splash of cold water. One minute, he was dreaming and the next minute, his eyes popped open and he was staring at the beige ceiling. He jumped from bed as fast as his eighty year old body could move, and slipped into the bathroom as not to wake his wife Michelle.

Michael took care of nature's call and freshened-up as quickly as he could. He crept out his side of the bathroom and tip-toed out the door, dressed in his pajamas and a bathrobe. Once he believed he was a safe distance away, so as to not wake Michelle, he moved at his normal pace, down the hall past the utility room, the library and past the grand guest room.

"Where do you think you are going?" shot Adam's voice from behind him in a low whisper.

Michael peered over his shoulder and with a smile said, "Do you smell that bacon?"

Adam motioned for Michael to lower his voice, and then pulled the door shut behind him. "Hell yeah, I smell the bacon."

"Let's go then," commanded Michael.

Both men, dressed in pajamas and robes, turned the corner and rushed through the living room into the kitchen area. Standing in front of the kitchen island was Angela, the maid, putting the finishing touches on a breakfast made for a king.

Michael rushed up to Angela, grabbed her by her waist, and planted a big kiss against her cheek. Angela smiled, and without turning or missing a beat in preparing the food asked, "How is the birthday boy this morning?"

Michael pulled away and moved towards the bay-windowed breakfast nook. "I'm no longer the birthday boy. My birthday was yesterday and it was great. Thanks for helping Michelle set it up."

"No thanks necessary," she said. "It was my pleasure."

"Hello Angela, nice to see you again," Adam interrupted.

"Hello Osguard Freeman," she responded. "I hope you and your wife slept well last night?

Adam walked to the seating area to join Michael, "Yes, we slept fine, thank you. You know, we didn't get to talk much at the party last night. I hope we can talk more during my stay. I would like to know what this old geezer has been up to."

"Old geezer? Why Osguard Freeman, you seem to be picking up English slang very well," Angela bantered back.

Michael watched as he became lost in thought. Angela was so lively that he continued to forget she was not human. Angela and her kind were another creation of Billy Red that Michael got to complete. Angela was an ARIT android, called a zyder; after Billy's Chaktun name…Mezhak Zyder, made to look and act human in every way.

Billy, who was crippled from the waist down since the house explosion, created a prototype zyder in hopes of transferring his consciousness into a living, breathing, able body after he killed Michael in the Unity Stream. Several years after Billy's accident, Michael discovered Billy's notes on the zyder and commissioned the science academy to continue working the idea.

The scientists worked for over a decade, using Billy's notes and prototype as a foundation, and soon after Michael retired and took over as caretaker of the science academy, the scientist rolled out the first zyder…*Angela.*

Angela was man-made, but contained the biological makeup and physiological characteristics of humans without the full emotional baggage. She ate, breathed, cried, felt pain and even aged and died like humans, but she was incapable of ambition, jealousy or anger. And when she died, her memories and experiences would be downloaded through ARIT gateportal technology to a master storage unit at the science academy, called the *Zyder Dome,* where it would be used to shape other zyder consciousness.

Due to accidents, death had occurred for a few zyders already, which allowed USSTAP to test and prove the theory; the Zyder Dome became the unofficial afterlife, or heaven, for the zyders. Five years ago, Michael successfully led the effort for zyders to be universally recognized as sentient beings; thus, creating a universe with two master races—humans and zyders.

Since then, USSTAP created zyders for domestic, military, police, agricultural and industrial jobs. USSTAP programmed zyders with certain and specific skill set and knowledge that allow them to thrive in chosen areas. But unlike indentured servitude or slavery, zyders were paid wages and allowed freedom to move on and do other things. Consequently, without ambition, jealousy or anger rooted in their program, most zyders elected to retain their original program— opting for upgrades rather than modifications.

Angela was the first and oldest zyder. She was made to resemble a human Caucasian from Earth, with shoulder-length brunette hair, which now was sprinkled with gray streaks; round dark eyes, framed with dark black rim glasses and a body which was more on top than the bottom—thanks to the immaturity of one of the scientist in the labs.

She, like all zyders, spoke English, Chaktun and Tuit. But she was unique because Angela upgraded her program to speak Spanish to accommodate the Spanish speaking Earthborn Osguards in Vader City; as well as Ganturi, to accommodate Tynala's passion to understand the Gigantur third of her tri-racial heritage.

Besides being the maid, Angela had become Michelle's best friend and confidant. They were almost inseparable. They shopped and went to the spa together. They were like sisters. There was genuine affection between the two. Conversely Dillon, the other zyder in the house, was Michael's best friend.

Unlike Angela, Dillon was made to reflect a human from Provello, with golden olive tanned complexion, curly greenish black hair and the distinctive Provello split tongue. Dillon was the butler, chauffeur and gardener, but he was also Michael's golfing partner and physical trainer. They hung out together, as much as Angela and Michelle, doing things that a woman just wouldn't understand.

Dillon was Michael's companion, who allowed him to be himself no matter what. Michael did not have to curve his words and actions through the lens of an Osguard with Dillon. He did not have to hold up his reputation or honor with Dillon. All he had to do was be Michael—the Michael he deemed he should have been if he never had joined USSTAP; a happy go lucky person without a care in the world.

Suddenly Michael heard the snap from Dillon's zyder chamber door echo down the hall. Dillon had just awoken from his slumber and disconnected from the chamber in which he slept. Then he heard a hearty yawn push through the silence of the hall. Seconds later Dillon emerged from the room, dressed in jeans and a T-shirt. He walked down the hall into the family room and sat at the bar.

"Angela, any coffee?" he asked.

"At the table with Osguard Michael and Osguard Adam," she pointed. Dillon looked over and shot an awkward smile, "Morning Osguard Michael…Osguard Adam. How'd you sleep?"

"Just fine," Michael replied with a smile. "Come join us. It looks like Angela is making one of her best breakfasts for us."

Dillon hopped off the stool, and walked around the counter to the breakfast nook. He pulled out the chair next to Michael and poured himself some coffee. He sniffed it and let his mind push away the fog of a zyder chamber sleep.

Michael and Adam laughed. Dillon gave a quick frown and then took a sip of coffee.

"Aye, that's some good coffee Angela," he almost sang.

"Glad you like it."

"Did someone mention coffee," Deuce yelled from the top of the stairs connected to the family room.

His announcement was like a fire alarm. Two minutes after Deuce entered the kitchen area to retrieve a cup of coffee, Michael's family room filled up with his children and grandchildren, all looking for coffee and something to eat.

After breakfast Michael found himself in the middle of the family room, with his family sitting quietly listening to him outline his findings from yesterday, and his plan to follow through with a search. When he was finished, the quiet of the room became deafening.

After a moment, Michelle stood. Her eyes were glistening with tears and her face in shock. "Michael, you are 80 years old. Space is for the young, and baby it's time for you to put up your space boots and call the game," she started, trying to mix metaphors to get her point across.

"This is the last one, Michelle. I promise," Michael began to beg. "This is just a cruise around the block; nothing dangerous. We will send Star Scouts in first; normal procedure."

"Michael…" Michelle began to scold.

"Mother," Edward interrupted. "I will go with him and make sure he doesn't do anything stupid."

"What?" Michelle said, choking back tears.

"Look, I have some time-off coming to me. If Dad can postpone this for another month, I can promise, I will be with him."

Michael looked at Edward and nodded, "Thank you, son."

Sharyla stood and said, "I can move some things around and go as well."

Michelle sighed, as she realized she was quickly becoming outnumbered.

Kashara stood and giggled to break the tension in the air. "I'm not going to let you have all the fun by yourselves. I can move some things and give you about a month of time as well."

Michelle pursed her lips and sat down. She stared at the carpet as her mouth dragged out the words, "Well you will need a doctor on this insane journey. So I guess you can sign me up too."

Michael cracked a big smile and rushed over, stood Michelle up and gave her a giant bear hug. "Thank you baby…thank you!"

"Don't thank me yet. Because if you don't come back alive, I'm going to leave your butt and get a divorce."

Michael pulled back, "What?"

"You heard me," Michelle quipped. "If you don't come back alive, I want a divorce."

Michael straightened up and saluted, "Tiah, sire!"

Deuce stood with Cheyenna and Tynala and took the center of the room vacated by his grandfather. "Dad, mom, mama, papa, nana, gramps, Aunt Sharyla and Aunt Kashara: we have something to say.

Michael looked up and saw the seriousness in his grandchildren's eyes. He knew they had just finished University and were in the process of selecting an Academy to go to, but there was still time. They had at least three more months before deciding. One of the few things Michael did, while he was CEO of USSTAP, was ramrod legislation giving children and descendants of Osguards from all Galactic Clusters the right of choice.

They now had the right to choose if they would rather go to a USSTAP Academy and become an Osguard of USSTAP, or do something else. It no longer was their destiny, but a choice to become an Osguard. Now that his grandchildren were of age and had completed University, it was their decision to follow in their parents footsteps or blaze a trail of their own.

Since the passing of the legislation, several third generation Osguards chose to leave USSTAP and fulfill their destiny in other ways. For example, Shawn's granddaughter, Karina followed her dream to be a reporter. Now she was the lead reporter for what translates in English as Star Universal News, also known as SUN in English.

"As you know," Tynala began, "we have a big decision to make."

Cheyenna jumped in, "Before we make that decision, we believe there is one more life experience we must have in order to understand our destiny and to learn something about ourselves."

Kashara interrupted, "You want to come along?"

"No," Deuce injected. "I mean yes…at least I do." The others nodded in agreement. "But we need to do something first."

"What's that?" questioned Michelle.

"On Earth, the U-day celebration is coming up."

Michael's heart sank. Immediately, Ed, Kashara and Sharyla gazed upon their father; concern blanketed their faces. It was like they were reading Michael's mind at the mere mention of Earth.

In all the years of his retirement, Michael had only mentioned Earth's U-day once. He had put Earth and its people behind him, and adapted Chaktun and Vader City as his new home. He felt betrayed by Earth. It hurt him to the core that he did all he could during his tenure as Osguard to help Earth—including saving it from multiple attacks that were unbeknownst to the people of Earth; only to be spit upon and to be considered so vile a human being, that he couldn't even settle on his own planet when it came time for his retirement.

"What's this about?" asked Adam.

"Look, Gramps, I know you haven't visited Earth," said Tynala. "But my mother, aunt, and uncle visited Earth many times; and we haven't. We just want to see what it is like. We want to see if we can get in touch with our roots."

"Earth isn't the place for that!" shouted Michael. His anger was only surpassed for the fear he had for his grandchildren going to Earth.

"Earth doesn't want us! It isn't safe!"

Jenna piped-in, "What do you mean it isn't safe? Earth is probably one of the safest places in the universe for them. It's your home planet. Besides, their technology is too inferior to ours to pose any type of threat. With the proper safety and security precautions, I bet Earth is as safe as Vader City."

"Jenna, I love you like a sister, but you don't know what you are talking about here," Michelle cautioned with her best diplomatic voice.

"Look, all of you," Deuce pushed. "We love you all, and we care about you all. But this is something we have to do. We are of age to make our own decisions. Furthermore, until we make the decision on which academy to attend, or if we will attend any academy at all, we are designated as Osguards-in-training, with all the rights and privileges of so."

"What are you saying?" Sharyla chimed.

Silence lingered in the air as the question echoed in everyone's head. Then Cheyenna spoke up, "Mom, we're saying with or without your permission, we will be leaving for Earth in three days."

"*What?*" Michael yelled. "Over my dead body!"

Michelle grabbed Michael's arm and pulled him close to her. "Michael, if I had reacted like that to your announcement to go chase after some fictitious golden spot in the universe, how would that had played out?"

Michael turned to look into his wife's eyes and saw the wisdom of her words. "Okay...okay, you're right, Michelle." He turned to his grandchildren and nodded. "If this is something you feel you have to do, you have my blessings...reluctantly...but you have them."

Kalina, who'd remained quiet throughout the debate, now stepped forward. "Okay, but I must insist you go with a security officer —and it will be a security officer of my choosing."

"Who do you have in mind, Kalina," Ed wondered aloud.

"I'm thinking of my security officer on my ship, Toniac...Toniac Good."

"Isn't he a zyder?" Deuce questioned. "A Tuit zyder? Is that wise?"

"You're half Tuit. Cheyenna is a third Tuit; and Tynala is a third Gantur. I want a Tuit watching you guys. The best Tuit I know is Toniac. And you of all people should know him being a zyder is not a problem. In this case it may be a plus. We can upgrade his programming so he can interface and integrate with Earth people better than you three."

"Okay, mom. I guess that's okay."

"What's your plan?" Jenna asked.

Deuce cleared his throat and said, "We want to visit New Haven where papa was born; and New York where Nausona and Laurona contacted their grandchildren Betty Nightman and Shirley Grace. Then we would like to see where it all began in Danville Virginia, where Osguard Gardens once stood and the site of the annual celebration of U-Day. We want to get there by August 30th to join in on the celebration."

Michael huffed. He knew that if U-Day was observed, it wouldn't be much of a celebration. He had lost all empathy for his brothers and sisters of Earth. His heart had already tightened by what he considered Earth's betrayal of him and USSTAP. Now it was about to explode from fear for his grandchildren. The only shining light in this conversation was Kalina's steadfast request that Toniac accompany them. He knew Toniac, and he admired Toniac's skills as a security officer and loyalty as a USSTAP sixana warrior. Kalina was right. If anyone could protect his grandchildren, Toniac could.

***

CHAPTER FOUR: BREADCRUMBS

Tasman Sea
Between Australia and New Zealand
Planet Earth, Millmum Galaxy, Rojam Os Cluster

The Sea Protector Atlantis ran deep and silent over what was left of the Norfolk Ridge. Her sensors and scanners were at a steady hum as the invisible fingers and eyes reached out through the murky black water and touched, probed and dug into the ridge and the corresponding trench below it. World General Akbar Zandi dispatched the Atlantis to investigate this sudden and, for now, inexplicable phenomena.

Above her, bore the beginning of an oceanic task force comprised of oceanic engineers, scientists, and navies from Australia and New Zealand. Like the Atlantis, they were dispatched by their respective governments to investigate what happened and how it happened. Presently several ships sat above them, pinging the area with sonar and underwater radar to capture the picture of the ocean floor.

For this reason, the Atlantis was cloaked in stealth mode ten, which was harder to do underwater than in space due to the acoustic characteristics of liquid. She was at all-stop with her slitanium hull fully energized to absorb all sound and energy waves. Inside, on her command deck, sat Centurion Christopher Byrd in the command chair. Chris was South African and of British descent. He'd grown up in Port Elizabeth on the Indian Ocean side of the country, where he fell in love with the sea and all of its glory.

When USSTAP recruited him he volunteered for all the sea duty he could, which took him to exotic water worlds of the universe. This was his first and possibly last assignment for USSTAP, training future USSTAP sixana seamen for sea duty on other planets in the safety of Earth's oceans.

He was thinking of his potential retirement back to South Africa, with the cool blue Indian Ocean water kissing the glistening white sandy beach he planned on having for a back yard.

Simultaneously, Byrd was thinking how the last thirty-six hours were atypical of a training voyage. His young seamen took part in a clandestine operation against Mother Nature that saved thousands of lives.

He knew his crew was stepping with a bit more pride and a great deal of satisfaction in their work today, and he was going to take full advantage of that. He understood that his crew was on a high that would take days if not months before normalcy crept back into their lives.

"Waterblade One has found something," his Centurion of Operations, Robin Force said, interrupting Byrd's thoughts of retirement.

"Report," Byrd grumbled.

Waterblades were the single seat submarines that were cousins to the defender starfighter. A Waterblade was slicker, smoother and slimmer than the defender. Its hydrogenic engines were connected to the main body of the sub, and not in the wing spares like its cousin, the defender. The concave blades that were set at a forty degree high angle ran the length of the sub, and were connected to the sub by swept spars. The blades generated the cut and dispersed the water, creating a hydro bubble for the waterblade to operate.

"Waterblade One reports the sentiment from the ridge that settled in the Norfolk Deep, is littered with dialairtic crystals."

"What? Is Waterblade One sure?"

"Yes, Sire, he is sure," Force told him, handing him her ARIT pad.

"That's odd," Byrd said to no one in particular, looking down at the ARIT pad. He scanned through the report and then looked at Force, "Is this connected to the underwater earthquake?"

Force took a deep breath, reached over to the ARIT pad and activated the next page button. "I believe so, Sire. But not in the way you are thinking."

Byrd reviewed the second page and as he read it one word stood out and took root in his mind—*microportal drill.* The report indicated evidence of a massive microportal drill had eroded the stability of the ridge.

The microportal technology disassembled things at a micro-cellular level and reconstructed it at pre-designated coordinates. But because the generators couldn't pass on the pulse that told a human's heart to beat or lungs to breathe, they were only used to transport inanimate objects and not living beings.

"Force, am I reading this correctly?" Byrd pushed in astonishment.

"Yes, Sire, I believe you are," Force whispered, looking around nervously. "Can we take this to your ready-room?"

Byrd looked up and saw the worry in Force's eyes and the nervousness of her demeanor, which was very unusual. He nodded and walked to the doors. As the doors opened, he yelled back, "Col Gabriel, you have the con!"

"Tiah, Sire, I have the con," Col Gabriel responded.

Byrd and Force stepped through the doors and as the doors swished closed behind them, they took the two steps down to the landing and turned right into Byrd's ready-room. The ready-room was the standard ready-room found on any USSTAP ship. It was half-elliptical, furnished with a desk with a leather swivel chair behind it, two leather free-standing chairs in front, a couch next to the door, and a kitchenette to the side. A bathroom was accessible behind the kitchenette. Opposite the kitchenette was the ARIT monitoring station on the other side. Byrd moved to the station and motioned for Force to continue.

Force activated the monitoring station. The report appeared on the right side of the holographic screen, and Waterblade One's pilot appeared on the left.

"Captain Joy, this is Centurion Force on secure channel beta four—do you copy?"

"Captain Joy here—I have you loud and clear."

"Centurion Byrd has reviewed your report. I want to run something by him, but I think you should hear it as well and offer any rebuttal or advice."

"Tiah," Joy responded.

"Sire," Force began, "I believe someone has been drilling for dialairtic crystals with microportal technology in this area...and they got sloppy and drilled too much and weakened the structural integrity of the ridge."

"Impossible!" Byrd retorted. "There is no way someone could have used microportal technology on Earth without us knowing it. We watch for this type of intrusion twenty-four hours a day."

"I know sire," Force pushed, "But I don't know any other way to explain the microportal residue."

"How recent is the residue and are you sure, Captain, it is microportal residue?" Byrd asked Joy."

"Tiah, sire," Joy said. "I connected to the Atlantis ARIT and that is what I got back. So I grabbed a piece with my sub's claw and brought it into the sub for me to visually analyze. My degree is in portal technology with a minor in microportal science. I wrote a thesis on using microportal technology to enhance gateportal travel; so I am very familiar with what microportal residue looks like. And I'm ninety-eight percent sure this is microportal residue. And for your last question, it is about forty-eight hours old."

"How did it get there?" Byrd asked.

"Like I said sire," Joy continued, "I did a thesis on enhance gateportal travel. It looks like someone else read my thesis, because there is enough radiation particles to suggest a gateportal opening occurred inside the ridge. I think a gateportal opened from space, in which a microportal drill was used to mine for dialairtic crystals."

Byrd's jaw dropped. Immediately, his mind raced to capture on the inconceivable possibilities that would fit the evidence. Someone, somehow, got past USSTAP security and safeguards and was drilling from space for the most expensive crystal in the universe.

Dialairtic crystals were the main power source used throughout USSTAP. Since the destruction of the Eierre System, which supplied one-third of the universe's requirement for dialairtic crystals, during the Tuit war, the demand had been insatiable. But no one could have by-passed USSTAP security and safeguard measures. It was impossible—impossible, unless they had someone's help on the inside —someone who turned a blind eye.

The realization sprung from Byrd's face—they had a spy. That's why Force was being so secretive. "Force, classify this report at level six; recall all waterblades and set course out of these waters and away from the topside force and get us to Lilly Station via gateportal routing."

"Tiah," Force responded with a sigh of relief. It was evident she didn't want to come out and say there was a spy in their midst, but she appeared damned glad the evidence she presented led Byrd to that conclusion.

***

Onboard Startram 01-7530038
Between Chaktun and Earth
Millmum Galaxy, Rojam Os Galactic Cluster

His cousins, Cheyenna and Tynala were asleep, but Deuce was wide awake. He was wondering if they were making the right decision to visit Earth. Their grandfather seemed awfully worried about their safety. But he was sure that was the paranoia of a broken heart speaking and not one of a calm man who weighed the facts equally. But there was still a tinge of doubt knocking at his consciousness, debating if his grandfather was right, and even if he wasn't right, what the hell he hoped to get out of visiting Earth.

He, Cheyenna and Tynala had always dreamed of visiting Earth, since they were little kids in primary school. He was well aware of his Tuit heritage, and was even quite proud of it. He was also aware of his Chaktun heritage, even though it was so distant in his lineage that it could hardly be counted. But he did not know anything of his Earth heritage…this American heritage, which at one point his grandfather and grandmother were so proud.

His grandparents as well as the other Earthborn Osguards living in Vedar City waved the United States flag proudly in their yards. They celebrated the Fourth of July and Thanksgiving, as much as they celebrated Christmas and Easter. They even had a small celebration of when some territories, called Puerto Rico and Guam, entered the union and added the fifty first and fifty second star to the flags. But they were unwilling, or unable, to talk about life on Earth to him or his cousins.

He tried talking to his father, but his father didn't have much to add. He was born and raised on a space station and only visited Earth to see his family a couple of times. He too had grown away from Earth; and Deuce thought that a shame.

He turned to look out the window of the startram. Its black wing-like engines, laced in the red power strip that energized its stealth capability seemed to meld into the darkness of space. The startram was the transport ship of USSTAP, meaning it had the characteristic design of USSTAP ships, but was considerably smaller. The middle segment of the startram was hollow and could connect to a passenger cabin that accommodated twenty-five passengers or a freight cabin.

This startram was equipped with a VIP passenger cabin; plush leather seating, spacious leg room, kitchenette with a bar, and monitors at every seat to capture the galactic network for entertainment and news.

They were fourteen hours into their eighteen hour flight. It would have been a lot faster if they used a ship that had gateportal engines, but they were reserved for the combat ships of the association. Deuce knew this was part of his grandfather's plan; having him and his cousins wallow through an eighteen hour flight so he could think about what they were about to embark on doing.

"Rise and shine," shot Toniac's voice from behind him. Toniac Good had a disarming smile...a good characteristic for a security officer. He stood six feet and two inches tall, with a lean, but muscular build. His skin complexion could be confused for someone of Latino descent, which was only enforced by his wavy dark hair. He had already donned the contact lenses to camouflage his Tuit cat-like eyes.

Deuce swiveled his chair around to face Toniac, as his cousins pushed the sleep from their minds. Toniac was at the main monitor in front of the cabin and he had his ready-to-teach look on his face.

"Okay kiddos," Toniac began. "Before we get to Earth there are a couple of things I need to go over with you." Toniac activated the monitor and several vidpics displayed across the big screen and on the individual monitors at their seats.

Cheyenna let out a loud yawn, while her arms reached for the ceiling in a long stretch. Tynala followed suit, but her yawn was a bit more petite.

Toniac then began to go over the history and the development of the country known as the United States, in which they were about to visit. Deuce soaked in every word, because this was the first time anybody really spoke to him about the United States.

Deuce learned that the United States was a staunch supporter of USSTAP, until a political organization with world-wide paramilitary capability rose to prominence in the country's political arena. This organization was known as Earth First, whose members were colloquially known as *Firsties*. The current president of the United States belonged to the Earth First Party. President Amanda Taylor was the third president in twenty years to belong to the Earth First Party, and she was presently running for re-election this year.

Deuce also learned that the Earth First party was responsible for shaping the negative attitude towards USSTAP, and that they had high leadership positions in many of the former countries that supported USSTAP. Toniac warned that finding friendly faces on Earth would be a challenge; therefore, they were to shy away from letting people know who they were.

Cheyenna raised her hand and asked, "Why?"

"Why what?" Toniac queried back.

"Why do the Firsties hate us so much?"

Toniac folded his arms across his chest and turned to the porthole next to him. He stared outside into the blackness of space. Stars were invisible since the startram was moving at MOP 50, which equated to fifty light years an hour. But one could still imagine the vastness of space still being littered with twinkling stars from heaven. Then Toniac stated, "They fear us."

"What do you mean they fear us?" Deuce asked.

"This is just my supposition," Toniac started to explain. "There is no written record, just a bunch of commentaries from different social scientist and talking heads on the galactic networks, but I tend to agree with them."

"Go on," Cheyenna urged.

Toniac turned to face his pupils. "They fear us because we don't fit into their paradigm, which means USSTAP is a threat. Some fear us because of religious beliefs. Their religion can't explain us, or doesn't even hint that there was life outside of Earth."

"Some fear us because we are aliens, and their xenophobic world cannot accept aliens. All of a sudden the leaders of the largest organization in the universe were Black, Latino and alien people with weird eyes, vampire teeth, horns, split tongues or a sixth digit on their hands—many with skin colors and complexions that they never saw before."

"To these people, who thought they were masters of their domain, they now have to cope with the realization that they are just ordinary citizens of the universe—nothing special or unique—just ordinary.

"Others fear us because we upset the economic order in which they can't control. In the early days of USSTAP's revelation on Earth, what are known as third world countries began to grow economically and challenge the economic power bases of the world. Some unstable countries became stable, and some technologically challenged countries started to become technology leaders."

"So those whose livelihood depended on taking advantage of these countries, unexpectedly found themselves being taken advantage of. And the list goes on. But the bottom line is fear. However, even though Firsties represent a powerful pocket of Earth's society, it is still a small pocket. Research indicates the majority of Earthlings are either neutral to USSTAP, or even supportive. Those who are supportive belong to a movement called Tappy. I guess that's a play on the English pronunciation of the association's acronym— USSTAP."

Deuce was pleased to learn there were USSTAP supporters amongst the people of Earth.

"They call themselves 'Tappies,'" Toniac went on, "Members of the Tappy movement advocate for more integration with USSTAP's technology and trade in an effort to catch up with the rest of the universe. To them it's about the holistic betterment of society in terms of economic growth and military stability."

"In the United States, the political arm of the Tappy movement is based on the newly forged political party made up of the remnants of the former Republican and Democratic Parties, now known as the Democratic Republican Party."

How original. Deuce thought.

As Toniac continued to talk, Deuce learned other countries had similar political parties that were loosely tied to the Tappy movement. This caught him by surprise, because he was used to planets having one government with one voice, not an independent system of governments with several voices. He always thought the U.N. spoke for the planet.

Toniac assured him he was mistaken. Toniac also described the state of technology they were about to encounter. Deuce imagined the country as an archaic, but comfortable, civilization since it still used fossil fuel modes of transportation and energy to drive its technology. Deuce realized this was why the planet had not achieved any type of substantial space travel. It seemed to refuse to move away from fossil fuel technology. He wondered if the leaders of the planet realized that the amount of fossil fuel was finite, and at the rate of consumption that the people of Earth were using their fuel, it would run out in a matter of decades. Also, he wondered if the leaders of the planet understood what the effects of burning of fossil fuel did to their atmosphere.

Before he could ask Toniac about this, Toniac moved on to talk about the population and the overcrowding that had occurred over the short time USSTAP had been actively involved with the planet. Deuce learned that thirty-two earth years ago, when USSTAP announced their presence to the people of Earth, its total population was approximately seven-point-one Billion. Today, in the Earth Year of 2044, that population was ten billion.

Toniac explained that food and water were scarce and not nearly enough to accommodate such a population growth. He warned that the Genesis children would witness, '*poverty up close and personal.*'

Tynala raised her hand and asked, "Why don't we help them?"

Toniac smiled and pushed a button on his remote. Several vidpics of Michael Genesis, in his younger days, flew across the screen. "Your grandfather tried," he responded. "That was the main reason he led the effort to recognize Earth. He planned on someday recruiting Earth into the USSTAP fold, and jump-starting them with technology in order to curtail poverty and illness."

"He started by offering medical assistance to cure fatal diseases like cancer, Alzheimer, and AIDS. The people took this assistance and continue to take advantage of this offer today through USSTAP medical facilities in the Central African Republic— the only property the UN-USSTAP Pact allowed USSTAP to purchase and maintain.

The Central African Republic government, also known as the CAR government, was one of a handful of African governments that rejected the UN-USSTAP Pact; and actually seceded from the UN in protest. Because of this, USSTAP chose Sibut as the home for its planetary hospital, The Susan Tillman Memorial Hospital, to administer to the health needs of Earth's fatally and chronically ill community. It was named after Dr. Susan Tillman, a dear friend of your grandparents, who died during the Kulusks' Terinolice Virus attack on Millmum Capitol Station, almost forty years ago."

"Through civilian doctor referrals, patients are transported to Tillman Memorial in the prefecture of Kémo via gateportal and treated. All-in-all, with USSTAP's assistance, the death rate from these diseases and others is down by sixty-five percent, compared to Earth Year 2012."

"The CAR is a landlocked country that was once a former French colony. When USSTAP offered the alliance, the CAR was marred in violence and corruption due to the fighting between the Muslim and Christian factions. The CAR is rich in minerals and gems like gold, diamond and uranium. USSTAP stepped in and offered profitable trade agreements and advocated peace between the factions; helping them to end the decades of instability, due to their internal conflicts and conflicts that spilled over from their neighbors."

Toniac changed the picture to a beautiful cityscape with elegant towers, buildings and structures. The streets were clean and the landscapes surrounding the buildings were manicured to perfection. "The special symbiotic relationship we have with the Central African Republic, helped turn it around from a third world country into a modern developed country in three decades. Life expectancy has risen two fold. HIV and other diseases are a thing of the past. Their economy is thriving. Their cities are growing. Industry has risen. The tourist trade is booming and the jobless rate is below three percent." "It is now the jewel of Africa and the envy of the world. The CAR is a prime example of how the rest of the planet could have benefited from establishing even a non-binding trade agreement with USSTAP."

The picture rotated to capture the full beauty of the city as Toniac continued, "Since the inception of Tillman Memorial, trade agreements with the CAR for the use of the land to build, maintain and sustain the hospital yielded wealth and rewards to the country in the form of oil and rare gems from other parts of the universe. Due to this newfound wealth, businesses sprang up, national security increased, crime dropped...the government became stable, predictable and more responsive towards its populations."

"This new fortune spilled over to the CAR's neighbors as well. Chad to the north, Sudan to the northeast, South Sudan to the east, the Democratic Republic of the Congo, and the Republic of the Congo in the south, and Cameroon to the west; are experiencing an economic revolution that make the area a true market competitor on the global stage. These countries, no longer being a puppet of the industrial nations of the north that control the UN, thrive like lions on the Serengeti in the midst of herd of wildebeests."

Toniac noticed the blank stares coming from his charges and realized they didn't understand what he meant when he metaphorically used lions and wildebeests to paint his picture. So he corrected himself using animals they were more familiar with from Chaktun, "Like jax on the Venolian plains in the midst of a coo of shredrants." The recognition in their eyes let Toniac know he had correctly conveyed his thoughts.

Tynala raised her hand. Toniac nodded to recognize her. "Toniac, why is that?"

"Why is what?"

"Why are Central African Republic and its neighbors the only ones taking advantage of USSTAP trade and technology?"

Toniac changed the vidpics to an elderly man. "This is Dr. Claude Chenault, former President of France, Former Secretary General of the United Nations, and founder and president of Earth First. He successfully led the effort that forted your grandfather's vision. And that's why we are where we are today. After the original sixty Osguards started to retire, or became caught up in other matters in the universe, the enthusiasm and motivation to challenge Dr. Chenault waned."

"That still doesn't explain why we don't help the entire planet," Deuce pushed. "I mean, this is my grandfather and grandmother's home world. Shit, it's the original sixty's home world! It would seem my grandfather and the others would fight tooth and nail for their people."

Toniac took a deep breath and let out a thoughtful sigh. "I know I do not need to remind you of the First Article." Toniac switched the vidpic to the USSTAP Charter, Article One; which read:

"Members of USSTAP will recognize the sovereign rights of territorial governments, and the people that government has domain over, without intervention or purpose of interference, without written authorization from Congress, Parliament or the Conclave. Said authorization can only be granted when a citizen or citizens of the United Science, Security Trade Association of Planets' life, or lives are unduly in danger. Said authorization will only be granted for short and limited time in order to rectify or secure the situation which caused the danger."

Deuce closed his eyes as if he was in pain. His father had taught him the First Article when he was four years old. But deep down inside, he knew his grandfather wanted to shred the First Article to save his home world from the path of suicide it seemed to have put itself in.

Nevertheless, he knew that his grandfather knew that going against the First Article, for the betterment of his home world, would only bring more angst than what it was worth. Breaking Article One would only put fear in other member planets' governments of the possibility that USSTAP would come knocking on their door if USSTAP didn't agree with the way they were handling their citizens. When Tynala and Cheyenna nodded at Deuce, he knew his cousins felt the same way.

"There seems to be so much animosity towards USSTAP. What about us? Should we hide our identities while we are on Earth?" Cheyenna asked.

Toniac nodded, "Of course, if asked or a need for introductions arises, you can state your name. We are not spying, and you are American citizens...by birth," Toniac instructed. "You will have the proper identification, identifying you as who you are. As for me, I carry USSTAP diplomatic identification. However, like me, you will be wearing contacts to hide your Tuit pupils; and Tynala, you will cap your Gantur teeth in order to appear more indigenous."

There were several more questions and answers transpired. Altogether, the lesson took two of the four hours they had left on the trip. When they neared the Earth's Solar System Startram 01–7530038 went pitch black, as the slitanium skin energized to absorb, bounce, and deflect any energy aimed at it.

The tiny ship floated through the Oort Cloud, surrounding the outer region of Earth's solar system, better known to USSTAP as the Gentry Star System. Startram 01–7530038 slowed to hypersonic speed and descended to negative two hundred on the galactic plane, putting it below the Gentry System and starting the Oort approach to Earth.

Looking out his window, Deuce asked, "Why the stealth entry?"

"It is a provision of the U.N.—USSTAP Pact of 2029," Toniac answered. "Even though we announce our presence and our comings and goings to the U.N. council for Space and Strategic Affairs, we must ensure our activity is out of sight of the public."

The Oort approach was a straight-in approach. Startram 01–7530038 flew below Earth's orbit, directly aligned with its southern polar cap where Earth's surveillance and tracking satellites were lacking. Then the startram rolled inverted, relative to Earth's position in the heavens. For in space, the definition of upright, sideways, or inverted was a relative term.

Most ships sailed the heavens using planetary northern hemispheres as reference to upright, but some galaxies used the southern hemisphere as their reference to upright, lending themselves to sail one hundred and eighty degrees opposite of the USSTAP norm. In those galaxies, the USSTAP instrumentation was altered to compensate and the ships rolled to match the norm of the galaxies. The galaxies using the southern reference were southpaw galaxies, and those using the northern hemispheric references were northpaw galaxies. Galaxy One, the Millmum Galaxy, was northpaw.

Startram 01–7530038 entered Earth's atmosphere, descended to five hundred feet off the surface of Antarctica, and pushed on a course bringing it out over the Atlantic Ocean. Moving at half hypersonic speed, puncturing the sound barrier and lifting heavy waves from the ocean under it, the startram sailed the dark skies of the night.

The low level flying was specifically designed to evade radar, thus complying with the 2029 Pact. The ship's scanner and sensor sweep reached out several hundred kilometers, to detect ships and other manmade objects that might be in the startram's path. When detected, the ship automatically altered course and altitude to avoid contact.

This part of the approach was very stressful, but also exhilarating for the pilots. They had to devote one hundred percent of their attention to flying the startram, which tested their skills in the most optimum manner. Any deviation in error while traveling over ten times the speed of sound could slam the ship into the ocean, killing its occupants and spreading wreckage over several square miles.

After twenty minutes, the startram slowed to a halt and hovered over the ocean surface. The ocean surface broke, revealing a platform pushing its way up. The startram settled onto the platform. A chromerion field enveloped the platform, and its content, in a bubble of scientific shielding. The platform descended, swallowed by the ocean as the sea returned to its natural state, leaving no indication of manmade disturbance.

Deuce had his face pressed against the porthole, staining his eyes to capture every moment of the capture. The elevator ride through the depths of the ocean was different than traveling through space. Deuce had traveled through space since he was a baby. He was used to it. He had forgotten the dangers of space, because of its beauty. It was a solid blanket of blackness, with the stars illuminating the darkness, shedding tiny sparkles of light. The ocean was different. It showed its dangers, with bold tenacity—water. Deuce never thought about dying in space; but all of a sudden he had a fear of drowning in water.

Even though both environments were just as dangerous as the other, he never thought of death from lack of oxygen—until now. Drowning in water or suffocating in space was equally abhorrent in his mind right now.

The platform descended deeper into the ocean, pushing volumes of water out of its way as the waves hugged the chromerion field shielding the ship from flood and pressure. The platform descended one thousand two hundred and fifty fathoms; sinking into the bowls of USSTAP Planetary Headquarters, Lilly Station, named after the Pathgo slave who demonstrated so much compassion to the Osguard sisters, ages ago.

It took several minutes for the crew to run their checklist and shutdown engines. In the meantime the moving corridor waded through the water to reach the cabin. Once the cabin and the moving corridor reached equal pressurization, and the water blown away, the cabin door opened.

Cheyenna, Tynala, Deuce and Toniac emerged from the cabin and walked to the main reception area. Deuce was still reeling from the startram capture procedures. It was probably the coolest thing he had seen in his short twenty Universal Years of life. He had heard about it, and even seen vidpics of USSTAP performing the procedure on other planets, but this was the first time he had experienced it.

When he and the others reached the reception area, there was a tall brunette with short curly hair and sparkling green eyes waiting for them. She wore the four dark starbursts insignia of a Centurion. He knew this was the welcoming committee by her stern professional demeanor.

She walked up to them and presented her hand to Cheyenna first, "Welcome aboard Lilly Station, I am Centurion of Operations, Jessica Jansen."

Cheyenna took her hand and gave it a hardy shake, "Thank you Centurion, I am Cheyenna Genesis…people call me Chey." Then she motioned towards Tynala, "This is my cousin Tynala Genesis."

Jansen nodded and offered her hand to Tynala.

"Please call me Nala," Tynala said as she greeted Jansen.

"And this is my cousin Michael Genesis II," Cheyenna continued.

"Call me Deuce," Deuce added as they shook hands.

"And this is Captain Toniac Good, our chaperon during this visit."

Jansen reached out her hand towards Toniac, "A pleasure to meet you captain. I've read about some of your dealings in Tuit space."

Toniac shook Jansen's hand, "Thank you, Sire," he managed to stammer.

Deuce half way expected some lame attempt by Jansen to bolster Toniac's pride, by mentioning how much he was an example to the Zyder race. But he was surprised by Jansen's casual mention of his military record and nothing else.

Jansen then turned to face her guests and said, "Sorry the general isn't here to meet you. We have had some activity in the last couple of days that is taking his attention. He is presently in direct conference with the Chief Osguard and the First Osguard."

"That important!" Toniac uttered.

"I'm afraid so," Jansen agreed.

"Is it something that'll damper our plans?" Deuce questioned.

"I don't believe so…at least not at the moment," Jansen reassured him. "But you must be tired from your long journey. Let me show you to your quarters so you can freshen up, grab a bite to eat and get some rest. We have you scheduled to step to New Haven at zero eight hundred hours, Earth Time, tomorrow morning. Until then, let us know if there is anything we can do to make your visit more comfortable."

Jansen pointed to her right, and motioned for her guests to follow her. "We will have your bags delivered to your quarters shortly."

"Thank you, Centurion, that sounds great," Toniac responded.

CHAPTER FIVE: UNRAVELED

USSTAP Lilly Station
Atlantis Continental Self-Atlantic Ocean
Planet Earth, Millmum Galaxy, Rojam Os Cluster

"Did you hear the *Atlantis* made port last night?" Sharon asked Phillip as she pulled up a seat next to him.

Phillip was eating his breakfast of eggs, toast and coffee. His mind was clouded with thoughts of his meeting with Claude last night. He had reviewed the data that Claude gave him and concluded the evidence was damning; mostly damning for him and his predecessor, who initiated contact with Claude decades earlier.

"Phillip...Phillip, did you hear me?" Sharon pushed.

Sharon's voice pulled Phillip from his thoughts as he turned and focused on her. His mind played back the last words Sharon said as it fought to push back the nervousness he was feeling inside. "Huh, what did you...hear what?" Phillip said, trying to bring his thoughts into the present.

Sharon Castle was the other controller of sector five, his sector. Sharon had the third shift, and probably had just been relieved by John Littlefoot, who had the first shift. Phillip was the second shift controller.

"I said did you hear the *Atlantis* made it back to port last night?" Sharon repeated as she poked at her breakfast yogurt.

"No, I didn't. I just got back from a day pass...visiting my father."

"Oh yeah, that's right. How's your father doing?"

"He's fine," Phillip regurgitated from his script. "Medicine is working and he should be back on his feet in a couple of days." Then he took a sip from his coffee. He was eager to hear what Sharon had to say, but wanted to portray that he wasn't. "So what's this about the *Atlantis?*"

"Yeah, she came back priority one and uploaded her report on secure channel beta five—General Akbar Zandi's eyes only."

"Came back from where?" Phillip asked.

"From the Norfolk Deep," Sharon responded, after gulping down a spoonful of yogurt. "Zandi sent her there to check out the cause of the underwater earthquake. If you ask me she found something."

"You meant to tell me Zandi sent a sea protector in the middle of all that activity, where she may have been seen by other ships?"

"Yeah, why not? With the stealth upgrade our submarines can float within ten feet of the Earth ships and still go undetected."

Phillip had not thought of that. He had counted on Akbar's aversion to keep him away from the site of the underwater earthquake. Worry forced its way to his eyes.

"What's wrong? It looks like you've seen a ghost," Sharon commented.

Phillip shook his head, "No I'm alright, just a little tired from my visit with my father." He took another swig from his coffee mug. "What do you think it's all about?"

"What?"

"The *Atlantis?* "

"All I know is she took soil and water samples at the bottom of the deep; and whatever she found, it must be good. Because, not more than an hour after the samples were analyzed she interlinked that she was coming home and all transmissions from then on went on the secure net."

Sharon's words rolled around in Phillip's mind. He didn't expect Akbar to move so quickly and so decisively. Hell, he didn't expect Akbar to make such a grand command decision as he did to stop the tsunami. He had always figured Akbar to be a cautious man…a man waiting his time for retirement, who would do anything to avoid the limelight of an incident…a man who wanted to keep attention away from him or his decisions. Conversely, Akbar turned out not to be that man.

"Yeah, Jansen is pulling all our data and records from the last year and running a level seven diagnostic on them," Sharon continued.

"Level seven diagnostic, for what reason?" Phillip asked.

"I don't know. I guess they are checking to see if there is something we missed, or if we made a mistake or something. Zandi knows that this Tsunami shouldn't have happened; at least it shouldn't have happened without some type of warning."

"All I know is my crap is tight and I don't have anything to worry about. I know your reports are above board, so that only leaves the young Lieutenant Littlefoot. I bet you he has something to hide.

All I can say is if he doctored the data to cover his mistakes, he must be good to fool both you and me."

Phillip nodded, knowing that a level seven diagnostic would uncover his duplicity in the Norfolk Deep disaster. He had underestimated the integrity of the ridge, and told his employer to drill at a point where the integrity was too shallow. The aftermath of the drilling eventually caused the ridge shift, which triggered the underwater earthquake. Unfortunately, the shift in weight happened after his shift and he wasn't in place to see it coming, and alter the records to make it look like something else.

"Oh, by the way, did you know we have Osguards on-board?" Sharon injected, changing the conversation.

"What?" Phillip grunted.

"Yeah, we have Osguards on-board," Sharon gleefully spurted. "Well, not exactly Osguards, but Osguard candidates. Michael Genesis' grandchildren are on-board, Michael II, Tynala and Cheyenna."

"Why?" Phillip asked.

"They are going to do some backpacking across America or some sort of nonsense like that," she stated. She straightened up like an epiphany hit her, "I think this is the first time since that ugly-ass U.N.-USSTAP Pact that a member of any of the Osguard families has stepped foot on Earth. I wonder if it has anything to do with the Tsunami and how Zandi handled it."

The information triggered something in Phillip. His frustration and nervousness had just turned into fear and he needed to do something. For the first time in his life he felt claustrophobic. He was over one thousand fathoms under water, in a metallic can with his enemies closing in.

"I got to go," he spurted.

"What?"

"Oh, I have to go back to my quarters, I forgot something," he stated with regained composure.

"Oh, alright," Sharon responded. "I'll catch you at shift change tonight."

"Yeah, shift change tonight," Phillip agreed as he stood.

The breakfast crowd seemed to be growing, and there were more people in the cafeteria now than when he sat down. He looked around to see if anybody was staring at him. He wondered if Jansen had put together the information, and if there was a security team watching him now, ready to pounce on him at any moment.

He shrugged the thought from his mind and waded through the traffic of people to the side exit. He pushed his way through the doorway and into the corridor that led to his quarters. He knew he had to execute his escape plan. He never thought it would come to this. He thought he'd never get caught and he would retire from USSTAP with a great bit of money from his other employer.

Now he had to escape and leave. He knew that it was only a matter of hours before Jansen would zero in on him; so he had to use the time wisely and efficiently to make his escape and insure USSTAP would never find him.

***

General Akbar Zandi stood in the middle of his communications center in his office. Around him were the 3-D holographic projections of the Millmum Galaxy Osguard: Jaquille Rican, Rojam Os First Osguard, Anthony Black, and USSTAP Chief Executive Osguard, Lillian Sario. This was the first time he'd ever spoken to the First Osguard or the Chief Osguard in his career; and all of a sudden he'd pushed the report from the *Atlantis* and had an immediate audience with the leaders of the Galaxy, Cluster and Universe within four hours.

"I believe we have a mole on your staff," Rican suggested.

"Maybe, maybe not; but all indications suggest that, and I am proceeding as if that is true," Akbar responded, trying to hide his irritation. "Only my CO, my Watch Officer and I are privy to the information the Atlantis provided. All communication about this is going through secure networks that are triple encrypted."

"This fits in on what USSTAP intelligence is telling me about some illicit activity involving dialairtic crystal smuggling," Black added. "I have a line on some companies that have gotten their hands on some prime crystals and are selling them to the highest bidder."

"Understood," Sario injected, "But I am more intrigued by the suggestion of a gateportal aided drill. The technology suggested in Joy's report isn't on our radar screen."

"Osguard Sario," Black interrupted. "I have known Captain Julie Joy since she was a cadet. She is a capable, intelligent and diligent sixana warrior. I read her thesis many years ago. As a matter of fact, I pushed for our science division to research her thesis. They were very impressed, to say the least. So if you are implying that this technology is impossible; I assure you, Osguard, it is very possible."

"Then we have a clear danger to USSTAP delicate interplanetary stability, in which USSTAP has governed for so long," Sario went on to say. "If someone other than USSTAP is in possession of gateportal technology and has found a way to integrate microportal technology with it, then we have a problem—a strategic problem. Not to mention the sale and distribution of unregulated dialairtic crystals...how that could collapse the universal market."

Now Akbar understood the reason for the immediate unity conference. It wasn't about Earth and how he handled the tsunami or the ramifications of how he handled it. It was about what was found in the aftermath and how it could affect the political, military and economic stability United Universal Science, Security and Trade Association of Planets. It was about someone other than USSTAP having gateportal technology, and their potential of using it against the common interest of USSTAP and its member planets.

"Osguards," Akbar pleaded, "I understand the severity of the problem, and I will do all I can to alleviate the situation. But first, and probably foremost, is the capture of the mole in my midst."

"I have narrowed it down to three people who were assigned to watch the sector where the incident occurred— Lieutenant John Littlefoot, Major Sharon Castle, and Commander Phillip Rand. I am having background checks completed on all three. If one of them is the mole, we may soon find the answers to some of the questions forming in your minds."

Akbar took notice of the Osguards pleasant nods. He took this as a form of affirmation for his directness to the situation. "Furthermore, I am running high-level diagnostics on their reports and data for the past year. When we find anomalies, and I'm sure we will, I will have that officer confined and questioned. We will know soon enough if this incident is connected to a higher game plan or not, soon enough."

"Understood, General Zandi," Osguard Sario acknowledged. "Please keep us informed. In the meantime I suggest we all run our own independent investigations to see what we can find out on our ends."

"Tiah," Black agreed. "Let's execute another unity conference in twenty-five universal hours and see what we have."

"Tiah," Rican added.

Sario nodded, "Twenty-five hours then."

One-by-one starting with Sario, then Black, and then Rican, a white light flashed and swallowed their images as the unity conference terminated.

Akbar sighed heavily and darted to his desk. He punched his command control module and activated his communicator, which was set on a scrambled net. "Jansen, this is Akbar."

***

Phillip entered his room and when the door closed, slammed his back against the door as if to hold something out. He scanned the room and thought that his privacy setting on his room ARIT might be compromised. He could be under surveillance right now.

It didn't matter anymore. He had to get off the station—now! He rushed to his desk and grabbed his secondary communication device from a hidden compartment in his bottom right hand drawer. He activated the blue button, which he hoped was the emergency beacon on a discrete frequency that was screened from USSTAP sensors and scanners.

He prayed that the plan would work as he filled an overnight bag with clothes and personal belongings. In his scramble he knocked a red vase over from his clothes drawer. The red vase with white lettering in Chaktun, rocked in a circle before gravity finally pushed it down. It smacked on top of the drawer, cracking it. Then it rolled. Phillip looked up in astonishment and watched the vase as it rolled. When the vase reached the edge, gravity again took charge and applied its magic. The vase fell...tumbling four feet in what seemed like eternity for Phillip. His mind somehow pushed and pulled time to distort his perception where a fraction of a second was vividly displayed. He watched the vase twist and turn. He saw every angle, curve, and sparkle, of the red vase as it plummeted to its destruction. When the vase crashed into the floor, it shattered into a cascade of fractured pieces.

Mesmerized by the incident, Phillip remained frozen. Staring at the mess on the floor, a thought penetrated his mind. He pulled one of his coronet energy packs from his personal delta belt, cracked the skin with his mation III, and placed it into the krigar: a food preparer, which looked similar to a microwave oven. The krigar used energy waves to turn gelatinous enzyme packs into full sustainable and tasty meals. He set the timer for one earth minute.

Looking around he grabbed the data crystal that held a record of all his communication with his other employer from his ARIT, and threw it in the krigar, slammed the door and rushed from the room with his bag. Once outside, he corrected his instincts to maintain a quick walking pace and not to go into a full sprint. He hurried to Gateportal Room Four

Gateportal Room Four door swished open and he stepped in. The controller looked up and saw him standing there, wet with sweat and holding an overnight bag. Just as the controller was about to greet him, Phillip pulled his pagenay.

***

The krigar counted down...five...four...three...two...one. When it reached zero, the krigar turned on and ignited a spark. The spark shot through the power pack in search of a certain enzyme, but only found the costolian power atom that was the center of the coronet fusion. The spark hit the costolian atom and ruptured its core, sending electrons and protons spiraling into each other.

Usually the costolian atom was the most stable power substance known to man, except when directly exposed to a high powered krigar energy wave. The costolian atom held the same properties as uranium, and reacted like a nuclear weapon when exposed to a direct krigar wave spark.

The explosion was just a nanosecond long, but the black costolian energy wave it produced shredded the krigar like it was a balloon. The energy then spread in an arch swallowing everything in its way and turning it into charred pieces of nothingness. No fire was born, but just pure black energy— like death reaching from the grave and pulling the world into hell. The bulkhead crumbled and the hull disintegrated, pulling the cold dark water from the Atlantic Ocean inside. The pressure ripped apart what the energy wave weakened but did not destroy.

The station's automatic fire and explosive compression system kicked in a nanosecond after the detection of the spark. The ARIT sealed off the room with double metal doors, and surrounded the explosive site with a chromerion field. The black energy punched at the chromerion field with the force of a two kiloton bomb. The chromerion field flexed and waned as the energy shifted, but maintained its strength, pushing the energy away from the station and out into the ocean. There another chromerion field enveloped the energy as it mixed it with the cold water, and provided a vortex tunnel for the black wave of destruction to go. It weaved and turned to finally it found an open outlet to release the energy into open water, where the magic properties of the ocean absorbed and dissipated the energy after traveling fifty miles.

***

Inside Gateportal Room Four, the explosion from Phillip's room rocked the floor. Phillip and the controller both swayed as the inertial dampers fought to keep the station steady. Knowing he had just a few minutes as the station's ARIT and the controllers would be concentrating on damage control, Phillip fired his pagenay at the controller. The blue beam of death popped from the pagenay and pierced the controller right through the heart, killing him instantly. The controller fell on his face, his head bouncing off the cold metal floor.

***

The station's ARIT activated the *Alert One* Warning horn throughout the station. On the bridge, warning lights lit up the chief controller's board like a Christmas tree.

"What the hell!" Epstein yelled, sifting through the lights.

"Report!" yelled Gray.

"Explosion on level four, ring eight! ARIT suppression protocol is venting the explosion seaward!"

"Evacuate and close off the section!" Gray ordered.

"Tiah!" Epstein responded. He turned to one side of his board and to the other. Anguish ruled his face. He definitely didn't like what he was reading. "I'm getting reports of multiple casualties and injuries!"

"Prep sickbay, activate rescue teams one, four and six! I want waterblades out there. Ships in dock…emergency launch; defense posture alpha two-six," Gray ordered.

A flash of activity ignited on deck as controllers hands glided over their control panels and the interlink chatter increased to an uncontrollable roar.

***

In Gateportal Room Four, Phillip set the coordinates for his escape route, inwardly praying that he could get off the station before anyone could catch him. He anticipated the explosion would keep the control bridge occupied long enough for him to escape. He expected they wouldn't notice an unscheduled activation of a gateportal during the crises.

He closed his eyes and then activated the control panel and a white light, of what he hoped was his salvation perched itself on the portal stage. He looked at the light, wetting his lips with his tongue and wondering what the hell was he doing. He knew there was no turning back now. He had just murdered the controller, a USSTAP citizen, and probably a dozen more with the explosion he set, which meant only life on a prison planet was waiting for him now. He had to leave.

He placed an ARIT eraser on top of the controller set for twenty seconds, and ran into the light. A second after he disappeared into the light, the invisible door to the gateportal closed. Fifteen seconds later the ARIT eraser activated, shortening out the control board and erasing all settings and memory patches. Commander Phillip Rand had covered his tracks.

In his wake he left a crippled Lilly Station, a sunken room containing charred remains of his life, a non-functional gateportal control panel and no witnesses. Commander Phillip Rand was gone—he'd vanished without a trace.

CHAPTER SIX: WHAT NOW

Miami International Airport
Miami, Florida
Planet Earth, Millmum Galaxy; Rojam Os Star Cluster

Miami International Airport was bustling with activity. Kerri Knight stepped out of the international terminal with purpose in her stride. She needed to get to the office and honcho over the activity in the newsroom. Her story started an avalanche of reports from competitors trying to pick up scraps from the U.N. team investigating the tsunami and the strange way it was handled.

Kerri made a beeline to the luggage carousel. She had several bags from her short-lived vacation she had to transport to a taxi. The area was crowded. Three international flights had landed at about the same time, and it was just her luck that the luggage carousels for all three flights were beside each other.

She pushed her way through the crowd, not bothering to smile or say, "Excuse me." She thought it somewhat demeaning that she even had to do this. If she had returned as scheduled, the network would have handled the bags and she would have not had to lift a finger. She huffed at the idea that she had to even think about gathering her belongings. She inwardly cursed that she was unable to get a hold of Manny.

She told herself that she would have to have a few words with Manny when she got to the office. She gathered Manny knew better to blow off her calls; especially, when she was on the trail of a very big story. She had single-handedly put USSTAP back on the front pages of every News link and television news channel in the world.

Because of her, the entire world was once again a buzz with what sophisticated technology USSTAP possessed that produced such an effect in the middle of the ocean.

She reached the carousel and noticed the airlines had not delivered the passenger bags yet. Now she had to wait. She wasn't used to waiting. She slapped a piece of gum into her mouth to curb her anger. Then she turned to the local common monitor hanging on the pillar next to her. It was on the local news station. She thought that so droll.

She made mental note to talk to the airlines about having WMN play on the airport monitors. People traveling from all over the world to Miami would like to see a friendly face; especially if it was hers, on the television; not some local two-bit nobody regurgitating the news they gleaned from WMN.

She studied the television and was able to capture the last comments on the story recounting last night's presidential debate between the incumbent, President Amanda Taylor, and her Democratic-Republican challenger, Governor Jackson Prichard of Connecticut. Jackson Prichard was fresh from the party's convention, where he beat three contenders for the nomination.

The newscaster concentrated on the last question of the evening where the moderator posed a question about USSTAP. *"Under your presidency, will the U.S. take a more active role in instituting diplomatic ties with USSTAP?"*

Kerri knew the questioned stemmed from her recent reports on USSTAP, where she colorfully extended the possibility that diplomatic ties with USSTAP would be very productive for America in specific but for the world as a whole. With a slight smile, she listened to the sound bites played of the two candidates responses.

First, after some political wordplay, President Taylor basically said, *"No,"*

She was very pleased with letting the U.N. Secretary General speak for the entire world, when it came to limiting the scope and power of USSTAP's reach in the world, and specifically in the country. She rounded out her answer by insisting USSTAP was a dangerous organization, filled with megalomaniacs who thought they were gods. She urged the American people not to be taken in by the shiny technology USSTAP had to offer. Then she made a veiled reference to *"Thirty pieces of silver,"* to punctuate her point.

Next, Governor Prichard did not mix words. He *"wholeheartedly,"* supported establishing diplomatic ties with USSTAP. He did not believe in abdicating his responsibility as president to foreign leaders, who may not have the United States best interest at heart. He reminded the audience that Michael Genesis and several others of the original sixty Osguards were born and raised in Connecticut, and all sixty were American citizens that this country had abandoned out of misplaced fear and misguided allegiance.

He then named President Taylor, as one who demonstrated misguided allegiance to the world political party Earth First. This sparked a heated rebuttal from President Taylor that made her come off petty and unprofessional.

A sparkle twinkled in Kerri's eye. What a welcome home present she just received. Her reporting had now influenced the presidential debates, and may even become a binding issue that could decide the next president.

Pulitzer, here I come, she thought.

"Kerri!" shouted a voice from behind her.

Kerri immediately recognized the voice of Manny Vazquez, her news producer. She spun around, still gleaming from the news report, "So you did get my messages," she bellowed.

Manny pushed his way past three women, who were standing around waiting for their luggage, and walked up to Kerri. His eyes were emboldened with power and his face brazen. "How could I not get your messages? You left about fifty of them."

"Good," she said scornfully.

"Good my ass!" Manny rebutted. "Listen Kerri, I don't know who the hell you think you are. But I am your producer, you work for me. I can't just jump when you say 'jump.' I have a station to run."

Kerri regarded Manny for a second, while smacking on her gum. "You're here aren't you?"

The bolster slipped from Manny's face, and he sighed, "Yes, I'm here."

"You feel better now?" Manny nodded.

"Good, now get my bags and have them sent to the apartment. I'm catching a cab to the station. Meet me in my office in an hour."

"Kerri...!" Manny said in a long drawn out grumble.

Kerri just winked and walked away. She knew Manny was the boss. But as long as she was the hottest ticket in the network stratosphere, she knew she could get Manny to do anything she wanted. He may not like it, but he would do it, as long as she continued to bring in the ratings.

***

Home of Michael and Michelle Genesis
Vedar City
Planet Chaktun, Millmum Galaxy, Rojam Os Galactic Cluster

Michael gave up drinking hard liquor several years ago for health reasons. He was healthy as a horse; but when he hit seventy-five years of age, his doctor recommended he change his social drinking habits. But Michael could never give up his eloquent wet bar in his man-cave. He told himself he maintained it for entertaining guest. But that was a lie. The only visitors he entertained were as old as he and had given up drinking as well for health reasons.

As he looked upon the wood-carved bar that sat six, a sense of pride ballooned in his chest. He had wines and liquors from all parts of the universe that his friends, co-workers and associates gave to him as gifts, layered on shelves behind a glass cabinet set on the back of the bar. In a way, the shelves held a history of his adventures, because there was a story behind every bottle and carafe he saw.

"Michael, did you hear me?" Shawn asked.

Michael emerged from his trip down memory lane, and stepped over to the leather recliner chairs centered in his man-cave. "No, sorry, I was deep in thought. What did you say?"

Shawn sighed and took a sip of his club soda. He laid the glass down on the side table. "Having another senior moment?"

"I guess," Michael admitted as he took a seat in the recliner next to his brother. "You know, every time I look at my collection of liquor, it brings back good memories. And you know with all the bad memories we've experienced as Osguards, reliving the good memories isn't a bad thing. Is it?"

"I suppose not," Shawn confessed, "I understand. Boy, do I understand." Shawn slowly shook his head as if trying to shake loose some memory from his mind. "But getting back to why I came over. I talked to Kang, and he talked to his daughter Lillian."

"Isn't she the Chief Osguard now?" Michael interrupted with a sly smile.

"You know damned well she is, Michael. You've nominated her as well as all the other Chiefs since you left the position." Shawn waved his hand towards Michael as they both released a slight chuckle. "Well any way, Lillian agreed to our little adventure on one condition."

"What's that?"

"It was to be a surprise, but the timing couldn't be better," Shawn pushed.

"What?" Michael asked, showing a little irritation.

"They've been planning this for about eighteen universal months."

"What?" Michael huffed.

Shawn's smile turned into a big grin and a beam of pride washed over his face. After a couple of seconds, he burst, "They are christening the first Delta Class Science Vessel next month."

"So," Michael said.

"So...so...I'll tell you so. They are naming her *The Parker and Elizabeth.* And Lillian said this mission would be the perfect maiden voyage for her."

Michael's eyes popped with delight, *"The Parker and Elizabeth*...named after mom and dad...an entire science vessel...with a crew?"

"Yup, and that's not all. Besides me, you, Patricia and your family going on this adventure, Patricia and my families will join you in honor of mom and dad."

"What? That's great!" Michael beamed with watery eyes.

"Since it is your mission, you will sire her," Shawn added. "You will sire the first USSTAP ship crewed entirely by Zyders."

"What?"

"Yup, I thought that strange at first, but Kang explained that Zyders' ability to calculate data at ARIT speed make them the best crewmembers for a science vessel. It is a great opportunity to forward the Zyder race and better integrate them into society."

Michael nodded, and then stared past Shawn. "Will it further their integration into society, or will it bolster the claim by those who think they should be separated from humans?"

"Michael, it will be whatever you make it to be. There is no greater advocate for the Zyders than you. Lillian believes having them on this mission will be a great step for them and us; and having you as the sire can only add to the prestige of the mission."

"I suppose so," Michael admitted, falling for the flattering words his brother was throwing at him. Then Michael focused on Shawn, "Either way, this will be another great adventure to add to the memory banks...aye."

"Tiah!" Shawn replied, raising his glass.

Michael raised his glass of chocolate milk he had been nursing throughout the conversation, and they touched glasses, saluting the next great adventure.

As the glasses touched and the cling echoed inside the man-cave, Angela stepped through the doorway. Her eyes were full of worry and her stature was somewhat wilted. She looked up and waited to catch Michael's eyes.

"Hey Angela," Michael greeted.

"Osguard Michael, Osguard Rican is on alpha line for you. She says it is important. It's about the grandchildren."

***

Earth First Headquarters,
Chenault Towers
Paris, France
Planet Earth, Millmum Galaxy, Rojam Os Galactic Cluster

Claude Chenault held the common to his face. It was projecting the image of Jerold Washington in his New York office. Claude was in no mood to talk, but he had to keep up the appearance of a leader. Deep inside, he was worried that he may have overplayed his hand with Phillip. He knew Phillip was just a hired hand; and the real boss, who he never met, was a super patient man, or woman, who probably didn't fare well with threats.

"Taylor is an astute politician," Washington said. "She did well last night accept for the last question. Pritchard made her look like she was your pawn and she is abdicating her duties as president to you."

"She's merely unofficially delegating her authority to deal with this one problem to us, not abdicating," Chenault snarled.

"Whether she's abdicating or delegating, the American people don't like it. To them there is no difference. Taylor needs to stand out on her own. She needs to be seen publicly challenging you on some level."

Chenault took a deep breath and sighed, "As you say, Taylor is politically astute. She knows how to sway with the political winds, and how to dance to the beat of public opinion. If that takes her to a point where she has to publicly challenge me, so be it. We all know who's in charge and whose philosophy she will execute."

"I hope you're right, sir," Washington said. "But I think she is weakening. As you say, she knows how to sway with the wind and dance to the beat. I just hope all that swaying and dancing won't take her off in a different direction."

"Talking about different direction," Chenault added, in an effort to change the conversation to what he really wanted to talk about. "What the hell were you thinking in your news report?"

"What do you mean?" Washington uttered.

"Giving credit for the Tasman Tsunami Save to Australia and New Zealand…to a made-up, non-existent organization?"

"I had to do something," Washington answered. "Kerri's news was starting to get ground swell. I needed to beat it back."

"You idiot!" Chenault bristled. "All you manage to do was keep it in the headlines longer. If you simply reported on the tsunami and reported that for inexplicable reasons the tsunami fell short, it would have been lost with the next news cycle. Instead, you entered into a debate with your ex-wife, all over the network that is forcing everyone from Chile to China to stake an opinion in the issue."

Washington lowered his head, visibly shaken.

"Now even the American presidential debates are taking sides," Chenault berated. "Your foolish reporting may have single-handedly set back the movement ten years," he lied. Chenault knew Washington's report was damaging, but Kerri's reporting was more damaging.

He could only hope now that USSTAP would stick to their play book and not publicly announce their part, if it was truly them, in the Tasman Tsunami Save.

It *had* to be them. *Who else could it be? All the latest polls have Taylor dropping three to eight percentage points. Hell, even the Atlanta-Richmond poll, which belongs to Earth First, has Taylor losing three percentage points. After last night's question heard around the world, Taylor is now in a statistical dead heat compared to the favorite before the debate.*

Chenault took a deep breath to steady the anger rising inside of him. He knew he had to fix this fast. There were less than three months left before the American election. And if his candidate failed in that election, other electrons he had a stake in would fail as well; especially in Australia and New Zealand.

"I want you to stop all reporting on this so-called secret Australian-New Zealand Emergency Management Organization,"

Chenault ordered. "They've flatly denied it several times, and what idiot would believe an emergency management organization would be secret? For what reason would an emergency management system be secretive; especially between allies?"

"Yes, sir," Washington mumbled.

"Washington, you look like a damned fool on this one," Chenault continued to chide. "Take some time away from the anchor desk. Tell your viewers you're taking a vacation and get the hell out of the lime light for a while. Wait for this shit to blow over. You understand me."

"Yes, Dr. Chenault," Washington mumbled again.

"And another thing…" Chenault began to scold.

The front door to his office banged open. The loud thud startled Chenault from his thoughts as he jumped in his chair. The thud's echo bounced off the cavernous office's ivory pillars and ceiling, like a gunshot.

Chenault looked up and saw Phillip with a crazed look on his face. Phillip eyes narrowed as his mind flashed over his self-defense actions. He automatically opened his right hand desk draw and started to reach for a pistol.

Phillip raised his pagenay and slowly shook his head. Chenault interpreted this to mean, stop reaching for the pistol. Phillip put his finger to his lips, indicating to Chenault to be quiet. Then he motioned for Chenault to hang up the conversation.

"Washington, I have to call you back. Something has come up that needs my immediate attention," Chenault hissed.

"Yes, Dr. Chenault," Washington replied.

"Washington?"

"Yes, Dr. Chenault."

"Don't forget, what I said…go on vacation."

Phillip's armed tensed up as if he was going to fire the pagenay. Chenault looked up with defiance and clicked the common off. Phillip tension eased and his arm drew a little slack.

"What can I do for you Phillip?" Dr. Chenault greeted him.

Phillip cleared the doors and closed them. He sauntered in, like he was the new boss, and took a seat across from Chenault. "The war has begun. I drew first blood. Now it's your turn."

CHAPTER SEVEN: AFTERMATH

USSTAP Lilly Station
Atlantis Continental Self-Atlantic Ocean
Planet Earth, Millmum Galaxy, Rojam Os Cluster

Akbar sat with a stoic look on his face at the staff table. Around the table sat the leadership of Lilly Station, Centurion of Operations: Jessica Jansen, Centurion of Watch; Richard Gray; and Chief of Controllers, Colonel Abraham Epstein. Joining them was Chief of Security, Colonel Victor DeJesus; Chief Engineer, Colonel Felix Wang; Chief of Maintenance, Colonel Jason Stars; and Chief Medical and Science Officer, Colonel Ericka Swan

In the middle of the table the ARIT projected a 3-D holographic view of the station with its damage. On the east side of the station on ring eight, just inside the outer ring, it displayed a gaping hole on level four with a cut into level three and five. The black char represented the boundary of the damage that the explosion caused.

"Five dead, including the portal gatekeeper in PGR-4," Swan reported. "Another twenty-three injured—eight seriously."

Akbar's face seemed to grow more stonewashed as the news drifted into his mind. "Who are the dead?" Akbar asked.

"Sentinel Richards, Ensign Mathews, Lieutenant Chernov, Captain McDaniel, and Major Richter," she solemnly announced. They were sleeping in their quarters right next to, above and below, Rand's quarters. Ensign Mathews was the gatekeeper found shot in GPR-4."

Akbar had never lost a crewmember due to violence. The sting of their deaths under his watch burred into his heart. But as Sire of the station, he had to present a balance between respecting the dead, mourning their deaths, and moving on with the mission. He nodded to Swan and motioned for Stars or Wang to speak next.

Wang took the lead, "The station is solid. The chromerion field is holding and the damaged areas are being drained of water. We should be able to get in those sections and start repairs in twelve hours." Stars nodded in agreement.

"Good," Akbar replied. Finally, he had some good news—well relatively speaking. He then motioned for DeJesus to give his report.

DeJesus cleared his throat before he began. Akbar took this as a sign that the security report would not be good news. "ARIT security captured images of Commander Phillip Rand entering GPR-4 just a second before his room exploded," DeJesus started. The image appeared in place of the image of the station in the middle of the table. "As you know, Commander Rand was under investigation in connection with the Tasman Tsunami incident, along with Lieutenant John Littlefoot and Major Sharon Castle. Upon preliminary investigation, I found out that Major Castle broke protocol and spoke to Commander Rand before we could question him on his shift. We believe Commander Rand had something to do with the Tasman Tsunami and the conversation with Major Castle spooked him." DeJesus then replaced the image of Rand with the station and drew the attention of the staff to the charred area. "The explosion originated from his room. I believe he used the krigar and a weapon power pact to initiate the explosion."

"Where did he get the weapon or a weapon power pack?" Jansen interrupted.

"I'm not sure," DeJesus answered. "We conducted a weapons inventory, and all our weapons are accounted for. That only leads me to believe he had a private weapon on-board."

"And how, pray tell, did he manage to do that?" Gray interjected.

"I'm not sure." DeJesus admitted. "However, we found out that his weekly trips to Paris to visit his father were a rouse. His father has been dead for over ten years. Further checks indicate he has no living relatives."

"Again, I ask, how?" Gray pushed.

"Again, Centurion, I don't know!" DeJesus snapped back. "Commander Rand has been a model USSTAP sixana for over two decades. He is decorated with multiple honors and citations; a few written by you Centurion Gray. So, I don't know how he got the fact that his father passed away ten years ago past our periodic security checks. But I would imagine the death of a love one is something a commanding officer should be aware of."

Akbar knew DeJesus had just thrown down the gauntlet and Centurion Gray was in his crosshairs. He didn't know if he should warn him off, or let DeJesus continue. With the surprises the last twenty-four hours had presented, he decided to lean on the side of caution.

He cleared his throat, indicating to the two officers to stop their bickering and directed DeJesus, "Do whatever you need to do to uncover what the hell is going on. Interview anyone you need, including me and my staff. I want to know how this traitor got on my station and who, if anyone, helped him. I also want to know what the hell happened in the Tasman Sea." He squinted his eyes, the happy go-lucky demeanor long gone, "Can you do that for me?"

"Tiah," DeJesus replied.

"Gray," Akbar called. "This isn't the time to point fingers...at least not yet. I want answers, not more questions. Am I understood?"

"Tiah," Gray said.

"As I was saying, Sire," DeJesus continued after several seconds of silence. "The ARIT security camera caught Rand going in GPR-4. ARIT security also captured enough of his presence to estimate he fired the weapon that killed Ensign Mathews. Then he used the gateportal to affect an escape."

Before leaving, he set some type of ARIT memory erase device on the console that destroyed the coordinates, along with itself, after Rand stepped out. Fortunately, we were able to retrieve the initial aspect of the coordinates. By our calculations, Commander Rand stepped somewhere in Western Europe."

Akbar's mind went straight to Chenault when he heard Western Europe. "Could it be France?" he asked.

"Yes, it could. Or it could be Germany, Spain, or even Portugal," DeJesus added.

"Okay, I want time-light satellites in the sky; let's see if we can capture an image of where Rand stepped to. I also want communications capture satellites in the sky, narrow in on Earth First and any of their affiliates in and around Europe. I have a hunch that Dr. Chenault and his xenophobic mutants may be behind this."

"Really, Sire?" Jansen interrupted. "You think Dr. Chenault has something to do with the gateportal, microportal integration that caused the Tasman Tsunami."

Akbar turned to Jansen and when he heard what he was thinking said aloud, he realized the foolishness of his thought process. But his gut still told him Earth First was involved somehow, even if it was a small part. "Humor me!" he insisted.

Jansen nodded, "Tiah!"

"Now, how about the Genesis Children?" Akbar asked, changing the subject so he would not have to defend his position any further.

"They and Captain Good used GPR-2 to step to New Haven Connecticut an hour ago," Jansen responded. "It was discrete and handled at high priority. I operated the gateportal. So, no one but the people in this room knows where they went and only you and I are aware of their agenda sire."

"Good," Akbar replied. "I understand their parents and grandparents were notified of the incident this morning by Osguard Rican. I halfway expected five galaxy protectors on my doorstep by now. But the word is they are satisfied that the Osguard kids are safe, and they will monitor the situation from afar."

"I guess that is some good news," Epstein remarked. "Because if we had those five starships knocking at our doorstep, the First Osguard's galactic guardian would not be far behind. And with the tensions here on Earth not favoring USSTAP, one galactic guardian and five galaxy protectors, loaded with enough military might to remake this planet three times over, orbiting on high, would not go over very well with the people of Earth."

Akbar glared at Epstein for a moment, regarding his remark. Epstein was correct, the extra tension brought about if the Genesis children were hurt would have caused a galactic crisis of enormous proportions; not that the illegal drilling of dialairtic crystals from the ocean floor with state of the art portal technology wasn't.

This is supposed to be my retirement job, Akbar thought.

Cursing the situation in his mind, Akbar turned to the rest of the staff, "You've got your orders. I have family notifications I need to attend to." He stood, signaling the meeting was adjourned. "I want an update in twelve hours…back in here in twelve, people."

With one final glance, assuring he made eye contact with everyone, he turned and left the room, leaving behind an agitated group of professionals who were trying to use their loyalty for USSTAP and respect for General Akbar Zandi to fight the bitter taste of betrayal that Commander Phillip Rand left in his wake.

***

Tri-Galactic Resource (TGR) Distributing Company Headquarters
Larmin City, Toloman Province
Planet Vellowhail, Telo Galaxy, Rojam Os Galactic Cluster

Seolin te Erucki, the president and CEO of Tri-Galactic Resource Distributing Company, also known as TGR, sat mesmerized in front of the ARIT player inside TGR headquarters in Larmin City, the capital of Toloman Province, on the planet of Vellowhail. Vellowhail was in the NGC-7793 galaxy in the Sculptor Star Group, better known on the USSTAP Map as Galaxy 5, the Telo Galaxy. Erucki was watching the Vellow planetary stock market results, as well as the Telo Galactic, Rojam Os Domain and Universal stock market data fly across his scanner.

His mind was almost as fast as an ARIT in calculating the data, their effects and trends. His fingers flew over his digital 3-D keyboard with the ease of a stenographer, matching, selling and buying stocks and bonds, across the myriad of investments and business opportunities sailing in the sea of commerce.

Erucki was an average size Vellow man. He stood about five feet and eleven inches, and carried a round but stout body. His dark brown, almost black skin, complexion was framed with a full salt and pepper beard and mustache that merged with his salt and pepper shoulder length thick stringy hair.

His piercing blue eyes seemed to peer through time and space, eating the data that dare fly into his view. His long flowing golden robe and flat round turban, were embroidered with brown square stitching and decorated with brown Telo diamonds—the most expensive gem in the Telo Galaxy—which were symmetrically placed within the squares.

Erucki was eighty-five universal years old and had run TGR for almost fifty years. In some circles he was considered a ruthless businessman; in other circles he was considered a political powerhouse; and still some found him to be the most pleasant philanthropist this side of the universal divide.

Besides being the president and CEO of TGR, and sponsor to many educational and business scholarships, he also had held the Chief Ambassador's position in the Telo Star Congress for two terms; was the Telo Ambassador to the Rojam Os Star Parliament for one term; and ran unsuccessfully for one of the four Telo Ambassador positions to the USSTAP Universal Conclave.

All-in-all, Erucki had a very successful life and as of now would leave a grand legacy; but that wasn't enough. Seolin te Erucki needed more.

As Erucki manipulated the information flowing through his ARIT scanner, he was hedging his bets on the dialairtic crystals he planned on mining from Earth. Until forty years ago, dialairtic crystals were the sole power source and the lifeblood of USSTAP's economic system. It powered everything from coffeemakers to space stations. Then the Tuit war happened.

His mind flashbacked to the time he spent as an ambassador to Rojam Os Star Parliament. It was during the end of the Tuit War and the aftermath of the Eierre solar system destruction. The five-planet Eierre solar system production of dialairtic crystals made Eierre Mining Facilities the fourth largest energy producer for the USSTAP economy and his number one supplier.

Even though their destruction ushered in USSTAP reliance and integration of the Kulusk; more stable but highly toxic pialairtic crystals and the less powerful jorelli plugs, his business took a hit. The commercial industry throughout Rojam Os still relied on dialairtic crystals. This meant he needed to find an abundant supply of dialairtic crystals in order to meet the demand. So far he had been sufficient in finding small pockets of crystals to stay afloat, but it was a year-by-year test to stay ahead of debt collectors.

As a star ambassador, Erucki served on the intelligence committee, which gave him the rare opportunity to review old classified documents. As a lover of history, he reviewed the top secret documents issued during the Ortho administration. Ortho Chting was the Interim Osguard between the Mother Osguards, Nausona and Laurona, and the original sixty Osguards.

During Ortho's tenure as the Lieutenant Osguard, he established Lilly Station on Earth. In the process of surveying the ocean floor, Ortho's scientific team discovered an abundant deposit of dialairtic crystals underneath it—the biggest deposit located right under Lilly Station. That's when he put the plan together to rid Earth of USSTAP influence so he could go in and mine the crystals for profit.

For years, he had led a plan to turn Earth's inhabitants against USSTAP, in an effort to force USSTAP to leave Earth and no longer declare it a protectorate; using Dr. Chenault as his hatchet man. According to his lawyers, USSTAP's abandonment of Earth would allow him to pillage Earth for the crystals with no legal action taken against him for harm done to the planet or its people.

He manipulated the stock market data, switching funds and pushing trades in favor of his overarching plan, as he salivated over the thought of getting his hands on the abnormally large deposit of crystals at Earth's core. The money he would garner would be well worth the risk.

It only sweetened the pot when his scientist invented the super drill, integrating both gateportal and microportal technology. With the help of a well-placed agent on Lilly Station, he used this invention for the last decade to covertly drill for the crystals while maintaining his anonymity.

A sound came from behind him, "Omgh…"

He had been so engrossed in the market manipulation and in his self-absorbed daydreaming; he had not noticed his intelligence officer, Elib fez Kolinera step into the office.

"What is it Kolinera?" Erucki snarled without turning.

"Word from Earth," Kolinera responded.

"Yes…yes…what is it?" Erucki snarled again, keeping his attention on the scanner.

"Well Chenum Erucki," Kolinera started, placating Erucki with the honorary title of Chenum, which meant 'master and lord' in Tolo— the language of his province. "As you know, our last excursion on Earth created a weather event that USSTAP had to intervene to stop."

"Yes Elib, I know that," Erucki grumbled, showing his agitation at the interruption. "I also know that fool, Chenault is trying to blackmail us. You've told me all that before. And I said, it didn't matter…the plan is still on schedule."

"Well, there is a winkle Chenum," Kolinera persisted.

Erucki found a place to stop his work and turned to face Kolinera, "What winkle?"

"It appears General Zandi has found evidence of our drilling and back tracked it to our guy on Lilly Station."

"Go on," Erucki urged.

"Our guy managed to escape and destroy the evidence connecting anything to you, and is now in Chenault's office awaiting further word."

Erucki moved to his desk and sat in his plush, brown leather swivel chair. Kolinera followed and stood in front of the desk with his hands folded behind him. Kolinera was a tall man, built to fight as evident by his rippling muscles, enlarged neck and shoulder physique, and his scared hands. He was two shades lighter than Erucki, with intense green eyes and clean shaven face. His robe was beige with no special accoutrements to note, indicating his stature in society as a mid-level worker.

Puzzlement occupied Erucki's mind as he tried to put the new information into place with his bold plan. He squinted as if to peer into the future and after several anguishing seconds, he finally lifted his head and looked at the cream colored ceiling. He never thought he would say these words, not aloud anyway. But he had to. He had to throw suspicion off his trail and keep his plan alive. He hated what he was about to do, but it was the only way.

He moved his head from side to side to release the tension that formed on his shoulders with the news, and then looked Kolinera in the eyes.

"Execute alternate plan bravo…start with Zandi."

"Nelx, Chenum," Kolinera replied in the affirmative. "It shall be done right away."

***

USSTAP City Tours
New Haven, CT,
Planet Earth, Millmum Galaxy, Rojam Os Galactic Cluster

The August sun was beating down, giving the day a balmy ninety-one degree temperature, which surprised Deuce. He was prepared for a cooler temperature with a long sleeve T-shirt and jeans. He rolled his sleeves up to his elbow, but the temperature had a muggy characteristic that caused Deuce to sweat more than usual.

He wiped the sweat from his eyes with his forearm and let out a slight, "Whew, it is hot here."

"It's called humidity," Captain Toniac Good offered, handing Deuce and his cousins a bottle of water. "Unlike Chaktun, where the temperature is high and the humidity is low, the temperature here can drive you crazy when accompanied by a high humidity. The weatherman says the humidity is around eighty-eight percent."

"You could have warned us," Tynala grumbled. "My sweat is getting in my eyes."

Toniac just shrugged, "Sorry."

"What's next?" Cheyenna asked, taking a sip of water.

Toniac turned and pointed to a tourist bus with no top. "I booked us on the ten o'clock tour. It should take us around the city to interesting points that are supposed to be connected to your grandfather and his relatives."

"We just want to go by my grandfather's old house and get a sense of what he was like as a child," Deuce complained.

"This is a four-hour tour that will end with a walk-around of your grandfather's old house," Toniac explained. "It also will take us to some of the other Osguard houses, their churches, the park where Billy Red stabbed your grandfather and the site near the Green where Ortho found your grandfather."

"Wow, they know all about that," Deuce asked.

"Yeah, they know all about that," Toniac assured his charges. "Movie producers had access to the holovidpic library and sifted through all the history of the Osguards and made several big budget films between 2015 and 2020—Earth years. Some say, Hollywood made billions off the USSTAP movies."

"Movies? What is a movie?" Cheyenna asked.

"Yeah, and who is this Hollywood?" Deuce added. "I don't remember anyone named Hollywood in my Earth History lessons."

Toniac giggled and shook his head. He then made a sucking sound between his teeth and let out a light sigh. "Movies are holovidpics without the holographic properties; and Hollywood is where they were made…at least one of the places they were made. I venture to say that other movie producers in other countries also made USSTAP films…I mean movies."

"Can we see one of them?" Tynala requested.

"Maybe," Toniac remarked. "I'll try to get my hands on one for the trip down south." Toniac then motioned for them to get on the bus. "It's almost ten, and a crowd is forming up. We should get moving so we can have a good seat."

***

Former Home of Shawn, Michael and Patricia Genesis
New Haven, CT
Planet Earth, Millmum Galaxy, Rojam Os Galactic Cluster

New Haven was the birthplace of the Tappy movement. The city was full of pro-USSTAP memorabilia and advertisements. Deuce saw dozens of people wearing; *I love USSTAP* T-shirts, hats and bags. Deuce did not see any evidence of Firsties in the city, or a hint of their anti-USSTAP propaganda. What Deuce saw on the tour, made his heart swell with pride.

After three hours the tour bus pulled up in front of an old white three-family house. The guide book said it was built in 1888. That made the house one hundred and sixty years old. It was an historic treasure. It was the only remaining house from that time on the block. It sat between two empty lots; laden with perfectly manicured lawns, gardens and brick walkways. A gray-stoned six-foot wall bordered the house and the empty lots which buffered the house from the community.

The house had two porches in front with a veranda on top of the bigger porch that led into the first floor. That porch wrapped around the corner of the house; while the second porch was merely a covered step way to the door.

The tour stepped into the house in groups of four. Deuce, his cousins and Toniac were the last group to go into the house. They walked up five granite steps onto a walkway. They then turned left and walked up seven wooden steps to the first floor porch. Sitting in an old fashion rocking chair waiting for them was a tour guide.

He was African American, about seventy years old with haunting eyes and gray hair. He stood and reached out his hand to Toniac, "Hi, I'm Alexander Kennedy. I will be your tour guide today. Welcome to the home of Shawn, Michael, Patricia, Paul and Peter Genesis."

Toniac reached out and shook the man's hand, "Hi, I'm Tony Good and these are my…my…"

"Friends," Deuce completed, holding out his hand. "Hi, I'm Deuce, and the lady in the red T-Shirt is my cousin Nala; the lady in the green T-shirt is my cousin Chey. We're from Texas." Deuce was proud of himself for having a story already made-up, but almost coughed when he realized he needed to stop blabbering like an idiot.

Alexander greeted each of the tourists with a hardy handshake and a big grin. "Oh yeah! Which part of Texas?"

"Victoria Texas," Cheyenna offered. Deuce new she was thinking of the Osguard community known as Osguard Village, which once was in Victoria Texas. That community once housed his Latin American relatives before the 2029 Pact.

"Isn't that were the second half of the Osguards are from?" Alexander commented.

"Yes it is," Toniac added. "You see me and my friends grew up learning about those Osguards and we wanted to take this opportunity to learn about the original sixty...so here we are."

"That's great," Alexander commented. "It's nice to meet some Tappies from the south; especially from Texas." Alexander pulled closer to the group and hid his lips with his hand as if he was about to tell a secret. "You know, I'm cousins to the Genesis."

"How's that?" Cheyenna asked.

"My mother was second cousins to Mrs. Elizabeth Genesis."

"Oh, that must be interesting," Toniac remarked.

"You said Paul and Peter Genesis; did they live here as well?" Deuce asked.

"Yup, this is a three-family house. Paul and Peter lived on the third floor with their father, Coltrane Genesis. Coltrane was Shawn, Michael, and Patricia's uncle—Parker Genesis' brother. Their grandparents Garrison and Victoria lived on the second floor."

"Oh, I didn't know that," Deuce allowed himself to say.

"Come on, let me show you around," Alexander commanded.

The group poured into the house, mainly to get away from the scorching heat. The caretakers had modified the house with central air and heat for the comfort of the patrons. The cool air was a welcome treat to them, as low moans of relief escaped their lips.

Deuce was the last to enter the house. It was smaller than he imagined. The foyer was tight and almost claustrophobic. He took a right turn into the living room. It was a small eight by nine foot room, with two chairs a couch and an old wooden stereo cabinet that took up the space between two windows. It opened up on top to an old fashion radio and record player. Deuce had never seen anything so archaic in his life.

Alexander went into his script, pointing out pictures and elements of the room that seemed to have some emotional significance to the family that once lived there. Alexander's passion and pride was evident in his tone and manner in which he delivered the script. Deuce knew Alexander was speaking of family as he pushed through his monologue.

To the left, the room opened up to what Alexander called the den. It had a gas stove attached to a chimney on the back wall, a couch and two more chairs, this time the chairs were recliner chairs. On the side wall was a bookshelf that took up the entire wall.

It was filled with books that Alexander called, "The classics." Alexander noted that Michael was an avid reader, and excellent student and Elizabeth purchased these books for him.

He also noted Shawn was an artistic genius who played the lead guitar and a natural athlete who won several trophies in basketball, football and baseball during his high school years; and the wall of trophies on the top shelf of the bookcase were Shawn's awards. Finally, he pointed to the ribbons and medals hanging from the side of the shelves and noted these belonged to Patricia, who was a model as well as a ballet and tap dancer.

Alexander said everything in the house was a complete replica made from old pictures donated by Mrs. Elizabeth Genesis years earlier. It appeared when the city of New Haven approached her with the idea; she loved the thought of her old home being turned into a museum. The city purchased the house and turned it into a tourist attraction; complete with a gift and souvenir shop across the street. The venture had been a money maker ever since. Even with the large amount of anti-USSTAP sentiment floating around the world, New Haven remained the centerpiece for the worldwide Tappy population to visit once in their lives—a pilgrimage. This sentiment seemed to keep the museum in business and the city well stocked in revenue.

Next, Alexander walked them through the pantry, where Deuce saw a refrigerator and old plates. The pantry led to the kitchen that housed a sink, another stove, this time to cook as well as heat the house, and a wash area where an old fashion washing machine and dryer was on display.

Deuce was surprised to see the house contained only one bathroom. At least it was indoors, and not an outhouse like his Earth History lessons led him to believe. In the back of the house was a long corridor that connected the three bedrooms. They were small—about eight by eight feet. The last bedroom they saw was the room his grandfather shared with his Uncle Shawn.

They slept on, what Alexander called, "bunk beds." Alexander said the lower bunk belonged to Michael Genesis.

Deuce put his hand on the bunk bed and closed his eyes. At that moment he had gathered a whole other appreciation for what he had growing up. Compared to what his grandfather grew up in, his life was one of a king. He also knew that his grandfather had it much better than his father, and his grandfather had it much better than his father. At that moment, Deuce understood the nature of progress. However, the feeling wasn't as intense as when he visited the prison were his other grandfather, Adam Freeman, was kept.

Where Michael was a descendant of slaves, Adam was a slave. His grandfather, Adam was a lolwe, the male half of the Tuit race. The half used for breeding and horrifically raised for medical experimentation and organ donations. Adam was a slave that never had any type of contact with another lolwe.

Adam would have lived his entire life, from birth to death, in solitary confinement, in stark isolation, only let out of an eight feet by five feet cell; to have the Tuits medically experiment on him and then humiliate him further by extracting his sperm to procreate the female half of the Tuit race. That's until the Tuit war with USSTAP, which enabled Michael David Genesis to save Adam, and others like Adam. Deuce was lost in thought, pondering how circumstance and happenstance came together to forge his very existence.

"Well that ends the tour," Alexander announced, drawing Deuce from deep thought. "I hope you had an interesting and informative visit. If you follow me, I will lead you to gift and souvenir shop across the street. There you can meet the rest of your group and maybe pick up a few gifts and souvenirs of your visit."

Deuce, his cousins and Toniac quietly exited the house; each lost in their own thoughts. Deuce continued to contemplate how fate forged his being and how destiny would highlight his life. Until now, he was truly contemplating not going to USSTAP Academy, and not following his parents' legacy of becoming an Osguard. But now he wasn't so sure.

***

Millmum Galaxy Osguard's Ready Room
USSTAP Galaxy Protector Campthor
Orbit around Millmum Capitol Station

The galaxy protector was the second largest starship in USSTAP inventory, next to the newly minted galactic guardian assigned to all the First Osguards and Executive Osguards. The Bravo Class Campthor was sleeker, sexier and faster than her Alpha Class predecessor.

Like the Alpha Class galaxy protector, the Campthor was coated with slitanium that absorbed light, and the characteristic red power rods that covered her seams. The ship was two miles in length, but one mile in width, with twenty decks—eight more than her predecessor. The engines were the USSTAP standard engines that were concave, and ran the entire length of the ship on the port and starboard side, and melded into a sharp edge point at her bow and stern.

The engines were connected to the main ship by spars. The main ship maintained its characteristic elongated elliptical shape, and flared at the stern where it contained its flight deck for her space fighters called defenders and her startram fleet. The bravo class galaxy protector was a collage of Tuit, USSTAP, Mosleck, Kulusk and Taiolian technology—merged into an eclectic masterpiece of human engineering.

This gave the protector the ability to transverse the space speed scale all the way up to MOP 105, equating to approximately 105 light years per hour; as well as improved gateportal engines that allowed her to jump 400 light years per step—a seventy-five percent increase from the forerunner alpha class in speed and step capability.

Her weaponry consisted of six coronet cannons, ten pagenay blasters, six K-guns and six Asher torpedo launchers—a twenty-five percent increase from the alpha class galaxy protector. She was lean, mean, powerful and imposing, but somehow kept her elegance with a refined and chic appearance.

Michael David Genesis felt odd and almost out of place inside the Osguard office. This was the first time he stepped foot on a Galaxy Protector since he relinquished command of the *Neraka* some fifteen Earth years ago. His "Alpha" class *Neraka* was decommissioned a year later; her properties recycled and smelted into resources to build the new "Bravo" class galaxy protector *Neraka,* which now patrolled the Telo Galaxy under the sireship of Osguard Perry Tower.

Moreover, since his retirement, Michael and his wife had relegated their travel to startrams and commercial space liners in an attempt to allay his critics bemoaning that he had built an empire with USSTAP that he did not want to relinquish control of.

But this was different. He was here for his grandchildren. He, Michelle, Adam and Jenna were invited guests of the Millmum Galactic Osguard, Jaquille Rican. Jaquille invited them on-board prior to putting the ship on Alert One posture due to the happenings on Earth. If General Zandi required back-up for any reason, Jaquille could have the Campthor in Earth's orbit within ten minutes; and he, his wife and the Freemans would be there to ensure their grandchildren's safety.

Since their grandchildren were on Earth, Michael understood Jaquille's offer was because she wanted Michael, and the rest, to be closer to the action in case something went wrong. Jaquille also let it be known that the First Osguard, Michael Black had put his Galactic Guardian, the Horizon, on alert and would be able to get to Earth within ten minutes as well. It didn't need to be said, but Michael knew that Ed, Kashara and Sharyla were probably unofficially in Alert One posture, orbiting their intergalactic gateportals, ready to lend a hand in a moment's notice.

"You know, Chief Osguard Genesis, I am honored that you, your wife, Executive Osguard Adam Freeman, and Osguard Jenna Freeman accepted my invitation to sit watch during this incident," Jaquille diplomatically said.

"No, Jaquille…it is I who am honored that you invited us. You did not have to do that," Michael responded. "It would have been well within your right to let us stay home and kept us informed on the situation."

"Osguard Genesis," Jaquille exclaimed. "It isn't in my blood or any acting Osguards' blood to do that! All of you here have been an important part of building USSTAP. So when you are in need of any service from anybody, you only need to say so." Jaquille licked her lips as she gathered her words carefully. "I assure you, your grandchildren are safe. I invited you here to witness that first-hand."

Michael nodded, as silence permeated the room.

"How's your father, Chiki, doing?" Michelle asked Jaquille, breaking the awkward peace.

"He's fine...doing well in Galaxy one-five-three."

"He should be up for retirement soon?" Michael asked, calculating in his head that Chiki was about to reach the mandatory retirement age of sixty universal years.

"Yup, he, my Uncle Tomi and Aunt Stelana will all retire within the next couple of years," Jaquille responded. "They are looking forward to it. They even are looking at buying some land together back on Chaktun and live out their golden years watching the stars from solid ground instead of a man-made starship traveling faster than light itself."

Michael gave a slight chuckle at the wisdom of her words. Being an Osguard was like being a nomad. You lived either on a station or a starship; but you had no world, no territory you could call home. At least Chiki, Tomi and Stelana were lucky in one respect. They were Chaktun and they knew their retirement, wherever it may take them, would be on Chaktun.

That thought enable Michael to let his mind wonder away from the pressing business of Earth. He remembered he was like that once. He had always thought he would retire in Osguard Gardens in Virginia, the community he had helped set up for their parents and grandparents. It was beautiful and quiet, set up next to a small but wholesome community of Danville.

Even though Danville had a dark history as the second capitol of the Confederacy during the last days of the Civil War, it was a bright spot of warmth and energy that had a mellowing effect on him. He loved the thought of living out his golden years there at one time. But the U.N. had other plans when they proffered the Pact of 2029. The very thought of the document made Michael ill.

Michael's demeanor physically changed as he took a sip of club soda. He sat quietly next to Michelle with his legs crossed and eyes staring out the porthole. In his view was the majestic Millmum Capitol Station.

The station was an amalgamation of seventy self-contained gray stations. They littered the space line like drifting snowflakes. Each station was diamond shaped. They were of different sizes and placements inside the area. The bigger stations had rings around them. A five-story ring, horizontally attached at the base, encased the biggest station. Around the ring several starships had docked, looking like bees in a honeycomb.

Michael concentrated on the biggest station, where he and Michelle spent most of their lives, raising kids and tending to the universe's problems. The biggest station was eight miles wide at the base and two hundred decks long from point to point. The nearby sun of the Chaktun solar system framed the beauty of the station.

The station had several window ports of different sizes and shapes. Some ports were oval, some square, some rectangular and some shapes only Picasso could describe. This station housed the star congress and the galactic parliament as well as the offices of the Galactic Osguard and the First Osguard.

In the last eight years of his tenure, the conclave ratified the plan that stated an osguard no longer maintain more than one responsibility. At one time, Michael held the position of Millmum Galactic Osguard, Rojam Os First Osguard and USSTAP President and Chief Executive Osguard. Now each position was separate, which allowed for separation of power and eliminated the appearance of conflict of interest.

"I know what will take our minds off things for a while," Jaquille finally mustered.

Michael arose from his daydream and turned to Jaquille, "What?"

"Can I invite you on a tour of this new class galaxy protector? I assure you, you will be amazed."

Michael nodded and looked around to the others, "I think that would be marvelous."

CHAPTER EIGHT: SEEING IS BELIEVING

USSTAP Connection Gift and Souvenir Store
New Haven, Connecticut
Planet Earth, Millmum Galaxy, Rojam Os Galactic Cluster

The group passed the bus and crossed the street into a large two story, spacious glass enclosed structure with the title, *USSTAP Connection Gift and Souvenir Store.* Again the blast of cool air that hit Deuce when he walked through the glass front door was refreshing and he again let out a small sigh of relief.

As soon as he walked into the store, the movie center caught his eye. "Let's go over there," he suggested, pointing to the display.

"You go," Cheyenna responded. "I want to check out these electronic books over here."

"Yeah, and I see some cool things back here, I want to check out," Tynala added.

Toniac looked at his watch and then scanned the room. "Okay, we have about a half-hour. Do what you want. Buy what you want. You have debit chips. But be back at the bus in twenty-five minutes." Then he squinted like a parent to a child. "No trouble...you hear me?"

"Tiah," they whispered in unison.

"That's what I mean...speak English only!"

"Okay," Deuce responded as the others nodded.

Deuce traipsed over to the movie section and looked through the stack of digital holographic strips. Each strip said, *"Digitally re-mastered from original 3-D format to holographic purity."*

Deuce didn't know what that meant, or even if the strips could be played on the new common that Toniac gave them earlier, but he knew Toniac would know. So he continued to look through the stack. He saw holo-strips for several movies that Toniac talked about. He saw a holo-strip titled the, *Homecoming;* he saw another titled *Revelation;* and a third titled, *Armageddon.* The last one he saw was titled, *Lost. Lost* was about the accident his grandfather had during the first use of the Unity Stream. It was the poignant moment when his grandfather decided to let Earth now of USSTAP existence. Then he saw a compilation pack that contained all four movies and a thirteen episode series that depicted USSTAP history from the Laurona and Nausona's days on Earth, until the moment that his grandfather announced USSTAP presence to the world. He quickly picked it up and scanned the contents.

It stated that it was over sixty hours of excitement, action and drama; filled with space battles, fight scenes and much more. Deuce wet his lips and decided this was what he wanted. He had seen the requisite HPV crystals, but he thought them boring. This holo-strip promised, 'not a boring second.'

Wow, Deuce thought. This is fantastic.

Deuce walked over to the cashier and dropped the package on the counter. The cashier looked at him with mouth agape. "Are you sure, young fellow?"

"Yes sir, I'm sure," Deuce beamed. Then he thought about the question and doubt inched into his world. "Why do you ask?"

"Nothing kid. It's been a long time since someone bought the combo pack," he explained. "I thought everyone had seen these movies already. It is kind of expensive."

"Oh!" he gulped.

"Listen kid," the cashier continued. "I'll give you twenty percent off and throw in a Tappy T-shirt for free. What size do you wear?"

"What?"

"You look like a large; maybe an extra-large with those biceps," the cashier noted. Then he put in a black T-shirt in the bag with the holo-strip pack. "That comes to three-hundred and ten dollars."

Deuce did as Toniac had instructed on the startram and pulled out his identification card and held it over the scanner. The scanner made a pleasant beep and a green light flashed. Deuce knew he then needed to press the scanner with his thumb to give what Toniac called fingerprint verification. The scanner flashed green once more and gave two pleasant beeps.

The cashier smiled and handed Deuce his package. "Have a good day kid. Nice doing business with you."

Deuce nodded and picked up his package, "Thanks!" He looked around and caught a glimpse of Cheyenna in the reading section. Happy with his shopping, he walked over to her and tapped her on the shoulder, "You find anything yet?"

Cheyenna glanced over her shoulder, and then went back to perusing the shelves, "Not yet."

"What are you looking for?"

Cheyenna shrugged, "I don't know yet. I'll know it when I see it."

Deuce had heard that before with his mom. He hated shopping with her; and he was about to become annoyed shopping with his cousins. He wondered why they just didn't know what they wanted before they shopped. It would make it so much easier.

He huffed and opened his mouth to express his thoughts, but then stopped. He knew saying what he thought would only cause trouble. Instead he told her, "I'll wait for you guys outside. I'm heading towards the bus."

"Don't you want to wait inside where it is cooler?" Cheyenna asked.

"No, I'm good," he said, not wanting to admit Cheyenna was right and it would be smarter for him to wait inside. His pride wouldn't allow him to stay inside and wait for them to finish.

"Okay," Cheyenna responded.

Deuce nodded and then walked through the corridor, up to the glass doors and put his hand on the bar. He hesitated, enjoying as much of the cool air that he could before going outside. Then with a sigh, he pulled open the door and stepped outside into the sweltering heat.

He walked over to the back end of the bus, and leaned into its shadow, trying to capture some shade from the sun. He swiveled his body around so he could keep an eye on the door for his cousins and Toniac, while at the same time being able to glance at his grandfather's old house.

Out of the corner of his eye, he noticed Alexander coming down the granite steps in the front of his grandfather's old house. Deuce turned and waved. Alexander waved back. Then Deuce noticed a young Black man moving quickly towards Alexander. Deuce's went into hyper-alertness and started to cross the street towards Alexander. Before he knew it, the young Black man confronted Alexander and began shouting and wildly waved his arms up and down. Alexander appeared frighten.

Deuce broke into a trot as he weaved between two parked cars. He saw the fright in Alexander's eyes as he approached. The man's back was towards Deuce and he did not see or hear him approach.

When Deuce was in arm's reach of the man, he heard the man yell, "You talk about these damned Osguards all day, like a fool!

Have you ever seen one? No, you haven't! So, where are they now? Where are your damned Osguards now? Can they save your ass from the beat down about to give you if you don't give me the money?

The man raised his fist over his head and was about to slam it down on Alexander's head, when Deuce grabbed the man's arm with his right hand, stopping the potential onslaught in mid-flight.

"Yes I can," Deuce growled

Startled, the man turned and tried to jerk his hand free, but Deuce had a vice grip on it. The man's left hand came up and he took a swing at Deuce. Deuce side stepped the swing and at the same time pulled the man's right arm back and around his back. Alexander jumped out of the way. In one swift move, Deuce had the man's arm twisted and pinned in the man's back with his right hand, and the man's neck pressed against the granite wall with his left forearm.

The man's face hit the top of the granite wall, busting his nose and inflicting cuts and scrapes onto his chin. The man squirmed trying to break free of Deuce's hold. Deuce applied more pressure to the man's arm, twisting it higher. The man yelled in horrific pain.

"One more ounce of pressure and I will snap your arm like a twig," Deuce told the man. The man continued to scream, but he stopped struggling.

"That's good," Deuce commented, releasing some pressure from his arm. The yell lowered to a whimper, laden with colorful explicative language that Deuce didn't understand.

"Deuce, don't hurt him," Alexander pleaded, grabbing Deuce's arm.

"What?" Deuce asked, showing his surprise mixed with a bit of irritation. "This jerk tried to hurt you!" Deuce grunted, as spittle sprayed from his mouth.

"Deuce!" Toniac yelled. "What the hell?"

Deuce shot a glance over his shoulder and saw Toniac and his cousins in front of a small crowd of tourists from the bus looking on.

"Don't hurt him Deuce," Alexander once again pleaded. "He's my grandson. He's my grandson, Gary"

"What?" Deuce yelled. "He's your grandson…but…but…he was about to attack you!"

"He's a drug addict," Alexander confessed. "He's sick. He's just looking for money for his next fix."

Deuce released Gary's arm and spun him around. He grabbed Gary by the shirt collar and pulled him close to him. Deuce now was eye-to-eye with Gary, glaring into his soul. Deuce witnessed the fright tear into Gary's eyes. Gary had now shut-up—his curse loaded language fell to a quiet whimper.

Deuce drew his lips to Gary's ear and whispered, "Your father is protected...don't you ever lay a hand on him again. Am I understood?"

Gary gave a quick nod, "Uh-huh!"

Satisfied, Deuce pushed Gary back onto the wall. Gary stumbled and fell against the wall. Gathering his composure, Gary shot up and looked around. The eyes in the crowd were looking at him like hungry vultures eyeing a dead carcass. With a quick breath, Gary shot down the sidewalk and ran around the corner.

The crowd erupted in cheers, laughter and hand claps. Deuce stood there with his fist balled up to his side. His mind was racing trying to make sense of what just happened, and why he jumped in the way that he did.

The crowd dispersed back to the bus, still loud with laughter and statements of cheer. Toniac, Cheyenna, Tynala and Alexander remained at the spot, watching a myriad of emotions play across Deuce's face.

"Son?" Alexander called.

Deuce emerged from his thoughts and turned to Alexander, "Yes sir."

Alexander motioned for everyone to come closer. When the group was huddled together, he whispered, "You are some kin to the Genesis aren't you?"

"Why do you say that?" Toniac whispered back.

"Deuce pretty much told Gary that he was, when he stopped him from attacking me."

"You are mistaken, Alexander," Deuce tried to bluff.

Alexander took Deuce's right hand in his and turned it over so he could see the back side. "The diamond shape on the back of your hand, and the way you were eating up every second in his house. I can tell you are some kind of kin, at least you three anyway. I don't know about Tony here," Alexander confessed.

"What if we are?" Cheyenna pushed.

"Nothing, I guess. I was just hoping," Alexander admitted. "I always wanted to shake a hand of an Osguard; specifically my kin before I die. I just thought I might have already."

Deuce looked at Toniac, and Toniac gave him a slight nod.

"We are Michael's grandchildren," Deuce confessed. "Not full-fledged Osguards yet, but someday we may be."

Alexander just smiled and patted Deuce on the back. The grin lit up his face with a warm glow. "Don't worry; your secret is safe with me."

"Thank you Alexander," Toniac said. Then he pulled out a card with a 1-800 number on it. "In three weeks, call this number. Leave a number you can be reached for Captain Toniac Good, and I will see what I can do about you meeting more of you kin folks that are Osguards."

Deuce huffed, licked his lips and mumbled, "Better yet, gather up your grandson and call that number. Tell them you are related to the Osguards, and you want your son cured of his addiction. Tell them Michael David Genesis II sent you."

Alexander's eyes lit up more as water pooled in them. "Thank you, son," he blurted. Then he hugged the three Genesis grandchildren, squeezing them tight. When he was finished, tears rolled down his cheek. He was so full of emotion; he simply nodded when he got into his old black sedan, wiping the water from his eyes. He started the car and eased out into the road. Seconds later, the car turned the corner and was gone.

Cheyenna smiled at Deuce, "That's mighty mature of you, cousin."

"Don't go getting soft on me now," Deuce reacted.

"I'm proud of you," Tynala added, punching Deuce in the arm.

"Stop," Deuce fake-pleaded.

"Okay, enough horseplay," Toniac bellowed. "We got a bus to catch."

CHAPTER NINE: STRATEGY BUILDING

USSTAP Lilly Station
Atlantis Continental Self-Atlantic Ocean
Planet Earth, Millmum Galaxy, Rojam Os Cluster

Twelve hours had passed and, once again, General Akbar Zandi was staring at his staff, hoping they had better news to report. He just had spent most of the twelve hours making contact with family members of the dead crewmembers, notifying them of their love one's death. He had no words to explain why such a senseless act took five brave family members from them. All he could say was an incident had occurred and that their love ones were dead. They wanted answers and so did he.

"Report!" he clamored. His face was visibly wrought with tension and his voice shaken with anger wrapped in professionalism.

Colonel Jason Star, the Chief Maintenance Officer spoke first, "The station's structural integrity is fine. Some support beams were damaged in the East Wing, but we shored them up and she's holding together just fine."

"Fine," Akbar nodded. "How about the damaged areas?"

Colonel Felix Wang activated his console and a 3-D holographic view of the stationed appeared. "We got outside and surveyed the damage. Good news is the ARIT estimated it correctly. We found no surprises. I have repair crews around the clock, sealing up the area and pumping out the water."

"With some luck and new supplies, we can have the section back up and operating in about thirty days. Right now, we are trying to make sure anything we do doesn't upset Jason's effort to maintain the station's integrity."

"Understood," Akbar responded. "I want end of shift reports on my desk until further notice."

"Tiah," Jason responded and deactivated the 3-D hologram.

"Anything from the satellites?" Akbar pushed, heading into what he really wanted to know.

Colonel Victor DeJesus cleared his throat. "Yes sire." He activated his controls and a 3-D picture of Paris France merged into view in the center of the table. Time delay satellites captured the characteristics of a gateportal anomaly outside the headquarters for Earth First."

Akbar leaned forward focusing on the hologram depicting the office spaces for Earth First, "Hmm," he managed to say.

"We also caught something else," DeJesus continued. "Marshal Keith Swan, sire of *Moon Base Set*, reported his people captured a nano-burst communication, using gateportal technology from a space debris field orbiting Earth. Marshal Swan sent a startram to capture the debris. The pilots report that it looks like a communications relay. They are bringing it back to *Moon Base Set* for the science boys to dissect."

"Do we know what the message was?" Akbar asked.

"No sire," DeJesus said.

"Do we know where the message came from or where it was relayed to?"

"No sire," DeJesus had to answer again. "But my hypothesis is that Rand stepped to the Earth First Headquarters and then contacted whoever paid him to look the other way during the micro-gateportal drilling."

Centurion Richard Gray, the Chief Watch Officer took his cue and began his report. "We went over the records, Rand's reports and compared them to other data from other controllers for the last year." Gray activated his console and the hologram of Paris dissolved and a hologram of the Tasman Sea floor appeared. "It appears every three or four days, some unknown person or persons have been drilling in this area using the combined technology of microportal and gateportal technology."

"A gateportal, with Viaminic resonation appears about twenty feet from the spot of drilling and pushes through a microportal beam that punches into the floor, finds the crystals, dissolves them at the molecular level, and transports them to somewhere. Where I believe they are reformed, packaged and sold on the black market."

Akbar sat back in his chair, mentally chomping on what he just heard. "Viaminic resonation?" he questioned. "Viaminic resonation could only mean one thing."

"Sire, let's not jump to conclusions," Centurion Jessica Jansen warned.

But it was already too late. Akbar had allowed his mind to fill in the gaps. He knew the small galactic republic, made up of about fifty or sixty planets called the Scolons occupied a nebula between

Telo and Sercey Galaxy. Intelligence had reported that the Scolonians were on the verge of gateportal technology breakthrough.

However, they were missing the catalytic ingredient in their technology, Siaminic resonance. They were using Viaminic resonance, which was dangerous for personnel transport, but perfectly fine for inanimate object transportation. So somehow, Earth First—specifically Dr. Chenault, Commander Rand and the Scolonians—were involved in this together.

But how, and for what purpose? Akbar thought.

"Let's see what the autopsy on the communications relay gives us," Jessica commented. "I know what we are all thinking—considering that last Intel report on the Scolonians. But they haven't indicated any untoward action since first contact over one hundred years ago. So why would they start now?"

Akbar turned to Jessica, his mind still reeling from the connection that Scolonians might be involved in the death of his crewmembers. "I want briefs on my desk in an hour. I need to pre-brief Osguard Rican as soon as possible."

***

Startram 01-7532666
On approach to Moon Base Set
Earth's Moon, Millmum Galaxy, Rojam Os Galactic Cluster

Major Seth Jones and Captain Turner Smith sat in silence, each executing their part of the approach checklist for Moon Base Set. In the cargo hold was the piece of space debris they had just salvaged ten minutes earlier. Primary scans indicated the ten foot debris, shaped like a hotdog bun with scorch marks covering its outer hull, had no power. So for all intents and purposes, it was just another piece of space junk out of a sea of space junk that orbited the Earth as a memorial to the planet's once striving space program.

Moon Base Set sat on the dark side of the moon, near the moon's equator. The lights, pouring from the portholes and the red power seams were the only visible sign of a manmade structure.

"Set Control…Set Control, this is Startram 01-7532666 requesting Zor approach for landing on docking bay Bravo Four." Major Jones said into the interlink.

"Startram 7532666, this is Set Control; we have you at twenty marks out; cleared Zor approach; vector five, two, zero, point five, five…announce beam rider.

Jones motioned to Turner. Turner set the marker and nodded.

"Tiah, Set Control; Startram 7532666 maneuvering to vector five, two, zero, point five, five…will announce beam rider," Jones responded; and then he turned on the startram tractor lights.

In the wash of the tractor lights and in the distance, the hexagon shape of the twenty-two deck moon base could be seen. Its rounded edges and smooth dome top, was a welcome distraction from the rugged and rocky surface of the moon. Concourses, connecting the landing bays to the base sprang from the rounded edges.

As the startram swung around to capture the beam rider to the Zor approach for landing bay Bravo Four, the space debris in the cargo hold, which was secured by galantic cables, shifted. The skin began to glow with an orange energy, and the temperature in the cargo hold shot up.

Turner glanced down at his instruments and saw the spike in temperature shot from 22 chimes in the cargo hold to 59 chimes. He flipped on the vidcam and saw the orange glow of radiation waffling around the debris.

"Major Jones, I think we have a problem," Turner announced.

Jones glanced up from his instruments and saw the worried look on Turner's face through his safety mask and helmet. But before he could form the words to ask what was wrong, the orange energy in the cargo hold ignited.

The space debris exploded, sending a powerful wave of energy out; cracking the spine of the cargo hold and cutting the startram in half. The orange fireball mushroomed in a spiral of gas, fire and radiation within .01118 seconds—not even enough time for the thought of danger to set into the consciousness. The crew compartment split from the ship like a bullet and slammed into the surface of the moon; cracking the seal.

Once the seal cracked, pure oxygen mixed with the strange energy and ignited. Blowing the crew compartment into four smaller pieces and leaving a trail of fire and gas spiraling back to the original explosion point in space. The engines blew off in the opposite direction; hitting and demolishing a stone mound before exploding into pieces, making another crater on the moon. It, too, sent a rope of fire to the original explosion point.

For a split second, the explosion made a rainbow of fire, gas and energy that lit up the skyline above the moon in a beautiful collage of orange and red lines. But as soon as the beauty was born, the cold blackness of space sucked the destruction into darkness. Like a jilted lover, the beauty of the fire left immeasurable destruction, for when the pitch black returned, Major Jones and Captain Turner lay dead on the surface of the moon, with their bodies badly burned and bones crushed.

* * *

I-95 North, Computer Aided Lane (CAL)
Southern Georgia
Planet Earth, Millmum Galaxy, Rojam Os Galactic Cluster

The computer aided lane, or CAL as it was better known, was the middle lane in the highway that used the National Transportation and Safety Board's computer to navigate private and commercial vehicle traffic. With an appointment, Kerri Knight was able to connect her car to the CAL and drive onto the lane in Miami.

After a forty-five minute wait at the on-ramp to I-95 North, the CAL wirelessly connected to her car's computer and took over all functions. With the destination set, the CAL pushed her car to ninety-five miles per hour onto the highway and effortlessly glided her into traffic on I-95 North. It was autopilot for her car; whizzing by other cars, changing lanes and calculating pit stops when she needed a bathroom break, gas or food.

Kerri happily relinquished control and sat back, regarding the view, while contemplating her next move. Kerri could have flown into Richmond, or even Washington, and rented a car and drove from there, but she was tired of airplanes. The trip from Australia was daunting and tiresome. She had enough of air travel.

But as she gazed upon the miles and miles of homeless camps that crowded the outer edges of the highway, where trees and lush grass once occupied, she wondered if she had made the correct decision. The world's population overgrowth was a distant story to her, inside the monolithic high society walls in which she lived within, inside of Miami Florida. Because of this, coupled with her air travel, she seldom witnessed the human toll of that scarce resource played on the unfortunate many, who survived day-to-day on government rations and the philanthropy of people like her.

Her heart tugged at her conscience, making her wonder what else she could do. Food, water and space had become the new currency of life, and with the world population encroaching above ten billion people, there was no relief in sight. No relief, unless the world could bargain with USSTAP. But that was impossible, as long as narrow minded baboons ran the world, preaching a loathing hatred that once was reserved for the criminally insane, and the political psychopaths of the world.

As the outside world whizzed past her at ninety-five miles per hour, Kerri could see only shadows of figures. She could not focus on the misery, or take in the stench of their existence at this speed. Kerri imagined that was the rationale for having the CAL travel at such a speed. Pit stops along the CAL were protected by high walls; said to be for security reasons.

But in actuality, was in place to keep the outside society from imposing in the inside society, like her. She shook her head and wiped a tear from her eye as she imagined the suffering and the turmoil that went along with the shadowy figures passing her by at a high rate of speed.

Kerri took a sip of her diet soda as she gazed out on the highway. The CAL was crowded today. In front of her were about fifty vehicles—tractor trailers, trucks, cabs and private automobiles—all traveling at a high rate of speed, using the CAL computer link to avoid accidents. Bounding the CAL were the local lanes, where cars traveled under the direction and control of the driver. These lanes were almost barren, where only one or two vehicles dare to venture due to the high proximity to the homeless tents.

After several hours on the road and two pit stops, Kerri knew she had to change her focus; she had to change from the outside world's misery to the fulfillment of her mission. Kerri was still in shock at how easy it was to convince Manny that she should go to the U-Day celebration in Danville Virginia.

She had practiced her speech on the airplane back from Australia for hours, but didn't get to use it. Manny agreed with her hypothesis that if there was any place on Earth USSTAP would covertly visit, it would be Danville Virginia during the U-Day celebration. The history of Danville was too strong for USSTAP to ignore.

It was the origins of the Pathgo and Gentry feud that flared with the arrival of Nausona and Laurona Osguard, prior to the civil war. It was also the land in which the "Original Sixty" had purchased to build homes for their families. It was the battleground on Earth where the Kulusks challenged the Osguards and lost.

Yes, there was too much history in Danville Virginia for the Osguards to ignore. When her common buzzed, she hardly noticed it. The fog in which her thoughts traveled had consumed her and the buzz floated into her consciousness like a butterfly to a flower. But the buzz was persistent, by-passing her voice mail feature. After a minute, she finally heard the buzz and broke out of her thoughts.

She tapped the common and the readout stated it was Jerold Washington. She huffed and groaned, wondering what her ex-husband wanted to talk to her about now. He had not called when she escaped death on the Australian Delight—not that it mattered to her. But it would have been nice to know he actually still cared for her; and that the years of marriage that they did share, meant something other than a competition between news reporters.

She smacked her common and activated the voice-only feature, "Hey Jerold, what do you want?"

"Hey Kerri," Jerold's voice came over the speaker. "I just wanted to check up on you. I heard you were back from Australia. Cut your trip short, eh?"

"I had to get back to work. You know how it is."

"Yeah, I guess I do. Well, I just wanted you to know I was thinking of you and that I am glad you are okay."

"Yeah right!" Kerri gasped. "What do you really want, Jerold?"

"Nothing, Kerri," Jerold squawked "Can't I check up on you once in a while? I mean we *were* married at one time."

"Um..." Kerri moaned.

"Besides, I called your office and your secretary said you were going on assignment in Virginia."

Kerri silently cursed. She made a mental note to fire her secretary when she got back. Her whereabouts were not to be released; especially to her ex-husband.

"No," Kerri lied. "I'm finishing out my vacation in Atlanta. I don't know what my secretary is talking about. She probably told you a story to get rid of you. I have to give her a bonus when I get back."

"Oh," Jerold responded. "Well, that's too bad. I thought you were going to Danville to cover the U-Day celebration. I thought we could meet for drinks or something."

"What do you mean—meet?"

"Oh yeah, I'm in Richmond now. I'm renting a car and will drive out to Danville tonight to catch the celebration. FNN wants me to cover the action there. See if I can find out something about these Tappy's and what they may be up to. You know what I mean."

Silence filled the airwaves as Kerri thought about a graceful exit out of her lie. Her mind twisted and turned, seething in her distaste for Jerold at the moment.

Then with a smile, and without much forethought, she blurted, "That sounds great. I think I can drive up and meat you there tomorrow afternoon. Maybe I can get my producer to approve a human interest story about Danville as well." She bit her upper lip, trying to hide the anger in her voice. "What do you say? It will be like old times. Both of us searching for a story together and seeing who will best whom."

"Looking forward to it," Jerold said. "I'll call you about five o'clock tomorrow and set something up."

"Yeah great…five o'clock then," Kerri confirmed.

"Five o'clock…right; see you tomorrow," Jerold reiterated before the common went dead.

Kerri slammed her fist on the dashboard, yelling at the top of her lungs—a grotesque and growling shout. Her eyes transformed from the living sparkle to a demonic stare, as the fiber in her muscles spasmed. What she was feeling was the true nature of hate.

She was experiencing the painful, but grueling dark side of her human nature. For the first time in her life, she wanted to murder someone. Right now she didn't know if it was her incompetent, half-wit secretary, or her devious, evil ex-husband.

***

USSTAP Star Cruiser Orangewood
Gentry Solar System
Millmum Galaxy, Rojam Os Galactic Cluster

Without the executing the fanfare of the Oort Approach, the USSTAP *Star Cruiser Orangewood* ripped into the Gentry Solar

System, bypassing Jupiter and Mars in a blink of an eye. The Star Cruiser was the smallest of the USSTAP starships and a nod to the days when Nausona and Laurona ran USSTAP.

The ship was half a mile in length and a third of a mile in width, with eight decks. This was the Delta Class type star cruiser with six pagenay blasters—three in the front and three in the back; two K-guns with three hundred and sixty degrees of freedom; and three coronet cannons.

The front of the star cruiser was shaped like an arrowhead, slicing through the thick darkness of space. The arrowhead narrowed into a shaft, which widened again, revealing long barreled pagenay gun blasters. The rest of the ship, behind the weapons grew in all directions in perfect symmetry.

The original USSTAP star cruiser, now known as the Alpha Class, was the predecessor to the galaxy cruiser, the grandfather to the galaxy protector and the great-grandfather to the galactic guardian. The Delta Class *Orangewood* was coated with a special black slitanium that absorbed light and red power rods covering the seams; giving it, like all of USSTAP ships, stealth capability.

But today, it ran with all lights on and stealth mode disengaged. The Sire, Centurion Porteriel was obeying orders straight from Osguard Rican: *Come in hard, fast and loud.*

Porteriel, a second generation Kulusk member of USSTAP, knew his job was to make his presence known. He had read the General Zandi's report as well; and knew something untoward was happening on Earth, and it wasn't just the people of Earth behind it. The explosion that took down Startram 01-7532666 bolstered his theory, and nudged Osguard Rican to act. He had to make it known that USSTAP was aware and ready to react as necessary, when necessary.

The *Orangewood* settled in high orbit around Earth, emitting several types of old radio signals known to Earth, awaiting a U.N. hail. It took five minutes before the U.N. Space Tracking station in Norway called the *Orangewood.* Porteriel ordered his crew to ignore the hail, and then ordered the *Orangewood* to assume stealth mode ten. Five seconds after the order, the *Orangewood* melded into the fabric of space, disappearing from Earth's radar and telescope observers.

"Notify Lilly and Set Stations, *Orangewood* is on station," Porteriel commanded. "Assume Alert posture Two," he pushed, readying his crew for combat.

CHAPTER TEN: BEGINNING LESSON

100 Miles outside Danville (U.S. 58)
Southern Virginia
Planet Earth, Millmum Galaxy, Rojam Os Galactic Cluster

The car was a USSTAP retrofitted black luxury sedan that sat six comfortably, but the long ride was anything but comfortable for Deuce. So far, the traveling had been disappointing; not at all what he expected. In New York City, he witnessed firsthand the poverty plaguing the planet; specifically the United States, the country his grandparents said they still loved.

Homeless people littered the streets, huddled in small masses in front of a fire dancing from a barrel at night; or in alley during the day for shade from the brutal heat. Unfortunately, the biggest homeless encampment was right at the place he wanted to visit. The homeless people, wearing tattered clothes that reeked of vomit, urine and feces, but filled with hope, engulfed the spot like a holy temple.

Only a small historical marker signified the place where once the famous shanty stood, where Nausona and Laurona met their grandchildren, and where Ortho's father met his demise. The historical maker, a plaque placed there by USSTAP Historical Society was tarnished, cracked and worn from years of neglect and weather. Now a tenement building, filled with the wretched and disparate members of society stood in its place.

It was no better in Washington. The city, which he thought was the power base for the United States was just as bad as New York. The poor and indigent roamed the street like zombies looking for their next meal, shelter or even some sort of safety.

The sight of the once illustrious *Rizza's Place,* the most prominent nightclub in Washington D.C., patronized by the Washington elite and giant power brokers in politics, was also a disappointment. *Rizza's* was one of seventy-six clubs that culminated into a worldwide franchise and served as a front for USSTAP personnel to go and let off some steam.

Deuce thought such an establishment would be a tourist goldmine; but it wasn't. Again, filth, dirt, and the poor met him as he and his cousins visited the old building; now laden with rats, garbage and unflattering graffiti. Deuce's heart was broken, and by the look he saw on his cousins' faces, so were theirs.

When they got in the car and headed to the I-395 North CAL, Tynala asked, "Why are so many people living next to the highway?"

Toniac explained that food and energy were scarce; and in such a scant supply that the planet had was not large enough to accommodate a huge growing population. Toniac also educated them on the Ortho models that predicted this situation would be exacerbated with the introduction of USSTAP technology, to heal the sick and save the innocent from naturally occurring phenomenon.

The words rang hollow inside Deuce's head as they left Washington. Were the agony and the plight that these people were enduring, the result of his grandfather's meddling policies which he executed in the name of compassion?

Was Earth's condition an example of what had come to be known as Ortho's principle, *"Stopping a world from naturally cleansing itself will induce certain consequences, which may be hard to overcome without doing something immoral?"*

Deuce had not quite understood the principle and why his grandfather stopped talking about Earth until now. This question must have entered his grandfather's mind; and that is why he remained neutral with the U.N. USSTAP Pact of 2029. Somehow, with his grandfather he concluded doubt gave birth to guilt; and guilt gave birth to acceptance of the status quo.

As they exited the I-85 South CAL and turned onto U.S. 58, Deuces mind had switched from numbness to irritation. Since they crossed into Virginia, Deuce noticed a plethora of denigrating electronic billboards against USSTAP, labeled public service announcements, cross their windscreen. Now that they exited the CAL, he saw physical billboards on the side of the road disparaging USSTAP. Deuce hoped the billboard they had just passed would be the last one he would see.

It was bad enough to have the CAL use its computer link to the car to systematically display electronic advertisements across the car windscreen while traveling on the CAL, but to have these insane, untrue public service announcements encroached on his beliefs, and upbringing smacked of pure hatred. Now, after they left the CAL and traveled on rural roads to their destination, he had to endure passing physical billboards that continued the insult him in larger than life pictorials.

There were three different signs that irritated him the most. All contained the logo of the letters *"USSTAP,"* circled in red with a red line through it—the universal sign for *"No USSTAP."* The most irritating sign was the one with a picture of Jesus crying and it read: *"Jesus wept when the Aliens came!"*

Deuce understood Christianity, because most of the "Original Sixty" practiced some sort of Christianity. He also knew how important Jesus was to them; and to have this sign displayed as a public service announcement was a slap in his face as well as a slap in the Original Sixty's face.

The next sign that irritated Deuce made him access his data banks on Earth's history to comprehend the meaning. The sign had a picture of Hitler, wearing a button that read, *"Fascism;"* Stalin, wearing a button that read, *"Communism;"* Bin Laden, wearing a button that read, *"Terrorism;"* and his grandfather, Michael Genesis, wearing a button that read, *"Socialism,"* playing cards around table with Earth in the middle of the table representing the pot. Underneath it read: *"Gambling mankind away!"*

Deuce didn't understand the full meaning; but he understood the Firsties who created this billboard as a "public service" announcement, were equating his grandfather to some of the most evil men known to Earth.

The third one had a picture of unrealistic looking aliens; some with two heads, some with multiple eyes; and others that looked like monsters from a horror HPV, chasing, shooting and stomping on humans. In the background was a depiction of a gorilla-looking creature that stood over all of the carnage, and his face was made to look like his grandfather's face. The caption of this billboard read, *"Stop the Alien Invasion!"*

Just as Deuce was about to suggest they go no further and head back to Lilly Station, he caught a billboard that announced the U-Day celebration in Danville. It was positive, upbeat and colorful. A sigh of relief, punched its way into his lungs. Five miles later, there was another upbeat sign welcoming all Tappies to the area. Then a third signed introduced the new amusement park called, *Osguard Gardens,* built over the same land the original Osguard Gardens was built. It boasted of a twelve story roller coaster, called *Star Rage* with a ten story drop. The next billboard for Osguard Gardens was two miles later with an advertisement for the gateportal and starship simulator ride.

Deuce now thought things were getting interesting. He wet his lips with his tongue and blurted, "I want to do that."

Cheyenna and Tynala who were sleeping in the back shot up with their eyes wide open and scanned the outside.

"What?" Tynala grumbled.

"I want to go on the Star Rage and ride the starship simulator when we get to Danville!" he bellowed with excitement.

"Yeah…right," Cheyenna moaned, as she laid her head back again. "Wake me when we get to Hatesville," she whispered and closed her eyes.

"Yeah…me too," Tynala added; she lowered her head and closed her eyes.

Deuce turned around in his seat and regarded both his cousins as they faded back to sleep. He knew that the trip wasn't what they wanted it to be, and now they were going through the motions to satisfy him and his quest. He realized the deluge of negative things they read on the way down to Danville had a psychological effect on them, and they would rather sleep than endure another minute in this hostile environment.

Toniac, who was at the steering wheel, sucked in some air and stated, "You quest is almost over. Tonight, we grab some shut eye in a hotel; and tomorrow we visit the festival at Osguard Gardens and see if there is anything you three can learn from this experience."

Deuce turned back around and smacked his teeth. "I hope there is something to learn more than we were stupid for even coming here."

"Well, I can't tell you if there is or not. But I can tell you that it is almost over. That I am sure," Toniac pressed.

Deuce closed his eyes and rested his head against the passenger side window. "Wake me up when we get there," he requested.

"Tiah," Toniac replied.

CHAPTER ELEVEN: CLEARING THE AIR

Osguard Gardens Hotel Restaurant
Danville VA,
Planet Earth, Millmum Galaxy, Rojam Os Galactic Cluster

The night had been surprisingly pleasant for Kerri. For the moment she forgot she hated Jerold's guts. He had turned on the charm that made her first fall in love with him. He was sweet, polite and even gallant. They had just finished dinner consisting of lobster tail and steak. The meal was delicious, the service great and the atmosphere was genuinely unique.

Kerri wore a red sleeveless dress that stopped two inches above her knees, accented with black two-inch high heels that made her calves pop. She wore her hair pulled away from her face in a pony tail that dangled around her shoulder. Dark mascara highlighted her green eyes.

She didn't know why she went out of her way to dress for the evening with Jerold. Something inside of her still wanted to be attractive to him, even though she loathed the very air he breathed.

"Another glass?" Jerold asked, holding the wine bottle up.

Kerri thought for a split second and then nodded. She knew she needed to keep her wits about her, but she was actually having too much fun. They had yet to talk about business or the reason they were both in Danville. The night was truly a date between old lovers.

Jerold recharged her glass with the dark red wine and then topped off his glass. He put the bottle down, picked up his glass and offered it in a toast, "To the most beautiful ex-wife I ever had the pleasure of being married to."

The toast stunned Kerri. Her eyes glistened with apprehension as she searched for a comeback. But then she realized the better part of valor was just to accept the compliment and add another compliment to him.

She tapped her glass to his and said, "Back at you!"

That wasn't the compliment she was searching to say, but it was all her somewhat intoxicated brain could conjure. She wanted to say something about how good he looked. But that might lead to an awkward moment, and even to a place she didn't want to go...like sleeping with him before the night was over.

Then she thought about complimenting his reporter skills; but that would be a lie that he would see through, no matter how drunk he was. So the best she could come up with was, *"Back at you."*

They both smiled and sipped from their respective wine glasses. The half-moon overshadowing the bay window, they were sitting near, pushed a glimmer of reality into the moment as Kerri sat her glass down.

Kerri cleared her throat, and began to ask the question that had been on her mind since the day she decided to file for divorce. "Jerold?" she asked.

"Hmm?"

"Jerold, there is a question I've been dying to ask you for some time now. And I thought it might be appropriate; now that we are divorced and no longer involved in each other's lives, that I should ask it now."

"Okay," Jerold said with trepidation. "What is it?"

"Okay," Kerri said again, trying to build up nerve to finish. "Why do you hate USSTAP so much?"

Jerold's eyes narrowed and his lower lip quivered.

"You don't have to answer the question. It's just it's been on my mind for quite some time now," Kerri backpedaled. "I don't mean to insinuate anything about your journalistic integrity; but it does appear you and the people you work for have an agenda against USSTAP."

"No...no," Jerold whispered.

Kerri could see in Jerold's eyes that she had hit a nerve. But she could also tell that Jerold wanted to answer the question, probably for the first time in his life. He wanted to answer the question with truth, and not with a talking point outlined by his network or the Earth First organization.

"I tell you what," Jerold started. "I will answer your question, if you answer one for me."

Kerri thought about it, taking another sip from her wine glass. She wondered what kind of question he could ask that would be worth him telling the truth about his odium for USSTAP. Then she thought if she didn't like his question, he didn't have to answer hers.

"Okay...shoot," she finally said laying the glass back on the table.

"Why did you divorce me?"

Kerri took a deep breath and sighed heavily, "You know why."

"I know what you said in court. I know what you said in the divorce decree. But no...I don't know why. I don't know the true reason."

Kerri pulled away and put her hands in her lap. She looked down at her hands as if the truth were in them. Deep inside she knew what she said during the divorce wasn't the true reason, but she didn't know what the true reason was at that time or now. She looked back up at Jerold and saw the wanting in his face. He was truly devastated by the divorce and wanted to know why it had to happen the way that it did.

"I don't know," Kerri whispered.

"What do you mean you don't *know?*" Jerold blurted. "No one throws away ten years of marriage on a whim."

"I know that," Kerri admitted. "It wasn't a whim."

"Then what was it?" Jerold pushed.

"Competitiveness and individual career goals...I was petty," she uttered.

"That's a start," Jerold said. "At least it wasn't me alone."

"Well," Kerri interrupted. "It was you in a way."

"How so? You just said it was your pettiness over our career goals."

"Yes, but it also was politics," Kerri confessed. She pulled forward and clasped Jerold's hands inside of hers. She looked deep into his eyes, and knew she was about to tell him the truth for the first time.

"Before you went over to FNN, you changed. You became evil and pointed in your reporting. You had a bull's-eye on everything not Firstie approved. Then you went over to FNN and drank their Kool-Aide. You went to the dark side of reporting. A reporter with an agenda isn't a reporter. A reporter with an agenda is a political hit man."

"I couldn't live with someone who lost their integrity...their lust for the truth. I couldn't live with a political hit man. It was too much for my career; too much for my integrity; too much for my humanity. You were— and still are—nasty, deceitful and...and...I didn't know you anymore. You became someone different. You weren't the man I married. You weren't the man I fell in love with anymore."

Kerri took a breath and whispered, "But tonight, I see a little bit of that man. So, that's why I asked the question. What changed in you? Why did you change? I believe it has something to do with you joining Earth First…something to do with their hatred of USSTAP."

"Is that why you are suddenly pro-USSTAP?" Jerold asked.

Kerri looked down at their hands. Jerold had just asked a very important question. Had she done the same thing, but just on the opposite end of the spectrum? She had never bothered to ask the question before.

So she just shrugged, "I don't know…maybe."

Jerold pulled away from Kerri, laying his hands on the table right in front of him. Kerri could see the words, she just spoken, were rattling around in his head. She knew he was having trouble digesting the information. She looked around, nervousness coating her stomach for the first time tonight.

"I'm sorry," she whispered.

"Don't be," Jerold said. "You're right. I did change. I see that now. I was consumed with…" his voice trailed off.

"Consumed with what?" Kerri pushed.

"Okay, I'm about to tell you something no one else knows. Maybe if you knew earlier we wouldn't have been divorced."

"Go on," Kerri urged.

"You know the story on how Ortho found Michael Genesis on the Fourth of July, back in the 1983?"

"Yup."

"You know it was all because of a kid named Billy Red, who tried to kill him?"

"Uh Hum."

"Well, USSTAP never said what happened to Billy Red, did they?" Jerold said in a low growl.

"He went to a USSTAP prison. I assume he is still there, or was released by now."

"Exactly. You assume," Jerold declared. "We don't know what happened to him."

"So what? He was a thug, with a record a mile long of murder and drug dealing…a mile long. He got what he deserved."

"Don't you think he deserved to be caught and tried in an American court, and not some alien witch court?" Jerold stated.

"I suppose so…technically yes," Kerri acknowledged. "So your beef with USSTAP is that they arrested this Billy Red, gave him a fair trial in their system, and punished him accordingly."

"No, my beef is they kidnapped Billy Red in 1983; and no one knew about his fate until 2013, when USSTAP released the HVPs to the world."

"Okay, the American government knew about it before them and sanctioned it," Kerri stated.

"What was the American government to do? USSTAP was Goliath, and the American government was David without the slingshot," Jerold quipped.

"So, this is why you are against USSTAP…over some low-life thug who would have been put to death in the American Justice system anyway?" Kerri surmised.

"That low-life thug as you call him was my grandfather!" Jerold confessed. "My mother was his daughter…a daughter he never got a chance to know because USSTAP kidnapped him."

Kerri drew back in horror. The conversation had just taken a turn that she didn't see coming. The line of logic she formed in her head was now void, unable to pierce truth through the midst of lies, because it was personal for Jerold. Now she saw Jerold was on a vendetta; and she just called his grandfather, "a low-life thug."

"What…? I'm sorry!" she exclaimed.

"Sorry for what?" Jerold pushed with anger in his tone, "sorry because Billy Red was my grandfather; or sorry for calling him a low-life thug?"

Kerri opened her mouth to explain, but the words wouldn't form correctly. She sat there staring into Jerold's eyes, at a loss for words. Her mind racing to find an answer to what he just asked. A feeling of hopelessness crowded her brain.

"I don't know," finally slipped from her tongue. "I honestly don't know," she reiterated. "When did you find out? Have you always known this?"

"No," Jerold answered. "My grandmother told me right before she died," he admitted.

Kerri thought back. That is when she had noticed the change in Jerold. She thought his grandmother's death had something to do with his personality change; but the change was so dramatic that she convinced herself the connection was minor if not irrelevant.

"What did she tell you?" Kerri asked.

"She told me that Billy Red was the love of her life," he began. "She had found out she was pregnant that summer. Her name was Jackie…Jackie Hightower, before she got married and changed her name to Jackie Ballard."

"You mean the same Jackie Hightower that Billy stabbed Michael over?"

"Yup, the one and the same," Jerold admitted.

"She said that Billy came back to the park about three years later and got into a fight with Michael. They ran off down the street and she never saw Billy again. She also said Michael's girlfriend beat her up that day— along with what I know now were storm troopers from USSTAP."

Jerold took a sip from his glass. "I believe they killed him that day, and took his body back to wherever they take dead bodies. They killed my grandfather and beat up my grandmother; before she could tell him he had a daughter…my mother." Jerold took a second sip from his glass. "You see that little bit of information was never revealed. USSTAP has never talked about the second fight between my grandfather and the great Michael Genesis."

Kerri noticed the anger spitting from Jerold's mouth as he recounted the story his grandmother told him. Now, she understood his hatred. She started to feel some of it brew inside of her. For if what Jerold said was true, the altruistic USSTAP she believed in may be a complete lie. They, like any big corporation or government, had deep dark secrets that could ultimately destroy their reputation or bring them down as an all-powerful entity.

"Listen, Jerold," Kerri opened, "If what you say is true, I believe you are going about it in the wrong way."

"How so?"

"If you want answers, you have to go to the source, not make the source your enemy." Kerri sat in silence to let her words sink in. When she saw enlightenment in Jerold's face she continued, "We, and I mean you and me as a team, need to find a way to ingratiate ourselves into USSTAP circle; and then ask some hard questions."

"Okay, but how?" Jerold asked.

"Well first, let me do all the talking tomorrow and you pipe down on your anti-USSTAP kick for a while. I believe there are some USSTAP people here and, if I can sniff them out, we may be able to find a source or two that are willing to speak about Billy Red…off the record of course."

Jerold smiled. "Of course."

"I mean it," Kerri pushed. "Your vendetta with USSTAP has to stop and if we find out anything, we must make sure it is worth publicizing before printing. I'm not in this to satisfy your vengeance. I'm in this to find some answers to the questions you raised. Is that understood?"

Jerold picked up his wine glass and gulped down the contents, seemingly to muster up the courage to accept Kerri's offer.

He slammed the glass down on the table and licked his lips. "Okay, just for tomorrow. But if you fall flat on your pretty face tomorrow, I'm going back to guns blazing on anything USSTAP. Am I understood?"

"Deal then?" Kerri said offering her hand to shake.

"Deal!" Jerold agreed shaking Kerri's hand.

***

In the background, unnoticed by the two usually sharp reporters, were four figures settling in for dinner…two gentlemen, one a bit older than the other, and two young women. Toniac, Deuce, Cheyenna and Tynala proudly sported: *"PROUD TO BE A TAPPY"* T-shirts, and ordering the house special: "Surf and Turf."

It would be the first time any of the foursome digested real meat from Earth. The smiles on their faces were truly like kids on Christmas morning, waiting to open their Christmas presents.

***

Osguard Gardens Amusement Park
Danville VA
Planet Earth, Millmum Galaxy, Rojam Os Galactic Cluster

In the dark, overshadowed by a low illuminating half-moon, several black clad figures with mask covering their faces, skulked between the Osguard Gardens Amusement Park rides, like cockroaches slithering between cans of food in a pantry closet. One particular figure scampered to the *Star Rage* roller coaster, and jumped over the four foot chain link fence with the mastery of an Olympic hurdler.

He moved with purpose toward the base foundation of the coaster. When he arrived, he knelt down and pulled out a metallic package from his backpack. He clicked a button on the package and then stuck it onto the pole. A loud metal click reverberated, signaling the package was now connected to the pole.

"Package one set," the figure said into his collar microphone.

Soon after, the other figures announced their package deliveries,

"Package two set."

"Package three set."

"Package four set."

"Package five set."

Satisfied, the first figure uttered a command to the others, "All packages set; fall back to rally point Charlie."

With the elegance of ballet dancers the five figures crept back, almost dancing between nooks to cranny to crevice, until they returned to the spot where they entered the park. Then with the magic of technology, the first figure tethered the hole in the fence, leaving no trace of their entry.

Before they left, the first figure announced in his microphone, "This is Eagle One…All packages delivered; set for thirteen hundred party at post one."

***

Osguard Village Amusement Park
Victoria TX
Planet Earth, Millmum Galaxy, Rojam Os Galactic Cluster

The owners of Osguard Gardens Amusement Park had another amusement park set up in Victoria Texas, the home of the Osguard *"Lost Lineage"* of Earth. It was smaller than and not as gallant as Osguard Gardens, because it lacked the same history, but it was as lucrative as its sister park in Virginia.

Under the half-moon, a thunderstorm drenched Osguard Village. However, in the radiance of the lightning strikes dark clad figures lurked between the rides and attractions. They too, left metal packages in their wake. When all was done, they shadowed their way back to the opening whence they came and reassembled. Between the sounds of the hard rain hitting the ground and the tin roofs covering the attractions, mixed with the clash of thunder produced by the storm, the lead figure radioed out to an unknown presence, "This is Eagle Two...All packages delivered; set for twelve hundred party at post two."

Another voice crackled over the radio, "This is Eagle Three...All packages delivered; set for thirteen hundred party at post three."

CHAPTER TWELVE: FINAL TOUCHES

TGR Distributing Company Headquarters
Larmin City, Toloman Province
Planet Vellowhail, Telo Galaxy, Rojam Os Galactic Cluster

Chenum Seolin Te Erucki didn't like being unaware of what was going on. He relished in the fact that his people always provided real-time updates and feedback during their missions. But since his communications relay station was no longer available, he had to wait to receive the word; using an encrypted interlink signal that piggybacked on the Star Universal News communications network.

In his wait, Erucki wondered if the station met an untimely demise from other space debris, stopped working due to mechanical failure, or was captured by USSTAP. Either way, he was assured any evidence it could render would be destroyed by the on-board self-destruct mechanism; which was automatically set to go off, if it did not receive an update signal from home base.

Erucki turned on his commercial interlink to see if the news could offer some insight to his questions. The side wall seemed to disappear as the realistic 3-D holographic projection took its place. The anchorman was speaking Tuit, one of the three mandatory languages of USSTAP; the others being English and Chaktun.

The anchorman appeared to be Vergani, as evident by his small elf-like ears. He was blathering about something called a Unity Point.

The Vergani anchorman stated that scientist at the USSTAP Science Academy claimed to have found the point of equilibrium between outerspace, innerspace, ultraspace and the elusive etion energy well phenomenon. He went on to describe it as the point of ignition where benion, trachion, restion and etion radiation are sourced.

Erucki took a mental note of it. If it was true it could be a new source of power, thus a potential business opportunity. It was an interesting news piece, but realized this wasn't the information he needed at the time.

SUN was the most reliable news network, but it covered a large swath since it dealt with all eight galactic clusters. Fortunately, the owners of SUN wised up and chopped their feed into nine distinctive news deliveries; one for each galactic cluster and one general news station that covered the big news from all the galactic clusters. He switched from the SUN general station, which he loved to watch to get the financial insight, to the Rojam Os distinctive delivery.

On this station, sat the anchorwoman he recognized. It was Karina Birdwell; Shawn Genesis' granddaughter. Her usual smile and graceful demeanor was supplanted with the serious but solemn face as she spoke.

"Authorities say that the explosion that killed two USSTAP pilots is unknown at this time. The startram they were piloting was reportedly just finishing a routine training flight, and was on final approach to Moon Base Set when it exploded. The identities of the pilots have not been released, pending notification of family members. Our hearts at S-U-N go out to the relatives and friends of the two pilots."

Erucki switched the interlink off and lowered his head. He knew the explosion had something to do with his communications relay. "They must've found it," he whispered to himself. "It must've been in the startram," he continued. Maddening thoughts crept into his once orderly mind. *Do they know? If so, how much do they know? Do they know it's me?*

He took a deep breath and held it for several seconds, and then he slowly released it. The orderly formation of thoughts once again bore into his mind, chasing the random thoughts of fear from his head. Panic melted away and confidence rode into his psyche. He raised his head, and summoned Kolinera through his private interlink.

Elib Fez Kolinera marched in several seconds later, "You called, Chenum?"

"Yes, I did," Erucki snapped.

"What is it that I can do for you, Chenum?"

"I need you to take down this notation. It appears our communications relay has been compromised, so we need to push all messages to Earth through the alternate signal we have on the SUN network."

"Nelx, Chenum," Kolinera said as he came closer. He pulled out his ARIT tablet and activated it. "Ready, Chenum."

"This is to Dr. Claude Chenault," Erucki began.

***

Dr. Claude Chenault Private Island
Tuamotu Islands, French Polynesia
Planet Earth, Millmum Galaxy, Rojam Os Galactic Cluster

Dr. Claude Chenault loved French Polynesia; he specifically loved the look of the Tuamotu Islands. He stood on the white sandy beach of his private eighteen by fifteen mile island and gazed at the setting sun, knowing his lifelong plan was about to come to fruition. He took a deep breath and exhaled. His spirit felt alive for the first time in years. He sauntered back onto his bamboo porch and into his stone house. He felt the evening breeze waft against his chest through his open white shirt, seemingly massaging his ego with invisible fingers.

When he entered the house, he went to the bar and poured a glass of red wine. Chenault swirled the wine in the glass by gently moving his hand in an exaggerated circle. He then sniffed the glass, allowing the sweet aroma to tickle his nose and excite his taste buds. Finally he sipped from the glass, quenching the eager expectation in his throat. Chenault smiled and put the glass down onto the bar. His face changed from amusement to determination. He knew it was time for business now. He turned and marched to the steel door elevator on the right side of the room.

He pressed his thumb onto the glass scanner, which instantly read his print. "Confirm, Dr. Claude Chenault," a computer voice announced as the scanner turned green. The steel doors opened, Dr. Chenault stepped in and pressed the button marked D. The elevator doors closed and the elevator descended. The shaft was twenty stories deep, passing through the island's base and into the bedrock. The descent took almost a full two minutes.

When the elevator reached level D, the doors slid open, revealing a cavernous underground hanger with concrete floor and rock walls. As Chenault stepped off the elevator his eyes darted from side to side, capturing the thirty Scolonian Aeroships lined up in ten rows of three spread over the three mile by one mile underground cave. The Scolonian Aeroship, camouflaged in sky blue paint was as long as a football field and shaped like an isosceles triangle. It contained six decks that housed a one hundred man crew.

Chenault smiled at the fleet. It was his pride and joy. He had worked with Chenum Erucki for almost thirty years, to build this hidden fleet of war machines on Earth right under the Osguards' noses. The fleet contained the state of the art weapons technology from the Scolonian military. Each ship was equipped with four laser plasters, two particle cannons and a host of kinetic nuclear tipped missiles.

It was all possible because of Erucki's connection and resources. Erucki used intergalactic microportal technology to transport the necessary equipment, parts and supplies to this underground bunker to build the ships; as well as the one hundred and fifty Kulusk planet-to-planet gateportal boxes he had confiscated from former prison planets in Scolonian space. Erucki upgraded the gateportal boxes and stepped 1,800 Scolonian and Vellow workers to the island to assemble the aeroships. It took over two decades to build the fleet.

Now the workers were gone. Trained aeroship crews had arrived through the same Kulusk gateportal boxes, to take command of those ships in the next phase of Erucki's plan—an all-out assault on the governments of Earth.

Chenault turned right and walked outside the guarded perimeter, toward his glass enclosed office built into the rock face of the wall. It was not as plush, nor did it have character like his offices in Paris, but this was the most important office he had. From this office he could command the fleet to take-over the world with the push of one button, or the utterance of one word into the interlink.

The door slid open, and a cool breeze from inside the office rushed out and enveloped him. As he stepped into his office, he could feel the mythical power surging through his veins. He was on the cusp of obtaining all of his dreams—ridding the planet of USSTAP interventionists and making the world into what he needed it to be.

He sat behind the glass desk and ran his fingers across the enclosed holographic keyboard. A live picture of Phillip Rand popped up.

"Yes, Commander," Dr. Chenault almost purred.

"All packages delivered," Rand snarled. The loathing in his voice was more than evident. "Your party will begin on time."

"Where are you? Why aren't you here?" Dr. Chenault queried.

"I'm running another op for the Chenum Erucki," Rand replied. "Besides, you don't need me for this. Although, I will be back after the party begins to make sure you don't screw things up."

Dr. Chenault nodded, "Indeed." He didn't care where Rand was, or if he ever joined him on the island.

"Okay," Chenault finally conceded. "But whatever ops you are running, it better not tip off USSTAP on what we are doing." Rand had served his purpose and no longer was useful. He just didn't want whatever he was doing for the Chenum to interfere in his portion of the mission.

"It won't," Rand growled. "Rand—out!"

Chenault ran his fingers over the enclosed holographic keyboard once more, and the picture faded away to be replaced by another picture of a man. He was Scolonian, evident by his bald head, lack of eyebrows. Scolonians contained no body hair, just smooth skin.

"I need you to check all conduits to the planet chromerion field generators!" Chenault bellowed. "If these things fail, we will be doomed!" he added.

"Nelix!" the Scolonian responded.

Once more, Chenault ran his fingers over the keyboard, and the picture of the Scolonian disappeared.

With a slight groan, Chenault stood and walked over to the glass wall separating his office from the aeroship field. He rested both hands on the glass and leaned into the wall. He could see his reflection from the glass as well as the sea of aeroships beyond the glass. This sight pumped more adrenalin into his system, as he let out a hearty belly laugh.

The laugh seemed to echo inside the office like the specter of death hovering over a dying body; knowing what was about to happen next was gruesome, but intoxicating at the same time.

"Tomorrow," Chenault whispered. "Tomorrow will be the dawn of a new age."

***

Osguard Gardens Hotel
Danville VA,
Planet Earth, Millmum Galaxy, Rojam Os Galactic Cluster

The sound of the shower woke Kerri from a deep sleep. She rolled her head towards the bathroom fighting to open her eyes. It was six o'clock in the morning, and she definitely had too much wine to drink the night before. She rubbed her forehead to massage the dull headache that was waking up with her. As consciousness returned she became aware of her surroundings.

This was not her room. This was Jerold's room and she was completely naked underneath the silk sheets. Her hand went from her head to her mouth, as the memory of the night she shared with her ex-husband invaded her mind in a blitzkrieg of flashes and feelings. She shot up in bed, letting the sheets float away from her body.

At that moment, Jerold slipped his head out of the crack of the bathroom door and shot his signature gallant smile at her. "Good morning, baby! I thought I heard you getting up."

Kerri's hand moved towards the sheets as she started to cover herself, but she stopped. Jerold's smile caused a flood of memories from when they were married, and a feeling of normalcy calmed her.

She lay down and smiled back. "Good morning," she responded as she bit her lower lip.

"Hey!" Jerold playfully scolded. "You better get up, go to your room and get dressed, or are you planning to go to the park wearing your evening dress."

At that moment, Kerri saw the spirited youthful man she fell in love with. Last night she could have blamed the wine for sleeping with the man she had come to loathe over the last couple of years, but this morning the effects of the wine had waned and she still had a longing in her heart to relive the experience of last night.

She turned over onto her side and patted the bed. "I'll go when I'm finished," she whispered.

Jerold stepped from behind the door. He had a towel wrapped around his waist and a puzzled look on his face. "Finished with what?"

Kerri threw the sheets from her, revealing her curvaceous body, and with a smile that could weaken the stoutest man said, "When I'm finished with you."

Jerold dropped the towel from his waist and slid into bed next to Kerri. For the next thirty minutes, they revisited each other's bodies and forbidden passion. When they were finished, Jerold was fast asleep, sate in his spirit.

Kerri slipped out of bed, dressed in her evening attire from the night before and then nudged Jerold awake. "I'll meet you in the restaurant for breakfast in one hour. Afterward, we can go to the amusement park like I told you last night."

Jerold nodded, "You know I have to take another shower."

"I hope it was worth it?" Kerri smiled.

Jerold nodded again, "Hell yeah, it was worth it."

Kerri giggled and kissed Jerold on the lips. She stared into Jerold's eyes, wondering what the hell she was doing. But in his eyes, she saw a hurt little boy, fighting for answers…answers about his grandfather…answers she promised she would help him find.

Because of that scared little boy, she was willing to put the last couple of years of fighting and turmoil on hold. Hell she was even willing to forgive him for the last couple of years.

She blinked and planted another kiss on his forehead. Then with a sigh, she stood up and turned towards the door. She walked toward the door without looking back. However, Kerri made and extra effort to put a little more *oomph* to her walk to remind Jerold of what he let go, and if he played his cards right, what he could have back.

When she exited the room, she closed the door behind her. The clicking sound emphasized in her mind, there was no turning back now. She had given herself to Jerold physically, and now she was about to give herself to him emotionally once more.

She sauntered down the hall to her room whispering, "What the hell?"

CHAPTER THIRTEEN: LET'S GET STARTED

Osguard Gardens Amusement Park
Danville VA
Planet Earth, Millmum Galaxy, Rojam Os Galactic Cluster

Deuce and his cousins had finished their third ride on the twelve-story, twelve hundred foot drop roller coaster, called *Star Rage*. It was the most impressive ride he had ever been on; almost as exhilarating as the defender simulator he flew last month.

They joined Toniac, who was patiently waiting for them next to the cotton candy vendor. Toniac was in the middle of devouring his second pink delight of cotton candy. His eyes were round with adrenalin, stimulated by the sugar his system was not used to digesting.

"Hey Toniac," Cheyenna called. "Don't you want to ride the *Star Rage,* it's…what did I hear that little girl call it…oh yeah; it's awesome…out of this world."

Toniac looked up at the towering medal monstrosity and watched as the passengers, who were strapped to a single chair with their feet dangling in midair, *whish* by him, screaming for their lives. He slowly shook his head, "I've flown defenders and startrams; I've piloted starships at speeds hundred times faster than the speed of light. I've risked my life more times than I care to count. But I will be a damned fool if I get on that rickety piece of crap and risk my life for some cheap thrill. Frankly, I'm surprised you three have ridden it as many times as you did. I thought you smarter than that."

His confession was rewarded with a burst of laughter from his three charges. Toniac frowned and looked away, feigning embarrassment. A few feet away, his eyes caught a sign that read, *Gate Portal Chamber and Galaxy Protector Simulator.* The arrow pointed towards the east.

Toniac's eyebrow raised in curiosity, "Okay, you guys have rode this so-called roller coaster all day, let's do something different."

"Like what?" Cheyenna asked.

"Like that," he said as he motioned towards the sign.

"Really?" Deuce complained. "You know how the real deal feels, why would you want to waste your time on an Earth cloned knock-off?"

"Look, if you don't want to go, that's alright," Toniac offered, but I think I will take a look. It sounds interesting."

Cheyenna and Tynala regarded Toniac for a quick second and smiled. Then they turned their attention to Deuce as they applied the universal famous guilt stare, made famous by their grandmother, on him.

Deuce knew he was outnumbered and he didn't want to fight the stare-down his cousins were applying. His record was something like zero to a zillion against the stare-down from Genesis women.

He simply shrugged in surrender. "Okay, it could be interesting!"

Then the foursome turned east and began walking, following the signs to their next agenda. They soon came upon a footbridge that crossed a creek. Instantly, Deuce knew this was the area where the Kulusk cave that housed the Kulusk gateportal once stood. The cave was demolished and bulldozed over, and in its place stood a three-story rounded building.

Its outer cosmetic, lighting and colorful façade screamed a futuristic aura. Deuce thought it a mixture of Kulusk and Chaktun architecture with a hint of Tuit elegance. He was extremely impressed with the detail in the construction.

"This may not be such a bad idea after all," Deuce said.

Toniac smiled and patted Deuce on the back, and the foursome crossed the bridge and got in line for the attraction. There were fourteen people in line. Unbeknownst to Deuce, Kerri Knight, and Jerold Washington, stood in front of them. The attendant stepped out of his box and grouped the line in sixes; pairing the USSTAP citizens with the American reporters: Kerri Knight and Jerold Washington.

***

Home of Rashid and Safia Zandi
London England, Great Britain
Planet Earth, Millmum Galaxy, Rojam Os Galactic Cluster

General Akbar Zandi stepped through the white light of the gateportal event. He landed in his old room in his parents' house. He really didn't want to leave his post at Lilly Station in a middle of a crisis, but it was his parents' fifty-fifth wedding anniversary. He'd promised he would take them to dinner at a new Iranian Restaurant that had just opened up in downtown London tonight. Besides, he knew Jessica could handle things until he returned.

The event closed behind him, taking the light with it. His room was pitch-black dark. He stumbled for the light switch, wondering why his parents' caretaker had left the light off. She should have known he was coming tonight, and that he would step into his room. It puzzled him for a split second.

He found the switch and turned it on. His reflection from the dresser mirror shot at him, startling him for a split second. After he regained his composure, he regarded his appearance in the mirror. He was wearing a navy blue suit and red tie; a far cry from his usually USSTAP charcoal gray uniform with chocolate bands around the neck, wrist and angles. His hair was neatly combed and his stencil mustached was thinly trimmed. He smiled, probably for the first time in four days, as he vowed to forget the crisis for this one night for the sake of his parents.

After a few seconds of primping in the mirror, Akbar opened the door to set out looking for his parents. Once again, he was met by the dark. It was seven o'clock in the evening and the sun had just gone down. The hall window was letting in the last hue of the burning sun as it made its mad dash for the horizon.

"Ub," Akbar called for his father in Arabic. "Umm," he called for his mother. Hearing no response, he instinctively reached for his pagenay in his right coat pocket. He placed his thumb on the yellow stun button. He then lined his body against the wall and slithered against it down the hallway.

He wondered if he should call the station to send an S-Team, but thought against it. He figured his mind was in hyper drive due to the crisis, and he would look foolish if he activated a security team only to find out some miscommunication between him and his parents caused them to leave without him.

***

Osguard Gardens Amusement Park
Danville VA
Planet Earth, Millmum Galaxy, Rojam Os Galactic Cluster

"Hi, I'm Kerri…Kerri Knight," the woman introduced herself to the group. "This is my…my…"

"Colleague," Jerold finished for her. "I'm Jerold Washington."

Deuce notice Toniac's mouth drop as the man introduced himself.

"The reporter for FNN?" Toniac questioned.

"Guilty," Jerold confess.

"Why would you be here?" Toniac inquired more.

"Just enjoying the day," Jerold announced. "Trying to get a feel for what this celebration is all about."

"From what I understand about you and FNN, this is the last place on Earth you would be, unless you are looking to besmirch the fine people here that support USSTAP."

"I invited him," Kerri interrupted. "You may have heard of me. I'm Kerri Knight from WMN. I used to be married to this lunk. I'm still trying to reform him. So I invited him here. Hopefully, the people here can get through to him and change his mind on USSTAP."

Toniac smirked. "Good luck with that,"

"And you are?" Jerold pushed, obviously trying to change the conversation and be polite in the face of a double insult.

"I'm Tony," Toniac offered. "And this is Deuce, my boss' kid and his cousins, Chey and Nala."

"Got stuck babysitting…ah?" Jerold commented, offering his hand to the group.

Toniac nodded as the children shook hands with Jerold.

Deuce grimaced, when he shook Jerold's hand; wondering if Jerold knew who they really were, how much of a verbal brow beating he would unleash on them. On the other hand, Deuce was quickly thinking of some verbal attacks to lay into Jerold if he became too combative during their time in the simulator.

***

Home of Rashid and Safia Zandi
London England, Great Britain
Planet Earth, Millmum Galaxy, Rojam Os Galactic Cluster

Akbar found the stairs and crawled down them, with his pagenay at the ready. The stairs took a ninety-degree turned at the halfway point. He stopped there and tried to peer down to the first floor. The lights were off and the daylight was fading fast.

He saw nothing, so he continued to crawl down the stairs, trying to be as stealthy as possible. He reached the bottom of the stairs and peeked into the living room. He thought he saw the back of his father's head sitting at the couch.

Fear gripped him as he steadied his heartbeat. He maneuvered into the living room, and around the couch. When he was close enough he saw his parents sitting quietly on the couch. He didn't know what to make of it, so he switched on the light on the table next to the couch.

The light flooded the room and illuminated the sticky red liquid flowing from his father's chest and his mother's neck. She was slumped into his father's lap. They had been stabbed. Akbar's eyes slumped with despair as he reached for his father and mother. In that split second, he was hoping against hope that they were still alive.

But before he could reach them, a pinching— then piercing burning sensation ripped through his side. He turned and grabbed the spot of the burn. It was a knife with a hand attached to it. He looked up and saw the smiling face of Phillip Rand.

He tried to push Rand away, but the pain was too great. Rand was now twisting the knife into his kidney. Cloudiness overtook him as his vision swirled into darkness. Soon the pain was distant, but so were his thoughts - except for one.

***

Osguard Gardens Amusement Park
Danville VA
Planet Earth, Millmum Galaxy, Rojam Os Galactic Cluster

Twenty minutes passed in pure silence, as Deuce fumed inside knowing he was so close to the Firstie mouthpiece that seeded all that garbage about his grandfather and his family. He fought the urge to attack Jerold, and found himself biting his lip to keep from saying something he would later regret. Deuce saw the same anguish he was feeling play across his cousins' faces. He knew they too were ready to spew out some Osguard justice.

The bell rang, signaling it was Deuce's group's turn to enter the building. The attendant motioned for them to step up to the entrance way. The smoky dark glass doors opened and a white light flashed in their face. Deuce raised his hand to shield his eyes from the light, but it was too late. When the light faded, bright spots clouded his vision.

"Please step forward," the attendant commanded.

Deuce and the others gingerly proceeded into the room. The glass doors closed behind them. The lights inside the room slowly illuminated to a dim glimmer. Deuce scanned the area and his eyes captured the scene resembling the inside of the Kulusk cave as depicted in the holovidpics he watched as a kid.

It was almost an exact replica. In front of them was the outlined of the old mechanical gateportal box with a control ARIT panel off to the side. It looked real.

A voice spoke from the corner speakers that were camouflaged as rocks, "You are now in the Kulusk cave where Nausona and Laurona Osguard tried to affect their escape from Earth in 1860, using the three century year old gateportal. They failed to fix the portal, but were rescued by a Chaktun starship later that year, after being brutally attacked by the Pathgo brothers."

Deuce and his cousins knew the story very well. They grew up with the story as part of their heritage. It was one of those points in time when tragedy bore the fruits of their existence and generated the core concept that produced USSTAP.

The voice continued, "The gateportal in front of you is an exact replica of the gateportal that once stood on this very spot, in which the Erif and Efas Ritchen used in the early years of the 20th century in their quest to find and kill the Earth-born Osguards."

Again, this was another story that Deuce, Cheyenna and Tynala knew all too well. It was another strange point in time that was a tragedy that produced the foundation of what USSTAP came to be. His grandfather said it was God's guiding hand that turned these tragic moments into something so grand.

The voice went on to say, "We are generating the gateportal for your step unto the Galaxy Protector *Neraka*. Please stand by for further direction."

The group roamed around separately, each examining some aspect of the cave. Deuce ran his fingers along the cave wall. It was foam and not rock, but still appeared realistic. On the side was a depiction of a Kulusk ARIT panel with the pictures of different solar systems.

The only solar system correct on the panel was the Gen solar system they were in. The other solar systems were pure fabrication and not even close to any known solar system in Millmum Galaxy. Deuce had to smile at the simplicity of the diagram.

"Step to the gateportal," a voice commanded over the camouflaged speaker. The metal doors squealed as they opened. A flood light punched out of the darkness in the metal box.

It wasn't the same welcoming, almost angelic light Deuce was used to from a gateportal, but a harsh, eye-burning light associated with electricity. Nonetheless, it was the best they could do to simulate the gateportal.

Kerri was directly in front of him. He witnessed her giggle as she walked towards the light. He turned towards Jerold and noticed he had a smirk on his face, and was visibly agitated by the experience. Deuce just smiled and placed his hands over his eyes in an attempt to shield them from the light. Tynala grabbed his left hand and began squeezing it, like she was actually scared.

The six people stepped into the box, which resembled an old style elevator upon closer examination. The door squealed to a close behind them and the light dimmed, allowing Deuce to lower his hand. Suddenly the doors in front of them squealed opened revealing a staged replica of the *Neraka's* command bridge. The bridge sat over the control bridge like a balcony. In the middle of the bridge sat six command chair mock-ups, in rows of three, instead of the usual three. Each command chair had multifaceted buttons. In front of the chairs was the ship's pilot and navigator stations. They had a miniature screen that sat between them. Around the outer walls were mock-ups of the ship's different workstations: the offensive weapons, defensive systems, communications, security, life-support and science officer stations.

Beyond the railing to the balcony were mock-ups of the seven rows of stations that controlled the defenders, startrams and long range ARIT scans. They were manned by uniformed manikins. In front of them sat a projection screen that took up the entire wall, simulating the ship's main viewer. It was the window to the outside for the ship. In the screen, as well as in the miniature screen between his pilot and navigator, sat a view of Earth.

They stepped out onto the bridge as the sights and sounds massaged their senses. Deuce eyed the command chairs and headed straight for them. He plopped down in the middle command chair on the bottom row, imagining how his grandfather must have felt at the helm of the mightiest starship in the universe during his day.

"Chromerion field up," Deuce yelled.

Cheyenna and Tynala giggled.

"Please take a seat and buckle up," the faceless voice commanded over the speaker system.

Cheyenna and Tynala took the seats left and right of Deuce, while Kerri, Jerold and Toniac took the seats behind Deuce. When all were seated, a bar slid across their laps out of the right arm of each seat and attached to the left arm of the seat—locking them securely into the seat.

The faceless voice over the speaker began its dialogue, "You are the Osguard of the *G.P. Neraka,* and today your mission is to deliver the Chaktun ambassador to Chaktun. Only one catch; there is a Kulusk armada between here and there."

The screen lit up and the floor began to move like a roller coaster. The screen simulated the ship moving through a gateportal and when it exited, facing four Kulusk starships. The Alert One sounded and the battle began. The screen showed the *Neraka* maneuvering and firing pagenay blasters and coronet guns at the enemy ships.

The sound effects matched the picture as the bridge waffled, tilted and shook in coordination with the maneuver that displayed on the screen. When the screen displayed the *Neraka* taking fire, the floor shuddered. When the ship turned, the floor tilted. When the ship descended or ascended on the galactic plane, the ship waffled accordingly. It was unrealistic, but somewhat fun. Deuce was enjoying the ride and laughing throughout.

***

Home of Rashid and Safia Zandi
London England, Great Britain
Planet Earth, Millmum Galaxy, Rojam Os Galactic Cluster

Akbar's finger twitched on the pagenay and clicked the yellow button. A yellow beam shot from his palm, hitting Rand in the leg. A shock, much like electricity, jolted Rand. The yellow beam briefly disconnected Rand's axons and dendrites in his nervous system, causing momentary sensory deprivation. His body convulsed and he let go of the knife. He hit the ground hard with his knees, as if gravity had just multiplied his weight tenfold.

Rand was aware, but unable to control his body. He was paralyzed, fighting for breath, fighting for his lungs to work again. Then, air magically rushed into his lungs and he could feel the floor beneath his knees and hands. However, he still didn't have command of his movements. He fell flat on his stomach and face with a hard thud. Saliva spewed from his mouth and his eyes rolled into the back of his head.

Akbar fell to the ground next to Rand, with the knife sticking out of his back. His breathing was labored, and his vision almost black. He mentally commanded his hand to move, but he couldn't tell if his hand obeyed the command or not. He wanted to activate his CD by touching the lower right earlobe.

With a gasp he said, "Warrior down...warrior down...S-Team...S-Team." The air escaped his lungs as he spoke and his eyes popped wide opened. Darkness took him and his soul was escaping.

A white tunnel opened up and Akbar thought it was a gateportal, but the figures stepping out weren't USSTAP warriors of the S-Team, but his mother Safia and his father Rashid. They looked young, like he remembered them when he was a child. His mother was so pretty, and his father a strong strapping specimen of a man. They waved for him to join them. Safia had a wide grin on her face and tears streaming from her eyes.

Akbar's soul got up from his body and walked towards the light. In an afterthought, he looked back over his shoulder. He saw his bloody body laying at the feet of his elderly parents, and the man he had just knocked down stirring next to him. His final thought was one of peace. His last act on Earth wasn't one of destruction. He hadn't killed Rand, he had let him live. His spirit was guilt free and now it was his time to journey into the afterlife as a reward for his life and deeds. He only hoped that his career with USSTAP was pure enough for the afterlife he prayed for.

With a smile, he turned back to his younger parents standing in the light and reached for their hands. They grabbed each other and hugged. Without a word, they sauntered together into the light. It was like stepping through a gateportal, but different. This time Akbar's destination was not of this universe. This time Akbar would not be coming back.

This time Akbar was dead.

***

Osguard Gardens Amusement Park
Danville VA
Planet Earth, Millmum Galaxy, Rojam Os Galactic Cluster

At 1:00 PM explosions rocked the park. The packages, left the night before by Eagle One and his team, were C-4 charges set on a timer. One package detonated at the base of the roller coaster, buckling the support. The explosion ignited in a puff spiraling white and gray smoke, ripping the support beam to shreds. The eight seat train was at its peak—twelve stories high—when the explosion tore through the beam, buckling and warping the track. The car jarred loose from the track and careened toward the ground.

The roller coaster crumbled, as if it was a quarterback being taken out at the knees by a linebacker. The sixteen people's screaming towards their horrible death could not be heard, because the other four packages were ripping the same level of destruction on the Ferris wheel, spin attraction, merry-go-round and the simulator building.

Deuce had just whipped his head around to look at Tynala. He saw her beautiful smile and her eyes glistening with enjoyment, when the screen exploded, sending glass, plastic and other embers flying. Deuce covered his face with his arms. Glass and metal struck his body like tiny bees stinging him. The support beam above them cracked and a portion tumbled down.

It bounced off the floor behind Toniac, Kerri and Jerold and then smacked Toniac and Jerold in the head, knocking them out cold. The floor beneath Deuce's foot cracked and then the room went dark.

A split second later, the red emergency lights popped on illuminating the smoke and haze that was floating in the room. Deuce pulled his bloody arms away from his face. He was in shock. He looked around and saw Cheyenna lumped over to one side, with cuts all over her face. He reached for her and checked her pulse. She was alive, but bleeding bad.

He turned to Tynala and saw she was awake. "Are you okay?" he huffed.

Tynala nodded. Her eyes were watery and her face was cut up as well. Her arms were sliced and laying in her lap. It appeared she could not move them.

From behind him, Kerri let out a blood chilling scream. Deuce turned around and saw Toniac and Jerold slumped over in their seats, with blood rushing from their heads. Deuce eyes popped wide open as fright hit him.

He tried to get out of the seat, but the steel bar was jammed into place. He could not remove the restraints. Deuce pulled and tugged with all his might, grunting like a wild animal as he tried to summon all the strength he had to break free. But it was useless. He was locked in place.

He banged at the bar with his fist in frustration and begged Kerri to stop screaming. "Quiet...quiet!"

"Call for help!" Tynala moaned. "Use your CD and call for help."

Deuce moaned, wondering why he didn't think of it at first. He touched his right earlobe and activated his CD. "Lilly Station...Lilly Station; this is Deuce Genesis."

"Lilly Station...controller five," rang a voice through his implanted receiver that he could only hear.

"Lilly Station, there's been an explosion! We are stuck and Captain Good is hurt! Send a medical evac team...Alert Code One!"

"Tiah," controller five responded. "Sending medical evac team to your location now...Alert Code One."

Deuce nodded, "They're on their way."

CHAPTER FOURTEEN: CHAOS

USSTAP Lilly Station
Atlantis Continental Self-Atlantic Ocean
Planet Earth, Millmum Galaxy, Rojam Os Cluster

One minute the observation deck was quiet, and the next minute all hell broke loose. Centurion Jessica Jansen jumped from her seat when she heard Akbar's voice crackle over the emergency interlink frequency. *"Warrior down...warrior down...S-Team...S-Team."* His voice was hauntingly faint and obviously in distress.

"S-Team gateportal eight...Alert One!" she commanded.

"Tiah," Epstein replied. His fingers moved like lightening over his holographic keyboard. "Dispatching Security Team Alpha One to GOW's coordinates!" he reassured Jessica.

GOW was the USSTAP title for the planetary commander. It stood for General of the World.

"This is Chief Controller Epstein!" he yelled into the station's interlink. "S-Team Alpha One report to gateportal eight for emergency step...warrior down...I repeat warrior down! Cleared hot, weapons foxtrot, alert one. I repeat...cleared hot, weapons foxtrot, alert one."

Jessica nodded. Epstein had just dispatched the station's top combat team in full offensive combat mode with clearance to use deadly force as necessary.

She pushed her interlink connection. "Warrior down is GOW!" she added. She didn't know if letting the team know that it was the general of the world, General Akbar Zandi, would push them even harder or not, but she felt like she had to let them know what the stakes were.

"S-Team Alpha One stepping now!" Epstein reported.

Jessica checked her watch and noted that from the time they received the call to the S-Team stepped through was fifteen seconds. She prayed that it was quick enough.

A second call rang through the emergency interlink frequency. "This is controller five. Medical emergency...Alert Code One...medevac team one to GPR-1...repeat...Alert Code One...medevac team one to GPR-1; sending coordinates now."

"What's happening?" Jessica bellowed.

Richard Gray, the watch officer spoke up. "The Osguard kids are in trouble. They reported an explosion at Osguard Gardens Amusement Park. I'm playing the call back for you now!"

The overhead speaker crackled to life, *"Lilly Station...Lilly Station; this is Deuce Genesis."*

"Lilly Station...controller five."

"Lilly Station, there's been an explosion. We are stuck and Captain Good is hurt. Send a medical evac team...Alert Code One!"

"Tiah, sending medical evac team to your location now...Alert Code One."

Jessica closed her eyes and wondered, *What the hell is going on here?*

When she opened her eyes, she noticed Gray and Epstein staring into her face. She knew they were wondering the same thing. If she believed in coincidences, this would be one. But she didn't believe in coincidences; especially ones with such horrific character as these two chilling calls portrayed.

"We're under attack," she groaned. "Epstein!" she barked, "dispatch an S-Team to the Osguard kids' location."

She looked at the threat board to her right. There were two Code One Alert events flashing. She balled up her fists. She wanted to hit something, but her professionalism kept the feelings in check. "Send two S-Teams to the Osguard kids' location, weapons foxtrot and send another S-Team to Akbar's location...weapons foxtrot. Put the station on Alert one...weapons delta!" she ordered. Before she sat down in her seat, observation deck personnel had rushed to implement her instructions.

All personnel went to their alert one station, armed with delta belts. The belt held a quick release holstered coronet side arm strapped low on the side of the thigh at hand level. The gun was a sleek sexy looking eight inch barrel black weapon with a curved hand-grip conformed to fit in the owner's hand. The gun shot rapid coronet energy pellets at the speed of light. The impact of anything traveling at the speed of light especially a coronet energy pellet not only put a hole in its target, it ripped through its target cutting clean seared grapefruit size holes.

The belt also contained a palm-size three-button pagenay strapped to the right hindquarter. The blue button fired the blue beam that quickly and neatly burned its target with high unbearable heat. The red button corresponded to a red beam of energy, which overloaded the human axons and dendrites in the nerve cells with heat, rendering its victim unconscious. Then the yellow button corresponded with a yellow beam that disconnected its victim's axons and dendrites causing momentary sensory deprivation and momentarily disorienting its victims.

The belt housed another weapon called a mation-G, the follow-on version to the mation II. Upon the call of the owner, this weapon shape-shifted a metal liquid polymer into any type blade. The operator pushed a button and mentally commanded the blade desired and the weapon would conform into that blade – a knife, axe, machete, sword, saber or even a saw.

The delta belt was the epitome of personal defensive weaponry for USSTAP. Due to DNA locking, each weapon on a belt could only be operated by its owner. It was the top level of defensive equipment right below full combat gear—weapons echo—and two steps below the offensive combat gear preferred by USSTAP S-Teams.

Weapons echo included a multi-facet rifle that contained the accoutrements of all three—coronet pellets, pagenay blaster and mation-G technology. While weapons foxtrot was the offensive gear that integrated a multi-selectable grenade launcher onto the rifle and included a full-battledress protective suit, helmet and gloves that integrated the owner's thoughts into an ARIT controlled assistant.

The remaining twelve S-teams on the station were in weapons foxtrot.

Jessica had just ready the station for an all-out armed assault.

"This is Alpha One Lead," the voice cracked over the interlink loudspeaker. His voice was solemn and full of despair. *"We have Commander Rand in custody. Send medevac team."*

Jessica shot up and moved towards the speaker as if the proximity to the voice would give here clarity on what was happening on the other side of the interlink. "What about the GOW?" Jessica asked.

"This is Alpha One Lead," the voice came again, followed by several seconds of agonizing silence. *"The GOW is dead,"* he huffed. *"Rand killed him...he stabbed the GOW to death!"*

Jessica fell silent, staring off into nothingness. Her body went numb. The words she just heard had psychologically knocked her down. She was lost.

"Are you sure?" Gray interrupted.

"Send medevac!" Alpha One Lead urged again.

"Medevac is in route!" Epstein informed Alpha One Team Lead.

"Tiah, Lilly Station," Alpha One Lead responded with calm. *"We have three bodies, two male and one female...initial identification is the GOW and his parents. Alpha One and Alpha Two are in the process of securing the premises now."*

"Tiah," Jessica whispered, clutching her fists against her legs. "Lilly Station copies all."

***

Osguard Gardens Amusement Park
Danville VA,
Planet Earth, Millmum Capitol Station, Rojam Os Galactic Cluster

The adrenaline that ravaged Kerri's system after the explosion was wearing off and the pain of her injuries were taken over. All of a sudden, it was hard to breath. She struggled to suck in air, but it was like breathing fire. Her lungs burned with each breath. Kerri slumped down in her seat, unable to move. The room began to spin and the lights were casting dark shadows in her vision.

Abruptly, multiple white lights flooded the shadowy structure as dark suited personnel emerged into the area. To Kerri, they looked like angels from God, coming to take here to the promise land. She wondered if she had died in the explosion and this was some type of out-of-body experience. But the pain that shot through her body as she tried to raise her hand told her it was not. This was real and somehow these people had used a heavenly entrance to get to her.

Her head was foggy and the pain was excruciating to the point where her vision was fading. She coughed and tasted her own blood exploding from her mouth. She tried to call out to the personnel, but only a whimper came out.

"Osguard...Osguard?" she thought she heard one of the voices say.

"Over hear," the kid in front of her yelled. "We're trapped."

Then her vision failed and her eyes closed. In the haze and fog of her pain, she only caught bits and pieces of conversations.

"Explosion...blood pressure...unconscious...concussion...they're coming with us...is that wise…it's an order…broken arm…head trauma…security team…"

Finally she felt a prick on her hand. Funny, she thought, with all the pain rattling around her body, she could discern a prick on her hand. And then nothing…lights out. Kerri fell into a big black hole of nothingness; no sound; no thought, not even the awareness of life. Kerri Knight was unconscious.

CHAPTER FIFTEEN: UNVEILING

USSTAP Star Cruiser Orangewood
Earth Orbit, Gentry Solar System
Millmum Galaxy, Rojam Os Galactic Cluster

Centurion Porteriel paced the command deck, listening to the reports flow in. He heard that the Genesis children were transported to the USSTAP's Tillman Memorial Hospital, in the Central African Republic, along with two civilians, and their caretaker Captain Toniac Good; and that Captain Good, Cheyenna Genesis and one of the civilians were in the operating room fighting for their lives.

He also knew that doctors were implementing medical procedures on Deuce Genesis, Tynala Genesis and the other civilian.

His security chief told him they were in one of three known explosions that caused multiple casualties. It went against his spiritual nature to only render aid to the two civilians trapped with the Genesis children. He wanted to send several medical evac teams to the sight of the explosions and render life-saving treatment. But Centurion Jansen had warned him it was against the UN – USSTAP Pact. Porteriel thought it was wrong, but he was a good warrior and obeyed orders; even though it made him sick to his stomach.

"Multiple gateportal openings…two light years in quadrant four…one decimal five…eight on galactic plane!" his defense officer yelled out.

Porteriel's heart jumped into his throat. He was on the cusp of going to battle stations when the defense officer said, "USSTAP signatures."

"On screen," Porteriel commanded.

The screen zoomed in on the coordinates and captured five gateportal openings, spread apart blinking into existence. The first gateportal bloomed to life and the *G.P. Campthor* jetted through at combat speed, a battle tactic usually reserved for quick and decisive strikes. *Campthor* didn't skip a beat, as it lurched into full hyper speed. The next gateportal shot out *G.P. Nightwing,* followed by another gateportal opening that spat out her sister, *G.P. Dragonstar;* both at combat speed. The fourth opening produced *G.P. Fantasia,* Osguard Edward Genesis' ship, followed by another opening that propelled *G.P. Sky Fire,* Osguard Kalina Genesis's ship into the dark blanket of space like a rifle bullet.

The galaxy protector was the flagship sired by the galactic Osguards as well as their immediate emissaries in the guardian ranks; Nolvars, Solvars and Vanguards.

Porteriel smacked his lips as he watched these giant battleships of space angrily screaming towards Earth. Those gateportal openings faded into closure as the next two blinked into existence. Almost in one simultaneous movement, Rojam Os First Osguard's *Galactic Guardian Horizon* pushed its massive body through the light and skipped into hyper speed. The second opening gave birth to Chief Osguard Lillian Saria's galactic guardian, the *Uno.*

There were sixteen Galactic Guardians in the USSTAP fleet, which were the flag ship of the First Osguards of the eight galactic clusters, the Chief Executive Osguard, and the Executive Osguards of the Guardian Supreme Council, and two of them just popped into view ready for battle.

Seeing two massive battleships of space flying in coordinated formation, speeding through space and ripping through the solar system like bald eagles on a hunt was both frightening and awesome at the same time.

Porteriel gave off a heavy sigh, "As they say in English, *the shit just hit the fan!"*

Porteriel watched with some trepidation as the seven ships raced towards him. He knew at once the Osguards siring these ships were angry, hurt and blinded with emotion. He bowed his heads and inwardly said a quiet prayer for those responsible for the explosions. Because he knew now, that whoever was responsible for hurting the Genesis children and killing all those humans on Earth, was about to feel the full wrath of the Osguards. And that was something he wouldn't wish on any human.

With the thunder and precision of Irish River Dancers, the seven ships formed up on the *S.C. Orangewood* in a synchronous orbit, separated by only five marks. When the sky show was over, a single voice rang over the interlink. *"Star Cruiser Orangewood,* this is Osguard Rican...Report!"

***

FNN Headquarters
New York City, NY
Planet Earth, Millmum Galaxy, Rojam Os Galactic Cluster

"This is Becky Love reporting from FNN Headquarters with a FNN News Break special report. Moments ago the United States was rocked with several targeted explosions. All took place at 1:00 PM Eastern Standard Time. One explosion happened at the United Nations; and is rumored to have taken place inside the U.N. Security Council, where members of the council were meeting to discuss the recent Tasman Sea incident. Two other explosions rocked both the Osguard Gardens and Osguard Village Amusement Parks. There are reports of multiple casualties."

"FNN is sending reporters to all three scenes and will keep our viewers informed as we get more details. To repeat, this is a FNN News Break special report. There have been three targeted explosions that have rocked the United States. One at the U.N. Security Council in New York and the others at the Osguard Amusement Parks in Danville Virginia and Victoria Texas. We are standing by for more news. I'm Becky Love for FNN."

***

The White House Oval Office
Washington DC
Millmum Galaxy, Rojam Os Galactic Cluster

President Amanda Taylor leaned against the Resolute desk. The desk was a large antique partners' desk used by several U.S. presidents since Queen Victoria gave it to President Rutherford B. Hayes in November of 1880 as a gift. It was built from the timbers of the British Arctic Exploration ship, *HMS Resolute*. The shiny brown stained desk glowed with majestic power that seemed to resonate through the president.

President Taylor wore a navy blue business suit with a skirt that hung just above her kneecaps and a white ruffled blouse. On another day, one would think she was about to embark on some official ceremonial duty, but the stern look on her face was telling.

Inside the oval office, sitting on the pair of couches that faced each other, were the core members of her National Security Council. To her right sat Vice President Calvin White; Secretary of State and the President's sister, Ann Farris; Secretary of Defense, Cory Sweet; and the Secretary of Energy, Donald Jones. To her left sat Chairman of the Joint Chief of Staff, General Felix March; National Security Advisor and the President's youngest sister, Alicia Cole; Chief of Staff and the President's husband, Richard Taylor; and the Attorney General, Simon Dylan.

Calvin White cleared his throat as the news from FNN played on the common monitor. "The casualty list is extensive," he managed to murmur. "Two hundred and fifty people, including women and children between the two parks and another fifty, including all the members of the Security Council and the Secretary General at the U.N. are dead. It's devastating."

"It's an attack!" bellowed her sister Alicia Cole. "We just sustained a terrorist attack on American soil...once again."

Amanda peered at her sister. The words flowed to her consciousness but faded as the numbness of the events clouded her ability to absorb the words into a coherent thought.

Ann Farris quipped back, "I don't think it is a terrorist attack, at least not one borne from this planet."

"What do you mean?" Cory Sweet asked.

"Just before I came here, I received a call," Ann continued. "It was Dr. Chenault."

"What does he have to say?" Amanda questioned fighting to bring her awareness back into reality. She folded her arms across her chest and crossed her feet.

"He believes this was an attack perpetrated by USSTAP," Ann pushed further.

"How so?" asked General March, now leaning forward as if he could physically catch the words that Ann would spout next.

Ann repositioned herself and explained, "Dr. Chenault believes USSTAP took out the amusement parks in a coordinated attack to cloud the issue of their real target...the U.N. Security Council."

Simon Dylan waved his hand in disgust, "That's preposterous. It's just more of Chenault's ideological bullshit."

Amanda shot a stern look at Simon, which cut him off from indulging in more comments. She never liked him. He wasn't a true believer like she and her sisters about Earth First. He was a concession to the more moderate Senate—an appointment to be the administration's watchdog when it came to civil laws.

Ann continued, "Look, USSTAP has one of their ships orbiting now. It didn't announce itself. It didn't go through the proper procedures set up in the U.N. USSTAP Pact; and it's been flying above our heads for two days and nights...doing God knows what. Dr. Chenault thinks taking out the U.N. Security Council under the guise of terrorist attacks against the Tappies is just the first step."

She swallowed to let the words sink in and establish a rhythm in which she could weave the story. "They killed all fifteen members of the council, including our own ambassador and the Secretary General; leaving the planetary militia that the U.N. built up leaderless and essentially leaving the planet defenseless against a USSTAP attack. Except..."

"Except what?" Amanda queried.

"Except that Dr. Chenault has built another planetary militia. Do you remember the aeroships he wanted to build when he was General Secretary?"

"Yes," Amanda nodded.

"Well he built them—thirty aeroships—the biggest, most technologically advanced flying battleships known to Earth. And he promises they can take on anything USSTAP can throw at us. He is willing to dispatch them to cities throughout the world. He says they will be a hovering protective cover that will ensure safety and security."

"Really?" Simon jested. "Have you seen the size of USSTAP's ships? Do you know what kind of armament they carry?

Ann shot a dismissive glance at Simon, "Really! Yes I have. But that should not be a problem. Dr. Chenault has built a planet wide force field that will keep us safe from any USSTAP weapons that can be shot from space. He has already activated it. I dare say that is why we haven't been bombarded from above thus far."

"What?" General March screamed. "What do you *mean?* What gives him the right to turn on some damned force field in our country...over our heads?"

Cory Sweet motioned for the general to calm down and then interjected, "Madam President, Dr. Chenault's actions seemed to interfere with our sovereignty as an independent state, and your powers as the leader of this country by taking on this unilateral move."

"It wasn't unilateral," Ann pushed back. "I told him we were good with it."

"You had no right!" murmured the Secretary of Energy, Donald Jones.

"Yes, she does," Amanda berated. "She is the Secretary of State and I delegated the power to intervene as necessary to protect this country from those USSTAP dogs."

Simon huffed and shot a daring stare at the President. "Madam President, hear me clearly on this; you don't have the right. It is not in your powers to delegate the sovereignty of this great nation to anyone —especially a foreign corporate entity."

Amanda stood straight and took a deep breath. Her bewilderment of the situation had now just given way to anger. "Mr. Dylan, I don't give a damn what you think! I'm the President of the United States, and I will not tolerate being spoken to in such a manner. You will apologize or leave the room this instant." A long agonizing moment of silence heated the room as Amanda waited for Simon Dylan's response.

Simon leaned back in the chair and slowly looked up at the ceiling. For a moment, he looked like he was about to acquiesce to the president's request for an apology. But in a sudden move, he closed the notebook in his lap and stood. "You will have my resignation in an hour."

Amanda Taylor was taken aback. Her mind raced for a retort, but no words could form on her lips. Instantly her political personality kicked in as she thought of the public damage Simon's sudden and unexpected resignation would cause in the middle of a crisis and three months before an election. His resignation would be political fodder for her adversaries; especially when they found out the root cause was the interpretation of her constitutional powers.

"Wait, Simon," she ordered.

Simon ignored her and continued to gather his belongings.

"I said *wait,* Simon!" she said with more force.

"Madam President," Simon responded without looking. "My resignation is effective immediately…good day!" Simon marched to the door, opened it and, with the fanfare of a Hollywood exit scene, walked out the door— slamming it shut behind him as a sign of his anger and disdain for the Taylor Administration that he so humbly served for over three years.

Amanda looked at the remainder of her core group and smiled, "I thought he would never leave."

The group offered a nervous chuckle at her poor attempt to defuse the humiliating moment. An uneasy silence fell over the council causing Amanda Taylor to search the faces of her closes advisers. She saw troubled and anxious faces—faces that didn't exude confidence in her leadership at the moment; but a wait-and-see demeanor that she didn't like.

She opened her mouth to speak, but no thought came to mind. She let out a silent sigh and shifted her hands to balance herself against the *Resolute.*

A beep from Alicia Cole's common interrupted the awkwardness. Alicia tapped her common and starting reading the message. After several seconds, she raised her hand, "I think you need to see this." Amanda nodded.

Alicia tapped her common and waved her hand in a slinging motion, pushing her data to the room's 52-inch monitor. The monitor screen popped alive, as images of the eight USSTAP bat-shaped starships hovering over Earth in formation crowded the screen.

"What the hell is *that?"* Richard Taylor asked in a raised voice.

"That, my dear brother-in-law, is USSTAP," Alicia noted.

"Look at the size of those ships!" Cory Sweet exclaimed.

"Yup!" Alicia responded. "Those ships are miles long and miles wide. They are the planet killers of the USSTAP military; and they are hovering over us as we speak."

Richard Taylor, her husband and Chief of Staff cleared his throat, "What next?"

"Ann," Amanda called out. "How many of those aeroships is Dr. Chenault willing to provide the U.S.?"

"Up to five for now," she responded.

"Good, I want one over D.C., New York, Chicago, Los Angeles and Dallas. And if he can give us more, I want one of those bad boys over Boston, Miami and Houston. Can you make that happen?"

"Yeah, I think I can."

"Then do it."

***

Dr. Claude Chenault Private Island
Tuamotu Islands, French Polynesia
Planet Earth, Millmum Galaxy, Rojam Os Galactic Cluster

The air in the cavern was dry and cool. The last of the Scolonian Aeroships were starting their engines. The sounds of the ultra-calogenic engines, and the facility industrial fans chasing the exhaust and fumes from the cavern and depositing them outside, produced a high pitched echo throughout the chamber that could shatter glass.

Dr. Chenault stood in the soundproof control booth that was buried into the south side rock face of the cavern wall. He was surrounded by Scolonian controllers, listening to the radio chatter as each controller passed on the instructions for their respective aeroship to maneuver to the top opening and exit the facility.

The opening was narrow, not giving much leeway for error for the big behemoth aeroships to exit. The exit broke through the surface within the deep forested area of the characteristically covered tropical island, some four miles behind Dr. Chenault's beach front house.

Chenault was as giddy as a child on Christmas. He had just received the last of the expected phone calls from the United States. All in all, it appeared the world leaders from Britain, Germany, Russia, Japan, China, Italy, Greece, Canada and the United States had come crawling to him, begging for him to defend their nations from the USSTAP's onslaught...or at least the perceive onslaught that Chenault had engineered.

As Chenault watched the last five aeroships maneuver and disappear through the opening, he smiled with satisfaction knowing his life-long dream and aspirations were about to come true. He had manipulated the world into thinking him as their savior. Moreover, he was more than willing to perform that role, as long as he was treated as the world's true and only monarch.

"Chenault-zero-three-zero is cleared and on track to Washington D.C." the last controller confirmed. "That's the last aeroship, Dr. Chenault."

Chenault nodded. "Proceed as schedule," he ordered. "Have my private jet ready to launch. I'm heading to New York."

"Nelix," the Scolonian responded.

***

FNN Headquarters
New York City, NY
Planet Earth, Millmum Galaxy,
Rojam Os Galactic Cluster

"This is Becky Love reporting from FNN Headquarters with a FNN News Break special report. We are getting multiple reports of large aircraft appearing over various cities in the world. Right outside our news studio, I can report one of these large aircraft floating over Manhattan now! The Taylor administration has announced it requested assistance from Dr. Chenault's Earth First Security Forces; as well as the United Nations Legionnaire Force to provide security from a possible USSTAP invasion."

"Additionally the U.N. has announced that Dr. Chenault has been appointed temporary U.N. General Secretary and Commander of the U.N. Legionnaires."

"The administration's tensions are high since the space observatory in Iceland reported several USSTAP starships hovering above the planet in what they call an attack formation. The EFSL has dispatched, what the administration is calling, aeroships to protect key cities in the U.S. from these starships of death that are hanging over our heads. These triangular shaped ships appear to be floating battleships, about a soccer field long and as equally wide."

"There is no report on the armament aboard these ships, or how exactly they will be able to protect the cities they are hovering over against an all-out USSTAP attack. But the administration assures us that the EFSL ships are more than capable of protecting these cities and, the entire planet, if needed."

"The last words from the administration to the Osguards were, 'Bring it, if you think you can handle it!'" So far all attempts to reach USSTAP officials have gone unanswered. For now, I can report that these EFSL lifesaving aeroships are on station over New York, Washington D.C., Los Angeles, Dallas, Miami, Houston and Chicago; as well as London, Moscow, St. Petersburg, Berlin, Paris, Rome, Hong Kong, Athens, Beirut, Tokyo, Beijing and other important strategic cities in the world."

"Altogether, our office has received confirmation of thirty EFSL lifesaving aeroships parked over cities ready to protect the world from the egregious self-serving maniacs of space."

"Obviously, since we haven't seen any action from these murderous psychopaths, since the initial bombing that killed so many innocent people and the ambassadors to the United Nations, we can assume that Dr. Chenault's forces have caused our enemies to pause in their attack plans. In that regard, I would like to send my heartiest thank you from the American people to Dr. Chenault, for being so foresighted, knowledgeable and courageous enough to take on this fight...thank you Dr. Chenault. This is Becky Love for FNN, New York City...back to you in the studio."

CHAPTER SIXTEEN: HOSPITAL

Tillman Memorial Hospital
Sibut, Prefecture of Kémo, Central African Republic
Planet Earth, Millmum Galaxy, Rojam Os Star Cluster

In the middle of the African continent, nestled between the nations of Chad, Sudan and Congo, the rolling beautiful savanna surrounded the newly minted skyscrapers of Sibut: the capitol of the Kémo prefecture in Central African Republic; also known as the CAR. The tapestry of yellow, brown, gold and black fingers of modern architecture glistened and sparkled in the African sun, as the buildings reached and kissed the wisping clouds in the sky. The three dozen buildings that made up downtown Sibut, were a crystal-clear sign of the relationship the CAR had with USSTAP.

The buildings' architecture carried the distinct geometric shape USSTAP signature, which were accented by an eclectic collage of Chaktun, Tuit and Kulusk design with a touch of Mosleck motif, all wrapped in steep Central African culture.

The outer edge of the patchwork of artistically pleasing buildings was USSTAP's 100-story Tillman Memorial Hospital. It was a rectangular-shaped white glass building with a courtyard in the middle. An enclosed truss bridge connected the inside west side of the building to the inside east side of the building on every even floor; and on every odd floor, an enclosed truss bridge connected the inside north side to the inside south side of the building.

In Tillman Memorial Hospital, on the thirty-second floor lay Michael David Genesis II; who was brought directly to the hospital by the emergency evacuation team three days earlier.

Sounds were distant, like echoes on a beach. But somehow he knew the sounds were beckoning him through the mist of unconsciousness. Deuce concentrated, focusing on the sounds. They were rhythmic—soothing and scary at the same time. Then he caught another sound, familiar and comforting. It was a voice. The voice brought peace to his mind. He focused on the voice, straining all his might to hear it. The cadence was peaceful.

After a few minutes, he recognized the first sound. It was now in the background, but he knew it. It was the Medical ARIT, also known as MARIT, tracking his heartbeat. Suddenly, the sights and sounds of the explosion ripped into his memory. He was hurt. His cousins were hurt.

Deuce began to struggle, his mind seared glimpses of Tynala sliced arms; Cheyenna crumbled in her seat; and the blood gushing from Toniac's head into his vision. His mind jumped from one image to another, flashing the horror of the explosion into his psyche.

His mind screamed, *No!* But the images persisted. His mind continued to scream in torment until he heard the comfortable voice sail into the hurricane of emotions. It was his mother calling his name —over and over again.

"Deuce...Deuce...wake-up Deuce...it's Mommy! Baby, please wake-up!"

Her voice chased the images away, and Deuce felt himself climbing out of the abyss. He fought to follow her voice. Soon his struggle gained some reward. His mother's voice became stronger and stronger as the seconds ticked by.

Finally with one mighty effort, he opened his eyes. He saw two figures above him. His vision was still hazy, but he could tell the figures were his parents Kalina and Edward Genesis. He blinked several times, trying to wash the haze from his eyes.

"Look Eddy, he's awake!" Kalina joyfully exclaimed.

"I see that Kal," Edward confirmed. "How do you feel, son?"

Deuce continued batting his eyes until his parents were in focus. But something was wrong. There was a glow emanating from them, like an aura.

"I'm a little woozy," he mumbled.

"That's alright, son," Kalina tried to comfort him. "You were in an explosion, but the doctors say you will be just fine. You lost a little blood, bumped your head a bit—a slight concussion, but all in all, you will be fine."

"Chey and Nala are fine as well," Edward Genesis offered. "They had a rough time. They had some surgery, but are resting comfortably in their rooms."

"Mom...dad?"

"I know son," Edward responded. "We are here...or at least we aren't far. You're at the USSTAP Hospital in Sibut. You've been here for three days. You've been unconscious the entire time."

"The glow?" Deuce mumbled.

"We're in orbit above Earth," Kalina responded. "We're only able to use the unity chamber because...because...well, because Earth has some sort of force field we cannot gateportal through."

"What?" Deuce coughed. He understood the inner workings of the unity chamber. It had been upgraded in the past decade with micro portal technology to project a holographic image of its occupants in the real world and not just in the unity stream, as it did when meshed with gateportal technology.

Each USSTAP ship had a unity room, which contained five pressure point beds that inserted into a tubular white ARIT-Micro Portal sleeve. Each ARIT-Micro Portal sleeve looked like a transparent Magnetic Resonance Imaging (MRI) machine. His parents were in that sleeve wearing a nanoflex suit soaked in MARIT fibers, having their conscious thoughts deconstructed, shot through the ethos and reconstructed in front of him as a holographic projection.

They could see and hear everything their holographs could see and hear. They were just unable to touch or feel anything— including him. That was a shame, because he really needed a hug from his parents, right about now.

"Yes, it appears the Firsties have built a force field similar to the planetary countermeasures grid we use to protect Earth," his father began to explain. "But this force field has characteristics of a second generation chromerion field."

"How?" Deuce asked.

Ed looked at Karina as if he was asking permission to continue. Karina nodded. "It appears we are under attack," Ed explained. "General Zandi and his parents were assassinated. The S-Team found the caretaker stuffed in the basement, also murdered."

"What?"

"Yes, baby," Karina took over. "They were assassinated in his parents' home, at the same time someone exploded bombs at Osguard Gardens, Osguard Village and the United Nations in New York City. Several hundred people were hurt or killed. The leaders of the United Nations were murdered."

Shock grabbed Deuce's heart as the news soaked in. He felt his body go numb in disbelief.

Ed took a deep breath, and summoned his command voice, "Authorities on Earth are saying the bombs were made from dialairtic crystals. The news organizations on Earth are pointing fingers at USSTAP."

"How does anyone on Earth know what a dialairtic crystal explosion looks like?" Deuce asked, pulling himself up to rest on his elbows. "People of Earth only know the term from the HVPs and the so-called movies they made about USSTAP ages ago!"

"They don't know what dialairtic crystals look like, and they sure as hell don't know what an explosion caused by a dialairtic crystal would look like! For heaven's sake, a dialairtic explosion would leave nothing but an empty hole. There wouldn't be any debris or bodies left to analyze."

Kalina bit her lip and sighed. When she opened her mouth to speak, Deuce could tell she was fighting back anger. "Centurion Jansen tells us that the leader of this so-called Firstie movement is leading the charge. His name is Claude Chenault, Dr. Claude Chenault."

"Toniac told us about him," Deuce responded.

"Well this Dr. Chenault is the one who has linked the explosions to dialairtic fracture, citing a source inside USSTAP. He is playing on people's fear of us and building an furor against us with these lies—"

Ed interrupted his wife, "He's behind all of this. He has been for years. Centurion Jansen's people caught General Zandi's assassin; or should I say, Zandi didn't go down without a fight and took his assassin out long enough for the security team to capture him at the scene." Deuce saw a shot of pride in his father's eyes as he talked about Zandi's efforts. Then the sparkle in his eyes faded, replaced by raw fire. "It was Commander Phillip Rand—one of our own— who murdered the GOW," his father continued. "Jansen used a MARIT interrogator on the traitor."

Deuce knew no one could resist a MARIT interrogator. It was a medical artificial intelligence device —about the size of a half-dollar — that attached to a patient's forehead. It used an energy source, he didn't quite understand, which connected to the brain and read the brainwaves.

Long ago it was used as a translator, but the intelligence community saw benefit in using it to read the minds of their prisoners. USSTAP rarely used it, but when it did, it was highly effective. Recently, USSTAP Keltar, the judicial and review arm of the organization, approved the use of the MARIT interrogator for police and security incidents that were deemed of grave importance.

Certainly the assassination of the World General would be considered in this category.

"Rand's interrogation proved most fruitful," his mother injected. "It appears we have a little uprising—one that involves a certain entrepreneur from Vellow and the Scolonians."

"It doesn't take a master of the science to see that," Ed huffed.

"What do you mean?" Deuce asked, laying back down and shutting his eyes to stop the headache that was now beginning to fight for his attention.

"Thirty major cities have Scolonian ships overhead, protecting them."

"Protecting them from what?" Deuce moaned, trying to stay awake.

"Protecting them from us, I suppose," his father concluded.

His father's last words faded away as the timed sedative pushed its way into Deuce's system and commanded him to sleep. Soon Deuce was traveling in the blissful darkness of slumber, warmed by the thought that his parents weren't far.

He could hear their voices but he could not make out what they were saying anymore. Just the tone and manner of their voices wafting in his fog of unconsciousness made him feel safe and comfortable. No matter what the news was he had just heard; he knew his parents were there and they would fix everything. Just like parents always did. Just like *his* parents always did; just like Osguards have always done throughout the years—fix it.

***

In another room, on the thirty-sixth floor, Michael Genesis's holographic avatar faded into existence. He was using the unity room on *G.P. Campthor* to make this visit. Moments before, Michael received word that his grandson was awake and doing well. This was pleasing news for him. His granddaughters had awakened the day earlier from their horrific operations and were doing well.

Tynala was cut up pretty bad, and lost a copious amount of blood, but faired surgery very well. The doctors sutured her wounds with MARIT stitching and replenished her blood via MARIT transfusion. Her cuts would heal any a couple of days, showing no evidence of their existence.

Cheyenna had a slight concussion, two broken ribs and a broken arm. Again the doctors worked their magic and mended her bones and mitigated the concussion. She would be as good as new in about two days. Until a few seconds ago, he was worried about Deuce. The MARIT concussion medication therapy had not produced the advertised results. He remained in a coma far too long than expected. But he was out of it now and on the right mending path for a full recovery.

His thoughts then turned to Captain Toniac Good. He, too, remained in guarded condition. The hospital did not have the medical equipment to fully heal a zyder with head trauma, so the doctors are doing their best to stabilize him. Tillman Memorial never expected to cater to a zyder; therefore, they didn't stock up on the special equipment needed to treat Toniac's condition.

They corrected and attended to his body, since the physiological differences between humans and zyders was so minute; but the brain was different. A zyder's brain was a composite of human tissue and living MARIT technology. Toniac needed a specialist, and there were no zyder specialist in Tillman Memorial.

The closest one was on-board *G.P. Skyfire,* and she was using the unity chamber to lend her expertise to the hospital's doctors as a holographic avatar. The best way to save Toniac's life was to get him aboard *G.P. Skyfire*. Michael had a plan to fix that. But for now he had another duty to perform.

The environment stormed into view. He squeezed his eyes shut as he attempted to orient himself to the situation. One minute he was lying down in the unity chamber and the next minute he was standing at the foot of Jerold Washington's bed. Next to him was the young lady that the team brought in with him, Kerri Knight: Washington's ex-wife. She was sitting in a chair next to him, wearing this big grin.

The doctors had fixed her up fairly quickly. She was lucky; she had only minor injuries...cuts and bruises mostly. But Jerold took a hard hit to the head, just like Captain Good. MARIT concussion therapy took some time. However, due to the medical miracles of USSTAP technology and the grace of God, Jerold pulled through. Michael saw that he too was smiling. Except in his smile, Michael saw a familiar picture. He knew instantly what that picture was, but he knew he wouldn't have ever guessed it without the blood test results that the doctors reported. Michael was looking at the direct descendant of his old friend—Billy Red.

Startled at the Michael's sudden appearance, Kerri looked up at Michael, covering her mouth to stifle the instinctive scream gurgling in her throat.

"Ms. Knight, I'm so sorry to frighten you," Michael began, still searching for words to continue the conversation.

"That's alright," Kerri pushed, dropping her hands from her mouth. "That's a new trick. I thought gateportal transfer was preceded by a white light."

"It is," Michael assured her. "But I'm not using gateportal transport. I'm using unity stream transmission."

"What?" Jerold growled.

Michael turned his attention to Jerold. He saw the smile that just occupied Jerold's face had disappeared only to be replaced by anger. Michael expected confusion, or even fright; but not the pure unadulterated anger he was witnessing from Jerold at this moment.

"It's unity stream transmission," Michael went on to explain. "I'm not really here. I'm aboard a galaxy protector orbiting Earth right now. This is just an avatar of my consciousness so I can speak with you."

"Why don't you just step down off that ship and face me like a man?" Jerold huffed. "Are you scared?"

"*Jerold!*" Kerri scolded while shooting him a dirty look.

"What?" Jerold pushed back. "Don't you know who this is? This is the high and mighty Chief Executive Osguard and President of the Universal Science, Security and Trade Association of Planets; the honorable do-what-he-wants, Michael David Genesis."

Kerri turned back to Michael, studying him with squinted eyes. Suddenly a flash of recognition covered her face. "Is it you? Are you Michael Genesis?"

"Yes, I am Michael Genesis. But I'm no longer President and CEO of USSTAP. I'm retired...Chief Osguard Emeritus, if you will."

"What are you doing here?" Kerri asked, letting her reporter skills come out.

"It's obvious what he's doing here," Jerold scoffed. "He's leading an attack force against us. Tasman Sea was just the beginning."

"Shut up Jerold...a good reporter asks questions...not answers them," Kerri admonished. Then she nodded towards Michael.

"First of all Jerold, I would step down here, as you say, if I could. But it appears Dr. Chenault...your boss...has a second generation chromerion field up, which prevents any gateportal transit; therefore, I must rely on unity stream transmission. Second, we are not attacking Earth. We were attacked. Those children that were in the simulator with you when the bomb went off in Osguard Gardens Amusement Park - they were my grandchildren. They almost died. Do you think I would be part of an attack that would jeopardize my own grandchildren's lives?"

Jerold's head snapped back as if he was slapped in the face. "Your grandchildren?"

"Yes, my grandchildren."

"Are they alright?" Kerri asked.

"Yes, they are fine. Deuce...Michael Genesis II...pulled out of his coma a few minutes ago. The doctors say he will be alright. My granddaughters, Nala and Chey are resting comfortably here in the hospital. Their parents are with them now. Thank you for asking."

"What were your grandchildren doing in Osguard Gardens Amusement Park?" Jerold asked, showing real concern for the first time.

"Kids!" Michael huffed. "They have a mind of their own and they wanted to visit Earth and see their heritage. I, my wife and their parents were against it...seeing how the people of this planet have treated us over the years. And now, they are almost killed by..." Michael cut it off; knowing accessing blame to Dr. Chenault would only infuriate Jerold at the moment. He had to wait and present the evidence at the proper time—a time where Jerold would be more susceptible to the truth.

"It doesn't matter. We'll get to that. Right now I fear there is something more pressing that we need to talk about, Jerold Washington," Michael continued. "You see, I know who you are...at least I know who your grandfather was."

Jerold swallowed as his eyes darted left to right, "So?"

"So I'm here to tell you that I did not kill your grandfather."

"Then who did?" Jerold shot back.

"No one killed your grandfather," Michael responded. "He's not dead."

"What?" Kerri interrupted.

"Jerold, your grandfather was one and still is one of the greatest minds I know. His discoveries and inventions have catapulted USSTAP into the technological giant we are today."

"If that's so, where is he now?"

"What I am about to tell you Jerold, is at the highest level. Only the Chief Osguards and the Ambassador Chancellor are read into the file. I had to get special dispensation from them to share this with you."

Jerold sat up in the bed; his eyes wide open with anticipation, "Go on!"

Michael looked over at Kerri, "I assume you understand, what you are about to hear is off the record and not for public consumption." Kerri and Jerold both nodded.

Michael wavered in his thoughts as he searched for a point in his story to begin or at least introduce the beginning. He stepped towards the window, and looked out at the great rolling Savanna surrounding the city. It was beautiful, elegant and haunting at the same time. He had always wanted to visit Africa—the mother land. This area was where Chaktun prisoners first stepped foot on this prison planet. The centuries old Kulusk gateportal chamber was in the basement of this facility as an old museum piece.

"Well?" an impatient Jerold persisted.

Michael turned to his two audience members and let out a long sigh. "Have you heard of Mezhak Zyder, our well renowned scientist?"

"Yes, he is the guy that lost his life saving you during the unity stream fiasco. It was portrayed in the Osguard holo-strip called, *Lost,*" Jerold answered.

"Well Billy Red and Mezhak Zyder were one and the same." Michael paused to let his words sink in. When he saw the quizzical looks permeate his audience's faces, he continued, "Billy took on the name after his last failed attempt to kill me in New Haven in 1985 or was it 1986...I forget just when."

"1986," Jerold said, "If you are referring to the fight you had with my grandfather in the park that summer it was 1986. My grandmother was in the park that day, and she told me the story before she died. I assure you, it was 1986."

"Right, it was 1986. I'd just graduated from Rutgers University," Michael smiled for a second. "Well, anyway, that attempt failed and I thought Billy had perished in an explosion in that old house on Whalley Avenue. But he didn't. He was badly injured but somehow survived and escaped to Chaktun, where he reinvented himself into the scientist we came to know as Mezhak Zyder."

"That simple?" Jerold huffed.

"Apparently," Michael concluded. "You see, Billy Red was able to do all these things because he is an Osguard descendant. He had Omega two-four-four DNA, which our scientist believed was altered and not eradicated through his years of drug use. Simply put, his drug addiction supercharged his brain."

"You mean I have *Osguard* blood in me?" Jerold almost shrieked.

"Billy Red was an anomaly; an Osguard from a bastard line USSTAP didn't know about or could trace. But blood tests revealed you are a descendant of Laurona Osguard, through your father."

Jerold's eyes glazed over upon hearing Michael's admission. Michael took a deep breath, deciding he needed to direct the conversation back to Billy Red's tale. "To make a long story short, Mezhak used the unity stream as a tool in an attempt to kill me once and for all. But it failed too. In the process, his body in this universe died and we thought that was the end of it."

"But it wasn't?" Kerri asked.

"No it wasn't," Michael admitted. "In 2020, Mezhak Zyder made contact with me through the unity stream during one of my transmissions. It appears Mezhak's consciousness bounced back to the other side, once he figured out Billy Red's body on this side was dead. He managed to take over the body of Billy Red on the other side."

"You mean he is *alive* in the parallel universe?" Kerri questioned.

"Yes, he is alive in the other universe," Michael nodded.

"I don't believe it!" Jerold spat. "You're making it up to save your own ass!"

"No I'm not," Michael responded. "It appears Billy and my alternate in the other universe made a pact, and began a science and technology company in which Billy could exercise his intelligence for the betterment of that Earth. He is a scientific rock star on the parallel Earth—bringing about new forms of energy, medical advances and ways to mitigate hunger. He is living it up as the most important man in the world on that side."

"How do you know this?" Jerold huffed, anger seemingly pushing from his eyes.

"I'm still in contact with him...at least through the unity stream. That is how I am able to continue his work on our side of the divide. He is guiding me."

"What do you mean, guiding you...how?"

"Maybe I should let him explain that to you himself."

"What?"

Michael closed his eyes and gave a mental command in one word, *"Now!"*

Next to Michael, another holographic avatar shimmered into existence. This one had the green glow of etion particles emanating from its aura. This avatar was one of an elderly man with a gray beard, and a band of gray hair wrapped around his bald head. There was a distinctive scar under his right eye.

Michael opened his eyes and looked over to the new avatar. "Hello old friend."

"Hello Michael. It's good to see you. I understand your grandchildren are on the mend."

"Yes they are; as is your grandchild," Michael responded back. "Mezhak, let me introduce you to your grandson: Jerold Washington. He's the son of your daughter Rose; and the grandson of your old girlfriend, Jackie Hightower, and his ex-wife, Kerri Knight."

Mezhak regarded Jerold for a few seconds, astonishment playing on his face. "You have her eyes. You have Jackie's eyes."

A tear formed in Jerold's left eye, "Is it you...are you really Billy Red...my grandfather."

Mezhak sighed and stepped closer to Jerold on the other side of the bed. "I am the consciousness of your grandfather, in the body of his alternate in another universe standing in front of you through technology I invented, as an avatar."

Puzzlement invaded Jerold's face, "What?"

"Yes, I am your grandfather!"

Jerold reached out to touch Mezhak's hand but only reached through the image as if reaching through light.

"Just like Michael," Mezhak began. "I'm not physically here, just my consciousness is here. I wish I could hold you in my arms, but I can't...at least not yet."

Jerold pulled back his arm in wonder, "Is this a trick?"

"No Jerold it isn't a trick. I'm sure you have questions. I'm here now. Let me try to answer them. Ask me anything that you know that I would only know."

"Okay," Jerold responded, "I have one. Why was my mother named Rose?"

Mezhak thought for a moment and then a sly smiled crept onto his face, "Roses were your grandmother's favorite flower. She had four tattoos of roses on her body; one on her left ankle, one in the small of her back, one on the right breast and one...well let's say one that could only be seen by a lover or a gynecologist."

Jerold eyes watered more as he listened to Mezhak speak about his grandmother and when he finished he simply stated, "It is you."

"Yes, Jerold, I am your grandfather. Now let me tell you my story and what is going on right now. It appears we need your help."

CHAPTER SEVENTEEN: CONNECTION

Unity Palace
Unity Chamber Fifteen
USSTAP Unity Virtual Stream

Unity was the virtual meeting placed used by USSTAP. It was the brainchild of Mezhak Zyder. Since its maiden launch over thirty years ago, USSTAP scientists implemented several safety measures that had made the system the main long-distance connection of USSTAP.

The Unity Virtual Stream in effect constructed the capital, known as Unity Palace in unity, a sort of cyberspace, which housed several hundred meeting rooms, two large chambers and social gardens. Here, the ambassadors from the Universal Conclave, representing every galaxy in USSTAP's sphere of influence and all the Osguards from the Guardian Supreme Council met, utilizing Zyder energy to connect their consciousness in a virtual world.

As previously, Michael Genesis was in the unity room aboard *G.P. Campthor.* Once again he lay in one of the five pressure point beds. This time the bed he lay in was inserted into a tubular white ARIT-Gateportal sleeve. The Gateportal, unlike the Microportal, transported his consciousness into the unity stream, projecting it as an avatar in Unity; instead of deconstructing it and reconstructing it into a hologram in the real world. The added advantage of this concept was that Michael had full access and ability of his senses. He could feel, smell and taste the environment in Unity.

After a few seconds of piercing light that invaded Michael's mind, the construction of Chamber 15 in Unity Palace faded into view. It was a medium size room with a large oak table in the center. The room had several picture-glass windows on the east side, where the sun was shining its radiance into the room with brilliant rage. Several high-back black leather chairs adorned the edges of the table. The room walls were the typical beige-brown USSTAP standard color, with splashes of silver, red and black edging to give it an exotic, but earthy feel.

Soon, other avatars shimmered into view. At the head of the table on the right, was Chief Osguard Lillian Saria, the President of USSTAP. On the right corner, First Osguard Anthony Black faded into view. Next to him, Osguard Jaquille Rican faded in.

At the head of the table on the left side, the leader of the Universal Conclave, Ambassador Chancellor Nestie Warwick washed into view. Next to her, the leader of Rojam Os Parliament, Prime Ambassador Felick Korish came into view. Finally, the leader of Millmum Star Congress, Chief Ambassador Ive Ove shimmered into view.

This was an emergency meeting of the leadership, from both the political and operational side of USSTAP, concerning the events of Earth. Ambassador Chancellor Warwick invited Michael to attend the meeting due to his personal involvement in the situation. After all, he was the Osguard-in-Charge of Millmum Galaxy, Rojam Os and of USSTAP when Earth was first inducted as a witting protectorate into USSTAP. Michael knew Warwick understood his thoughts and his history with the situation would weigh heavily on which direction the meeting would take.

After several minutes of social pleasantry and political procedure, the meeting finally wound down to the business at hand. Michael listened as the political winds pressured for USSTAP's complete withdrawal from Earth, using the rationale that the leaders of the planet had come to a decision to not be involved with USSTAP; and like with other planets that demonstrated that type of commitment, USSTAP should honor the wishes of the planetary leadership. However, the operational side of the house argued that the Scolonians had interfered with Earth while under USSTAP's protection, and had manipulated the leadership into making an unwise decision. This, in the long run, would be detrimental to the organizational security of USSTAP.

Michael could see both sides of the argument, and had to push back hard on his on bias opinions. He sat in the room, remaining quiet as his own internal debate thrashed inside of him. Michael was of three minds.

First, he wanted to exact revenge against Earth First and all that they stood for the attacks on his grandchildren and the innocent civilians that celebrated USSTAP in Osguard Gardens and Osguard Village. He wanted to annihilate them by bringing all military weapons to bear. But he knew this was not doable without bringing about a large scale casualty count of innocent civilians. So, he struggled to figure out a way.

Second, he agreed with the Osguards sitting at the table. The Scolonians had manipulated the leadership of Earth, while helping

Chenum Seolin te Erucki pilfer dialairtic crystals from the Earth's core. This was in direct violation of USSTAP rule and needed an immediate response. Whether this was a diplomatic response or an armed response was debatable to some, but to Michael the armed response seemed to be the best course of action.

Third, he had leanings to just pack up and leave, and let the Firsties deal with the mess they made when it came to the Scolonians and Chenum Erucki. He knew if USSTAP left Earth, that it would be open season to any and all scavengers and pirates who weren't under the rule of USSTAP to pillage and plunder Earth for all its resources, without thought to the population. Again, the countless scores of civilian casualties would be too hard to bear.

Michael realized that USSTAP had several planets that did not rise to the knowledge of their presence under their protectorate law. This allowed for the population of those planets to grow and mature at their pace; without interference from those that would do harm to them in the name of profit, technology or expansionism.

Earth was different. It was different because Michael and the other Osguards bore from the planet. This was the main factor that caused Michael not to heed Ortho's words not to introduce USSTAP to Earth's citizenship. Michael wanted so fervently to bring his home world into the USSTAP fold that he ignored the warning signs exposed by ARIT simulations. He thought he could control the situation. But he couldn't.

The UN-USSTAP Pact was the telling straw in his failure to control the situation. When the Pact was offered by the Firsties, and accepted by USSTAP's political arm, he knew right then he had failed in his endeavor to push a technological renaissance unto Earth. So he tried to salvage what he could.

But the ostracism he and the other Earthborn Osguards received played raw on his nerves and he could not function in the planet's best interest anymore. So he'd retreated. He'd retreated to Chaktun, his now adopted planet, and the origins of his Osguard bloodline. He'd retreated to Chaktun, placing Earth and its people in his past; hoping one day to forget them. Now the situation has brought back that wound—reopened the cut, letting the blood of his decisions poor out on the floor for all to see as the debate on what to do next, raged on. But leaving Earth defenseless would be unconscionable.

"What do you think, Chief Osguard Emeritus?" Ambassador Chancellor Warwick posed.

Michael heard the question, but did not recognize it was meant for him, for his internal debate between revenge, retaliation and retreat —fueled by anger, duty and self-pity— still occupied his mind.

"Michael!" Warwick gently called.

Upon hearing his name, Michael eyes fixed on Nestie in a quizzical manner.

"Chief Osguard Emeritus Genesis, what do you think? Do you have something to offer in this debate?"

Michael looked around and saw that all eyes were on him. Now was the time to speak. This is why he'd been invited to this unity discussion. His words would persuade the chamber on which way to act. He did not appreciate the position he was now in, but it was a position he knew he was walking into when he accepted the invitation to join the debate.

He searched the eyes of the political side of the table. He saw years of peace and the fear of war plastered on their faces. Then he looked to the operational side of the table. The three Osguards seemed to express the same worry. But their worry was surrounded with the need to keep the association strong. Whatever steps that came next were needed to project USSTAP's strength, in order to persuade others not to challenge USSTAP's authority in the future.

Then an inner voice rose in Michael's psyche. It was a voice he hadn't heard for years. It was a voice that guided him in his early years of command and guided him to introduce USSTAP to the citizens of Earth. It was the driving voice of his fortune.

It rang loud and clear, as it said, *You are to embrace a new world and design a new universe. The Beginning and the End has chosen you to lay out a path so humanity can begin its journey to the next level.*

Michael closed his eyes, now praying for guidance and to maintain his sanity. Suddenly Michael was hit with an epiphany. The struggle in his mind settled as a plan began to form. His eyes popped opened and a smile broached his face. In an eureka moment, he bellowed, "I have a *plan!"*

***

USSTAP Galaxy Protector Neraka
Precinct Station twelve
Telo Galaxy, Rojam Os Galactic Cluster

The starship looked like a black bat gliding through the rays of a bright full moon. Flying away from the regal white light, the giant galaxy protector lumbered through the intergalactic gateportal. Her engines fanned out like wings. Her arrowhead bow resembled a bird's face peeping into the darkness of the cold and desolate space. USSTAP *Galaxy Protector Neraka*–Bravo Class–was the flagship of the Telo Galaxy.

Her emergence through the gateportal at Precinct Station Twelve was a grand but surprising event. Osguard Perry Tower was not scheduled for a visit for another two months. But Tower wasn't here for a visit. He was on a mission from First Osguard Tony Black.

Perry Tower stood in front of his command chair with his hands on his hips. The son of retired Osguard 16, Kenny Tower, he had sired the Telo Galaxy for almost thirty years as Osguard 05, when he assumed sireship from Peter Genesis. As with most Osguard descendants, Perry had deep hazel eyes, auburn hair, laced with gray, and the birthmark diamond; but his birthmark was on his back.

He watched the main viewer as the black cover of space with twinkling stars washed the white luminance of the gateportal away.

Perry walked up to his navigator and pilot, putting his hands on their shoulders and ordered, "Set course to Vellowhail; MOP-30."

"Tiah!" the pilot responded.

With a swift motion of his hand, the pilot activated the ship's engines and pushed her through the speed scale, jumping from hypersonic speed, to hyperlight speed, and finally igniting the MOP engines; which catapulted her to a speed in which she ate up thirty light years of distance per hour. To the naked eye, it looked like she simply vanished from sight in a purple haze.

***

TGR Distributing Company Headquarters
Larmin City, Toloman Province
Planet Vellowhail, Telo Galaxy, Rojam Os Galactic Cluster

Elib fez Kolinera moved without haste, through the large doors marking Erucki's inner sanctuary. Erucki looked up in amazement, his lips poised to spit venomous words of punishment at Kolinera, for entering without being summoned or without permission. Erucki's deathly stare stopped Kolinera in his place. Kolinera lowered his head in shame.

"This better be important," Erucki hissed.

"It is," Kolinera assured him.

"Well, what is it?" Erucki rose from his plush brown leather chair, perplexed at Kolinera's demeanor.

"We have word from our agent on Precinct Station 12. It appears *G.P. Neraka* has unexpectedly showed up and is on a direct course to Vellowhail."

"Do you know why?" Erucki asked, leaving the venom out of his voice.

"News reports say the Earth's GOW was assassinated, along with his parents," Kolinera began.

"Oh, that's too bad. But what does that have to do with the *Neraka* visiting our fair planet?" The coy smile on Erucki's face indicated he knew exactly why the starship was visiting their planet.

"It appears they captured the assassin and have successfully interrogated him," Kolinera explained. "Additionally, USSTAP's interest is more than high, due to the fact that Chief Osguard Emeritus Michael Genesis' grandchildren were severely injured in the bombing in Osguard Gardens."

"Chief Osguard Genesis, his wife and his children as well as Executive Osguard Emeritus Adam Freeman and his wife Osguard Jenna Freeman were on the scene within minutes of the explosion. The entire episode was elevated much faster than we anticipated. The Chief Osguard, the First Osguard and the galactic Osguard are on scene running the situation."

The smile disappeared from Erucki's face. He was stunned by the news. He did not anticipate the situation would exact such a high profile so soon. He thought he had time to let human tempers simmer to a boil on Earth before it reached priority one with the Osguards.

Additionally the fact that his operative was captured did not bode well either. He thought his plan was perfect. But Rand's capture put a slight wrinkle in the arrangement. Now USSTAP had proof of his involvement in the entire episode; especially if they used their MARIT interrogation technique.

His plan was supposed to be flawless. In the confusion of the bombings and the GOW assassination, the Firsties and the Tappies were supposed to point fingers at one another. Each was supposed to escalate in response in order to exact revenge, and ultimately, USSTAP was to bear the blame and be asked by the world governments to vacate the planet. Therefore, leaving the planet available for his excavation efforts, unhindered by universal law. He didn't account for Michael Genesis' grandchildren to be involved; let alone severely injured.

Kolinera continued, "I also heard word that the local authorities will execute a hold order on one of our citizens based on a writ of intrusion issued by the Ambassador Chancellor. Once the writ makes its way through the Star Parliament and the Telo Star Congress, I imagine it would be a matter of time before the Vellow security forces execute the hold."

"I suppose that writ is for me?" Erucki surmised.

Kolinera nodded, "That's a safe bet." He paused for a second and then added, "It will probably take about two hours before the Vellow government receives the proper notice."

"Call our Scolonian friends and ready the planet-to-planet gateportal. I think it is time for us to take that long extended vacation we talked about," Erucki ordered.

Erucki didn't know exactly how USSTAP planned to act on the knowledge they gathered, but he recognized that his presence on the planet may not be a great idea when the galactic osguard reached orbit.

"Nelx!" Kolinera responded.

CHAPTER EIGHTEEN: REALITY CHECK

Tillman Memorial Hospital Court Yard
Sibut, Prefecture of Kémo, Central African Republic
Planet Earth, Millmum Galaxy, Rojam Os Star Cluster

The *Susan S. Tillman* statue stood in the middle of the hospital court yard, surrounded by an array of beautiful and vibrant flowers. Its life-like essence hovered over the flowers like a nurturing mother. Her hands were open in a welcoming gesture and her body language exuded a peaceful presence.

As typical for all USSAP statues, the *Tillman* statue was infused with lively color, similar to a Madame Tussauds' presidential wax figures in Washington DC. The intensity of color highlighted Susan's brown eyes, brunette hair, accented her black uniform with shades of light, and captured the infectious smile she always sported in life.

Michael's avatar stood in front of the statue, tears swelling in his eyes. He had never visited his friend's name sake and technically, he still hadn't. He was stuck in a star ship miles above Earth, laying in a pressure point bed and stuffed in an ARIT-Micro Portal tube having his consciousness thrashed around heaven and Earth like e-mail sailing through cyberspace.

A pain of guilt shot through his heart, for this was not the way he wanted to pay tribute to Susan's memory. Susan was a kind and gentle soul, with a passion to cure the sick and heal the wounded. She deserved his physical presence at her namesake, not a shoddy facsimile of his consciousness.

Her spirit for life is what he loved about her. He knew her love for people is why she went into medicine. Her spirit for life and her love for others is why he recruited her into USSTAP all those years ago. Michael also knew that Susan was a strong advocate of sharing USSTAP technology with the people of Earth…something Michael once believed in himself at one time.

Where did that belief go? he wondered.

He closed his eyes and let the memories, he had locked away in his mind years ago, flood out like waters breaking through the levees. He let the currents of his guilt sweep his consciousness away as his mind flashed back to what he had deemed was the turning point in his life—when he lost faith in his fellow man of Earth.

Thursday, June 20, 1996

It floated in the recesses of space, a war-gray painted diamond hovering in the midst of a man made metal asteroid belt. Millmum Capitol Station, the center of the Universal Science, Security and Trade Association of Planet's power overshadowed the seventy smaller diamond shaped stations packing the area. Inside the clubhouse bar, Dr. Susan Tillman stared into the sea of blackness, lost in thought, contemplating mortality for the first time in her ten-year career.

The thoughts floating through her mind wet her eyes with tears. In ten years, she had never felt as much fright as she felt at this moment. Even the majestic beauty of God's lawn, the space that surrounded her, couldn't comfort her. Despair floated in her soul and showed on her face.

The bar was crowded. Warriors were getting off shift and stopping by to fuel their thirst before retiring for the night. The cacophony echoed in the room, but Susan remained oblivious to the dull roar. A beautiful brunette, with an infectious smile, was alone in a room full of friends.

"Susan!" a voice came from behind her. However, she did not hear it.

"Susan," Michael repeated, putting his hand on her shoulder, breaking her from her trance.

Startled, Susan turned. She took a deep breath realizing it was Michael tapping her shoulder. He stood almost a half foot taller than her, his skin glowed with an almond complexion and he sported a rare smile.

Susan noticed he never smiled much anymore, not like he used to when she first met him on the Rutgers University campus twelve years ago. Back then, he was a happy person; somewhat mysterious, but playful with a comic's wit for one-line jokes. But since then, the weight of command had stripped him of his happy character. She had known of his double life for the last ten years. But during that time, Michael Genesis, as the First Osguard, had led USSTAP into what the "in" crowd considered the golden days of the universe.

Michael had inducted thirty new galaxies and introduced an Osguard as the overseer of each galaxy, bringing the grand total of the USSTAP universe to sixty galaxies with over fifty thousand planets.

"Susan," Michael said with more concern. "What's wrong?"

Susan nodded toward an empty table, where they made their way through the crowd and sat. Michael studied her for a moment, and then ordered two drinks. She tried to fight back the tears, but one sneaked out and spilled down her right cheek. After a second, she wiped the tear from her cheek and took a sobering breath.

Soon the waitress came with their drinks, a rum and Coke for Michael and a Kuruth wine cooler for her. She drank from the wine cooler, mustering up the courage to ask Michael for the biggest favor of her life.

Michael watched as his doctor and his friend fought for courage, something he never imagined she ever needed to do. "Take your time, Susan," he prompted. "We've been friends for a long time. You know you can tell me anything. I may be your Osguard, but foremost, I'm your friend. Please tell me what's wrong?"

Susan looked up at him, searching his face for an opening. She saw Michael giving her his most passionate look. It was the same look that made her trust him twelve years ago, when he saved her from being kidnapped into slavery. It was the same look that recruited her into USSTAP two years later. It was a look that had been missing from him for years. His hair was shorter, his face fuller and his eyes more mature. But here it was, awakened by her plight and released by his concern.

"Sire," she began. "I just received a call from my mother in Massachusetts."

"Ah!" he responded. "How is she doing?"

"That's what's wrong," she said, trying to keep her voice from cracking. "She has breast cancer," she blurted out.

Michael's eyes widened. The revelation was not what he expected. His thoughts choked in his throat.

"The doctors only gave her three months to live. They caught the cancer too late. It has metastasized throughout her body."

"I'm sorry," he offered in a soft whisper.

"Michael," she begged, reaching for his hand, "I can save her...I want to save her...I need to save her."

"I know," he interrupted, and then fell silent. He took a sip from his glass, never taking his gaze from her. He put the glass down as if to punctuate his thought. "You never knew Ortho, did you?"

She shook her head while releasing his hand.

"Ortho and I always had a philosophical difference when it came to how to handle Earth. As you know, Earth is the only planet under our protectorate that does not benefit from our technology—except the select few from the Osguard family."

A touch of shame crept into his voice as it trailed off. He took another sip from his glass. "Ortho's been dead for almost ten years now, and the decision rests upon me and my family on how to deal with Earth. But I've been too busy building USSTAP up in my ancestors' vision. I've put that decision off." He sighed, wiping the imaginary strain of life from his face with his hand, stopping to rub his chin. "It's about time I make that decision, and there's no better time than now."

Susan's eyes brightened with hope, but a tinge of fear still remained. She knew from Ortho's teachings he did not trust Earth with the knowledge of the universe. Ortho assumed Earth would destroy itself, if it had access to USSTAP technology. She never quite understood why, but she abided by the edict in order to practice the state of the art medicine of the cosmos. But now a family member was in need of that technology; the same technology that had saved several members of the Osguard family—saved them without their knowledge or acknowledgement. Now the pain of conscience became a sting of duty—family duty. Would Michael follow his heart or his rules? She didn't know, but prayed he would follow his heart.

"You know, I'm not that same cool kid from New Haven you met at Rutgers," he continued. "No, I've changed. Now I have to be a crafty politician dealing with impetuous galactic governments."

"I have to be a respectable diplomat appeasing immature ambassadors on the station. I have to be a visionary statesman for my ancestors' grandiose dreams. I have to be a dauntless soldier for the fearsome sixana warriors. I have to be a smart chief executive officer, running trillions of light years of space for the known universe. I have to be the ever watchful chic chief financial officer overseeing monstrous fortunes in trade."

"And let's not forget, I have to be the intellectual leader of the scientific community, directing the fair sharing of technology without compromising the security of the association. That's a lot to ask from a guy with an International Science Degree. I've been so busy being so many things for so many people, that I forgot who I am or where my real duties lay!"

Susan tilted her head in confusion. She didn't know where he was going with his comments, and she feared wherever he was going she wouldn't like it. She took a deep breath and held it, bracing herself for the bad news she feared he would say.

"Go!" Michael said. "You have my blessing and my approval to treat your mother. Save her life."

She smiled. The words lifted the burden of decision from her.

"Lord knows you'd have gone with or without my permission," he continued. "But remember, once she is treated, she will be under the medical care of USSTAP. She can no longer see a regular doctor. And until I convince the parliament, she must not know of USSTAP. Your treatment must be like it is with my parents, without her knowledge. Do you understand?"

Susan nodded, "Don't worry; I will treat her at USSTAP's Boston precinct clinic. I will make sure the doctors there are assigned to her from now on."

"You'd better!"

***

Sunday, July 7, 1996

Her mother was sleeping so peacefully, she dared not wake her. It had been a long grueling six-hour operation, but for some reason Susan felt refreshed. The technique was very simple, but the execution was very time consuming. Susan had to search and map every minute speck of the cancer using the Medical Artificial Intelligence—MARIT for short.

Then in small patches, invisible to the naked eye, she had to inject the T7-90U nanobiotics. The gold colored serum, made from the Edute root on Chaktun, trapped the cancer cell and eradicated it, leaving a by-product of healthy skin tissue and cells. This process took seven to ten minutes, limiting the amount of area the doctor could treat at one time.

The healthy cells and tissue replaced the ones the cancer had eaten up, reacting like the body's immune system and incubator at the same time. The new cells grafted onto healthy cells, replicating the

DNA from the healthy cells, copying and morphing in a strange bubbling effervescent splurge of life. Susan always thought of the T7 family of drugs as the primordial ooze from which life sprang.

In her limited research, she realized the T7 family of nanobiotics aided in the cure for many of the deadly diseases plaguing Earth, from AIDS to Leukemia. It was what appealed to her when Michael asked her to join USSTAP, a secret united nations of the stars—secret to Earth only. Again, a philosophy she couldn't quite come to terms with, but abided by for the sake of learning.

With all that pecking at the back of her mind, she sat, watching and thanking God she was allowed to have a hand in saving her mother's life and wondering if destiny was the watch word of the day. Was her fateful meeting with Michael preordained? Was her acceptance into medical training with USSTAP in God's plan? Was her life, up to the present, a careful road to follow so she would have the knowledge and ability to save her mother's life?

In the sunlight flowing through the window, she saw her mother stir. Her mind was digging its way out of the darkness and trying to grab on to the day, somehow knowing the danger to the body was over.

Susan went to her side. She wanted her face to be the first thing her mother saw when she woke up. It was selfish of her, but she felt she had the right, besides her father was asleep in the private hospital room next door. The ordeal had been taxing on him, so Susan prescribed a sedative for her father while her mother recuperated from the operation.

Victoria Tillman's eyes crept opened. Susan saw the pupils scream confusion, and then fear and finally relief as they focused on her.

"Hey, Mom," she greeted.

"Hey, baby," Victoria responded, fighting the grogginess that enveloped her world.

"How do you feel?"

Victoria tried to raise her head, but dizziness forced her to abandon the attempt. She plopped her head back into the soft pillow with her eyes closed, taking a mental inventory of her feelings. "Tired," she mustered, "but somehow complete."

Although Susan should have been surprised by Victoria's response, she wasn't. Most of the patients she had treated with the T7 family of nanobiotics said the same thing upon awakening.

They felt somehow complete.

She often wondered about that. She wondered if the T7 family of nanobiotics affected the mind or exerted some type of mind control. But if it did, she always found that odd affect dissipated within a few hours—overwhelmed by the pure euphoria of being cured.

"That's nice, Mom," she said. "The procedure went well," she informed her while hovering over her.

"Are you sure?"

"Yup, I can say you are now cancer free."

"I don't believe it," Victoria huffed. "But I do feel…I do feel…better."

"See, Mom, I told you this would work."

"I don't know how you talked me into this. Common sense tells me there is no cure for cancer. Dr. Conrad said I was too far along for any type of treatment."

"Dr. Conrad was wrong," she assured her. "I told you, this is a secret government experimental treatment," endorsing the lie. "I've been running medical experiments for the government for years. They allowed me to treat you under the strictest confidence. You can't go back to Conrad ever again. You come here for your medical needs from now on…you and Dad."

"How do I know I won't grow a second head or a third breast from this treatment?"

"I promise, Mother you won't!"

"How come the government allowed you to treat me? Am I a Guinea Pig or something?"

"Mom, we've been through all this before. My boss pulled some strings and gave me permission to treat you. He didn't want to see you die any more than I did."

"Why? Who's your boss?"

Susan looked away trying to dodge the question for the twelfth time since she arrived back on Earth last week. Finally she decided to allow some truth in her story, hoping to give the lie some dignity in the meantime. She turned back and looked her mother in the eyes. "Michael…Michael Genesis."

"Michael Genesis? You mean that boy who saved your life in college?"

"Yes, the very same guy."

Victoria's eyes widened with curiosity "Are you two—"

"No…no, Mom. We're just friends. Besides he's married to a beautiful woman, my old roommate, Michelle. They have two beautiful daughters."

"Oh!" Victoria responded.

"Mother," she warned.

"What? All I said was…oh."

"It was the way you said…'oh.' I'm surprised at you Mother." Then she tilted her head as the question that nagged her for years formed on her lips for the first time in her life. "You mean it wouldn't have bothered you if we had gotten together?"

"No, why should it?"

"The obvious, Mother."

"You mean the fact he's Black and we're White?"

"Yeah, Mother. How would that have set with your friends at the country club? Wouldn't you have been ostracized or something?"

"Well, I thought he was a pretty nice guy…very polite and a wonderful gentleman. Your father and I both knew he was such a pillar of strength during the trial. We both thanked God he was there for you."

"And then he disappeared, never to be heard from again. Imagine my surprise to find out, you've been working with him all these years, especially on some super secretive government program. I'm just shocked, that's all."

"Okay Mother," Susan surrendered, standing up, "I see Daddy's judicial tricks have rubbed off on you, and you won't give me a straight answer."

"I gave you a straight answer," she asserted.

"Yeah right," she rebuffed. "Let me go get Dad. I'm sure he will want to see you."

"Susan," Victoria beckoned, "How about the others?"

"The others?"

"Yes, the others…like me…who are suffering from cancer."

Susan lowered her head, hiding the guilt that harbored in her heart for over ten years. She released a heavy sigh and looked back at her mother. "I'm working that one out, Mom…I'm working that one out."

"And Michael…what does he say about the others?"

Susan shrugged, "I honestly don't know." She turned and exited the room. "I honestly don't know," she repeated under her breath.

Inside, Victoria closed her eyes in thankful prayer, accented by a tear flowing down her cheek dividing her blessing from her apprehension.

A few minutes later, Judge Rutherford Tillman rushed into the room to visit his bride of thirty-five years. The smile he wore told Victoria he was happy to see her. In his hands, he carried a bouquet of flowers. He handed the floral rainbow to her and laid a big open mouth kiss on his wife.

Their lips rekindled a fuel that had burned in their hearts for over forty years. Victoria was his first and only love. Once the spark lit, he gave her a great big bear hug.

"Susan told me the treatment was a success and that you're cured," he pronounced when their lips parted for air.

"I know, she told me the same thing," she giggled losing herself in his embrace.

"Thank God," he praised. "I can't believe it…you're cured."

"I can't believe it either," she repeated. "And I won't believe it until Dr. Conrad checks me out."

Rutherford broke the embrace and glared at her, "You can't do that. You heard what Susan said."

"Yes, I heard what our daughter ordered," she rephrased. "But, Dr. Conrad has been my doctor for a long time. I won't believe I'm cured until he says I'm cured. This is some type of government experiment inside of me. Who knows if I'm cured or not, or if I just traded the cancer in for something far more deadly? I have to get Dr. Conrad to make sure I'm okay. Don't you see that?"

"All I see is that our daughter, a doctor herself, says you are cured. That is good enough for me," he said, trying to control his anger. "You're cancer free…I know it…Susan knows it. Why can't you accept it?"

"Supposedly, I'm cured because of some type of government experiment. I just don't believe it."

"If you don't believe it, then you don't believe our daughter, or at least you don't believe *in* our daughter. Either way, it's wrong. You are cured and that's the end of it." His anger was no longer hidden. His emotional roller coaster had just hit the frustration high. "You will live to see our grandchildren have children. Please Victoria, don't question God's blessing. He gave you a gift…take it…thank Him for it…and use it…period."

Victoria saw the pain she had just inflicted in her husband's eyes and decided to retreat from the conversation. "Yes baby, I do thank the Lord, and I will use the gift he gave me." She paused to watch the tension fade a little from his face. "Don't worry. I don't know what I was thinking. I won't go to Dr. Conrad. You're right, if I can't trust my daughter about this, who can I trust."

"That's better," he laughed, rewarding her with another passionate kiss and bear hug.

***

Monday, July 29, 1996

"Your tests are back, Victoria," Dr. Conrad announced.

He sat behind an old desk carved out of mahogany. His leather chair squeaked with every movement of his body. His large frame, gray hair and mustache gave him a grandfatherly character, which always put Victoria at ease; even on that dreadful day last month when he announced she had malignant breast cancer, which was incurable due to its advanced stage.

She sat on the other side of the desk, wearing a red jacket and skirt combination with a blue vest and white hat. She felt patriotic today. She didn't know why, but she guessed it might have something to do with her acceptance that the government saved her life and this was her little way of thanking them.

"Yes, Dr. Conrad...what do the tests say," she asked with a voice wrought with tension.

"I ran the tests three times," he murmured.

"And?"

"And, Victoria, I must offer you my sincerest apologies."

"Why?"

"Because last month, I could have sworn you were suffering from malignant breast cancer that had spread throughout your body. But your tests show you don't have cancer now, nor did you ever have cancer. I'm sorry for the fright I must have put you through in the last month."

Victoria smiled, "Are you sure? You mean I'm cured?"

"Well Victoria, you're not just cured. You were never sick. My lab must have made some type of mistake. I really don't understand. According to these tests, you aren't sick at all. In fact your tissue samples indicate that your body has regenerated into a woman half your age."

He put on his glasses and opened the chart again, comparing the test results from last month to the new ones. "Remarkable...I don't understand."

"You don't understand what, Dr. Conrad?"

"I don't understand this...you...your tests." He closed the folder, pushed his glasses halfway down his nose and stared at Victoria. "I've been your doctor for over thirty years, and there is no way I can explain what happened to you. It's a miracle."

"Yes, Dr. Conrad. It's a miracle," she repeated, finally accepting what her daughter and husband had been trying to tell her for the last three weeks.

"Look, Victoria," Dr. Conrad began to beg. "I need to study you...I need to study this. Maybe I can figure out the miracle and harness it somehow to help other cancer patients."

Fear groped at her, as the words hung in the air for what seemed like an eternity. "What, Doctor," she responded.

"I need to find out what happened. I need to know what you did to cure yourself of cancer."

"Doctor, you said yourself, your lab must have made a mistake. I never had cancer."

"I don't believe that. I've studied both test results and you definitely had cancer. But now you don't. I can't explain it. But with your help, I will."

"No, Doctor, I don't think so."

"What do you mean, you don't think so?" he asked.

Victoria had practiced what to say and how to say it for the past couple of days, just in case she was cured. But now it seemed hard for the words to flow from her lips. She looked down, gathering the strength to tell the lie. She wanted to help Dr. Conrad in his quest. Only weeks before she would have gladly joined him in pursuing a cure for cancer. But now she wasn't so sure. Plus, she had promised her daughter to keep her treatment a secret.

"Well, Dr. Conrad, I had a second opinion after you diagnosed me with cancer. They told me I didn't have cancer. I went for a third opinion, and they confirmed it as well, I didn't have cancer. So my only conclusion was you had misdiagnosed my symptoms."

She took a deep breath. She was on a roll, and the lie seemed to spurt easier from her mouth with every word. "Dr. Conrad, you are almost seventy years old. I think it is time for me to see another doctor. And, Doctor, it might be time for you to seriously consider retirement. Medicine is becoming a game for the young. Technology is advancing faster than ever."

Dr. Conrad removed his glasses, the pain of her words tearing into his confidence. "I'm sorry, Dr. Conrad. I have to move on to another doctor," she continued in her most compassionate voice.

"I understand, Victoria," he said with a cracking voice, "but I think you are making a terrible mistake."

Victoria stood and offered her hand, "I hope not, Doctor...I sincerely hope not."

Dr. Conrad stood and shook her hand, "Where do you want me to send your records?"

She handed him a card from her purse, nodded and left his office without another word. When the door slammed shut, it echoed in Dr. Conrad's imagination signaling the end of a brilliant career.

He sat back in his chair and signaled his secretary to cancel the rest of the day's appointments. He took the card and stared at the words as if he was staring into a crystal ball, *Unlimited Associates Medical Center.*

***

Tuesday, October 15, 1996

"Dr. Conrad," the voice rang from the speakerphone, "this is Dr. Marcus Hoyt. I'm with *Pyramid Pharmaceutical.*"

"Yes, I've been expecting your call, Dr. Hoyt," he said trying to hide his enthusiasm.

"First, let me congratulate you on your retirement. I hope everything is treating you fairly."

"Yes, I must say, the wife and I are enjoying the retirement. I didn't realize what I was missing, because if I did, I would have retired much earlier."

"Well that is great to hear," Dr. Hoyt replied. "I'm sorry to interrupt your retirement, but I was looking at your report and the test results you sent on your patient."

"Yes, I figured that is why you called."

"Very interesting case...very interesting indeed," Dr. Hoyt continued. "Did you know we found traces of an unknown agent in the tissue sample you gave us? It was where the cancer cells appeared to have been in the earlier test."

"No I didn't," Conrad admitted. "But I figured something was there. That's why I sent everything to you. I heard you have a state of the art laboratory set up and if there was anything in the test, you would be the ones to find it."

"Yeah, we found it, but we can't identify the substance. Is there a way you can bring the subject in for more tests?"

"I'm afraid not," Conrad admitted. "The subject is uncooperative and is under the care of another doctor at the *Unlimited Associates Medical Center.*"

"That's too bad."

"I know. I tried to convince her it was her civic duty to help. I even called her several times after she left me. However, my pleas went unheard."

"Maybe we can give it a try. Our people may be able to offer incentives she'll find hard to refuse."

"She won't take my calls anymore. So I will be unable to set up a meeting. I'm sorry."

"Just give us her name and address, we will contact her."

"Sorry, I can't give out a patient's name or number without their consent," Conrad reminded Hoyt.

"Look, Dr. Conrad, if we can get our minds around this we can all make a fortune. We will be able to save millions of lives as the men who cured cancer."

"I'm not in it for the money," Conrad reported. "I just want to find a cure for cancer."

"I understand that," Hoyt apologized. "I won't lie; my company is in it for the money. And something this big will make *Pyramid Pharmaceutical* the number one pharmaceutical company in the world." His voice trailed off. "Besides, she's not your patient anymore. All I'm asking for is the name and number of a potential donor to our cancer research."

"Well, when you put it that way." Conrad was already reaching for his Rolodex. He plucked the card marked *Victoria Tillman* and read it to Dr. Hoyt.

***

Thursday, October 24, 1996

The night was briskly cold. The New England trees had laid down their blanket of brightly colored leaves that swam in the air as each car passed on the dimly lit road. Victoria was driving back from her weekly visit to the Unlimited Associates Medical Center. The doctors gave her a clean bill of health, which planted a never-ending smile on her face.

Since her brush with death, she had drunk all that life had to give her. No more sulking about the little things—like the color of her living room curtains, the maid's affinity to irritate her, or her husband's cigar smoke. Life was more than that. It was about seeing, hearing, feeling, and tasting new experiences. It was about the obtaining and the transfer of knowledge. It was about people.

This was why she had volunteered her time at the local church soup kitchen. She needed to share her blessings with those less fortunate. And this was where she was heading, to the soup kitchen, like she did every Thursday night after her visit at the clinic. It seemed the most appropriate thing to do after being examined for over thirty minutes, like a human test subject.

But the procedure was never invasive. She just lay on a table and let the doctor run a machine over her body. It mapped every part of her and displayed the results on a screen to her left. It was like some high tech ultrasound device. However this device painted the cells of her body in color and at different depths.

The picture always started out at the skeletal level, then added tissue, muscle, organs, and skin. At each section of each level a number registered to the left of the display. As long as the number remained above ninety percent she was considered in top health. Today, the lowest number she received was during the inspection of her liver. It was at ninety-five percent. Her heart registered at ninety eight percent and her bones registered at ninety-six percent. She didn't understand the methodology, but she sure was pleased with the results.

Her headlights gleamed onto the bundle of clothing in the middle of the road. She was so wrapped up in thought over her new found life; she barely noticed the obstacle sprawled out before her. The sight penetrated her psyche as wrong, but her brain did not decipher the picture right away. At first she had the instinct to just run over the bundle of cloth, thinking it trash that dropped from a truck or something.

But in the instantaneous time it took to form a thought, her mind recognized the image as a person lying on his or her stomach.

She slammed on the brakes, bringing her BMW to a loud, piercing screeching halt. The midnight blue metallic carriage of death skidded several feet, and then swerved left, kicking sand, dirt and leaves up in the air like a surf and missing the body by inches. When the car came to a complete stop, it was turned one hundred degrees, facing the wooded area and in the opposite lane.

Victoria, shaking from the incident, took a deep breath while checking herself for pain. She stared at her trembling hands, still glued to the steering wheel, oblivious to the outside world. Then she looked out her window, surveying her handy work, until her eyes gazed upon the object of the entire episode—a body in the middle of the road.

She leaped from her car and rushed to the body. She turned it over and to her horror, realized it was nothing but a department store manikin dressed in a suit and overcoat. Fear and then relief flowed through her body. She picked up the manikin and began to walk it to the edge of the road when a sharp pain pierced her neck.

She dropped the manikin and reached for the pain—but before she could raise her hand, her knees slammed into the concrete. Before her face hit the ground, her mind had already said goodnight to the day. She fell, unconscious to the ground with a tranquilizer dart protruding from her neck.

***

Friday, October 25, 1996

The eight hundred and fifty thousand dollar house sat in the old Bunker Hill district, surrounded by all the trappings of success—a manicured lawn, long driveway, iron bars, and brick fencing running along the boundaries and the note of wealth—a swimming pool and tennis court in the backyard. Judge Tillman had planted his wife and daughter in the lap of luxury, by putting in long hours and working the social and political network of the rich and famous.

Every time Susan visited, it was a reminder of her privileged youth. Not that she felt ashamed of her youth, but she now was more mature and understood privilege was an uncommon commodity in the universe. She had battled plagues and famine on many planets, satellites, and space stations, which would make the staunchest member of the Peace Corps, shy away.

She drove her white Ford Mustang through the gate and up the drive, parking it right at the front door. She slid out of the car to be met by the most devastating look she had ever witnessed on her father. Rutherford stood at the front door, his shirt ruffled and his pants wrinkled as if he had slept in them all night.

Immediately, Susan realized something was amiss and raced to her father, "What's wrong? Is Mother all right?"

Rutherford stared past his daughter. Susan saw nothing in his eyes. He was there physically, but wasn't there mentally. She guided him into the house and into the large living room. She placed him on the couch and retrieved her medical kit from the car.

She scanned him with her portable MARIT disguised as a mobile phone. Her father was distraught, but not going into shock like she feared. She poured him a glass of cool water and helped him drink several sips.

"Dad," she summoned again. "Where's Mom?"

In a feeble voice he responded, "I don't know."

"What do you mean, you don't know?"

"She never came home last night. She never made it to the soup kitchen after her appointment at the medical center."

"Did you call her mobile phone?"

"Yes, no answer," he said, bringing life to his words. "I called the police and they found her car four miles from the medical center...abandoned."

Susan turned away in thought. She had no time for emotion, even though she knew she should be scared, she knew it wasn't the time or place to show fright. Her mother was missing, and with all the nanobiotics floating around in her body, she needed to find her.

"Dad, you rest now. I'll find Mother."

"How?"

"Never mind how...just rest. I'll have Mother home for dinner."

***

Friday, October 25, 1996

Lilly Station, the home of the Earth Forces of USSTAP, sat on the Atlantic floor on the continental shelf, once known as Atlantis. The old Kulusk station was the spherical hub, housing the command section and gate portal room. Several wings extended from the hub like spokes of a wheel. Extending at the end of the wings were concourses where the sea cruisers docked and where the startram catcher was housed.

In this underwater palatial command center, Susan stood speaking with the General of the World, GOW, General Paul Westbrook, and a former aide to Michael.

"Because of the T7 and your mother's DNA pattern we have on file," General Westbrook explained, "we were able to pinpoint her location."

Westbrook turned to the left-hand screen in the front of the command center. It displayed a map of the Boston area. A blinking star danced in the northeast corner of the map.

"Maximum magnification," he ordered.

Soon the display changed to an outline of a building, with heat signatures representing people inside the building.

"Your mother is here, on the top floor of the Pyramid Pharmaceutical Research Facility. As far as we can tell, she is unharmed. However, I don't know how long that will remain."

"Now what?" Susan asked.

"I spoke to the First Osguard."

The news hit Susan like a ton of bricks. For some reason, she hoped the incident could escape Michael's awareness bubble. But in the end, she knew she was hoping against the inevitable.

"And?"

"And I presented two options," the general continued. "We go in with an S-Team, and take your mother by force and apprehend anyone who stands in our way."

"Sounds too John Waynish!" she responded. "What else?"

"Or we wait until your mother is alone, step into the room and quietly step her out," Westbrook added, referring to using the gate portal system, that used the fourth dimension of innerspace to transport living matter by stepping into one side of the white light from one spot, and stepping out of the other side of the white in a different spot. "The Osguard liked that idea better," he added.

"Either way, my mother is exposed to USSTAP technology."

"Not necessarily. Not if she is sedated before we step her out."

"But she will see us step in?"

"We can step in the hallway, a closet, anywhere but in front of your mother," he explained. "The First Osguard wants this incident contained with minimal exposure…understood Captain Tillman?"

Hearing the rank thrown in her face instead of the customary title of Doctor, made Susan realize it wasn't her call and that the decision had already been made.

"Tiah, sire!" she responded in the USSTAP vernacular, meaning she would comply with his orders. "Where do we step my mother to."

"You will be waiting at the medical center." The display switched to a map area of Boston. We will step her to you there. You check her out and if she checks out fine, drive her home and gently interrogate her and find out what happened."

"And if she isn't fine?"

"Well, then it becomes a medical call and you do what is best," he stated.

"Tiah!"

"Fine," Westbrook concluded. "We begin in thirty minutes. You'd better get in place."

"Tiah!" she said, turned and exited the command center.

***

Saturday, October 26, 1996

Dr. Hoyt looked down on Victoria. She was in a hospital bed suffering from a drug-induced unconscious state. Two nurses stood behind Dr. Hoyt busy preparing medical instruments. Victoria was connected to several machines, measuring her heart rate, blood pressure and oxygen level.

The room had no windows and one door. Other than the bed and the medical equipment, the room was a cinder block Spartan prison: equipped with the coldness of evil greed.

"We've run every test we know of," Dr. Hoyt said to no one in particular. "We have tissue samples, blood samples, urine samples and fecal matter to test. All show normal. But there is a high concentration of this material I can't quite decipher."

"What can we do to help?" the tall blonde nurse asked from behind.

"I didn't want to do this, but the circumstances leave me no other choice."

"Do what?" the plump red head inquired.

"We will have to do a total mastectomy, so I can continue testing the affected area."

"You're going to remove her breast!" the tall blonde exclaimed.

"I'm afraid I have no other choice," he stated. "Prep the patient for the procedure."

"Yes doctor," the plump nurse agreed.

Dr. Hoyt left the room assured his nurses would carry out his request. The two nurses began as the doctor ordered, preparing Victoria for a major operation. Once satisfied she was ready, the nurses left the room.

Finally, the long corridor leading to the makeshift hospital room was empty. And in a split second a low hum rumbled in the corridor, the air pushed aside and a shimmering haze took root, like the heat dissipating off the sands of the desert. An invisible door slid open, spewing the immaculate and blinding white light of innerspace into the corridor.

Out of the light, a black clad figure emerged. It was Michael Genesis, the First Osguard of USSTAP. He wore four gold lightning bolts on the right and left side of his collar, the USSTAP symbol on his right breast, the corps patch on his left shoulder and the number *"1"* on their right shoulder; signifying that he belonged to the USSTAP first galaxy of responsibility, the Millmum Galaxy.

He also wore the Charlie belt, containing the palm size pagenay and palm size mation II. The pagenay shot energy rays to incapacitate, knock out or kill. While the mation II formed liquid polymer into any type of blade he wanted. He forewent the Delta Belt combination, which would have added the deadly coronet pistol to his arsenal. He wanted to keep this a simple extraction, and he wanted to do it himself.

The invisible door closed behind him and he crept to the outside of Victoria's room. His Portable Artificial Intelligence, PARIT for short, registered that Victoria was the only one in the room. He rushed in, knowing his time was limited. He checked her vitals and realized she was already asleep, so he decided against sedating her any further. He disconnected all the devices attached to her, wrapped her in a blanket, and with one sweeping motion, slung her over his shoulder. An alarm buzzed through the air announcing his intrusion and attempt to retrieve the golden goose from the greed laden giant of the *Pyramid Pharmaceutical Company.* He then activated his portable gate portal, PGP, summoning the white light of innerspace. Without looking back, he stepped into the white light. The door lowered behind him, seemingly whisking him into nothingness.

Michael emerged out of the light in the emergency ward of Unlimited Associates Medical Center. Susan looked up, more shocked than surprised at the sight of Michael carrying her blanket-wrapped Mother over his shoulder. Without a word, Michael lowered Victoria onto a gurney.

She ran her portable MARIT along her mother's body. "Drugged and unconscious…but nothing that a good night's rest won't cure."

"Good," Michael said. "Get her home then."

"Sire, I'd rather keep her here overnight for observation."

"Spoken like a true doctor," he rebuffed, taking a seat in the chair against the wall.

Susan signaled the attendants to take her mother to a room and then joined Michael.

"I'm sorry for this mess," she started.

Michael raised his hand for her to stop. "Don't be sorry. It was my call. Besides, your mother is safe and sound."

"Yeah, but I jeopardized USSTAP."

"You didn't…your mother did," he said with earnest. "Perhaps this is what Ortho was afraid of." He blew out a hard sigh.

"I suppose Ortho was right," she conceded, "Earth isn't ready for us."

"Perhaps…perhaps not!" he puzzled. "All I know is this wasn't the right way to introduce our technology to them. Your mother should have heeded your advice. Now I expect you to make it clear to her in no uncertain terms, she is to follow the rules…understood," he admonished.

"Tiah!" she replied, "but what about *Pyramid Pharmaceutical?"*

"There is no way they can synthesize the T7-90U nanobiotics," he assured her. "But if they are good enough to do so, I say let them." He smiled to relieve the tension and then stood. "Take care of your mother. I've got to go. I have a galaxy to run."

He activated his PGP and disappeared into the light, leaving behind a grateful, but weeping Susan.

***

Friday, December 12, 1997

Over a year later, in the Tillman living room, Rutherford and Victoria watched to the latest news surrounding *Pyramid Pharmaceutical* on TV. She smiled as she watched the young reporter standing in front of the *Pyramid Pharmaceutical Research and Development* laboratory outside of Boston. The same facility where she was unceremoniously held captive and rescued—a secret she promised her daughter she would keep, even from Rutherford.

"The medical division of Unlimited Associates announced today that they are buying out the defunct Pyramid Pharmaceutical Company. Unlimited Associates is the world's largest privately owned company, dealing in commodities and advance technologies."

"Until a year ago, Pyramid Pharmaceutical was the nation's sixth leading pharmaceutical company. Their stocks rose to an all-time high, when they alleged they had found the cure for certain cancers. Their announcement led to a six month investigation by the FDA and the Justice Department."

"At the end of the investigation, Pyramid's CEO, Ralph Venturites, and the head of their Research and Development Department, Dr. Marcus Hoyt, were indicted and sentenced to ten years for three counts of medical fraud and four counts of embezzlement. The company declared bankruptcy two months ago."

"With the news of the buyout by Unlimited Associates, the company employees and those who counted on the drugs they manufactured will have a new source of income and life. However, there is no relief in sight for Pyramid's investors. As of today, Pyramid has been released from public trading and investors will be paid according to current stock prices—fifteen cents a share."

"Reporting from Pyramid Pharmaceutical Research and Development Laboratory outside Boston, this is Brian Summers for Cable Television News."

***

Eight hundred light years away and through USSTAP communications technology, Michael and Susan watched the very same broadcast. When Brian Summers signed off, Michael clicked his receiver off, put his foot on the desk and his hands behind his head.

"Well that's a start!" he stated to Susan. "Now we can produce the drugs needed that are organic to Earth. We can ease the suffering and prolong the life of the terminally ill. Then someday, we can introduce the drugs like T7-90U nanobiotics."

Susan looked out the port and gazed at the star line, mesmerized by its beauty. A look of incompleteness occupied her face. She wanted more. Her Hippocratic Oath demanded more. But for now she had to settle for what she could get.

She forced a smile and turned toward Michael, "Like you said Sire, it's a start."

***

Friday, September 9, 2044,
Tillman Memorial Hospital Court Yard
Sibut, Prefecture of Kémo, Central African Republic
Planet Earth, Millmum Galaxy, Rojam Os Star Cluster

Michael's eyes popped open and he took another long look at the statue. His guilt jumped into the realization that he was mostly responsible for the deteriorating situation between USSTAP and Earth. If it wasn't for his pride and bravado getting in the way of his duty, he would have found common ground and reached out to the people of Earth like he did countless times with people of other planets. His diplomatic skill was the instrument of power he needed to wield early in the relationship with Earth's people, not his military strength led by his emotions.

Michael always knew that the silent majority of Earth's population was on his side or neutral at best. It was the vocal minority that made things difficult. And instead of exploiting the vocal minority's size as inconsequential, he combated them head on, making them more powerful in the world's eye than necessary; while ignoring the pleas of the silent majority. Now it was time for him to change that. It was time for him to fight for the silent majority.

"Susan," he whispered. "I'm going to fix this. I'm going to fix this for you…in your memory. I'm going to fix this. It may not be exactly how you wanted, but I will fix this."

CHAPTER NINETEEN: TAKING THE OFFENSE

White House
Washington DC
Planet Earth, Millmum Galaxy, Rojam Os Galactic Cluster

This was his fourth trip into the unity chamber, and Michael Genesis dreaded it. But this was his plan, and he had to execute it this way. The tight fitting black nanoflex suit attached to his body like a second skin. Coupled with the full-face hood, the nanoflex suit was definitely claustrophobic. With the added physical discomfort of being rolled into an ARIT tube, like a corn dog, the experience was much more challenging to bear.

The light rushed into his eyes. Michael thought he should be accustomed to the piercing light invading his consciousness. After all, he had used the unity chamber almost three hundred times in his career; albeit, he only used the microportal adaptation of this technology about a dozen times in the past.

Yet the piercing light was always uncomfortable, almost to the point of being painful—no matter if it was the gateportal adaptation that sent his consciousness to the virtual avatar in the unity stream, or the microportal adaptation that sent his consciousness into a holographic avatar in the real world.

The light faded and shadows started to form in his vision. Soon colors began to swirl into place. It took a full four seconds before Michael could get his bearing, and a full visual picture of what was in front of him. He knew his holographic avatar was shimmering into sight behind the black mist of microportal energy; which could be frightening to the occupants of the room.

When Michael's avatar fully assembled, he was standing in the middle of the Oval Office of the White House, the seat of power for the United States of America. The ARIT outfitted Michael in full diplomatic formal apparel. He was wearing red tunic that covered his black jumpsuit. The red tunic had the USSTAP elongated diamond encased in two orbits centered in large print.

A black four-inch wide belt that made the tunic flare a little, wrapped his waist. He also wore a black cape with silver embroidery that draped his back all the way just below his buttocks. He wore the five silver thunderbolt insignia on his high-neck collar —indicating he was a retired Chief Osguard. Four two-inch silver braids adorned his cuffs, indicating he was a retired member of the Guardian Supreme Council. His calf-high leather boots, which sported a glossy shine, rounded out the pageantry of his uniform.

In front of him and behind the giant desk, known as the Resolute Desk, sat President Amanda Taylor. Behind her, stood her sister and Secretary of State, Ann Farris, and her younger sister, the National Security Advisor, Alicia Cole. Michael saw the frightened look on their face as they watched him shimmer into place.

"Don't be alarmed," Michael said. "This is just a holographic avatar sent here to communicate with you. I am Michael Genesis onboard the USSTAP *Galaxy Protector Campthor,* orbiting Earth."

President Taylor raised her hand to her mouth. She still displayed a touch of fear, but Michael could see she was fighting that back with her need to project an air of authority. However, her sister Ann was emanating pure vile disgust as she picked up a letter opener from Taylor's desk and hurled it at Michael.

Michael's first reaction was to duck, but he fought that impulsive self-defense maneuver and stood his ground. He knew he had to show the president that he was indeed a hologram, and therefore incapable of presenting a physical threat to her. So he stood there as the letter opener flew through his avatar and lodged into the door frame behind him.

As the silver dagger of death flew through his holographic avatar the energy field that made up his avatar was disrupted, sending a short high pitch sound throughout the room, like feedback through a microphone. The sisters instinctively covered their ears in an awkward attempt to protect them from the sound. When it passed, the sisters uncovered their ears and regarded Michael with evil eyes.

"See," Michael said. "I am a hologram. I cannot hurt you even if I wanted to."

Ann's eyes burned with rage, as she looked for something else to throw.

Alicia turned to her sister and asked, "Should I call security?"

Amanda Taylor shook her head, "What for...they would only shoot up the room. If the letter opener flew right through him, what do you think bullets would do? Besides, I would like to know why the great Michael Genesis would grace us with his presence."

She turned towards Michael, "Jesus! I thought you were dead."

"You thought or did you wish?" Michael responded.

President Taylor shrugged, "Does it matter?"

"I guess not," Michael admitted. "Let's get down to brass tacks," he pushed more forcefully.

"Brass what?" Alicia questioned.

Michael looked at the ladies and realized his colloquialism was a bit outdated. "Never mind," Michael pushed, shaking his head.

He then stepped closer to the women and began his rehearsed speech. "I am here at the behest of the Chief Executive Osguard, Lillian Saria; Rojam Os First Osguard, Anthony Black; and Millmum Galaxy Osguard, Jaquille Rican to speak to you about the events that have taken place over the past four days, and see if we can resolve this situation peacefully."

"A situation *you* created," Ann pushed back.

"No madam," he said. "I assure you, this is not a situation of USSTAP's doing. It is a situation created by someone on Earth; and that someone is Dr. Claude Chenault."

President Taylor huffed, "Oh! Here we go. Here come the lies!"

Michael closed his eyes, fighting back the emotions boiling in him. In all his years of running USSTAP he had never been called a liar by another head of state; not even one in which he was adversary to. He realized the president's statement was an omen of the difficulty he was about to encounter in telling her the truth about what was going on. He opened his eyes and continued.

"Madame President, I am not a liar and I'm not your enemy. Even though you and your organization, that you call Earth First, have treated me and my family as enemies since we revealed ourselves to you. I am an American citizen, born and raised in the United States of America, just like you and your sisters."

"I am proud to be an American and proud to have brought something to America, and this planet, from my dealings as a USSTAP Osguard. But you and your organization, which Dr. Claude Chenault started, have ruthlessly pushed me away. In order to keep the peace, I and my family accepted the rejection, with the comfort that at least we were providing some sort of relieve to our home planet through medical technology."

"But that comfort is no longer present. Because of Dr. Claude Chenault and his association with the Scolonians...who are flying over your major cities in their aeroships as we speak...Earth has been robbed of precious resources from its core, making the planet unstable."

"Because of Dr. Claude Chenault, the General of the World and his parents were assassinated. Several USSTAP warriors have been killed. My grandchildren were severely injured and hundreds of innocent lives were killed or injured, in the three explosions that happened on U-Day."

"What are you talking about?" Ann growled, not holding back her anger. "Dr. Chenault is a great patriot! He has come to our rescue and stood up to you and the rest of the devils of USSTAP. He is a great man poised to take over the U.N. forces and beat you back to the hell wince you came from!"

"Really?" Michael sighed. "You think, even with Scolonian aeroships and this second rate chromerion field you have generated around the Earth's surface, that you have the resources to beat the mightiest military known to humans?" Michael paused to let his words sink in.

"USSTAP is made-up of over 100,000 worlds in eight galactic clusters; incorporating over 900 galaxies. And you think Dr. Chenault can save you from the can of whop ass we can lay on you if we really wanted to?" Michael took a deep breath to capture his composure that he felt was unraveling at the moment. "Dr. Chenault is the problem...not us. We caught General Zandi's assassin and we interrogated him." Michael closed his eyes once more and gave a mental command, *Port now!*

The black mist of a micro port showered a small spot on the Resolute Desk. When the mist cleared a common strip appeared.

Michael opened his eyes. "That is the assassin's interrogation," he told the ladies. "Play it, watch it and, when you are ready, call the USSTAP hotline and use the code word 'Silk.'"

"I will return to you and we can discuss your arrest of Dr. Chenault for the murders of those innocent people in Osguard Gardens, Osguard Village and the U.N." Michael took a step back. "You have 72 hours to contact us. If you don't contact us we will take action."

"Are you threatening us?" Alicia asked.

"If you don't arrest Dr. Chenault and order the Scolonians to surrender to us, we will take Dr. Chenault and destroy the Scolonian ships."

President Taylor shook her head, "You keep saying these ships are Scolonians. Who the hell are the Scolonians and why do you think these ships are Scolonian?"

Michael blinked. He was trying to see if President Taylor really didn't know the ships weren't from Earth. He decided to take a chance and believe Dr. Chenault had played her like he played the rest of the world.

"Scolonians are a group of people that are not members of USSTAP. They are a ruthless people that occupy about eighteen parsecs of space in what your scientist call NGC-7793 galaxy in the Sculptor Star Group. The Scolonians govern about twenty planets, using sheer terror. They spit on everything we stand for. They have no respect for human rights; and USSTAP will have nothing to do with them."

"But, it appears Dr. Chenault somehow has been working with them through a third party within USSTAP to steal dialairtic crystals from the Earth's core." Michael pointed out the window to the aeroship hovering above Washington. "Do you really believe Dr. Chenault built that thing without alien technology or alien help?"

Amanda Taylor shrugged. Silence fell over the room for a couple of seconds, as Michael noticed the ladies actually mulling over his words.

"What's in it for us?" Amanda asked. "It seems like you get your way no matter which way we act."

"You arrest Dr. Chenault and order the Scolonians to surrender to us and we will leave Earth. You will no longer be a protectorate."

"Meaning?" President Taylor asked.

"Meaning...you're on your own. If the Scolonians or any other people want to do business with you, or come and take what they want, it will be up to you to negotiate or defend yourselves. We will leave you alone to handle your business as you see fit."

"Let's start with that...let's start with you leaving us the hell alone!" Ann pushed.

"When this is all done, and Dr. Chenault has met justice, we will leave...as long as those who want to come with us are allowed to leave with us. I'm talking about everyone who wants to leave Earth and join USSTAP."

"That will only be a handful," Alicia responded.

"Maybe...maybe not," Michael reacted. "Remember, you have 72 hours. After that, you will be picking up the pieces...not me." As Michael said those last words, his avatar shimmered out of sight, surrounded by a cloud of black mist generated by the microportal.

"That sounded eerily like an ultimatum!" Alicia said.

President Taylor continued to stare at the spot where Michael's avatar had disappeared and said, "No, it wasn't just an ultimatum...It was more like a promise...a promise he has every intention of keeping, if we don't do as he says."

***

Lilly Station
Atlantis Continental Self-Atlantic Ocean
Planet Earth, Millmum Galaxy, Rojam Os Cluster

When the doors slid open, Deuce realized he was in it for the long haul. In front of him lay the command deck of Lilly Station's control center, with all its glitz and glory. The circular shaped room was somewhat daunting. The three empty chairs that sat in the middle of the room facing each other were equally as intimidating. The guard at the door looked into Deuce's eyes as if he was sizing him up. Then he scanned Tynala to his left and Cheyenna to his right.

Deuce knew the guard was acutely aware of the four green thunderbolts on their collars, wondering what to do next. The thunderbolts signified he and his cousins were Osguards in Training; but still Osguards nonetheless.

With the look of understanding, the guard, hopped to attention and bellowed out, "Osguards on deck!"

The buzz of activity lowered to a hum as people turned to see the young Osguards in the doorway. No one was expected to jump to attention other than the guard. It was simply a warning to let people know that a command structure had entered the room. This was militaristic protocol carried over from a Chaktun ritual of the Maxum, moving from the political leader of the government to a command position of his forces.

Deuce and his cousins stepped into the room and made their way to the command chairs. Deuce took the middle chair as his cousins sat in the other chairs.

Centurion Jansen stepped up to the chairs and nodded. "Welcome aboard. I hope you found your accommodations satisfactory."

Deuce nodded, "Yes, Centurion, I found everything well." Tynala and Cheyenna both agreed.

"Osguards, I think you will be pleased to know that the *Skyfire* was able to microport the needed additional equipment to Tillman Memorial for Captain Good's surgery. Dr. Aswabinot from the *Skyfire* is overseeing the operation via microport hologram. Osguard Kalina Genesis assures me that Captain Good is in good hands."

Deuce felt a warmth of relief wash over him as Centurion Jansen spoke. Deep down he was worried about Toniac and wondering if he would pull through. But now knowing Dr. Aswabinot, a specialist in zyder brain surgery was overseeing the operation, was reassuring. It would have been more reassuring if Dr. Aswabinot could perform the surgery.

But the second rate planetary chromerion field that Dr. Chenault erected over the planet was disrupting the innerspace field around the planet's stratosphere; thus making gateportal travel from the ships orbiting the planet and Earth too dangerous to attempt.

However, microportal beams went unhampered by the second-rate chromerion field. The microportal energy beam mapped the micro-cellular structure of its subject, disassembled them into cellular pieces and shot them through the cold vastness of space toward its destination. Using the coordinates provided by the ARIT, the micro portal reconstructed its contents at a set point.

Microportal technology wouldn't work against modern chromerion fields, but the one surrounding Earth was an inferior duplicate of Scolonian technology that had apparent gaps that USSTAP was able to manipulate.

Unfortunately, microportal technology couldn't be used on living things, because it could not transport that all important essence of life; the signal that told the heart to beat, the brain to function or the lungs to breathe. It would be so simple for the ships orbiting Earth to bypass Earth's chromerion field, if microportal technology could be used to transport the ships into Earth's atmosphere. But doing so would kill every living human and zyder on the ships. USSTAP had relied on gateportal technology for far too long and this incident was a reminder of that situation.

Now USSTAP had to rely on another one of his grandfather's exquisite and elaborate plans. Although it was complex, it also was beautiful in its sophistication. Michael David Genesis was a master strategist and a chief technician, and right now, Deuce was beaming on the inside with pride that he and his cousins were an intricate part of the plan.

Deuce counted his blessings that their involvement was directly due to an archaic but chivalrous rule, created long before he was born; stating no military action could be executed on Earth without the direct participation of an earth-blood Osguard. His grandfather mentioned that this was why Osguard Angela Santos was thrust into the thick of things as an uninitiated OIT during the Tuit crisis on Earth in 2002.

"Your grandfather has completed his visit with the United States President and has exited the chamber," Jansen announced.

"Are Washington and Knight ready?" Tynala asked.

"Tiah," Colonel Abraham Epstein, the Chief Controller said, stepping into the command center housing the command chairs. "They are set up in our media center on Deck Five."

Tynala looked at Deuce and Cheyenna and received nods of concurrence. Tynala took a long glance around the room. Deuce realized that she was savoring the moment, where she was about to give her first ever command as an Osguard—even though she was just an OIT, it was still a command that would be followed without hesitation. Deuce smiled and nodded once more.

"Good," Tynala said. "Proceed with broadcast."

"Tiah," Epstein replied. He stepped down from the command center and pushed out orders to his staff to cut into the Earth's common links and frequencies, and pipe in the broadcast from their media room.

Earth common was the multi-media device that practically all humans owned and wore. It was the culmination of television, internet, smart phones and cloud servers into one device. Deuce knew the Tynala had just ordered USSTAP to hack into all common operating links and frequencies, disrupting whatever program or communication was in progress and push Jerold Washington and Kerri Knight's broadcast.

Deuce inwardly prayed that Jerold Washington would live up to his end of the agreement and not backstab USSTAP. Deuce didn't completely trust Washington; especially after watching some of his reports on USSTAP while he was traveling down the east coast to Virginia.

In front of Deuce and the others, the big monitor popped on. On the monitor, Deuce could see Jerold Washington and Kerri Knight sitting behind a USSTAP smoked glass desk with all the complementary holographic control panels. Jerold had a big grin plastered on his face. Deuce thought of an old term his grandfather used to say about someone that showed that much teeth when they smiled. He'd called it, "a shit-eating grin." That's what Jerold had on his face to Deuce...a shit-eating grin.

"Hello, my fellow people of Earth," Jerold began. *"This is Jerold Washington."*

"And I'm Kerri Knight," his ex-wife chimed in.

"We are reporting to you from deep under the Atlantic Ocean on USSTAP Lilly Station."

"We are sorry to interrupt your common," Kerri went on to say. *"But we have breaking news to report to you."*

Deuce moved to the edge of his seat, followed by his cousins as they watched the two perform this back-and-forth news reporting as if they were reading from a synchronized script. The two went on to report the meeting that Michael had with the President of the United States, and then introduced the HVP that USSTAP secretly recorded of the meeting. The full discussion, from the point his grandfather shimmered into the Oval Office until he shimmered out played over all common links and frequencies.

When that was complete, the couple reported on the incidents that happened since the tidal wave, including the murder of USSTAP warriors on Lilly Station, the startram explosion, the assassination of General Akbar Zandi and the explosions in which they were inadvertently caught up in. They spoke of USSTAP coming to their rescue, and the fact that Deuce, Tynala and Cheyenna were almost killed in the explosions at Osguard Gardens.

Deuce was impressed by the matter-of-fact tone the two reporters relayed the news, showing no emotions or pushing any slant one way or the other on what they were reporting. They were just reporting the facts as they saw them.

When they completed their version of the facts, they reported on Commander Phillip Rand's capture and interrogation. Then they introduced the HVP that recorded Rand's interrogation—with and without the MARIT interrogator – and his final confession that implicated Dr. Chenault, Chenum Erucki and the Scolonian High Council. This HVP played in its entirety without any edits or commentary; altogether taking exactly five hours and twenty-three minutes.

Deuce's concentration waned during the Rand's interrogation HVP. He had already seen the important parts and knew the outcome. His grandfather had instructed him that it was important that the interrogation be played in its entirety, to stave off any accusations of creative editing or manipulation. The people of Earth needed to know exactly how USSTAP extracted Rand's confession.

Afterward, Jerold and Kerri engaged in about an hour of discussion and debate. But at the end both reporters agreed that USSTAP was not the perpetrator of the events that wreaked havoc on the Earth, but that Dr. Claude Chenault was the main person to blame. This was evidently hard for Jerold to admit; he even said so during the discussion and debate. He tried somewhat to defend Dr. Chenault by stating his reasons were pure, but his execution was poor. Yet even Jerold knew this was a hollow excuse and backed off his defense of Dr. Chenault's motives.

As one of Dr. Chenault's hard core supporters, it was a masterful victory to have Jerold Washington transition through this crisis of faith on air for all his fans and supporters to see. Deuce hoped Jerold's admission would change the hearts and minds of the Firsties that were pushing for an armed conflict with USSTAP.

After six hours of transmission, USSTAP relinquished control of the common links and frequencies; and Jerold Washington and Kerri Knight took a long and well deserved break.

Deuce smiled as the screen faded to black. "Okay," he said to Tynala. "I hope that did it and the President of the United States will lead the rest of the world into adhering to Papa's demands."

"I don't think so!" railed Centurion Richard Gray, the Watch Officer of the deck. "We are getting reports that the Dr. Chenault is amassing the U.N. Legionnaire Force on the Saudi Arabian peninsula and in the Red Sea. He also has five aircraft carriers sailing towards the Gulf of Guinea through the Atlantic Ocean. It appears they are about to attack the CAR."

"Damn-it! I hate it when Papa is right," Cheyenna pushed.

Deuce shook his head, "I really thought that showing the people the truth of what happened by their own reporters would be all it took to end this shit."

"Apparently not," Tynala observed.

"Okay," Deuce pushed. "It looks like we are going into phase two of Papa's plan." Then he looked to Centurion Gray, "Notify all ships and subs...Alert two...position the forces in alpha formation, in the Gulf of Guinea, Red Sea and Indian Ocean; ready gateportal nets."

"Tiah!" Gray said. "That's a lot of area to cover."

Deuce saw the worry in Gray's eyes and tried to calm him with a reassuring voice, "Centurion Gray, even though we are here barking the orders, we are working in concert with the ordained Osguards orbiting this planet."

"Whatever I order has their full support and authority behind it. Besides, this plan, no matter how far-fetched it seems on the surface is one that my grandfather devised and was blessed by the Congress, Parliament and Conclave as well as simulated by several hours of ARIT scenarios. It will work!"

"Tiah, Osguard," Gray said. "I know it will work. I just hate that we have to do it. I hate that we are using our technology against our own people."

"I know," Cheyenna chimed in. "But if all goes as planned, no one shall be hurt."

"I hope you're correct, Sire," Gray said as he stepped back.

Deuce nodded, dismissing Gray to carry out his assigned duties.

***

Star Universal News (SUN) Broadcast Ship 01-441
Gentry Solar System News Staging Orbit
Millmum Galaxy, Rojam Os Galactic Cluster

Karina Birdwell was sitting in the news anchor chair as the make-up artists scurried around her, working to put on the last of her make-up before she went on the air. With the holographic technique SUN ARIT used, Karina's avatar would be projected into every living room in the universe as if she was sitting with her audience. With that much clarity, it was important to address, mitigate and remove all blemishes from Karina's face in order to present the most perfect image of her as possible.

But Karina was not concerned about that. She was actually worried about her cousins on Earth. As a news anchor, she had to report their situation as dispassionately as a computer, while deep down inside, her guts were screaming for revenge and her soul was praying for healing.

Because of this closeness to the situation, her news manager allowed her to be the point person on the story. However, her journalistic integrity and her passion for her cousins were at odds with one another and not in synch like her news manager would hope. Even with the make-up artists scurrying around her, slathering her face with powder and cream, she told herself, she needed to be a professional. She needed to do her job, and the best way for her to help her cousins and the rest of her family was to be the best person in the universe at that job right now.

"Ten seconds to air," the director announced.

The make-up artists put a feverish rush on their last-minute touch-up job. Karina could feel the panic in their movement and decided to quell the quiet storm that raged in their minds. "That's fine...I'm good. Thanks for the work!"

With that, the artists scrambled off set. Karina turned her swivel chair around toward the ARIT imagery cameras, also known as imcams, which would broadcast her report to both the universal channel and the Rojam Os distinctive channel. She took a deep breath as the director counted down the remaining seconds...going silent and using his fingers to count down the last three seconds before the red light illuminated on imcam one.

"Hello, this is Karina Birdwell reporting to you live from the Gentry Solar System," she spoke in Chaktun, one of the universal languages of USSTAP, *"where it appears USSTAP is in somewhat of a standoff with the governments of the protectorate planet Earth."*

Karina went on to explain the situation, similarly to the way Jerold Washington and Kerri Knight had, just a few hours earlier. However, her explanation was abbreviated to accommodate the short attention span of her viewers that really didn't care or want to care about what the reason behind the dust up was. According to her news manager, the viewers only wanted to know the results of the controversy and what USSTAP was going to do about it.

Karina introduced the Rand HVP'd confession, which to her viewers had a more universal wide implication than what was happening on Earth. Rand's confession literally pointed to a conspiracy hatched on the Vellowhail involving the Scolonian High Council. This could eventually lead to a war if not handled correctly.

Now that Karina had introduced the problem and the problem makers, she had to introduce the updated news.

"We just received this clip from USSTAP Intelligence, indicating that the governments of Earth have chosen to fight rather than give into USSTAP's demands. The clip you are about to see was taken from a secure link. In it, Dr. Chenault is speaking to the leaders of several Earth governments; including the United States, Russia, China and Great Britain."

The screen faded to black for a quick second and then popped to life with the image of Dr. Chenault sitting behind the U.N. Secretary General's desk, with his hands folded on top of the desk in a leadership manner.

"I assure you that I am innocent of these charges," Dr. Chenault seemed to plead. *"I categorically deny any involvement with any alien or alien government. I am a true patriot, who espouses Earth First in all things. Haven't I provided the force field that keeps the alien bastards at bay? They cannot attack us as long as the force field is up. Didn't I provide aeroships to protect your cities from any attack USSTAP Earth forces may trigger?"*

"I'm the one that has Earth's interest at heart...not any half-breed alien from another planet. I tell you, now that you've given me control of the U.N. forces, and I have integrated them into my Firstie Legion. I will dispose of this threat immediately...in a way that USSTAP will know we mean business! I will mount an attack on their African holdings and pummel their footprint on this earth into dust, so the winds of time will blow them away for good!"

The clip stopped there, and Karina popped back into the visual. *"Response from USSTAP was quick and united."*

She faded away, to be replaced by the images of Chancellor Ambassador Warwick, flanked by Rojam Os Prime Ambassador Korish and Millmum Galactic Chief Ambassador Ive Ove. Ambassador Warwick had a determined look on his face, one which indicated he considered the entire event to be an insult that needed to be rectified immediately.

Warwick spoke with strong emotion as he said, *"In response to the clip I heard from USSTAP intelligence, where Dr. Chenault defies the request of this body to surrender himself to us, I have issued a writ of intrusion for his capture, which has met with the requisite concurrence of two thirds majority from both the Rojam Os Parliament and the Millmum Star Congress."*

"We have knowledge that Dr. Chenault is building his forces in the area of our African allies and is planning to attack. All I will say is, if Dr. Chenault launches one asset in anger against our African continent allies, or our interest in the Central African Republic, we will be forced to take action. And believe me when I tell you, USSTAP will not deter from taking that action."

The image flipped away from the three political leaders and back to Karina. Karina looked straight into the imcams and said, *"USSTAP has lived in peace for almost thirty universal years. USSTAP has even integrated two more galactic clusters to its ranks during that time; expanding the economic boom we have been living in to other parts of the universe. Now, because of the greed of Chenum Erucki, the audacity of the Scolonian High Council and the xenophobic ravings of Dr. Chenault of Earth, that peace may be shattered.*

All I can say is the combined might of these three seriously cannot stand against the single might of USSTAP. May the spirits of the universe help them if they continue down this reckless path. Reporting from Gentry Solar System, this is Karina Birdwell...good life."

***

Scolonian Situation Room, Scolonian Palace
Vannillusk City, Finogina Province, Eenerdrolet Prefect
Planet Scolon, Telo Galaxy, Rojam Os Cluster

Tezlete Gzaheit, the leader of the Scolonian High Council, also known as the Consman, sat in at the helm of his situational room still stewing over the SUN broadcast he heard several hours earlier. He was unaware of his planet's involvement in Earth's affair and was totally taken by surprised.

At first he thought the broadcast was the opening salvo to a propaganda campaign against the empire, until he realized the abundance of dialairtic crystals they had been receiving in the past several years originated from TGR. And now the Vellowhail government was looking for Chenum Erucki.

He quickly added up all the facts and came to the conclusion his cousin, Velman Gzaheit was behind things. An hour earlier he had sent guards to bring his cousin to him so they could have a chat about what was going on with USSTAP.

He was taking his third sip of Scolonian Harbor Tea when the bell rang, signaling someone was about to enter the situation room. He placed the orange cup down and looked towards the glass doors. Outside the doors, he saw the commander of the Council Guards with three of his men towing two prisoners.

Tezlete nodded and swiped his hand over his desk's panel. The glass door lifted up into the ceiling with an electronic hum. The commander entered the room and rendered the Scolonian customary salute by placing his left fist into his right hand in front of his chest and nodding.

"My Consman," the commander said.

"Speak!" Tezlete commanded.

"We went to your cousin's house and could not find him. Instead we found these two."

"Who are they?" Tezlete asked.

The commander motioned for the two guards to bring the prisoners forward into the room. "Quick identification shows these two are not Scolonian, but Vellow."

"Vellow?" Tezlete inquired as the guards brought the two men forward.

Both men were clean of hair, including their eyebrows, which made them appear to be Scolonian. The elderly man was stout with dark skin and piercing blue eyes. The other man was younger, bigger and more muscular, with angry green eyes.

"Who are you?" Tezlete asked, staring at the older man.

The man stood straight in an effort to regain some dignity and cleared his throat as if gurgling the stench of shame from his soul. "I am Chenum Seolin te Erucki, president, owner and executive director of TGR Distributing. And this is my humble operations and intelligence officer, Elib fez Kolinera."

Then with the sudden power of indignity in his voice he asked, "Why are we in shackles and why do you disrespect us in this manner? Don't you know we are guest of the Consman?"

Tezlete eyes widened. "No, I didn't. Why are you here?"

"Because your men woke us from a sound slumber and dragged us here," Kolinera injected.

"No, you idiot...! why are you on Scolon?"

Erucki turned towards Kolinera and back towards Tezlete and repeated, "We are the guests of the Consman."

"I am the consman and you are certainly no guests of mine."

"You're not the Consman Gzaheit!" Erucki blasted. "Your men snatched us from the consman's private residence, just outside the city!"

"The house my men snatched you from belongs to my cousin, Velman Gzaheit. And let me be the first to tell you, my cousin Velman is not the Consman...I am!" Tezlete roared back. "*I* am Consman Tezlete Gzaheit. My cousin is the Shunduff, the military leader of Scolonian Forces. He answers to me and the High Council."

Now Erucki's eyes squinted as if he was peering through the fog of night. "What do you mean?"

"Are you deaf as well as stupid?" the commander of the guards chastised. "The man we stand before is the Consman, not Velman."

Erucki head lowered as the shame of his stupidity rushed into full view. His mind raced from one conversation to another where he spoke to Velman. Now he realized that Velman never introduced himself as "the Consman," but only inferred he was the Consman.

"I think you better start from the beginning and tell me what connections and dealings you have had with my cousin," Tezlete urged as the full picture of what was going on around him started to take shape. "But first, *where* is my cousin?"

Kolinera sighed and looked up at the ceiling. His despair was more than evident. "Consman," he started. "You're not going to like this, but your cousin is gathering your First fleet in preparation of a USSTAP attack on your planet. He has forces on Earth, prepared to do the same thing."

Tezlete sighed and regarded his prisoners for a moment. Then with the authority of a world leader, he switched his gaze to the commander, "Confirm this."

The commander nodded, "Owtow!" he replied in the affirmative; and walked over to a wall console and began maneuvering switches, dials and toggles with ease. Holographic diagrams drifted in and out of focus, figures shimmered alive and star charts wisped into view.

"My Consman, it appears the prisoner is telling the truth!"

"Issue countermand now... authority... Consman...five... two... eight!"

"Owtow!" the commander replied. After a few seconds the commander looked up at the screen and reported, "My Consman, I'm not receiving receipt code for the countermand order."

"Try again!" Tezlete sneered. He turned towards Kolinera, "You seem to be the smarter of the two. I suggest you tell me more."

Kolinera displayed a bewildered look. The obscurity of their situation was written all over his face, painfully framed with guilt. Tezlete knew the younger man was not where he wanted to be, but now had to pay the consequences of the older man's overreach for power.

It only took a few seconds of soul searching before Kolinera agreed with a shameful head nod.

CHAPTER TWENTY: BATTLESTATIONS

Lilly Station
Atlantis Continental Self-Atlantic Ocean
Planet Earth, Millmum Galaxy, Rojam Os Cluster

Deuce sat in the command chair, pondering over the situation. The report from *G.P. Neraka* was not good. Osguard Perry Tower admitted that there was no sign of Chenum Seolin te Erucki on Vellowhail. It was like he disappeared into thin air. Osguard Perry ordered the *G.P. Trailblazer,* sired by Vanguard Ketchin Moroko, to travel to Vellowhail and continue the search.

But all indications were that Erucki found out USSTAP had a writ on him and escaped the planet. This was why First Osguard Anthony Black allowed his name to be released by USSTAP Intelligence to the media. Deuce knew that Osguard Black wanted to put more pressure on Erucki. Erucki, being one of the most recognizable faces in the galaxy, would make it even harder for him to stay in hiding with the public on watch for him.

In the meantime, Osguard Black ordered the *Neraka* to rendezvous with *G.P. Kiliough, G.P. Filloughby, Galaxy Cruiser (G.C.) Pasi, G.C. Naylan, Star Protector (S.P.) Worro* and Star Cruiser *(S.C.) Snitlio* and push towards Scolonian space in preparation.

Additionally, Tynala had ordered Karina's broadcast to be translated into several Earth languages and pushed on the world's common links and frequencies. She thought it only proper that the people of Earth knew what their leaders were about to embark on.

A blinking red light on the overhead holographic monitor caught Deuce's attention. Jessica Jansen stepped up into the command area, her eyes wide with adrenaline, "Legion ships in the Gulf of Guinea have just launched a volley of missiles towards the CAR."

"How many?" Cheyenna asked.

"The ARIT calculates twenty missiles in the air."

"Should we have *Campthor* intervene?" Jansen asked.

Deuce thought for a moment as he regarded the board, and then he shook his head, "No, it's too late for the missiles. There's no way to activate the gateportal net to capture them. Activate chromerion field around Sibut; ready pagenay self-defense weapons in case something gets through the field."

"Gutsy call, cuz!" Tynala whispered.

Deuce understood it was a "gutsy call," because if one of those missiles got through the field due to some alien technology he didn't account for, the mission would take a drastic wrong turn. He regarded his cousin for a split second, beckoning her with his eyes for support rather than doubt.

"I suggest we incapacitate those ships, so they don't send another missile volley," Tynala whispered.

Cheyenna surmised aloud, "If they see what our chromerion field can do against their missiles, they may change strategies or maybe give-up. My bet is they will continue firing thinking they can weaken the field. I think Tynala is right. Take the ships out of the equation."

Deuce nodded, stood and went to the monitor, "ETA to impact?"

"Twenty minutes!" Richard Gray responded, as he pushed some triggers on his holographic keyboard.

"Two minutes before the first missile impact, have the *Campthor* incapacitate those ships," Deuce ordered. "Taking them out will add confusion."

***

African Battles Space
African Area of Operations
Planet Earth, Millmum Galaxy, Rojam Os Galactic Cluster

In the dark skies covering the African continent twenty Legion made Berserk Cruise Missiles, colloquially known as BCMs, screamed across the sky at 0.95 Mach; sailing at an altitude of 30,000 feet. The missiles were bunched in five groups of four adhering to a protocol of two-mile separation.

The BCM was the latest cruise missile in the Legion inventory. It was twenty-five feet long with a 15-inch diameter; weighting almost 4,500 lbs. Unknown to most governments of Earth, the BCM had the most sophisticated guidance scheme, highlighted by Scolonian technology and a dialairtic warhead.

As the gray javelins of destruction hurled their explosive load across the deserts of the Cameroon, air raid horns sounded, blasting the quiet into a frenzy of activity. Inside Cameroon and the CAR, the local governments pushed a shelter in-place call. Citizens of both countries scrambled to underground shelters; hard steel doors closed; windows with metal bars clanged shut and the militaries manned their position...searching the skies for a target to hit.

Unfortunately for the militaries who pledge to defend the sovereign country with their dying breath, the targets they were searching for had radar evading properties that tricked the computer search programs on their weapons systems. The darkness brought an added protection to the BCMs, because visual acquisition of the flying death darts was impossible against the night sky.

***

Sibut Regional Military Force General, Keno Tiangdio rushed into the USSTAP Sibut Precinct Headquarters, screaming at the top of his lungs, "We're under attack and it is your fault!"

USSTAP Commander, Richard Dingwello, stood from his command chair, and raised his hand to stop the general from speaking again. This stopped the general in his tracks, but his anger was steaming from his trembling lips and red shot eyes.

Dingwello, satisfied that the general was stopped for the moment, turned to his right and asked, "How soon to impact?"

The defense operator to his right said, "Five minutes, Sire!"

Dingwello turned to the general and plastered a big grin on his face. "Dear General, if we were truly in danger, do you think I and my people would still be here?"

Tiangdio looked around the room and noticed that the area was packed with USSTAP officers, all wearing side arms and other armament he never saw them wear before. He knew the armament they wore around their body was what they called a delta belt, and he also realized at that moment they weren't afraid or panicked.

Tiangdio took a deep breath and blew it out hard. "What are you doing about this attack?"

"Nothing," Dingwello pushed. "This attack is a waste of time and energy. There is no way the Legion will do anything to this city or this country. We are protected!"

Tiangdio shook his head, "What the hell do you mean, we are protected?"

"Sit down, general, watch and learn!" Dingwello responded taking his seat. "Watch the overhead monitor."

Tiangdio moved to the command center where Dingwello was sitting and turned to face what Dingwello was watching. In the monitor, he saw the map of the CAR and blips that he assumed represented the BCMs heading towards them. He also saw a blue circle encompassing Sibut like a fence.

He pointed to the blue line and asked, "What's that?"

"That dear general," Dingwello began, "is a chromerion field. We stepped four chromerion field generators to the city two days ago in case Dr. Chenault did something like this. We also stepped four pagenay batteries as back-up."

"You did not get our government's position to do this," Tiangdio protested.

"You're right!" Dingwello admitted. "If you wish, we can step them back to Lilly Station now."

Tiangdio squinted one eye, showing his disapproval, but he also showed confusion in his face. He huffed and looked away. "Okay," he murmured.

"What's that?" Dingwello asked.

Tiangdio looked up, his face washed with defeat, "I said okay. I will clear it with my government."

"When you do," Dingwello began, "I bet if you make it sound like it was your idea, you will be praised by the president herself."

Tiangdio nodded as the thought played in his head. "Thank you!" he mumbled as he looked back at the board. He then activated his common, "General Tiangdio for President Dejouriata."

***

Two minutes before the first group of BCMs impact the chromerion field protecting Sibut, *G.G. Uno* and the *G.P. Campthor* reached out through the sensor spectrum with their invisible fingers towards the west coast of the African continent. The invisible fingers ranged through the spectrum identifying all in its wake. Within forty nanoseconds the ARIT on both ships identified the five large aircraft carriers in the Gulf of Guinea.

A nanosecond after that, the ARIT passed the aircraft carriers coordinates to the microportal control center in the cargo bays. There, the ARIT fine-tuned the microportal subject search for fuel, explosives, gunpowder and copper wiring. Once the subject search concluded, the microportal beam shot down through Earth's atmosphere, cutting through the Scolonian chromerion field with the precision of a heart surgeon.

The microportal beam appeared as glistening black micro dust particles. The two beams swept over the five aircraft carriers; capturing the target search matter, deconstructing them into micro dust and reconstructing them within the electromagnetic pull of the sun.

Inside the carriers, the beams siphoned the fuel from the carriers' tanks, BCMs bladders and the ship's engines like a huge invisible vacuum. It also targeted, captured and expunged explosive materiel, including gunpowder, grenades and the BCM warheads, as well as miles and miles of electrical wiring.

Within five seconds of the beams crossing the ships, the aircraft carriers lost all power; causing the lights to extinguish, the engines to sputter and freeze and all the instruments to go dead. Radios, flashlights and emergency generators were inoperative, causing massive confusion that could not be calmed. Yells for help and shouts for coordination, collapsed into screams of fear echoing in the dark moonless night.

Two minutes later, the first of the BCMs crashed into the invisible force field, known as a chromerion field, protecting Sibut. Five horrific explosions spotted the field; in forty meter circular patterns. The BCM warheads exploded like fireworks, shredding blue, yellow and green light particles in a blossom array. The chromerion field smoked gray for a split second as it absorbed, neutralized and dissipated the harmless radiation into the night sky.

Thirty seconds later the next volley of BCMs hit the chromerion field; resulting in the same nighttime fireworks display. This display happened three more times, each ending with a Fourth of July atmosphere of blue, yellow and green blossoming explosions. From inside the chromerion field it appeared as if the missiles smacked into a wall and disintegrated into fine colorful fibers, which floated gracefully to the ground.

***

Lilly Station
Atlantis Continental Self-Atlantic Ocean
Planet Earth, Millmum Galaxy, Rojam Os Cluster

Deuce watched the entire episode play out in the overhead monitor. When it finished he allowed himself to breathe for the first time since the first impact. When Gray announced the field held up to the missiles with little degradation, it was like a great weight was lifted off his chest.

"The carriers?" Deuce asked.

"Incapacitated," Gray said. "ARIT scan indicate no injuries."

Another breath of relief shuttered through Deuce. "I'll be damned," he said. "Who'd a thought...targeted microportal beams?"

Cheyenna looked at Deuce with a slight smile, "I really thought the microportals would not be able to discern the targets and those entire ships would have been hurled into the sun."

Tynala studied the board once more, "Thank the spirits of the universe!"

Deuce still smiling with relief added, "Haven't we learned not to doubt Papa, yet?" The three chuckled.

Gray interrupted the moment of levity, "Osguards, it appears Chenault has launched bombers from the Saudi Peninsula."

"Damn-it, can we get a break!" Cheyenna expelled in exasperation.

CHAPTER TWENTY-ONE: BOMBER ATTACK

African Battles Space
Red Sea/Indian Ocean Area of Operations
Planet Earth, Millmum Galaxy, Rojam Os Galactic Cluster

The Legion's newly minted bomber, the DeGualle 2000 was another example of collaboration between Earth scientist and Scolonian technology. The DeGualle was 415,000 pounds of destruction wrapped in Scolonian machinery. The two-man bomber was a 70-foot long trapezoid with a wing span of 150 feet, with the same radar evading property inherent to the Berserk Cruise Missile. But like the BCM it was only capable against Earth known radars and not the sensors and scanners operated by USSTAP.

USSTAP world-wide sensors and scanners aided by the eight starships hovering in orbit in Earth's Thermosphere, captured the launch of five DeGualles from what Chenault thought was a secret airbase near Al Madinah, Saudi Arabia. The data fed directly to the alert board in Lilly Station. The board also captured the Legion's launch of ten Mirage 4000 fighters from the same base.

***

Lilly Station
Atlantis Continental Self-Atlantic Ocean
Planet Earth, Millmum Galaxy, Rojam Os Cluster

Deuce knew he had to act quickly. These jets were flying over the Red Sea now, but the counterattack would not work if he waited until the aircraft crossed the water and entered Sudan airspace. All had to work on crack precision timing.

Epstein, the Chief Controller gave the signal that the subs were in-place below the projected flight path of the fifteen-ship fleet.

Deuce nodded and pointed to Jessica, "It's your show...proceed as discussed."

Jessica nodded and bellowed orders to several positions. Deuce knew he didn't know how to articulate the plan in the distinct order pattern that Centurion Jessica Jansen was now accomplishing with such professionalism and proficiency. He knew that the picture perfect timing needed to pull off this part of his grandfather's plan was in good hands with her. He just sat back and admired leadership in motion, mentally taking notes.

***

African Battles Space
Red Sea/Indian Ocean Area of Operations
Planet Earth, Millmum Galaxy, Rojam Os Galactic Cluster

Out of the heavens the black beams of microportal technology from *G.G. Uno* and *G.G. Horizon,* pierced through the gases that made up Earth's Thermosphere, Mesosphere, Stratosphere and finally Earth's Troposphere; where the Legion had erected the Scolonian force field. The black sparkles of radiation made a wall that lay directly in the path of the oncoming bomber fleet. The radiation was transparent to the DeGualle bombers and the Mirage fighters. To their pilots, it was a clear, moonless night with no obstacles in their way.

When the first DeGualle penetrated the misty wall of black radiation, the microportal searched and found the liquid fuel of life that fed the four engines and instantly deconstructed them into energy, grabbed it and shot it at three times the speed of light towards the sun, as directed by the starships' ARIT, where it was faithfully reconstructed and there pulled into the sun by solar wind activity.

The bomber's four engines coughed and sputtered as the tubes that once held the fuel of life tightened and constricted from the vacuum pressure of an empty tank. The last sight the pilots saw before the lights extinguished was the fuel meter rapidly dropping to zero— an unlikely scenario to the mind of the command pilot.

The co-pilot switched to battery power and a red glow pushed back the darkness, showing a dead instrument panel. The pilot attempted to gain control of the stick and rudder that now had loss all power. His controls were sluggish and he was quickly getting disoriented with no discernible horizon to look at and no instruments to correct his situational awareness.

The pilot began the emergency engine restart checklist, running through his boldface with marked efficiency. The engines sputtered one more time, then finally went quiet. Eerie silence filled the cockpit. The pilots could only hear themselves breathing as they sucked in air through the oxygen mask.

The pilot reset his equipment and rushed through the emergency engine start check list again. This time, the engine didn't even shutter a cough. Panic now pushed the pilots' actions. They had no control authority with the stick and rudder, they had no power other than the lighting from the emergency battery; and they were clueless on their altitude, pitch or bank. In reality they were no longer pilots, they had just become passengers of fate.

The copilot clicked his radio to make a radio call. In French he reported, "Legion Fleet, this is Anvil Lead...our engines are dead, we are descending, we have no power...last known coordinates 20.9692 North...38.1297 East...I repeat...Anvil Lead last known are 20.9692 North...38.1297 East. We are bailing out. Repeat Anvil Lead is ejecting...repeat...Anvil Lead is ejecting."

Three seconds later, the crew compartment detached from the aircraft with an explosive kick. Soon nature's forces of gravity and friction acted on the crew compartment, slowing it down from Mach flight it was executing to a wavering rapid descent. Ten frightening seconds later a parachute deployed, snapping its passengers back and knocking the wind from their lungs.

***

Lilly Station
Atlantis Continental Self-Atlantic Ocean
Planet Earth, Millmum Galaxy, Rojam Os Cluster

The main battle board lit up like a Christmas tree. Deuce licked his lips in anticipation, as he saw the entire episode play out in front of him. He watched as the airplanes crossed the black microportal line. Then he saw the rapid deceleration of each aircraft followed by the crew compartment ejection. Soon there were lights indicating all fifteen aircrew were gently riding the sorely winds above the Red Sea in floating parachutes.

Centurion Gray called out each ejection as the board displayed the separation. Finally he reported, "All butchers disabled."

Centurion Jessica Jansen smiled and walked over to the Chief Controller, Colonel Abraham Epstein. "It's your turn now!"

Epstein nodded, turned to his display and started rhythmically maneuvering instrument triggers. "All subs in place and ready to activate the gateportal net," he reported.

It was quite a feat Epstein pulled off. During the Alert he had repositioned ten sea cruisers and five sea protectors in the Red Sea in the direct path of the Legion strike force. Like they did during the Tasman Sea emergency, the ships used their gateportals to step to the coordinates that he provided. The he ordered them to reconfigure their gateportal beams in order to capture and step the falling crew compartments.

"Engage gateportal net!" Deuce said, trying to control his excitement.

Epstein pushed the orders to his controllers, who pushed the orders to their respective subs.

***

African Battles Space
Red Sea/Indian Ocean Area of Operations
Planet Earth, Millmum Galaxy, Rojam Os Galactic Cluster

As the dark gray shells floated passed 20,000 ft., circular white cylinders of light shot from the sea and captured the crew compartments, including their parachutes in an angelic blinding beam. Once caught in the beam, the crew compartment seemed to vanish in the white light. When the beam turned off, the crew compartments were gone. Only the still darkness of the night remained in the spot where the crew compartment was once seen.

Fifteen seconds after the last crew compartment disappeared, blue lights of destruction pierced through the water, reaching up into the sky. The particle generator array beams, also known as pagenay beams, initiated from the ten sea cruisers and five sea protectors, sliced the darkness with the furor of lightening and the heat of the sun, connecting to the falling carcasses of the DeGualle bombers and the Mirage fighters. The airplanes evaporated, like ice in a frying pan, leaving nothing but small amounts of gas steaming off.

***

Al Madinah Legion Air Base
Saudi Arabian Peninsula
Planet Earth, Millmum Galaxy, Rojam Os Galactic Cluster

Al Madinah Legion Air Base was in a buzz of activity. The command post had just lost contact with the first bomber wave, somewhere over the Red Sea and with the Legion Navy force that led the attack from the west coast of Africa. Confusion seemed to permeate the air as General De Havard, the Commander of the Legion Forces, tried to make sense of what was happening.

Unbeknownst to General De Havard, walls of black microportal beams were presently washing over the camp. USSTAP galaxy protectors *Campthor, Nightwing, Dragon Star, Fantasia* and *Skyfire* were spurting the microportal beam in a constant stream like a dog bathing his favorite fire hydrant. The beams search function were calibrated to search and capture gun powder, explosive materiel and fossil fuels; in an effort to render combat weapons, guns, rifles ineffective, and neutralize the aircrafts and their armament.

As the black wave of microportal cleansed the base of its war-making capability, it deconstructed the materiel to its cellular level; turned it into energy, swallowed it in the beam and shot it towards the sun. Where once again, the materiel was reconstructed only to be picked up by the solar winds and swept into the sun's radiation to be incinerated.

The black beams emptied every fuel tank from every airplane, car, truck, and storage area in a matter of seconds. It also found every bullet, whether in a gun, rifle, clip or in storage and robbed them of the much needed gunpowder; essentially neutering the weapons and causing them if used to shoot blanks.

When the duty officer informed General De Havard that the base was now effectively inoperative and unable to rage an operational offensive or even defend itself against an attack, the general eyes rolled in his head in an apparent show of despair.

"What the hell has Dr. Chenault got us into?" he whispered.

The duty officer lowered his head and mumbled, "That crazy asshole will send us all straight to hell."

"What?" General De Havard asked with agitation.

"My General," the duty officer finally said, building up his nerve to continue. "USSTAP wasn't doing a damned thing to us. In fact, they were adhering to the U.N.-USSTAP pact, when they had the force and the power not to and dare us to do anything about it. Look around you! They have taken us out of the fight without firing a shot. If they had that ability all this time and they had nefarious intent, wouldn't they have used it years ago?"

"Maybe it's a new weapon?" the general proposed.

"Whether it is or not, they have it and they are using it, and we can't do a damned thing to counter it."

"What do you suggest?" the general huffed.

The duty officer sighed. He was about to say something, but thought better. He knew he had already said too much. He looked around the room as if the next words he would say were written on the walls or the ceiling.

Then he stopped and looked straight at the General. His brown eyes were cutting and filled with angst. "You're the commander. Whatever you decide we will follow. But I offer this suggestion that a wise commander once told me."

He wiped his lips with the back of his hand and continued, "Don't start a fight you know you can't win. If you can't win by fighting, find another way to win. If you can't find another way to win, find a way for your opponent to lose. If you can't find a way for your opponent to lose, then get out with as much as you can."

"That's from my speech at the Legion Academy almost twenty years ago," the general remembered aloud.

"Can we win in a direct fight?" the duty officer questioned.

The general shook his head.

"Can we find another way to win?"

The general shrugged.

"Can we find a way for USSTAP to lose?"

The general again shook his head.

"What's left?"

The general shrugged once more. Then he looked at his hands as if he was seeing them for the first time. "Call all forces to stand down," he ordered.

CHAPTER TWENTY-TWO: IMPROVISE

U.N. Underground bunker
New York City, New York
Planet Earth, Millmum Galaxy, Rojam Os Galactic Cluster

It was a tough decision, but Deuce thought it needed to be done. He was going off script from his grandfather's plan, but he saw a ray of light that he thought would be a crime not to take. He knew it was a bold move.

Washington and Knight had just completed their report on how USSTAP thwarted the Legion's attack on Sibut over the common. The fact that the Legion found their pilots fifteen clicks to the west of Al Madinah, gave credence to the power of USSTAP's military might. Yet, the U.N. still had not given USSTAP a response to his grandfather's offer.

Because of the delay in the U.N.'s response, Deuce ordered the intelligence community to microport several imcams into the U.N. Security Council chamber. Imcams were cloaked in stealth mode 10 technology, which made them virtually undetectable to the U.N.'s security measures. Deuce, Cheyenna and Tynala listened and watched with more than mere curiosity.

The fifteen new ambassadors of the security council, who were sworn in hours earlier, mingled around the oval table that was their new home during the USSTAP crisis. The new U.S. Ambassador to the U.N., Yolanda T. Perkins captured Deuce's attention. Ambassador Perkins was President Amada Taylor's former college roommate and the former president of Yale University, before accepting this post. The intelligence dossier, which Deuce had read earlier, stated that Ambassador Perkins was one of the original founders of the Firstie Political movement, which brought President Taylor into office.

But with the recent events overcoming the world stage, her recent comments indicated that she was now faltering in her stalwartness for the cause. The intelligence community believed Ambassador Perkins, like many other of the new ambassadors, was thinking about accepting Michael Genesis' offer.

Imcam surveillance had captured Ambassador Perkins advocating that arresting Chenault and allowing him to have a fair trial in the American court system, was much more acceptable than allowing USSTAP to capture him and do whatever they pleased. She justified her statements by stating a fair trial would prove Dr. Chenault's innocence. This was the crack in the armor that Deuce had hoped would come.

With a mighty flash of light, two dozen sixana warriors armed in weapons foxtrot configuration stepped into existence. Their full-battledress protective suit, helmet and gloves, along with the multi-selectable rifle-grenade launcher seemed like something from a futuristic video game. The warriors proceeded with mark efficiency to cover the exits and surround the fifteen ambassador delegation.

Several ambassadors attempted to reach for their emergency beacon to let the outside world; especially their personal security details to let them know they were under attack. But, unbeknownst to them, USSTAP had already jammed those beacons and piped in a timed loop video of the proceedings to the security cameras. Therefore, to the outside world looking in, it would appear that the ambassadors were still milling around the table engaged in private discussions.

Other ambassadors screamed, while others attempted to dash towards the twelve-inch thick concrete and steel door that locked them inside the underground bunker.

"Please quiet down and take your seats," came a computerized voice from one of the sixanas.

At that moment the French ambassador pulled 9-mm Luger from under his coat and fired at the warrior speaking. The warrior's protective suit, which acted like a chromerion field, absorbed the bullet's impact and stopped the bullet. The bullet fell to the floor with a clang. A micro-second after the shot, several yellow pagenay blasts sailed through the air from those warriors that had a clear shot at the ambassador.

The blast hit the ambassador in his upper torso like bolts of lightning. The ambassador's body convulsed as the blasts lifted him off the floor. His arms extended as the gun dropped from his fingers. His eyes rolled back in his head and he began to jerk as if he was having an epileptic attack. His mouth opened as if it were about to scream, but a copious amount of pink liquid was all that came out, spraying out like a fire hose dousing a flame. Five painful seconds later, the ambassador was on his back, heaving for air.

The other ambassadors watched in horror, some with mouth agape and others covering their mouths with their hands as to hold in the curdling scream that was forming in their guts.

"I won't ask again," the computer generated voice said. "Take your seats."

After several seconds of terrifying chaos, the ambassadors settled down; fright and disbelief ruling their faces as they made it to their assigned seats. One of the warriors then pulled out a ARIT scanner and waved it at each ambassador. He was checking for more weapons. When he was satisfied the danger had passed, the nodded to the lead warrior.

The French ambassador, still on the floor, was dazed and heaving for air to fill his lungs. Another warrior grabbed the French ambassador, secured his weapon and pushed the ambassador to an empty chair.

On the stage in front of the oval table sat a podium with the U.N. symbol plastered on front. Behind the podium appeared three more white lights. From these lights Deuce and his cousins emerged, wearing the USSTAP uniform with the four green thunderbolts on their collar. They walked up to the podium as the angelic light faded behind them. Deuce looked around and saw the fright in the ambassadors' faces.

This was not exactly what he wanted, but it would do for now.

"Good evening ambassadors. My name is Michael David Genesis II, and these are my cousins, Cheyenna Michelle Genesis and Tynala Elizabeth Genesis. We are the grandchildren of Michael Genesis and USSTAPs' envoys here on Earth during this crisis. I thought it appropriate that we take this time to talk about what is going on."

***

Sector twenty
Border between USSTAP and Scolonian Space
Telo Galaxy, Rojam Os Galactic Cluster

Osguard Perry Tower stood tall in front of the command bridge monitor. In the monitor, he saw the greatest gathering of starships in his life, poised to do battle. The *G.P. Neraka* had rendezvoused with *G.P. Kiliough, G.P. Filloughby, G.C. Pasi, G.C.*

Naylan, S.P. Worro and *S.C. Snitlio.* The fleet hovered on the USSTAP side of the border of Scolonian Space.

Osguard Tower reviewed the intelligence reports on Scolon. It was not impressive. Scolon was a category III, known as CAT III planet. This meant that its technology, although behind USSTAP, was advanced enough to be included into USSTAP; but its rudimentary application of law to advance human rights was not adequate for acceptance. It was an oligarchy based on a class system that most of the universe had abandoned a century ago.

Perry understood that oligarchies like Scolon would almost definitely fight to prove themselves worthy in the universal context. Thus he had to be ready for anything, even an all-out military assault. USSTAP Intelligence, also known as U.I. had a list of Scolon's military capability and capacity.

Scolon had fifty starships that made up four battle fleets. Their starships, whose name was loosely translated into English as 'Devilstars', contained a complement of Zhenista missiles similar to USSTAP's Asher Missiles; four Ehellatz weapons ports that shot laser like beams similar to USSTAP's pagenays, and assortment of kinetic weapons resembling bullets wrapped in energy fields, called *"shockers."* ARIT simulation results indicated that USSTAP Chromerion fields could withstand both their Ehellatz lasers and shockers. However their Zhenista missiles would be somewhat formidable.

Perry took a deep breath and nodded to the communications operator, "Open hailing frequency to the Scolon High Council!"

"Frequency opened!" the communications operator reported after wisping her hand over her console.

"Scolon High Council," Perry began. "This is Telo Galactic Osguard Perry W. Tower with a message from USSTAP."

***

U.N. Underground bunker
New York City, New York
Planet Earth, Millmum Galaxy, Rojam Os Galactic Cluster

Deuce finished his statement, but he could tell by looking at the ambassadors that it might have been a waste of time. Their demeanor had not changed one bit. He tried to assure them that

USSTAP was still their ally, and not their enemy. He explained that they could have killed the Legion soldier, sailors and airmen that waged war against USSTAP just hours ago. But USSTAP had bent over backwards to assure no loss of life on either side.

He also pleaded with them to accept his grandfather's generous offer. But the frightened looks that were on the ambassadors' faces when he stepped into the chamber had now been replaced with faces of omnipotent defiance. This only burned into Deuce's soul more as he felt the diplomatic tone in his voice slip away into one of pure authority.

Flashbacks of his grandfather's lectures on how Earth was and how it could grow with USSTAP's help fueled his speech. He once again assured the ambassadors, USSTAP did not interfere in a planet's sovereignty. USSTAP did not police or occupy any land, their domain was open space He spoke of his grandfather's wishes to help the people of Earth, save lives and ease suffering; only to be thwarted by the Firstie movement whose only goal was to manipulate the system for economic reasons, by fueling the psychosomatic xenophobic attitudes that resided in the population.

Cheyenna and Tynala joined in like a choir, right on cue speaking of the different humans that made up the universe and how their difference really made them the same. All three shared accounts on how USSTAP's richness in diversity and wealth in sharing had renewed humankind and uplifted humanity to a better place; and how Earth's reluctance was causing the population to miss out on the enlightenment.

They praised USSTAP's charter to ensure "Life, Liberty and Opportunity" throughout the universe. This included ensuring humanities basic needs of health, shelter, food and education was met at all levels of society. Cheyenna stated that the inner working of USSTAP's economic structure was a true blend of a government organization and civilian freedom. Through various methods and options, USSTAP provided food, shelter, clothes, medical care, dental care, education, training, and free transportation to its members and their families.

Tynala preached that profiteering was relegated to human wants; and USSTAP tried to veer it away from turning to abusive practices that subjugated human needs. Unfortunately, this was not aligned to the leaders of the Firstie movement, who supported the greedy corporations and power-hungry politicians that preyed on people' basic human needs. These architects of the new world order regulated and sold resources that satisfied basic human needs strictly as a commodity on the stock exchange; so only those who could afford it, received it and the hell with the rest. Ergo the multitude of poor living in poverty quadrupled in the new world order.

As Deuce and his cousins spoke, the upturned lips amongst the ambassadors seemed to sour with each word. Instead of convincing the ambassadors of USSTAP's goodwill, it appeared that Deuce and his cousins were hardening the ambassadors more against USSTAP. Deuce now hoped these words would find some solace in the heart of the population which would hear this conversation broadcast over the common when they were done.

Deuce raised his hands in defeat. Tynala stopped speaking and looked over the podium at the ambassadors and finally realized she was wasting her breath. Cheyenna slowly shook her head, visibly showing her disgust. Her eyes that once burned with ire now were filled with sadness. Deuce, Cheyenna and Tynala now felt the hurt that their grandfather had expressed over the years. They felt the sting of betrayal and the heartache of sorrow.

Suddenly, their gateportals activated and they stepped backwards into the light. Before the white angelic light swallowed them into innerspace, Deuce calmly said, "May whatever God you pray to have mercy on you, because today our mercy has run out."

The light disappeared, taking with them the three young Osguards. Then as suddenly as they appeared the two dozen sixanas stepped into their own white light of heaven and disappeared. Around the room, the ambassadors took a collective sigh of relief. To them, they had just escaped death, but in reality their stubbornness may have just signed the planet's death sentence.

CHAPTER TWENTY-THREE: TIME IS UP

White House, Oval Office
Washington DC
Planet Earth, Millmum Galaxy, Rojam Os Galactic Cluster

President Taylor sat behind the Resolute desk with a stone face. In the Oval Office with her sat her inner circle, the SECDEF, Ann Farris; the CJCS, General Felix March; her National Security Advisor, Alicia Cole; and her husband, the Chief of Staff Richard Taylor. In the background, playing over the common, the former Attorney General Simon Dylan's voice echoed in the office lambasting the administration for following the Firstie's discriminatory practices, which led to USSTAP's compassionate military action and their unorthodox appearance in the U.N. bunker.

President Taylor studied the group with intent. They remained silent, soaking in the verbal lashing Simon was delivering with fire and brimstone. When Taylor heard Simon calling her a weak follower of an "evil mind-controlling cult," she snapped the common off and snarled.

She allowed a few seconds to pass, while she collected her calm and then she addressed her inner circle, "I just got off the common with the leaders of China, Russia and Great Britain. They want to acquiesce to Michael Genesis' demands. I said no! The United States of America will never give in to the demands of terrorists." Suddenly, without thought she asked, "What the hell have I've done?"

March let loose a heavy sigh, looked around and knew it was his turn to say something. "Madam President, USSTAP aren't terrorists. We just got our asses handed to us on a silver platter by a supremely organized, super disciplined and well trained foe." He shook his head in disbelief. "The legionnaires lost…plain and simple. USSTAP disabled the carrier fleet and the airplanes without firing a single shot. They destroyed—no…disintegrated the most modern planes known to man after disabling them."

"Then they had the gall to transport the pilots hundreds of miles, fifteen clicks to the west of Al Madinah; almost back to base they took off from. No, Madam President, USSTAP aren't terrorists.

They are probably the most formidable opponent we ever had the misfortune to face."

Ann grunted, "Even without their precious starships they had the superior technology to invade the U.N. underground bunker, shoot an ambassador, give a state of the union address, and leave; unscathed by any U.N. security force."

"That's ballsy!" Richard commented with a hint of admiration.

Alicia stood and walked over to her sister's desk and with fear in her eyes, began to speak, "I'm afraid Simon is right. I don't know what we were thinking, taking on an organization with such sophisticated technology and exquisite machinery. I know we thought we were David and they were Goliath, and with God's blessing, we were ordained to take down the evil giant."

"But let's stop kidding ourselves. Hell, we are centuries behind them. It wasn't David versus Goliath; it's more like the Roman Empire taking on a fleet of bombers loaded with nuclear weapons."

General March groaned, wiping his head with his hands, as if he was nursing a migraine. "She's right, Madam President. We need to withdraw our support from the U.N. Legionnaires and order those aeroships to leave our airspace."

President Taylor's eyes narrowed, her lips slowly parted, and with a deep sigh of despair said, "I can't do that."

Richard jumped to his feet, "Why not?"

"To retreat would admit defeat. It would admit we were wrong. And the United States of America is never wrong. The United States of America would never retreat in the face of adversity. And I damned sure won't be the first President of the United States to admit defeat and run with our tails stuck firmly between our legs, even if we were wrong…which we're not."

General March chuckled, "Korea, Vietnam, Iraq, Afghanistan and Iran."

The President's voice bolstered with anger, "Those weren't retreats. Those were graceful and strategic withdrawals—"

"Then make this a graceful and strategic withdrawal," Alicia interrupted. "Because if you don't withdrawal; it will be a painful and unplanned defeat that will be the end of this nation and our way of life."

"Don't be so dramatic," Richard countered. "Nothing that USSTAP has done in the past suggests they would take over the United States."

"That's what the Native Americans said about the British colonists. You see how that turned out," President Taylor commented. "No, we stay the course. God will see us through."

"Are you sure?" Ann asked.

"I'm sure." President Taylor responded. "I'm declaring marshal law. Activate the military, reserves and guards with orders to defend our cities."

"But..." General March began.

"But nothing!" President Taylor barked. "Do as I say...now!"

"Yes Madam President."

***

Unity Palace
Unity Chamber Millmum Room
USSTAP Unity Virtual Stream

This was Deuce's first time. Red, white and blue lights spiraled in a candy cane effect. Deuce felt his consciousness fly into the lights. It was truly an out-of-body experience. The lights bent right and left, they curved up and down. Outside the cone of twisted colored light was pitch-black darkness. The darkness was bold and forbidden with evil characteristics. Something told him that this void contained no life...a black hole that could devour his consciousness with marked efficiency. He knew to stay on the lighted path.

In actuality, Deuce's body and mind was safely nested in the unity chamber. According to Dr. Mezhak Zyder of the Chaktun Science Academy the lights were energy connecting his consciousness with the virtual stream, called *Unity*. With advanced ARIT and gate portal technology, these lights traveled through the heaven, reaching out for and combining with other energy with the same configuration.

After a few more seconds of the disorienting light show, the lights faded, and in front of Deuce stood his father and grandfathers. He, as well as they, were wearing the crimson robs associated with the status of being an Osguard. They stood in the Millmum Room, one of several hundred-conference rooms representing each of the

242

galaxies. The room was pentagon shaped with four walls and bay windows in place of the fifth wall. The walls were angelic white, radiating light as they reflected the sun's rays shining through the windows on the south side. In each corner stood a large gold pillar with strange alien symbols curved from top to bottom. The gigantic double door was opposite the bay windows, reaching from the vaulted ceiling to the brown stone floor.

Each exchanged pleasant nods of acknowledgment toward one another before Edward Genesis spoke, "You know why you are here, son?"

"Yes, father, I do." Deuce responded. "I take full responsibility for what happened at the United Nations on Earth," he continued with more bravado.

"And what was that?" Michael piped up.

Deuce took a deep breath and looked up to the ceiling as if the answer was up in the air. His eyes slowly lowered and fixed on Michael. "I thought we had a window of opportunity to talk to the ambassadors at the U.N."

"What made you think that?" Adam asked.

Deuce paused and wet his lips with his tongue. He wanted to get his thoughts straight before answering. "Ambassador Perkins," he began, "her comments to the others led me to believe she was turning towards our side."

"Then why did you barge in with overwhelming force, instead of letting things run its course?" Michael said with a stern voice.

"I don't know," Deuce admitted. "Maybe I thought a show of power would be the extra push she needed to come fully around. Maybe I thought we needed to speak from a position of power."

"And you consider scaring her with force a position of power?" Michael chided.

"Yes...no...I don't know," Deuce responded, obviously flustered.

Michael shook his head, disappointment bathed his expression. "Deuce," he called. "Sometimes I forget how it was to be so young with so much responsibility." Michael moved closer to Deuce. "I once thought all I had to do to be a good Osguard was to use brute force to make people do what I wanted them to do. But I was wrong. I found out the hard way at Talion, when I lost half my crew."

"That mistake convinced me that the greatest power an Osguard had at his disposal was true leadership, not brute force. You're lucky; this mistake didn't cost any lives...at least not yet. Hundreds of people died at Talion under my command...died because I made a mistake in judgment and thought force was all I needed. I failed my crew. I failed USSTAP and worst of all I failed myself. Son, you need to learn now rather than later; force is the last resort, not the first option." Deuce nodded.

"See son," Edward interrupted. "True leadership is to know when and where to use your strengths, and when and where to mitigate your weaknesses. Using the security force at the U.N. bunker was an example of not optimizing your strengths."

Deuce's face scrunched up in confusion. "I saw an opportunity, what should I've done?"

"Besides checking with us?" Michael said with authority.

"Yes, Papa, besides checking with you." Deuce pushed back.

"If I am to be an Osguard, I need to make decisions like an Osguard."

"Deuce," Adam called, "You are not an Osguard. You are an Osguard in Training. No one expects you to make decisions on your own. You have us to bounce your ideas off. You have the entire Osguardian leadership at your beck and call. You have the Chief Executive Osguard, First Osguard and Rojam Os Osguard hovering above you who are the true Osguards responsible for how this thing plays out. Then, you have me, Michael, your Nana, your father, your mother and your aunts to guide you."

"It isn't your job to make decisions that have not been delegated to you already. Do you understand?"

Deuce eyes squinted in disbelief, for he had never been scolded by his Grandfather Adam before. "What would you have told me if I came to you and said I wanted to speak with Ambassador Perkins?"

"We would have said do it," Ed pushed in support of his son, "but not with brute force." Ed nodded to Michael and Adam, signaling this was his time to educate his son.

Michael and Adam stepped back, clearing the way for Ed to come closer to Deuce. "Your instincts were correct. What you saw in Ambassador Perkins' was an opening. You were prudent to act, but the actions you chose were less than desirable. You could have found another way to communicate to Ambassador Perkins...a quieter way…a less violent way. You may have gotten through to her. You may have gotten through to them all—at least some of them. But we will never know now; because brute force only hardened their position and solidified their resolve."

"How would you have handled it, father?"

Adam squinted his eyes in thought and postulated, "If I was alone, and didn't have others to consult I may have tried contacting the U.N. via interlink hologram, or like your grandfather did with the United States President and used the microportal chamber. Either way, I would not make them fear for their lives as I spoke to them."

Deuce nodded. "I see father!" Then he looked at Michael. "Papa, am I relieved?"

"No Deuce, you're not relieved." Michael smiled. "The Galactic Keltar Supreme, Tony Musoto sanctioned your actions as within the USSTAP Charter. He noted the U.N. had already used force to attack USSTAP, therefore the rules of open combat applied to your actions."

Adam interrupted, "That doesn't negate what we are trying to teach you here about your actions."

"I know, Gramps."

"But I must say, you were correct in one aspect," Michael interjected.

"What's that?" Deuce responded.

"You were correct in broadcasting that conversation to the planet," Adam said in a congratulatory tone. "Even though your actions hardened the hearts of most of the ambassadors at the U.N. and may have swayed those on the fence to go against us; your speech may have swayed public opinion and garnered more support for USSTAP amongst the populace." Deuce smiled as the tension released from his body.

"Now go back and finish what we started…and this time stick to the script as much as possible," Michael ordered.

Ed looked at his son with painful eyes, "Even though we taught you about limiting the use of force to achieve your objective, don't shy away from it. Today my son, you may have to give a command that will end someone's life."

"I know father."

"Are you ready for that?"

"No father. No one can ever be ready to take a life. But I will do what has to be done."

Ed smiled, "May the spirits of the universe guide you today my son."

"May the spirits of the universe guide us all," Deuce replied back, signaling for the unity stream to bring him back. The red, white and blue candy cane effect crowded his vision as the chamber mechanism swooped his consciousness back into his body. He woke up in the chamber sleeve fighting an uneasy dizziness from the experience.

***

Lilly Station
Atlantis Continental Self-Atlantic Ocean
Planet Earth, Millmum Galaxy, Rojam Os Cluster

Deuce, Cheyenna and Tynala watched the overhead monitor from the command center in Lilly Station. Jerold Washington and Kerri Knight had spent the last four hours promoting life under USSTAP; describing the economic foundation which they coined as responsible capitalism. The term made Deuce squirm in his seat as he listened to the two reporters banter about the pros and cons of the system over his interlink connection. All the while, a digital clock ticked down on the screen under their images. The clock was now hitting ten minutes. When the clock reached zero, the 72 hours his grandfather gave the President of the United States to accept USSTAP's offer would expire.

On the monitor, Jerold and Kerri went on to explain how most of the worlds that were former members of the Tuit Consortium modeled their financial infrastructure after USSTAP economic model when they joined USSTAP. Using this model, these worlds struck poverty from the populace by eradicating hunger and eliminating homelessness. Albeit, there still remained social economic classes, the system encouraged social economic mobility. It also ensured the poorest of the classes no longer suffered under unbearable conditions of poverty, and richest of the classes appeared to maintain wealth stability.

Deuce understood the message no longer targeted the decision makers of Earth but now was tailored to the populace who may want to join USSTAP after the crisis was over. Deuce had written off any idea that USSTAP would be able to recover their previous standing in the eyes of the world leadership and was now ready to abandon Earth to its own devices. Deuce's priority was his grandfather's wish to bring Dr. Chenault to justice and removing the Scolonian threat from Earth's sphere of influence.

"We have a little over five minutes left," Cheyenna said to Deuce and Tynala. "I want to make one last final plea to the captains of those Scolonian ships."

Deuce turned and looked into Cheyenna's eyes and saw a flicker of hope twinkle within them. He nodded and gestured with his hand to proceed.

"Colonel Epstein, can you open hailing frequencies to the thirty Scolonian ships at the same time?" Cheyenna asked.

Colonel Epstein stopped what he was doing and walked up to Cheyenna with curiosity plaguing his face. After a split second of reflection he answered, "Tiah!"

"Open hailing frequencies, translate my transmission to Scolonian."

"Tiah!" Epstein responded.

"Wait!" Tynala injected. "Interrupt the common broadcast. Play the transmission on the world common...all Earth languages...all frequencies and channels."

Epstein nodded, "Tiah!" and then jotted off the platform to follow out on the young osguard's orders.

A few seconds later, Epstein yelled out, "Hailing frequency opened to all Scolonian ships and Earth common communications tied in."

Cheyenna cleared her throat, stood and walked to the monitor. Standing there for a moment to gain her composure she licked her lips and then began, "Scolonian aeroships hovering over Earth cities, this is Osguard Cheyenna M. Genesis. I along with my cousins, Osguard Michael D. Genesis II and Osguard Tynala E. Genesis, are in charge of USSTAP Earth Forces. Your presence on Earth is a violation of USSTAP Protectorate Law Alpha One."

"Although you are not a signatory of USSTAP law, universal precedence and tradition call for you to abide by this law within USSTAP space. Therefore, I respectfully request you retreat from Earth cities and fly to a designated airspace for detainment and eventually return to your home world. If you do not comply with this demand, we will consider this an act of war and be forced to take action."

"And you should know by now, we are authorized to use the full force of USSTAP to expel you from this planet. Additionally, your non-compliance to our request may cause repercussions to your home world in the form of sanctions and or force. You have four minutes to comply. Do you understand?"

Several seconds ticked by as Deuce swallowed a couple of times to soothe his parched throat. He finally cleared his throat with a cough, ready to declare his cousin's attempt at contact a failure, when the interlink crackled to life.

"This is Cutavif Gzechize, commander of Scolonian Earth First Force air battalion. We reject your offer and are prepared to defend these cities with our lives. So, I suggest you think it over before you start any attack on us."

Deuce nodded. Finally, there was an admission that the aeroships flying above Earth's cities were Scolonian. Of course he knew the diehard Firsties would insist that the transmission was a fake or altered, but at least he had something that should push those that were on the fence to lean in the direction of USSTAP.

Cheyenna cracked a smile, "We won't attack the cities of our home world. We will attack you and your home world. If you are prepared to die today, we are prepared to make it happen. You have three minutes."

Deuce thought Cheyenna put a nice touch by declaring Earth as their home world. That made the fight more personal and connective to Earth's populace. USSTAP was fighting for them.

Deuce looked up and saw the clock ticked down to just less than two minutes. He knew there was no turning back now. The world was about to change in less than two minutes, and he had his finger on the trigger.

"Ready the subs!" he commanded.

Centurion Jessica Jensen nodded, "All submarines in position."

"Signal the starships," Tynala added.

"Starships ready," Jessica added after checking her monitor.

Cheyenna gave a faint sigh, "I guess I better go and get ready."

Deuce nodded, "Let the spirits be with you."

"And you too, my cousins," Cheyenna responded. She turned and exited the command bridge.

Deuce felt his heart pound inside his chest. He had not imagined a few short days ago, when he was discussing their visit to Earth with his parents, he would be in this position. He had always tried to shirk the responsibility of being an Osguard off his shoulders and enjoy life. He thought this visit would be another fun thing to do to help him forget the large responsibility of command that awaited him. Now he was smack in the middle of exerting that responsibility in a possible beginning of a galactic war.

He looked at the clock as the last ten seconds ticked away. Five...four...three...two...one...then finally the display blinked all zeroes. Deuce stood and said, "Signal the fleet ...execute...execute ...execute!"

***

The seven USSTAP starships orbiting Earth energized their microportals. The black mist of beams sailed through the Scolonian chromerion field with ease, just like the night before. Each black mist cracked through the clouds and pushed through the chromerion field protecting a Scolonian aeroship hovering over a city. The seven beams simultaneously hit the ships hovering over Washington D.C., New York, Boston, Chicago, Miami, Dallas and Houston.

The beams punched through the chromerion fields protecting the ships and connected in the rear storage bay. Each beam sparkled as a five-foot silver cylinder materialized. When the cylinder was whole, the beam dissipated. An ARIT sensor in the cylinder registered it was complete and activated an automatic gateportal opening. The cylinders were gateportal flash canisters.

The white light of a gateportal illuminated from the canister radiating benion particles in a wave pattern, swallowing everything in its wake into innerspace. To the outside observer, a white flash exploded from within the ship, blinding the surrounding area. When the white flash snuffed out the ship was gone—zapped out of existence in a blink of an eye. Instantly, the skies over these seven cities were clear of Scolonian aeroships.

***

In the same instant the ships disappeared in a flash of lightening over the largest cities of the United States, they popped into existence from bursts of white lights that danced in the night sky. The aeroships were now 5,000 feet over the middle of the Pacific Ocean in the dark, disoriented with inoperative navigation equipment trying to reconcile the sudden change of location. The ships were within a five mile radius of each other.

Deuce's voice rang through the Scolonian Aeroships' hailing frequencies, "Scolonian Aeroships...this is Osguard Michael D. Genesis II...surrender now or be fired upon!"

Six of the seven ships powered up their weapons.

***

The threat board on Lilly Station lit up, identifying Zhenista Missiles charging. Deuce couldn't believe his eyes. His jaw dropped as he saw the entire episode play out in the holographic display. The aeroships were searching the ocean for his subs. He had placed five sea cruisers and two sea protectors right under the aeroships, with full armament unlocked.

"Sire," Jessica urged.

Deuce knew his next command would end in deaths. If he allowed the Scolonians to continue the Zhenista Missiles would cause fatal damage to his subs. If he ordered his subs to fire, the Scolonians would surely be obliterated into pixie dust.

"Sire," Jessica urged again. Deuce understood the impatience in her plea. He closed his eyes and lowered his head, "Weapons free...lock onto the six butches with weapons energized...fire at will."

***

The ocean below the Scolonian aeroships bubbled. Then razor sharp pagenay beams punched through the surface of the water and pierced the night, sailing towards the six aeroships. The blue rays of death connected to each ship, momentarily pulsating at the chromerion field barrier before pushing through to its target...the Scolonian hull.

Direct hits roared like thunder as the beams struck their targets. The Scolonian ships lit up in a blue haze as the pagenay blast spread over the entire hull. Cracks and fissures soon prickled the hulls surface. The fractures spread like streams of water racing downhill as the continuous power of the pagenay beams laid all of the energy of a small star unto the hull.

Six seconds of power was all it took. The hulls imploded in bright colors, as micro bits of the ships sprayed in an ugly design in the sky; radiating in waves of blue, red and orange embers. Like a thunderstorm the flashes of light broke the darkness into colorful patchwork of death and destruction, raining blood and metal into the ocean; leaving a lone aeroship in the sky.

***

"Six Scolonian aeroships destroyed," Jessica Jensen reported. Her tone was professional, but obvious filled with relief.

Deuce nodded, "What about the seventh ship?"

"Receiving surrender hail now, sire." Centurion Richard Gray reported.

"Good," Deuce said. "Quarantine the ship, board her and take the prisoners to the holding area."

"Tiah," Jessica replied.

For the next hour the fury of activity in Lilly Station command center orchestrated the surrender of the lone aeroship. Using gateportals, sixana warriors boarded her and escorted the hundred Scolonian airmen off the ship unto a holding cell reinforced with a chromerion field on the African savannah outside Sibut inside the Kémo Prefecture. The sixanas then attacked the aeroship computer system and ripped thousands of terabytes of information from its memory; including ship-wide command codes.

Two hours later, learning all they could learn, the sixanas retreated from the ship. With the abandoned ship hovering in autopilot, and no human onboard to work her controls, a sizzling blue beam of death sprouted from the ocean surface and connected to her hull. The ship exploded on contact, meeting the same demise as her sister ships over two hours ago. However, this time there were no flesh, blood or bone mixed in the haze of micro-dust that slowly floated towards the ocean.

"Sire, we're ready to proceed," Jessica reported as soon as the threat board recorded the destruction of the seventh Scolonian aeroship.

Deuce lifted his head from the report he was reading on his ARIT table, "Signal the starships to deliver the next seven."

"Tiah," Jessica replied.

CHAPTER TWENTY-FOUR: MEXICAN STANDOFF

Sector twenty
Border between USSTAP and Scolonian Space
Telo Galaxy, Rojam Os Galactic Cluster

In the monitor screen, Perry Tower was staring at half the Scolonian fleet. Twenty-five Devilstars sat on the other side of the border. So far they had not powered up their weapons, but they also had not responded to any hails that Perry pushed out. It was an old fashion *"Mexican Standoff."* Perry did not appreciate that term, but it was more than apropos for the situation he now found himself in.

"I have contact with twenty-five Devilstars, eighteen light-years away...on a rendezvous course with the other twenty-five," the defense officer reported.

"Oh great, now the other half of their military is coming to join the fight," Perry said, showing his exasperation with the situation. "Call the nearest station and see if you can get us some back-up out here."

"Tiah," the communications officer replied and began to work his magic over the communications station.

After a few seconds a puzzled look came over the communication officer's face. Then a shot of recognition twinkled in his eyes. He switched some triggers at his station and then nodded. "Sire, I'm getting a hail from those approaching Devilstars."

"On speaker," Perry commanded.

The speaker cracked with electricity. The connection had an irritating buzzing noise. The voice that spoke was faint...almost distant...overpowered by the buzzing noise, "USSTAP ships, this is Consman Tezlete Gzaheit, leader of the Scolonian Empire. The ships you are confronting on our border are not under my command. They are rogue ships led by my cousin Velman Gzaheit."

The connection dropped off. The communications officer maneuvered his hands over his equipment, moving triggers and switches in rapid succession, but to no avail.

"Sire, we lost contact," he admitted. "It appears the Devilstars in front of us are now jamming the signal."

"Fight through the jamming," Perry ordered.

"Trying, Sire,"

Perry caught himself as he started to tell the young communication officer to, *"try harder!"* But he simply nodded. "How about our call for reinforcements?"

The communication officer looked up and switched some toggles on his holographic board. *"G.P. Cloke, Pucmeil* and *Venner* are responding...top MOP speed. The *Cloke ETA* one hour. *Pucmeil* and *Venner*...twenty minutes after."

"How soon before the Consman and his troops get here?" Perry asked.

"Nine minutes," the defense officer reported. Then an alert signal caught his attention. After analyzing the signal he added, "Butches powering up weapons!"

"Okay," Perry said. His decision was already made. He needed to prepare his people for battle.

It would be his crew's first battle and his first time at the helm in battle. He had to distribute the next set of commands as if he was an old hand at this. He had to push out a sense of confidence for his people to feel secure as they performed their jobs. He took his seat at the command helm and ran through the scenarios in his mind. Training now was kicking in.

He took a deep breath and looked up at the large screen. "Alert One. Fleet go to stealth mode ten. Defense posture lateral alpha. Depth range—negative ten to positive fifteen on the galactic plane. Heading ...four, six, zero, one, decimal five, four...Report all stations!"

As he bellowed his orders, they were relayed with market efficiency. The *Kiliough, Filloughby, Pasi, Naylan, Worro* and the *Snitlio* vanished in a wave of electromagnetic ooze as they energized their slitanium hull through the stealth mode power rods. Once safely hidden from sensors and scanners, including human sight, they used their hydrogenic engines to maneuver as Perry directed. When complete they were separated vertically as well as horizontally in a defensive fighting alpha formation, weapons at the ready.

The next six minutes were nerve racking. The *Neraka* sensors picked up the twenty-five butches frantically scanning the area for them, but in stealth mode ten there was no way they could get a solid lock on them to fire any weapons. However with each scan that passed over their starship, he found himself holding his breath and not moving as if he could accidentally make a noise that they could pick up.

Right now all ships were running silent...no transmissions. All actions would be off his cue. Presently, Perry didn't know what else to do but stay hidden. He knew he could dispatch the butches without much problem if he took the first shot. But he was told to wait for further instruction prior to engaging, or crossing the border.

Then it happened. On the screen he saw the second wave of butches approaching. But the first wave turned to engage the second wave and without notice a firefight began. The two waves were fighting each other. Ehellatz beams shrieked across the dark space between the two waves of Devilstars. A collage of bright colors, yellow, green, blue and red beams, flew through space displaying a disco laser show of confusion.

Bright red dots darted the space between the ships. Perry saw the threat board identifying the dots as shockers. The second wave of butches were spread in a massive attack formation, and seemed to be gaining ground as the first wave lay in a straight line with the border and the USSTAP forces behind them like a stone wall.

Perry was confused and didn't know if he should intervene. His finger rested on the communications button that would relay his orders to the fleet. He licked his lips as the thought of engaging the foe and wiping out the entire military in one swoop danced in his head.

On the screen and confirmed on the threat board, Perry saw the first wave firing their Zhenista missiles. The large kinetic bombs of destruction pushed towards their target at hypersonic speed, eating up the space between the firing starship and the target starship at a slow rate compared to the Ehellatz and the shockers. But the level of destruction the Zhenista missile carried in one punch was ten times as devastating as either Ehellatz or shockers could bring to bear.

The first couple of missiles seemed to explode against the protective force fields surrounding the second wave Devilstars. However, with each shot of missiles, the protective field seemed to be collapsing. By the fourth volley, the protective field was completed depleted and the ships were now vulnerable.

The first wave of Devilstars released the fifth volley of Zhenista missiles. According to intelligence reports that would be the last volley they could shoot. Their missile inventory would be exhausted. The first wave would be Winchester after that volley and would have to rely on energy weapons from then on. But it also meant that the second wave would be destroyed...crippled at best. Either way, the fight would be over.

Perry replayed in his mind the message he received from Consman Tezlete Gzaheit. The word *rogue* played over and over again. Before he knew it, he had hit the communications button and ordered, "All ships, lock on and fire on those Zhenista missiles. Blow them out of space."

Before he released the button, all seven USSTAP starships fired their pagenay weapons. The uncertainty of which starship locked onto which Zhenista missile caused some missiles to be double targeted, and left seven missiles to be untargeted. The targeted missiles exploded in a fire of bright red and yellow light, while the seven untargeted missiles sailed through the cloud of debris undaunted.

"Reacquire and fire!" Perry yelled into his communications microphone.

The seven missiles were closing in and were between twenty-five hundred and two thousand feet from the second wave Devilstars when the seven USSTAP ships fired once more. This time they were joined by the second wave of Devilstars as they shot their Ehellatz. The dazzling laser show crossed beams and connected to the closest Zhenista missiles first and then worked their way back in a serenaded dance step of flashes; ending with a brilliant explosion punctuating the demise of the kinetic flying death rods of doom.

Perry took a deep breath, hoping he had made the right decision and interceded on the right people's behalf. "Open hailing frequency to the consman!"

A split second later the communications officer reported, "I have the Consman on frequency."

"On speaker!" Perry commanded. "This is Osguard Perry W. Tower to Consman..."

A piercing crackling sound interrupted Perry, followed by the Consman's voice, "Osguard Tower this is Consman Tezlete Gzaheit, thank you for your assistance. Please stand by. I'm in the middle of something here."

"Yes, Consman, USSTAP standing by," Perry said with some sarcasm in his voice.

On the screen and through the threat board, Perry witness the mop-up operation, as the first wave of Devilstars ceased their aggressive action. It appeared they surrendered believing the

Consman had successfully co-opted the USSTAP forces towards their side. Again, Perry was fighting that sinking pit in his stomach.

Forty excruciating minutes passed when the *G.P. Cloke* rendezvoused with her sister ships. She engaged her stealth mode power rods, energizing her slitanium hull and maneuvered quietly into formation. Twenty minutes later, the *Pucmeil* and *Venner* joined the formation, maneuvering in stealth mode ten. The ships' approach did not go unnoticed, adding to the vagueness of how many USSTAP starships were hovering on the border in stealth mode.

Ten minutes after the *Venner* joined the group, Consman Tezlete Gzaheit hailed the *Neraka,* "Osguard Tower, this is Consman Tezlete Gzaheit. We have Chenum Seolin te Erucki and his minion, Elib fez Kolinera. I believe your hail to our High Council said you were looking for them. Our High Council was unaware of their presence on our planet or my cousin's involvement with them in corrupting your planet Earth."

"We are ready to transfer them into your custody, in exchange for any traitors that are still alive that broached your planet Earth. I stand ready to discuss the particulars."

Perry smiled. His gut feeling had paid off. He had sided with the correct party—so it seemed. He still had to proceed with caution. He did not know what exactly happened between the two forces on Scolon, but he knew he didn't want to become an unwitting pawn in any further action.

Perry keyed his mic, "I stand ready as well, Consman. How do you propose we proceed?"

"I prefer a private audio-visual interlink between you and I, Osguard Tower."

"Consider it done. I will send you the interlink frequency and we shall continue this conversation...let's say in an hour. That should give you some time to finish dealing with your situation."

"Concur, Osguard Tower. An hour will be sufficient."

CHAPTER TWENTY-FIVE: ENDGAME

Makeshift USSTAP Holding Facility
Outside Sibut, Kémo Prefecture, CAR
Planet Earth, Millmum Galaxy, Rojam Os Galactic Cluster

Osguard in Training, Cheyenna M. Genesis sat behind a brown smoky glass desk in the startram, readying herself for the next step. She sipped the pure cool ice water from her glass, as she went over her questions in her head. She needed to find out as much as possible about the connection between the Scolonians and Earth First. She needed to know how deep this conspiracy ran.

The buzz of the door chime interrupted her thoughts. She looked up and told herself to be calm. She knew any sign of nervousness would be conveyed as a sign of weakness to her prisoner. She gently cleared her throat and said, "Enter!"

Three sixanas marched in with Cutavif Gzechize, commander of Scolonian Earth First Force air battalion in tow. The Scolonian was completely hairless. She saw no eyebrows or a hint of eyebrows on his face, which made his piercing red eyes seem that more horrifying. He stood about six feet tall and wore a tight blue mesh-like uniform that conformed to every ripple of his body. He was muscular, built for hand-to-hand combat. He sported an evil grin that the red hue of his skin only made much more menacing.

Cheyenna took regarded the figure that was walking in with the sixanas as a prisoner; and she did not feel any fright from the view. She felt disgust. She reminded herself that this man had ordered several hundred people to fight to the death, while he surrendered without a shot. He was a coward hiding behind the persona of his rank.

At first she was going to offer Gzechize a seat; but now her blood boiled and she thought against the idea. She wanted him to stand in front of her in shame. She motioned for the sixanas to bring the prisoner forward, while at the same time activating the microport control and ordering the chair in front of her desk to disappear from sight. A black mist engulfed the brown leather chair and de-materialized it within a second.

Gzechize's eyes widened for a split second and then returned to the normal grizzly trance he had when he walked in. The sixanas remained professional, wearing weapons echo configuration. They pushed the prisoner forward into the startram cabin. Their demeanor was stoic, but informative that they were armed and ready to end their prisoner's life at any sign of aggressiveness.

Cheyenna stood, she was in weapons delta. She walked from behind the desk and up to the prisoner. She peered into Gzechize's eyes. She wanted to let Gzechize to know his act did not scare her and that she was the boss in this room.

Ten long seconds passed as she stood within a breath's distance of Gzechize, when Cheyenna finally spoke. "I am Osguard Cheyenna M. Genesis, tri-chair commander of USSTAP Earth Forces and you are our prisoner."

Gzechize began a hawk in his throat as if to spit. Cheyenna recognize the movement and slapped Gzechize across the face. The force of her slapped made Gzechize's face spin to his right sending the now blood-soaked phlegm spraying. Gzechize's knees buckled as he stumbled to regain his balance. The sixanas held him firm. Gzechize then turned back and sneered at Cheyenna.

At this time, Cheyenna snapped the interrogator MARIT unto Gzechize's forehead. The half-dollar size instrument dug into his skin and sent electronic signals to his brain. The connection was somewhat discomforting, but the discomfort eased after a few seconds. When Cheyenna was satisfied the connection was complete, she moved to the other side of her desk, all the while keeping an eye on the prisoner.

She sat in her chair and pulled up the holographic monitor connected to the I-MARIT. "Okay, Gzechize, let's begin," Cheyenna started. "What can you tell me about Earth First?"

Gzechize eyes narrowed, beaming his detest towards Cheyenna. Conversely, his mind was sifting through the answer; establishing plausible lies to cover the truth. Unbeknownst to him, the I-MARIT recorded the truth and the lie; and instantly compared the electrical impulse from his memory to what it was recording.

When the I-MARIT matched a memory to an unspoken statement, it labeled it the true statement. Gzechize was spilling his heart out without even knowing it. He believed he was withstanding a simple interrogation by maintaining his silence. When in actuality, maintaining silence was the worst way to combat the I-MARIT interrogation.

Cheyenna shouted, "How did the Scolonians get here? Who built those aeroships and where did they come from?" Cheyenna kept her stern look and did not react to the wealth of information streaming across her monitor. She pretended to be angry and frustrated at Gzechize refusal to speak, which emboldened Gzechize more—making the interrogation go smoother than Cheyenna anticipated.

After an hour, Cheyenna couldn't think of anything else to ask and angrily dismissed Gzechize with a wave of her hand, "Get this waste of protoplasm out of my sight. Put him with the others. Maybe they will find a way to reward him for his cowardice."

The sixanas grabbed Gzechize and ushered him out of the startram. Cheyenna hit her interlink and requested the next prisoner be escorted to her in ten minutes. For now she needed to take a break before she interviewed the aeroship's pilot-in-command. She knew she needed to confirm the I-MARIT's findings with at least four more interrogations.

This was going to be a long day, but well worth her time.

***

Dr. Claude Chenault Private Island
Tuamotu Islands, French Polynesia
Planet Earth, Millmum Galaxy, Rojam Os Galactic Cluster

Osguard in Training, Tynala E. Genesis was in full combat gear, weapons foxtrot, leading four S-Teams. They had stepped to Dr. Claude Chenault's Private Island after the third gateportal bomb transport of aeroships to the decision box was complete. Five miles off the coast lay her re-enforcement: five sea protectors and one sea cruiser.

She lay just inside the beach near the cliffs as she reviewed the latest report streaming across her face-mask. After twenty-one ships transported to the decision box, only eight had surrendered, the others began to engage USSTAP forces which ultimately ended in their demise; thirteen aeroships blown to smithereens; totaling approximately over 1,300 dead. She knew it was a huge death tally that would weigh heavily on Deuce's heart. She wondered if she would have been able to make the call as easily as Deuce made in destroying the aeroships with their crew onboard.

She swallowed hard, realizing she may be making that call soon. She was about to lead four S-Teams in an all-out assault of Chenault's compound with two objectives. The first objective was to capture Chenault; the second, to turn off the chromerion field surrounding the planet. U.I. reported Chenault flew back to the island from New York after the failed attack on CAR.

Presently, Chenault's compound was surrounded by a secondary chromerion field. Similarly to the world-wide chromerion field, USSTAP gateportal technology was unable to step through this field. Luckily, Deuce's forces were able to get the command code to allow temporary passage through the field.

She keyed the command code in her personal ARIT, also known as a PARIT and activated the sequence. The momentary disruption should not appear on any monitor in the command area, as long as they kept it to only a few seconds. This was meant to allow people to walk through the area without disruption as long as they had the right key.

When the doorway opened, the four five-man S-Team used their personal gateportals, PGPs, and stepped through to the other side. The entry shut down after three seconds with Tynala and twenty sixanas inside prepared for battle.

Tynala activated her PARIT connection to her helmet visor and reviewed the island schematics. "Overlay body signatures onto schematic," she commanded. Red dots appeared where interpreted heat signatures emanated. "Total count of humans?" she requested. The number sixty-three appeared in the upper right part of her visor.

"Can you isolate Dr. Chenault?" A target pixel circle surrounded a red dot in the command chamber bunker. There were two more body signatures with him. "It figures!" she mumbled. A cluster of about thirty appeared to be in the south side of the cavern.

Tynala thought this to be the control room for the aeroships. She knew that they must be going crazy about now, trying to figure out what happened to their ships.

Using the PARIT interlink, she shared the view with the S-Team leads. "S-4, I need you to secure the east side of the island. There are eight sentries on duty. S-3, you take the north side of island and S-2 the south. Then S-2 and S-3 make your way west, securing everything back to this point. Sweep and neutralize as necessary, but try to take them alive."

Tynala knew she just gave them the go-ahead to kill if necessary. However, with all the non-lethal weaponry at their disposal, she knew that taking a life would be the last resort. "S-1 you're with me. We are going to breach the command chamber. S-4, join us when the east is secured."

The four groups separated and discussed their individual missions. Tynala had enough sense to allow S-1 lead to come up with the plan. She knew she was just there as the Osguard top-cover.

The command chamber, which originally housed the aeroships, was twenty stories deep, buried deep into the island's bedrock. PGP coordinates needed to be accurate or they could find themselves stepping into a stone wall. The PARIT correlated the information Deuce's team downloaded from the captured aeroships and calculated the best point of entry.

After several minutes, the S-Team leads reported they were ready. Tynala set the mission clock and networked it to all the members. She nodded and started the count down. "Moving in five...four...three...two...one..." then she activated her PGP along with the other members. Instantly a white oval of light appeared out of thin air. All the members jumped in with their weapons unlocked and in the ready.

Tynala popped out the other end of the white light, exiting innerspace with a zap. Her feet hit the ground with a loud thud. Next to her, S-1 Team Lead punched through his gateportal opening. Her rifle was set on pagenay and in the knockout option, as was S-1's rifle.

She scanned the room. In front of her were two Scolonians standing on either side of Dr. Chenault. As plan she took the one on the right and left the one on the left to S-1 lead. She pointed her rifle and squeezed the trigger. A red beam sailed from her rifle and connected on her target's chest; overloading his axons and dendrites in the nerve cells with heat, rendering instantly unconscious. He fell face first.

His face hit the stone floor with a healthy thump. It appeared he broke his nose in the fall. Blood was seeping from his nostrils and spilling into the cracks of the stone floor like a river. Tynala turned to the second Scolonian, but he was already on the floor, quickly dispatched by S-1 lead.

Dr. Chenault eyes enlarged and fright plastered its way onto his face. He sat in his chair, apparently too scared to move. A flash of red light from behind her caught Tynala's attention. She turned to peer out the wall window and saw the rest of the team maneuvering towards the control room. Several of the controllers were outside the room, meandering in the huge cavern. She thought they may have been the controllers of the missing aeroships and with no ships to monitor had idle time to waste in the cavern.

Next she heard S-1 yell, "NO!"

Tynala turned back to look at Dr. Chenault. He had collapsed on his desk, white liquid foaming from his mouth. She raised her rifle at Chenault, keeping him covered as S-1 rushed to him. S-1 checked Chenault's pulse using his PARIT sensors in his glove's fingers.

"Nothing!" he roared, and turned him over. S-1 pulled out a MARIT inducer from his buddy pack in his leg pocket and punched the needle into Chenault's shoulder. "It's cyanide. He must have had in his mouth already before we stepped through. It looks like it was part of his dentures."

Tynala keyed her microphone. "S-1 Team...shut down the chromerion field around this island. Lilly Station...Lilly Station...this is Osguard Tynala Genesis, I need a medevac team my location...repeat medevac my location as soon as we get this damned chromerion field down."

Sixty long seconds later the S-1 team inside the control room disabled both the worldwide chromerion field and the chromerion field surrounding the island. The three-man medevac team stepped into the room through gateportal openings. They rushed towards Dr. Chenault and began reviving procedures.

Tynala stepped away and went outside into the cavern. She opened her PARIT communal connection and read through the reports that were rapidly coming in. The island was secured...no casualties. Twenty out of thirty aeroships chose to make a fight in the decision box and were completely annihilated. The Scolonian High Council disavowed any knowledge of the Scolonian actions on Earth and handed over Chenum Seolin te Erucki, and his sidekick Elib fez Kolinera, to Osguard Perry Tower. The final report she read was the medevac team confirming, Dr. Claude Chenault was dead; an apparent victim of suicide by cyanide poisoning.

She disengaged her helmet, allowing it to reshape and fold into her collar pouch. She told herself to breathe, as she pulled air into her lungs. It was over.

CHAPTER TWENTY-SIX: NEGOTIATION

Former house of Shawn, Michael and Patricia Genesis
New Haven, CT
Planet Earth, Millmum Galaxy, Rojam Os Galactic Cluster

A week had passed since the battle and the uproar it caused was still blazing. However, Michael still needed to do this. Moments earlier he stepped into his former house. It was the first time he had been on Earth since 2030. That was the year after the U.N. USSTAP Pact was signed, and he realized he was no longer welcomed on his home world. More to the point, it had been almost fifty years since he stepped into his old house.

Presently, he studied the kitchen, specifically the stove. He stood in front of it, rubbing his finger over the old style burners willing his mind to remember. After several seconds a memory emerged.

The ghost of his mother popped into view as his mind took him back to his childhood.

He saw his mother, Elizabeth, standing over the stove, cooking scrambled eggs with that old black cast-iron skillet he used to admire. He remembered how she hummed gospel songs as she cooked breakfast for the family every Saturday and Sunday morning. It was the only time the family was able to get together for breakfast.

During the week day they had such a varied schedule that they hardly saw one another in one setting. Mom worked second shift and Dad worked third. Patty, Shawn and he had school, work and sports that kept them out of the house. But somehow, Saturday and Sunday morning was always reserved for family time, and that brought a song to his mother's heart.

The memory faded as a heavy weight began to form on his spirit. Michael bowed his head with closed eyes as if to mentally shake the weight from his soul. Then he moved through the pantry, into the den. He saw his father's black recliner chair.

This brought back a rush of warm memories of when he was a small child of six. He remembered he used to fall asleep in his father's lap, while Parker sat in that recliner chair and watched football games on Sunday. He remembered how safe he felt wrapped up in his father's arm. He remembered pressing his ear against his father's chest and hearing Parker's heartbeat. The sound of his father's heart beating while snuggled in his strong grasp was probably the safest feeling he ever had.

He knew that his father was strong and powerful and would protect him, his mother and his siblings at all cost. There was nothing his father wouldn't do for his family. Similarly, there wasn't anything Michael wouldn't do for his family. Now staring at that old black recliner chair pushed those treasured feelings to the surface.

Michael's eyes began to water and he took a seat in his father's old chair. A myriad of thoughts bubbled in his mind. He always understood and cherished the thought of family, but now he was having comparative thoughts of home. This house wasn't just the house he, Shawn and Patricia grew-up in; it was a home that he, Shawn and Patricia were raised in.

"Papa," called a voice from behind Michael

Michael looked over his shoulder and saw Deuce standing in the doorway with an elderly gentleman. "Yeah, Deuce."

"Papa," Deuce began stepping toward his grandfather, "this is Alexander Kennedy. He is…well he is family."

Family? How apropos it was for Deuce to introduce Alexander as family, just at the moment when Michael was relishing in the thought of family and home.

Maybe this was why Deuce picked his old family home for this meeting. Michael stood and walked over to Alexander. "My grandson said you wanted to shake the hand of an Osguard one day. Although I am retired now, I hope my hand will do for now." Michael put his hand out.

Alexander readily grabbed Michael's hand with both of his and shook it with the glee of a kid meeting Santa Claus for the first time. "Sir, your hand is the main hand I wanted to shake."

Michael smiled, "I'm honored, but there are several hundred Osguards in the universe that would be happy to shake your hand, and thank you and the other Tappies for keeping faith in us."

Alexander let go of Michael's hand, and said, "No problem. It was my honor."

"Well soon, we hope to repay you and the others by offering you the chance to join us."

"You mean Earth will become part of USSTAP?"

Michael shook his head, "No, I'm afraid not. What I'm talking about is our offer to you and others who believed in us an opportunity to become citizens of USSTAP, travel the stars, settled on new worlds, or old worlds within our purview."

Alexander slowly shook his head, "That sounds fine sir, but I'm too old for all that. I'm too old to leave my home and seek out adventure. New Haven is my home and I am not ready to leave it...even for the promise of adventure and new things that I have dreamt about all my life."

"I'm sorry to hear that," Michael responded.

"I'm sure there will be a lot of people that will take you up on your offer, but there also will be a lot of people who will refuse to leave. We want to be part of you, but not at the cost of leaving what we know is our home."

The word *home* hit a nerve with Michael, since he was just wrestling with the notion of home. He slowly nodded, "I understand. I didn't think of it that way. I was just thinking of it as a chance to immigrate to a better life...like the Europeans did to America."

"Yeah, I understand that," Alexander admitted. "But life here isn't bad enough to make me leave my home. In fact life is good."

"With the poverty, overcrowding and political infighting, you still say life is good here?" Deuce interrupted.

"Son, I didn't say life was perfect. Life is never perfect, no matter where you live. I just said, life is good; especially if you have God on your side."

"But with us, it could be better!" Deuce pushed.

"Yeah, I bet you that was what Marcus Garvey said to get Blacks to move back to Africa in 1937. Segregation didn't work then, and it won't work now."

Michael was stunned. His right eye squinted as if to peer into the words lingering in the air. After a slight pause Michael responded. "No one is talking about segregation. I'm advocating immigration from Earth to another world...a world you can begin again with a clean slate."

"Thank you, Osguard, but no thank you." Alexander sternly said. Then his demeanor softened as he spoke, "We appreciate what you have done for us, and we will appreciate what you will do for some of us. It's just that migrating from Earth to another world or into the stars is not exactly what some of us want."

"Then what is it that you want from us?" asked Deuce.

"Really I don't know...maybe to help us make our home better."

Michael nodded. "I understand Alexander, and if I could I would. But my hands are tied. We offered to leave this place and I have to stand by my word."

"I know that," said Alexander. "I just wish you hadn't given your word to leave us. I imagine you were mad or frustrated, because the Michael Genesis I've studied wouldn't have agreed to leave his home so readily. The Michael Genesis that I believed in all my life would have fought for his home, his family and his people. He would have found a way to turn lemons into lemonade."

"He always did in the past with the Moslecks, the Kulusks and the Tuits. I expect the Michael Genesis I know could do it again with the Firsties." With expectation highlighting his eyes, Alexander went on to say, "Don't you have a plan to do that. You always have a plan."

Michael sighed, "Do you think people of Earth want that?"

Alexander smiled, "Yes, people want it. Look at the cheers around the Earth since you defeated Chenault and his storm troopers. Yes I know people want to be engaged by USSTAP."

Michael looked up and then closed his eyes, searching his soul for what to do next. Nothing came to mind. He felt helpless. His emotions were biting at his professional mind to do something other than continue down this course he had laid. He sat back down in the recliner chair and stared at the old style television set in front of him.

"Alexander," he called still staring at the television set. "I can't promise anything, but I will think about it." Then he turned to Alexander, "If an opportunity presents itself, I will consider your words."

Alexander smiled. "You promise?"

"Yes, cousin, I promise. You are family and I make this promise to you. I will consider acting on your words, if the opportunity presents itself."

"That sounds like a challenge to the Tappies to make the opportunity present itself." Michael nodded.

"Challenge accepted."

***

United Nations Private Conference Room
New, York City, NY
Planet Earth, Millmum Galaxy, Rojam Os Galactic Cluster

Michael David Genesis surveyed the room. He was on his guard, wondering what diplomatic gobbledy gook double-talk the new U.N. Secretary General, Yolanda A. Perkins would spout. It had been six months of testimony from USSTAP officials, including his grandchildren, since hostilities ceased. and the U.N. was still trying to flex their muscles and drum up some blame to pin on the association. Even after the emergence of Dr. Chenault's taped confession that littered the airwaves after his death, the U.N. appeared to be more emboldened than ever.

Right now, because Ambassador Perkins requested, the most powerful people of Earth and in the universe he had ever had the opportunity to be around in one venue occupied the. They sat around the usually diplomatic circular table that neutered any feelings of superiority from its occupants. The circular table indicated that all were equal in stature in this room, which he knew was a diplomatic necessity.

Representing the powers of Earth were the new President of the United States, Jackson Prichard, who hailed from his home state of Connecticut; along with England's Prime Minister, Robert Grant; and the leaders of Russia and China, President Vlad Trosponov and President Xin Xing. He thought this was very presumptuous of the new secretary general to summon only these leaders as the voices for the entire planet.

Besides him, as the appointed USSTAP Ambassador of Goodwill to Earth's United Nations, representatives for USSTAP at the table were: Ambassador Chancellor Nestie Warwick, Prime Ambassador Felick Korish, and Chief Ambassador Ive Ove. It was their first visit to what was once known as a Kulusk prison planet – Ea rth—now known as Earth.

All of them had rid themselves of the garb that were usually adorned with accouterments signifying their stature within USSTAP, for regular Earth business attire.

Checking his watch, Michael felt uneasiness overcome him for accepting the secretary general's invitation. The U.N. Secretary

General was now more than fashionably late. The meeting was to start ten minutes ago. He looked over at Ambassador Warwick and with an apologetic smile shrugged. He knew it was more than an insult to keep the political leader of the free universe waiting; not to mention the leaders of the galactic cluster and the galaxy that had offered Earth unconditional protection for almost two centuries.

Michael turned to the U.N. protocol officer, "What's the hold up?"

The protocol office shrugged, "I don't know ambassador, but I'm sure the secretary general will be here shortly."

Michael squinted and let loose a gentle sigh. He was now stewing on the inside. He turned back towards Ambassador Warwick and said, "It appears the U.N. Secretary General is not quite ready for us. Maybe we should step back to your transport ship and give the secretary more time to finish whatever she deemed more important than this meeting."

Ambassador Warwick nodded, "Perhaps you are right, Chief Executive Osguard. I believe we shall retire until the secretary general is ready to meet with us."

Michael turned back to the protocol officer and saw the color flush from his face. It was a sign of panic, which made Michael relax a little. The USSTAP ambassadors stood and nodded to the Earth world leaders.

President Prichard's eyes lit with recognition and offered, "Maybe we should retire as well!"

The protocol officer held out his hands as if he wanted to use telekinesis to push the USSTAP ambassadors back into their seats. "Hold on ambassadors, I'm getting word that the secretary general is on her way. She should be her any moment."

Warwick looked at Michael. Michael knew Warwick was looking for advice on how to proceed. Michael then offered, "Well, if she is on her way, I would recommend we continue with the meeting."

Warwick and the others sat back down. As soon as they pulled their chairs closer to the table, Ambassador Perkins stepped into the room, followed by an entourage of associates.

"Sorry, Ambassadors, Prime Minister and Presidents," she offered in haste. "I just finished up meeting with the Security Council, and it ran a little longer than I expected. Please accept my apologies. I did not mean to keep you waiting, but this was important."

"How so?" Michael asked, as Perkins pulled up a chair to the table and sat.

"Well, Ambassador Genesis," she began while looking at Warwick, purposely snubbing Michael. "It appears the Security Council has come to a decision."

"That's fine," Warwick said. "And what did they decide?"

"The security council is willing to put this entire episode behind us. They have found that there is sufficient evidence to declare Dr. Chenault's involvement in this episode was clearly a violation of the U.N.-USSTAP Pact and warranted intervention."

"Is that so?" Ambassador Korish said, not hiding his sarcasm.

"Yes, Ambassador," Perkins added with her own sarcasm. "In that light, the security council finds USSTAP actions in this episode within acceptable diplomatic parameters."

Michael rolled his eyes. There it was: the gobbledy gook he knew was coming. Warwick shot a glance at Michael, followed by Korish and Ove.

Michael chuckled, "We did the right thing."

Perkins shook her head, "I didn't exactly say that."

"Then what are you saying?" Ove pushed.

Perkins interlaced her fingers and rested her hands on the table, "Even though this little episode required intervention, I believe it was not in USSTAP's purview to take action. It was the U.N.'s responsibility. USSTAP's hasty action prevented the U.N. from executing an acceptable course of action for all concern. With that said, I believe USSTAP owes us an apology."

"Is that so?" Michael reflected aloud. "Forgive me, Madam Secretary, but wasn't the Legion forces that attacked USSTAP outpost in the CAR under the auspices of U.N. control?"

Perkins cleared her throat, "That's correct. And since you mention it, I believe USSTAP owes us monetary recompense for the airplanes you shot down."

"Madame Secretary if I may," President Prichard interrupted. "As far as the United States is concerned, Ambassador Warwick, Ambassador Korish, and Ambassador Ove—USSTAP saved the world and we agree USSTAP did the right thing."

"Mr. President!" Perkins exclaimed.

"Wouldn't you agree?" Prichard asked the other world leaders at the table. The three leaders nodded and gave their verbal concurrence.

"Madame Secretary," President Prichard went on to say in a stern voice. "We sat through your fact finding trial—"

"Hearing," Perkins interrupted. "It was a fact finding hearing."

"Fine...hearing," Prichard acknowledged. "As I was saying, during this fact finding hearing you dragged out every conceivable witness, analyzed every piece of evidence and put the leaders of the entire known universe in a witness box. To testify to a body of people, who in my opinion, were directly responsible for what you so lightly call: an episode."

Prichard stopped and took a sip of water from the glass in front of him. As he drank, he saw the approving eyes of his fellow world leaders. He put the glass down and continued, "As far as I'm concerned, Dr. Chenault is a product of this organization...Geez, he was one of *you*. He used your forces to mount an attack in my country. He killed your predecessor and the former Security Council."

"Then he attacked USSTAP under the U.N. flag. USSTAP protected themselves and retaliated, using minimum force and remarkably, no loss of life—at least, no loss of life of any Earth citizen. The bottom line here, Madam Secretary is the U.N. committed an act of war on my country and on USSTAP, and you have the audacity to ask for an apology and restitution. Madam Secretary, I think you need to stop this and stop it right now! It's over!"

Perkins sat back in her chair, noticeably shocked at what she just heard. She opened her mouth to counter Prichard, but then noticed the agreeing head nods from the other leaders. She closed her mouth and took a deep breath.

After a second of reflection she said, "You are correct Mr. President. In retrospect requesting an apology and restitution may be in poor diplomatic taste in this situation."

Prichard smiled, "Good that's settled. Now let's talk about renegotiating this so-called U.N.-USSTAP Pact."

Warwick deferred to Michael with a head gesture. Michael took the cue and placed his hands on the table. "Our original offer during the Scolonian crisis still stands. USSTAP will leave this world by the end of the year."

"What?" Prichard shot back.

"Sorry, Mr. President," Michael offered. "I made an offer in good faith during the crisis and USSTAP intends to honor that offer."

"You *can't,"* the Russian President interjected.

"Yes we can and we will," Ove responded. "You see the human influence from Earth is dwindling. Chief Executive Osguard Genesis and the surviving members of the original Osguards are the only ones that have any type of attachment to this planet."

"No ambassadors in the Millmum Star Congress, Rojam Os Galactic Parliament or the Universal Conclave have any reason to justify continued resources being dedicated to this planet anymore. We were just honoring the wishes of our legendary heroes and leaders—the original Osguards. We were being patient with you. And quite frankly, the last three decades of the U.N. - USSTAP Pact has taken its toll on our patience."

"The ambassador is right," Michael added. "This isn't the planet I vowed to protect when I was the First Osguard. The hatred we experienced over the last three decades and the indignation we suffered during this crisis has soured any attachment I had for this world...and I know I speak for the all the surviving original Osguards." Michael's voice cracked as the pain of what he was saying beat inside his throat. "This world almost took my grandchildren away from me; and when I confronted you with it, you practically spit in my face."

"Chief Executive Osguard," Trosponov interrupted. "You are taking these events personally. It isn't wise to make these kinds of decisions when your heart is under such distress."

Michael looked at Trosponov and smiled, "Those are wise words and, believe me when I tell you, I didn't make this recommendation to USSTAP lightly."

"Michael," Warwick interjected. "I have to lend some credence to my friend from the land of Russia. I agree that your recommendation was made under emotional duress. Therefore, I would like to modify your recommendation with Ambassador Ove's and Korish's permission." Both ambassadors nodded.

"Mr. President, this is my one and only offer to solve the situation."

"Go ahead, we're listening," Prichard said.

"USSTAP will leave this planet at the end of the year as promised. We will take all those from your planet that want to relocate to a fresh new untouched world, and who are not criminals running from your laws. We will take all, no matter what they are, what their condition is, or what their profession is—as long as they agree to abide by our constitution and laws."

"In exchange, you will remain a protectorate. We will ensure you aren't bothered by any other people who would want to do you harm. And when you are ready...you contact us for full membership into USSTAP."

"You will leave Earth...lot...stock and barrel?" Perkins inquired. "Even Tillman Memorial Hospital?"

"Not quite," Ove responded. "We will close Tillman Memorial Hospital, but we will maintain contact with our friends in Africa that stood by our side. We will continue are trade agreements with them."

Michael kept his stoic demeanor, but his heart sunk when he heard about USSTAP closing Tillman Memorial. He didn't realize the hospital was on the table as part of the deal.

"Unacceptable!" Perkins pushed back.

"I'm sorry, Madam Secretary," Korish countered. "This is not a negotiation. This is what we are going to do, with or without your concurrence, and there's not one solitary thing you can do about it. I suggest you walk out of this room as a victor in the eyes of your people, and sign on to this agreement. Or walk out as an enemy of USSTAP and lose with your people."

Michael never saw the ambassador so heated before. Perkins had managed to push the wrong buttons. Watching Perkins, he knew she realized it as well. Perkins gulped and her eyes went wide. The color drained from her face as the Korish's words echoed in the room.

Prichard looked down at his fist on the table, visibly uncertain on what to do next.

Then he asked, "Those that leave with you, will their families still have contact with them?"

Michael fielded this question, "Mr. President, there is nothing more important than family to me. I'm sure we can work out something where contact is maintained. I recommend a travel agreement between us that will allow families to visit each other." Michael looked over to Warwick.

Warwick smiled, "I'm sure we can work something out."

Prichard nodded, "Okay, that sounds like if those that leave want to come back to Earth, you will allow it; and those on Earth who decide later to move to this utopia world, you will have some type of arrangement for that."

Warwick sighed, "Agreed, if that is acceptable to Michael?"

Michael nodded, "It's Unity."

"What?" Perkins asked.

"The world...it's not utopia...its name is Unity."

"Unity...that has a nice sound to it," Prichard admitted.

"I know! It's kind of corny, but I think it fits," Michael added.

"Yes it does fit," Prichard agreed. He took a sip of water from his glass. After putting the glass down, he cleared his throat and continued, "I understand we aren't negotiating. But in the spirit of friendship and, because you have been so amenable in adjusting your offer, I would like to run something by you that we...Prime Minister Grant, President Trosponov, President Xing and I discussed earlier."

Warwick nodded, "Go on."

"First, let us apologize for what this planet has done to you, Chief Osguard Genesis, your family and especially to USSTAP, Ambassador Chancellor Warwick. What the Firsties did is unforgivable and we deeply regret that we as a people allowed it to happen."

"Thank you," Michael replied. "I'm sure that wasn't easy for you to say."

"Easy or not, Chief Osguard, it is the truth. We as a planet are very sorry."

"Mr. President," Perkins interrupted him, "I don't think you can speak for the entire planet."

"Madam Secretary," Prime Minister Grant called shooting her a stern look. "You had your say. And it was a pitiful display of diplomacy. Now let the professional leaders speak. I advise you to be quiet, or you can leave the room."

Perkins's jaw dropped as the astonishment of what the Prime Minister said to her washed over her.

A slight smile crossed Michael's lips, displaying the pleasure he felt at Perkins being put in her place.

"Please continue, Mr. President," Grant urged.

"Thank you Bob," Prichard sighed. "As I was saying, Ambassadors, the United States and her allies, including China, Russia, Great Britain, Australia and others have been diligently working to bring those members of the Firstie movement and others responsible for the attack on your association to justice. We have captured several members of Dr. Chenault's inner circle and they will be tried appropriately. We are still investigating some people...world leaders and even United Nations members."

Nervousness exuded from her Secretary General Perkins as all eyes in the room turned toward her. She grabbed her glass of water and gulped down the entire content as the silence in the room framed the atmosphere.

"That is very comforting to know," Warwick said. "But we are satisfied with Dr. Chenault's passing that the matter is settled."

"You see, we want to apply for full membership to USSTAP as soon as possible and we will do what's right to prove our resolve in this matter."

"Again, that is encouraging, but not necessary," Warwick responded.

"Thank you Ambassador Warwick. But it is something we feel we must do."

"I understand President Prichard, but please do not do this for us. If you are, I must ask you to cease. We are satisfied that the guilty have been punished," said Warwick.

"It is something we do for ourselves," Grant added. "But continuing with the matter of full membership application, in that regard, I understand that there is a home world amendment making its way through your legislative system; which will actually replace capitol stations for ground based structures on member planets."

"That's correct," Michael chimed in. "In fact Unity will be home to Unity Hall."

"We understand that," President Trosponov pitched. "But what of Millmum Capitol? Where will that reside?"

"That hasn't been determined yet," Chief Ambassador Ove admitted. "There are several planets in the running, but no planet has won it out right. Why do you ask?"

President Xing piped up next, "There is nothing more honorable to us as a united people than for our planet to become a regular member of USSTAP."

"That will take some time," Prime Ambassador Korish responded. "There are some trust issues we must overcome first. I dare say on both our parts."

"We understand that," Xing admitted. "All we ask is that you consider it."

"Understood," Michael charged. "Of course we will consider it. But as Chief Ambassador Ove alluded, 'what's in it for us?'"

Prime Minister Grant smiled and said, "Put your capitol here on Earth."

"Say what?" Michael almost gagged. His mind jumped back to the conversation he had with Alexander Kennedy months ago. Was this Alexander's idea of an opportunity presenting itself? If so, it was a big leap from what he expected. Michael knew he had to continue with this line of discussion in order to see if he could fulfill his promise to Alexander and his Tappies.

"Put Millmum Capitol on Earth, and while you're at it, move the Parliament here as well. Let us show you we are changed people and we support USSTAP."

"Yes," Trosponov pushed. "Russia would be happy to host the Rojam Os Parliament."

"And China would be honored to host the Millmum Star Congress," Xing added.

"Great Britain would love to host your Rojam Os Osguard Senate."

Pritchard smiled and looked straight at Michael. "The United States would be overjoyed to welcome its children home again and place the Millmum Osguard Executive Building in Virginia…in Danville…Where the original Osguard Gardens once stood and where Laurona and Nausona gave birth to the USSTAP concept."

"What about the Firsties?" Michael choked, visibly honored by Prichard's words, knowing Alexander somehow had something to do with it.

"What about them?" Prichard huffed. "Besides Perkins and some of the old guard left in the U.N. the Firstie movement is dead. The people of Earth are more than overjoyed to have you and your organization on our world."

Warwick looked over to Ove and Korish, who gave a noncommittal nod. "How say you, Madam Secretary. Are you willing to stand by this offer?"

Perkins eyes widened. Fright seared on her face.

"Yeah, she will stand behind it," Prichard assured Warwick. "She will stand behind it or she will lose our nations as members of the U.N. and I will personally pull her ambassadorship as well."

Perkins closed her mouth, shut her eyes and gave a sheepish nod.

"Then, that's settled," Xing gleefully announced.

Michael shook his head, acting as if he was in disbelief, "Okay, if we are truly going to consider this, I would like to add one more amendment to our agreement."

"What's that?" Ove asked.

"I would like to keep the Susan S. Tillman Memorial Hospital open and add a dozen more satellite hospitals throughout the planet. It is the least I can do for Susan. It is what I think she would want."

Ove nodded.

Warwick then slammed his hand on the table. The noise startled everyone as the bang reverberated throughout the room. "Is everyone forgetting we just fought a battle here, and I'm not so convinced that our presence on this world would not ignite another one?"

"I'm not sure our people would be safe here. Now you are asking me to place our top ambassadors and their families on a planet that just a few short months ago openly and publicly despised our very existence. Not to mention, assassinated USSTAP's top leader of the planet and his family."

Trosponov cleared his throat. "That was a sad and tragic event. But, Ambassador Chancellor the problem you speak of was an anomaly perpetrated by the vocal minority, not a reflection of our true nature as a people."

"Of which one sits in our presence purporting to be the planet's authority. Furthermore, this anomaly you speak of lasted almost thirty Earth years. I hardly suspect it has been eradicated in six short months."

Michael sighed, "Agree. I don't see the sudden change of heart happening. But I am willing to put it to a test."

"How so?" asked Korish.

Michael knew it was now or never to put his plan to work. "I suggest we institute restrictive five-year probation for Earth, during which we exercise full visa privileges and rights for USSTAP citizens to visit. We also build and operate open precincts and stations. If in that time, we watch, observe and evaluate. If at the end of five years we deem the area sufficiently safe, we entertain their proposal to host the capitol and maybe even honorary membership into USSTAP."

"That seems fair," Ove injected. "How say you Madam Secretary?"

Again, Perkins was speechless. She threw her hands in the air in a defeatist manner, "Sure…whatever!"

A smile registered on Michael's face. This was going better than he could ever imagine. "In the meantime, we will still accept people from Earth who want to relocate to Unity as we stated earlier."

Prichard, Grant, Trosponov and Xing gave a measured patient nod. "I think that is still acceptable," Prichard concluded.

"Okay," Warwick declared. "I'm still somewhat hesitant about this. Then he turned to Michael. "Are you good with this?"

Michael took in a deep breath and slowly exhaled. "I suppose I am…yeah, I'm good with it for now. But, if anything untoward happens to any USSTAP citizen, their family or our property during the probation, the original agreement will be reactivated."

Warwick looked around as if someone else in the room should give the final word. After a few seconds, he stared at the four world leaders and said, "I will have our diplomatic corps get with your ambassadors to work out the details, and then I will have our legal departments draw up the papers for your signatures."

Pritchard sat back in his chair, "That will be fine." Once again Grant, Trosponov and Xing nodded in agreement.

Trosponov turned to Michael, "Unity, huh!"

"That's right…Unity!"

"I like that. It's not corny at all."

"I'm glad you agree, Mr. President."

EPILOGUE: EXODUS

USSTAP Science Vessel Parker & Elizabeth
Geosynchronous orbit
Near Planet Unity, Zyder Solar System

The equilibrium point between outerspace, innerspace and ultraspace, which Michael Genesis dubbed, *Unity Point* was actually the location of a habitable planet orbiting a binary solar system in a figure eight pattern. Michael liked to think of it as an infinity pattern. It was the perfect symbol of the humanity's future—infinite! It perpetrated hope, embodied the human spirit of continuous growing, and reminded him of the endless resourcefulness of humanity.

The solar system, in which Michael named after Mezhak Zyder, occupied ten light years of space, in the middle of the endless void of nothingness that usually separated galactic clusters from one another. It was an island in the middle of an ocean of darkness, hidden by nebulas and other giant gas clouds. All intents and purposes, it was a one-planet galaxy in a one galaxy cluster.

The planet was about two-thirds larger than Earth with eight giant landmasses framed by endless blue oceans. The landmasses connected to each other by long slivers of mountain ranges at different points. This reminded Michael that no matter how large or small or how different humankind was, there was always a link...a bond...that connected all humankind together. Michael hoped that this world would be that link.

The planet had four moons. Two were large enough to contain an atmosphere and sustain life, if necessary. The other two were just like the moon orbiting Earth; rocky barren and devoid of life. This allowed more options for settlements for USSTAP to develop.

With the final ratification of the home world amendment to the USSTAP Charter under his belt, Michael picked a site on the eastside of the largest continent for a capital city, which he dubbed Unity City. He planned to build the capitol, Unity Hall in the middle of Unity City. Unity Hall would physically mirror, in every detail the virtual Unity Hall, where USSTAP leadership had met for the past thirty years using the unity stream. Unity Hall would house the offices and the chambers for the Universal Conclave, the Guardian Supreme

Council, the Justice Review Board Keltar, and all the supporting departments.

This was Michael's twelfth trip to the area. His first trip was the adventure that he and his family took when they sailed the *S. V. Parker & Elizabeth* on her maiden voyage over a year ago. Michael sat back in his easy chair on the observation deck, watching the planet through the large port screen. It was a beautiful untamed and virtually an untouched planet.

Almost as pristine as the day God made her. Now he was about to lead a contingent of human colonist from Earth to settle on her. He felt a melancholy come over him as he squeezed his wife's hand. It was like walking through a fresh patch of fallen snow. The planet was so beautiful and peaceful...so perfect, he hated to disturb it. He knew the settlements would alter the beauty of the planet's nature forever. He was taking one last look at its perfection before mankind instilled its footprint forever on its surface.

He flashed back to the first time he saw the planet close up. He was like a kid in a candy store. He was so happy and full of wonder, he could not contain his joy. They slashed through the super gateportal almost five light years from the solar system and approached the anomaly with excited caution. He sat on the command deck with his brother and sister next to him, while their children operated the ships key systems.

Kashara piloted the ship, while Sharyla assumed navigation duties. Ed was monitoring the life science station. Maji, Shawn's son, was monitoring the weapons and defense, while his daughter, Nausona was completing the star mapping. Mitiah, Patricia's son took on engineering duties, while her daughter Laurona and Shawn's youngest son, Vedar, operated the sensors, scanners and unmanned probes. All the grandchildren, except for Karina Birdwell, were on the observation deck, which sat below the command deck.

Karina was on the command deck, broadcasting the event live for Star Universal News; along with the very pregnant Kerri Knight and her husband Jerold Washington, who were broadcasting the event live to Earth. Small imcams hovered around the command deck like humming birds, trying to get a glimpse of every key stroke tapped, every button pushed and every holographic picture displayed. It was a little nerve racking at first, but the crew soon learned to ignore the imcams and the constant chatter the reporters were involved in while filing their reports.

That day was special for Michael, to have all his parents children, grandchildren and great-grandchildren on one star ship, embarking on a mission that would extend humanity to the very spot the universe may have first ignited into life. It was a great tribute to their memory and a defined triumphed to their life. But he knew that moment couldn't have been done without his former arch nemesis and now best friend Billy Red, aka Mezhak Zyder.

And for that very reason, the voyage was delayed until Mezhak could really join them. On that special day, Mezhak Zyder, in his fully energized avatar, stood behind Michael with a beaming smile. Driven by the prospect of hugging his grandson and now his great-grandchild, Mezhak built a holographic avatar with the physical properties to fully interact with all human senses, in the physical universe using magnetized force fields and electromagnetic stimulation, enveloped in chromerion technology.

Mezhak Zyder found a way to produce the same type of avatar used with gateportal technology to interact in a virtual world to now interact in the real world. Although he could only maintain connectivity in this universe's real world in this form for only six hours at a time, it was well worth the effort to touch and hug his grandchild and his granddaughter-in-law.

Mezhak put his hand on Michael's shoulder, and Michael reached across his body and laid his hand upon Mezhak's. Tears clouded their vision as both men became misty eyed at the sight of Unity orbiting the two suns.

Mezhak whispered, "There she is...Unity, the original garden of Eden. She is circling the first lights of life, Adam and Eve."

The hovering imcams captured the solemn moment and emotional wording and beamed it throughout the universe to zillions of people throughout eight galactic clusters; forever sealing the name of the planet as Unity, and the name of the two suns as Adam and Eve.

The Genesis family and the 100-man Zyder crew spent forty-five days exploring and mapping the planet and the surrounding space. They took and analyzed thousands of thousands of samples. They explored the jungles, deserts and mountains of the planets as well as the surfaces of the moons.

It was a scientific adventure of a lifetime; one that Mezhak spent his entire professional career preparing. The readings were excellent and indicated the planet, which had no life other than trees, plants and vegetation was ready to sustain humans. In fact, thirty days into the exploration, Kerri Knight gave birth to a son, named William —the first human born on Unity, making him the first native of the new world.

Now eighteen universal months later and after a very exhaustive vetting process, 4.3 billion people from Earth, nearly half the planets population, were on their way to settle the planet that will ultimately become the USSTAP's home world. Michael used the blueprints from the Mosleck Reformation Act, which was used to resettle the entire surviving Mosleck population onto the Hustain moon after USSTAP terraformed it, to help plan the cities and the planet's infrastructure.

Although, Unity did not need to be terraformed, the Reformation Act blueprints were the right starting point to plan the transition stations, architecture and infrastructure to house the 4.3 billion colonists to help them adjust to their new world.

Michael now saw that Michelle was asleep. He let her hand loose and walked toward the port screen. The strange voice that haunted him so many years ago now whispered in his head but instead of saying, *"The Beginning and the End has chosen you to lay out a path so humanity can begin its journey to the next level,"* it now said, *"The Beginning and the End are proud of you. You have laid out a path so humanity can begin its journey to the next level."*

He smiled for now he felt his destiny was fulfilled. The ache that drove him all his life to be perfect was now gone. The pain of command now seemed worth it. The sorrow of death he witnessed seemed less. The guilt of so many lives lost under his command became lighter. He was on his journey now of becoming complete.

He stepped up to Mezhak, who was taking in the glory of the planet and said, "Who would have thought that one fight between us in the park so long ago, when we were teenagers, would lead to this."

Mezhak turned towards Michael with a big grin. "Boy, I wanted to kill you that day."

"I know that!"

"I wanted to kill you for so long afterward as well," Mezhak confessed.

Michael looked down at his feet and swallowed hard, "I know; I was there. There were times I thought you were going to kill me." Michael looked up and peered into Mezhak's eyes, "What changed?"

"I did...I changed," Mezhak responded. He closed his eyes as if to recall some long lost memory. "Your alternate on the Earth I live on now changed me. He made me see who I really was." Mezhak's eyes popped upon as if he had an epiphany, "He became my friend, and he told me I needed to make amends with you here. So I worked to traverse the alternate divide and do that."

"Even though I'm really in some ARIT sleeve in an alternate universe right now, I am glad God gave me the knowledge to make my spirit...my mind...traverse the divide; and be with you on this momentous occasion."

Michael bumped his shoulder against Mezhak's, "I'm glad you did my friend...I'm glad you did."

The two men stood in silence, looking over the new world. The two former enemies, now best of friends, soaked in the view, drinking in their accomplishments and silently praying for this moment would never end. Unity's blue majestic oceans, mountainous continents and large plains were so beautiful and inviting, the picture exuded the warmth they craved their entire lives.

In the background, the gateportal flashed to life with the angelic white light of innerspace. Through the holy haze, the first of a multitude of personnel transports floated into view, bringing its precious human cargo of space pioneers to the new wilderness. Soon the space above Unity will be filled with wide-eye, enthusiastic immigrants, in search of a new life and a new beginning.

Mezhak wrapped his arms around Michael's shoulder and with the pride of a new father stated, "We did it...we did it, my friend. We have brought our people home!"

Michael wrapped his arm around Mezhak's avatar's shoulder and took in a deep breath, "Amen, brother...Amen!"

Guardian Supreme Council		Universal Conclave	
Chief Executive Osguard		Ambassador Chancellor	
Executive Osguard One / Cluster (8)	Osguards One / Galaxy (900)	Executive Ambassador One / Cluster (8)	Conclave Ambassador Four / Galaxy

Galactic Senate	Galactic Parliament
First Osguard	Prime Ambassador
Osguard One / Galaxy (Varies)	Galactic Ambassador One / Precinct (Varies)

Capitol Station	Capitol Station Star Congress
Osguard	Chief Ambassador
Staff	World Ambassador One / Planet (Varies)

Table 1: USSTAP Executive and Legislative Organization Chart

ABOUT THE AUTHOR

Nationally award winning author, Malcolm Dylan Petteway is a military analyst and a twenty-year veteran of the United States Air Force. He flew B-52's as an Electronic Warfare Officer and has 3,000 flight hours and 300 combat hours.

In his distinguished career, Malcolm has used his knowledge in the art of war, military weapons and combat defenses in planning over 400 combat sorties. Besides his Meritorious Service Medal with three oak leaf clusters and numerous other awards, Malcolm is the recipient of the U.S. Air Force Air Medal and the U.S. Air Force Air Achievement Medal for his actions during OPERATION ENDURING FREEDOM. Malcolm Petteway is a graduate of the U.S. Air Force Academy and California State University Stanislaus.